Darker Days

By

AJ Powers

Editing by: Talia Philips & Edits by V
Cover design by: AJ Powers
Stock Photography: Adobe Stock Images
ISBN: 1973737264
ISBN-13: 978-1973737261

DEDICATION

To my Creator and King.
To my loving wife, Talia. There is no other
person I would rather share this journey with than
you. I am so blessed to have you as my wife. I love
you.
To my daughters and son. Thank you for being
the best children a dad could ask for. I love you so
much.

IN MEMORY OF

Deborah O'Connell. A wonderful woman who
always went above and beyond. You are deeply
missed.

ACKNOWLEDGMENTS

To Doug and Melanie. Thank you for your friendship, feedback, and expertise. I am deeply grateful.

To Joe O'Connell, thank you for pushing me to become a better writer. Your feedback is priceless and appreciated.

To Robert. I also have you to thank for pushing me to become a better writer. Your encouragement and support have been nothing short of astounding. Thank you. PS – Get more Roberts down!

Brad. Thank you for sharing some of your winter experiences in the Dakotas.

To Faxon Firearms. Thank you for graciously allowing me to use the likeness of the ARAK-21 in this book. I look forward to owning one of my own someday!

To Geoff and Phil...What can I say? You guys are great. Thanks for your friendship and support.

Chapter 1

"I don't like this," Clay said while looking through a pair of binoculars.

"What's the matter?" Geoff asked.

Clay lowered the binoculars and wiped the lenses with his sleeve. The light rain—virtually a mist—quickly collected on the optics, distorting the image on the other side. Handing them to Geoff, Clay pointed towards a parking lot about a half mile away.

"Hmmm," Geoff grunted, echoing Clay's concern.

If the deal didn't seem too good to be true or wasn't fifteen miles east of Dallas in Mesquite, Clay might have been a little less edgy about the arrangement. At first, he balked at the notion of traveling so far to do business with a man he had just met a few months ago, but his sister's persistence quickly convinced the whole group.

I really need to stop listening to her, Clay thought.

Geoff handed the binoculars back to Clay who promptly looked through them again, studying every aspect of the location they would visit at dawn. Nothing about it seemed out of the ordinary, but then again, Clay wasn't sure if anything qualified as "ordinary" anymore. His gut told him this trade couldn't be taken at face value. Every unknown situation needed to be treated cautiously, and in this situation, that meant there probably was an ulterior motive at play.

As he continued gazing through the binoculars, Clay wiped at the lenses again, leaving behind a trail of smudges and a slight scratch from the metal snap on his cuff. He sighed because of the stupid mistake, but continued scanning the target up ahead. They were to meet the man in the Sears parking lot at the Mesquite Towne Mall on the morning of August 2nd. The man said he lived in Wichita Falls, and felt Mesquite would be a reasonable halfway point for both parties.

The location wasn't bad, actually. It was a wide-open parking lot, though still filled with many abandoned vehicles that hadn't turned over since the ash fell a decade ago. After spotting a Stingray, Clay was consumed by the memory of announcing to his dad that the Stingray would be the perfect graduation gift. He could still hear his dad's roaring laughter at the thought of buying a $60,000 car for his son because he completed high school. "Besides," his father said to him, "we're a Ford family." There was no denying that fact, but there was something about that particular Corvette's design that justified an exception.

"So, what's the plan?" Dusty spoke up, pulling Clay back from his memory.

Clay was tempted to give into the nagging feeling telling him to abort and find a place to camp for the night before starting the first leg of the nearly 200-

mile trip back to Northfield. But it had taken the three of them over two weeks to get up there, and Clay was reluctant to scrub the effort based on a hunch. And now that they had arrived, Clay's hope that the trade was legitimate trumped his cynicism.

Deciding once again to continue with the trade, Clay responded, "We need to be in place at least an hour before sunrise so we can watch the parking lot beforehand." Clay looked to his left, "Dust, you see that pylon over there?" Clay asked as he pointed to an overpass on Interstate 635.

Dusty nodded. "Yup."

"That looks like the best spot for you to perch with the .270. Use that column as cover and watch our backs."

"No problem."

Clay looked through the binoculars at the bridge and then over to the parking lot. "That's probably close to a two-hundred-yard shot. Maybe more. You good with that distance?"

"Pffft!" Dusty scoffed. "Remember that doe I dragged home last month? I nailed that sucker from at *least* two-fifty," she said as she held up her Browning X-Bolt.

"Sure ya did," Geoff interjected with a friendly grin.

"Oh, I'm sorry. When was the last time *you* bagged a buck, Geoffrey?" Dusty shot back.

"Touchè," Geoff quickly conceded.

Clay chuckled at the healthy dose of camaraderie the three of them shared. Although Dusty had grown into a beautiful young woman, she never bothered to try and pretty herself up—to be like the other girls back home. Instead, she was always more interested in hunting, security detail, and other tasks that the guys on the farm usually handled. She always said

3

she would rather get her hands bloodied and dirty than cook, clean, and swoon over babies. She often wore a cowboy hat and was pining for a pair of boots Vlad had agreed to set aside for her. She was a tomboy through and through and could more than hold her own. So, both Geoff and Clay just looked at her as one of the guys most of the time.

"Anyway," Clay continued. "Geoff and I are going to hide beneath that same overpass. We'll keep an eye out for anything strange. We will *not* head to the parking lot until the man arrives. If he doesn't show up, we don't move."

Both Geoff and Dusty nodded.

"Man, I really hope this works out. I'm gonna be pissed if we walked all this way for nothing," Geoff commented.

"Me too," Clay agreed as he stuffed the binoculars into his pack. He grasped on to his Larue AR-15 hanging from the sling and said, "All right, let's go find some shelter for the night."

It didn't take long to find adequate lodging. As they were coming in, they spotted a large movie theater just south of the I-635/Highway 80 junction. Movie theaters were always a goldmine for Clay in the past. He never walked out of one empty-handed, and the projector rooms always made for cozy sleeping spots, typically with only one entrance to cover. This theater, however, broke Clay's streak. Though he didn't spend a whole lot of time searching, he was surprised with how little there was inside. It was clear that numerous people had been through the multiplex, and he was going to be hard-pressed to find anything of real value. Most pre-packaged foods had become nearly unpalatable anyway. From time to time, they found an item that still retained *some* of its original taste and nutrition, and on rare occasions, they discovered freeze-dried foods that were as good as the day they were canned. By and large, however, they needed to rely on food they could grow or butcher themselves, which was why they were in Dallas in the first place.

With his Arsenal SLR-95 at the ready, Geoff cleared the projectionist's room. Much to Clay's surprise—and frustration—it wasn't the little chamber he expected at all. The theater, having been remodeled a short time before Yellowstone's caldera exploded, was state of the art and built for efficiency. This meant *all* the projectors on that side of the building were in one long room—five screens on either side. There were doors at both ends, too. The ceiling was riddled with water stains, several of which had small holes toward the center, allowing the rain to trickle in.

So much for cozy.

Despite the unwelcoming accommodations, it was the best spot in the theater to hole up for the night. And since daylight had already departed, it would have to do.

"All right, let's get to work. Dust, you want to get started on a small fire and dinner?" Clay said, realizing such a large room provided at least one benefit—ventilation for a fire. "Geoff, help me block off one of these doors so we don't have to worry about covering both."

Swallowing her retort about such domestic responsibilities, Dusty dropped her pack and fished through it for her supplies. Geoff also dropped his pack, which produced a hefty thud as it hit the floor. The pair of spam cans—each containing 640 rounds of 7.62x39, which was part of the trade tomorrow— weighed close to fifty pounds. The other items they were parting with in the morning only added to the

AJ POWERS

weight of his pack. Geoff stood up and stretched his back trying to work out some of the kinks that had developed during their travels.

"Help me move this," Clay said as he rested his hand on a large metal cabinet.

Clay and Geoff lifted the cabinet and walked several feet before putting it down to rest. It weighed far more than either expected, and instead of making a lot of noise to drag it across the floor, they hauled it in twenty-foot increments. They eventually placed the large metal box in front of the door and both leaned up against it, panting for air.

"That ought to do it," Clay said as he gasped between the words.

Clay felt out of shape. It had been three years since his average day consisted of climbing hundreds of stairs and hoisting up gallons of water 160 feet. Though he was still extremely fit, the daily tasks that came with living at the top of an office building for years gave Clay a workout unlike any routine he had established on the farm. *Still*, he thought, *I wouldn't trade Northfield for anything.*

"Whoa!" Dusty shouted from the other side of the room as the fire roared to life inside a metal wastebasket.

Clay and Geoff walked over and sat down next to the fire. Though the summer temperatures were still present, nightfall was always accompanied by a chill in the air. Clay took his gloves off and stuck his hands out by the flame while Dusty prepared the rabbit she had killed earlier that morning. Geoff popped off the top of his AK-47's receiver and wiped down the insides with a rag. When out "in the wild" as he called it, he never fully fieldstripped his rifle unless it was absolutely necessary. Even though the inner workings of the weapon were exposed, it was still a fully functional gun in the event they were ambushed.

After dinner, the three of them played cards for a couple of hours. As always, Dusty had the most bullets—their form of poker chips. Clay looked down at his pocket watch. It was a little after 9:00, so he forced an exaggerated yawn and stretched his arms over his head. "We should get to bed. Need to be out the door early tomorrow."

Even though Geoff and Dusty agreed, none of them were all that tired. Clay really missed his MP3 player whenever sleep evaded him. He hoped to find a working replacement someday, but he had little hope he ever would since the last three years yielded nothing. Dusty had made a makeshift bed out of seat cushions she found in a storage closet. She slept relatively close to the door, putting herself between Clay and Geoff and the only entrance into the room. Clay always gave her grief about it, but she never took the hint that he wasn't a fan of her placement. Or, maybe, she didn't care.

The sound of the dripping water coming in through various holes in the ceiling was almost maddening. Normally, Clay found the rain relaxing, but the sound of individual droplets splashing incessantly into a pool of water grated his nerves.

"So, you think he'll show?" Geoff asked quietly, uncertain whether Dusty had fallen asleep or not.

"Dunno," Clay said. Part of him hoped he would, another part of him hoped he wouldn't. Situations like this were uncharted territory for all three of them, and while Clay wanted to believe the best in the stranger, he found it increasingly more difficult to find good in humanity anymore. "Show or no show, all that matters is we get back home in one piece."

"No arguments here," Geoff said before rolling over.

Clay eventually fell asleep, but a loud crack of thunder woke all of them up. He heard Geoff shout something, but it was incoherent. Clay was uncertain if Geoff's words were the disjointed babble of someone waking from a deep sleep or his own mind lagging in its ability to process the nonsense. He looked down at his watch, certain he had just fallen asleep, to find it was 4:45. They had overslept and Clay was thankful for nature's wakeup call.

As his adrenaline picked up in anticipation for the morning, Clay pulled himself from his sleepy stupor and prepared to leave. They took a few minutes to pack everything up and chow down on a few bits of leftover rabbit before leaving the projection room. As they walked through the lobby, Geoff's flashlight hovered over some garbage on the floor.

"What is it?" Clay asked as he walked up next to Geoff. Clay looked down at the floor and saw a faded cardboard cutout of a woman. He strained his eyes then racked his brain to remember the name. "Sigourney Weaver?"

"I have no idea who she is," Geoff said as he looked on, "but she's freakin' hot."

"Yeah. Not bad for a seventy-year-old," Clay said with a grin as he smacked Geoff's shoulder. Dusty silently rolled her eyes as she scanned the empty lobby.

Geoff's smile twisted into a look of confusion. "Seventy? Really?" he asked, seemingly disappointed as if *that* fact ruined his chances of meeting her someday.

"Come on," Clay said as he headed for the door.

The storm had weakened a little, and the random zaps of lightning in the sky provided them with sporadic light to help navigate. They reached the I-635 junction, and Clay stopped to go over the plan one more time.

"Dusty, take this ramp and get yourself set up on the bridge we talked about yesterday."

"Got it," Dusty replied.

"Make sure you take that thing off once you're in position," Clay said as he smacked the brim of her hat. "Make yourself blend in as much as possible, okay?"

"I will, I will," she sighed.

"Remember, if he doesn't show an hour after sunrise or if Geoff and I don't go out to meet him, then regroup at the theater and we'll head home. Nothing this guy has is worth dying for," Clay said with a serious tone. "All right?"

"You got that right," Geoff said.

"And Dusty, one more thing," Clay said as he gently grabbed her arm, all joking replaced with a serious, protective tone. "That spot on the bridge may be the best vantage point for our meeting, but you are also very exposed up there. Don't forget to watch your own back, okay?"

"This ain't my first rodeo, Clay," she said with a confidence that no sixteen-year-old girl should have about being a sniper. "Don't get in over your head," she jabbed as she started up the exit ramp onto I-635 north, heading toward the mall.

Clay and Geoff followed the access road, walking cautiously and quietly. Once they reached the bridge that was soon to be Dusty's perch, they climbed into the cab of a stalled out semi-truck. The painfully slow passage of time increased their anxiety as they waited in near silence for several minutes. Before long, they started whispering back and forth to distract themselves. They talked about their families from before the earthquakes, which was something they rarely did, but it helped the daylight come faster. As the sun rose, their conversation died down, and Clay kept his eyes glued to the binoculars

With the rising sun, the rain began to fall again and the visibility worsened as the rain picked up. Clay didn't feel like going out in it, but in all reality, it was a light drizzle compared to some of the storms they slogged through on the way up. It wasn't even the cold that bothered him so much as the sticky film that covered his skin after the rain evaporated. Nobody knew for sure what it was—most people just assumed it had something to do with the ash—but it made for an unpleasant, itchy experience. One time, after an extended hike through a heavy downpour, Clay actually peeled it off his skin—much like a bored fourth grader with access to a bottle of Elmer's glue.

An hour passed and the man was still a no-show. Despite being a little disappointed, Clay's stomach started to unknot. He had been so indecisive about the whole exchange that his thinking had become muddled and he second-guessed every decision. And when Clay's judgment was impaired, he made mistakes; missing minute details that could be the difference between life and death.

"All right, I'm calling it," Clay began before he suddenly stopped talking. He held up the binoculars once again and saw a man come around the side of the mall, a small cow trailing behind him. Clay sighed. "Crap."

"What?" Geoff asked before helping himself to the binoculars. "Sweet! He's here!"

"Yeah," Clay said, conflicted.

"What? He's here and he brought the cow. That's what we came for."

Clay took the binoculars back and looked all around the mall. The only sign of life was the old man and his cow. "Did you happen to notice he's alone?"

"Yeah, so?"

"What if I told you I was going to travel all this way to meet up with a few strangers for a trade—what would you have said?"

"I would have said you were a moron," Geoff said. He sat in silence as his words sank in. "Oh. Right."

They waited in the truck while Clay contemplated their move. Should they stay put until the man leaves? As Clay observed the man check his wristwatch on several occasions, he knew that moment wasn't far off.

"Well, whatever you decide, dude, I'm behind ya one hundred percent," Geoff said. "I trust your instinct."

Clay wrestled with himself for several more minutes as he tried to make a decision, but he was no closer to an answer than he was when he first saw the man round the corner. "Screw it," he said as he jumped out of the cab onto the asphalt and into the rain. Geoff followed closely behind and they walked toward the mall's parking lot. The man finally spotted them and gave a friendly wave from afar.

"Keep your head on swivel," Clay said out of the corner of his mouth.

"Hello there!" the old man said as they approached. "I was beginning to wonder if you were going to show. I hope the trip up here wasn't too much trouble."

Clay held out his hand, palm up, and let the raindrops hit his skin. "It was wet," he said gruffly.

The man let out a gravely laugh followed by a few coughs. He was an older man with a bit of a waddle in his gait. He didn't seem to be in all that great of shape or health. Something wasn't adding up; the nagging voice screamed at Clay to walk away.

"I hear ya. I got hammered hard most of the way here from Wichita Falls."

"So," Clay said, shrugging off the man's comment, "we have what you asked us to bring, so if you don't mind, let's wrap things up so we can be on our way." Clay looked over and nodded. Geoff slid the bag off his shoulder and placed it on the ground.

"Well, hold on there," the man said. "I would like to get to know a little bit about you, first. I've had this girl for four seasons now," he said as he stroked the cow's head. "We've been through a lot together, her and me. And I would like to make sure she's going to a decent home. You say you have a farm or something of the sort?"

This is bad, Clay thought.

"That's right," Geoff said wearily. "We'll take care of her—she'll be fine."

"That's good. Got plenty of drinking water? She looks like a cow, but drinks like a camel," the man said with a chuckle.

"Why are you stalling?" Clay barked, his grip tightening around the handle of his AR-15.

The man stepped back, acting offended. "Stalling? I guess I'm just from a different era than you two youngsters. Back in my day, folks took time to get to know—"

CRACK!

Both Clay and Geoff whipped their heads around in the direction of the gunshot.

The bridge.

As Clay and Geoff turned back to the man, they noticed he had distanced himself from them and brandished a sawed off double barrel. Clay and Geoff immediately raised their own rifles.

"Drop it, old man!" Clay ordered.

The man kept his shotgun trained on the pair. "Now, come on fellas, you didn't really think we wouldn't find your sharpshooter up on that bridge, did you?" he said with a slight grin of satisfaction. "We've been at this racket for a long while; there ain't much we haven't seen."

Clay's mind was split between Dusty's predicament and his own. The old man kept his scatter gun trained on them, his finger resting on the trigger. He was about twenty feet away, and Clay and Geoff stood shoulder to shoulder. The fact that his barrel was cut short didn't help matters, either. At that distance, if he pulled the trigger he would deliver a nasty blow to both Clay and Geoff. Nobody moved.

The sound of galloping hooves echoed around the parking lot as four men came into sight, two from either side of the storefront. They were all armed, and their allegiance was obviously to the elderly man with the cow.

Three of the horses spread out, keeping their distance from each other, while the fourth horse stopped a few feet short of the old man. The rider quickly dismounted and walked over to him.

"So, what do we have here?" the younger man questioned the old man, readjusting his red trucker's hat. He had a sinister, toothless grin on his face and a worn-out lever action rifle—he certainly enjoyed his post-society vocation.

"All right, boys, enough playing around. Get those hands up, and don't try anything foolish or I'll show you just how quickly I can empty both these barrels," the old man said.

Clay and Geoff dropped their rifles, letting them hang from their slings. They both slowly reached their hands into the air. Geoff looked over, expecting for Clay to have some sort of plan; he was not comforted with the blank expression on his friend's face.

"Wilber, why don't you go ahead and see what our friends here brought for us," the old man said.

"Sure thing, Pops."

Wilber handed his rifle to the old man and walked toward Clay and Geoff, holding some zip ties in one hand and reaching for his Beretta with the other. He was about five feet away when Clay felt the shockwave of the bullet zooming past his head. A cloud of blood exploded out of Wilber's chest before he crumpled to the ground. The sound of the powerful rifle finally caught up with the bullet, booming across the small downtown scene.

"Wilber!" The old man cried out in anger and confusion. By the time he realized what had happened, Clay and Geoff had opened fire. The man's body shook as he absorbed the symphony of bullets from Clay and Geoff's rifles.

Gunfire erupted from the other three men who were still on their horses. One of the horses, being startled by the barrage of bullets, bucked his rider off and stormed away from the scene. The man never returned to the fight.

Clay and Geoff split up and sought cover behind different cars. The last two men continued firing, raining glass down on Clay's head as he flattened himself up against the door. He swung his body up over the hood and shot at one of the men, but was quickly suppressed by the other. Geoff then stood up and took some of the heat away from Clay, but was also forced back down.

Geoff looked over at Clay who held up three fingers, then two, then one. Both swung out of cover and opened fire. Geoff successfully took down his target, but Clay missed his. Geoff's voice ripped through an eruption of more bullets as he screamed out in pain and frustration.

"Geoff! You all right?"

Geoff had dropped down to one knee as he clutched a shoulder. "Yeah, I'm fine. Just take care of *your* guy, would ya?" he said, ribbing Clay for his inaccuracy.

Unsure of how much ammo was left in his magazine, Clay dropped it and replaced it with a full one. The sound of falling rain was interrupted only by a single potshot Dusty had taken at the man. She didn't have much ammo left and Clay knew it. He couldn't count on her to lay down suppressive fire for them, so Clay took a sharp breath in and readied himself. He spun around the front bumper of the car and took aim. Nothing. Panic rose in his chest as he quickly scanned for the last man but was unable to locate him. He had comfort in knowing Dusty was watching the exchange through her optics, so any chance of the man ambushing him was slim, but the situation still unnerved him.

Clay was considering different reasons for the man's absence when he saw him pop out from behind a minivan. Clay fired two shots before he heard a click.

Misfire?

Clay tugged back on the charging handle and fired again. Click.

Hearing a slew of profanity leave Clay's mouth, the man suspected a gun malfunction. He spun around the van and sprinted toward the car Clay used as cover. By the time Clay heard the splashing footsteps, the man leapt onto the car. As soon as his feet planted onto the rusted-out hood, the attacker swung his rifle around and aimed downward.

That was when Clay saw the flash from the bridge—then he heard the sound—it was over.

The man's bulky frame fell forward, nearly pancaking Clay in the process. He turned away from the gruesome cadaver that remained after Dusty's shot. He had seen his fair share of blood in the last ten years, but sometimes it was still too much to look at, especially up close. He wasn't sure how much time had passed, but when Clay opened his eyes, both Geoff and Dusty stood in front of him.

"Well, that kinda sucked," Dusty said as she swiped at her wet, disheveled hair clinging to her face.

"You don't say?" Geoff said as he held his shoulder, his grip doing little to reduce the blood leaking between his fingers.

Dusty looked around, spotting several bodies within eyeshot. "Well, on the bright side, it sucked a whole lot more for them."

Chapter 2

Clay stared down at his fieldstripped LaRue trying to figure out why it wasn't firing. He had wracked his brain throughout the slow, wet day of travel, trying to figure out what had gone wrong. Before they left the mall, Clay had tried to fire it again—no joy. Everything, including the trigger assembly, worked well as far as he could tell. The problem had to be something with the bolt carrier group, most likely with the firing pin--the part of his rifle that Clay was least familiar with. He would have to dig a little deeper once they got back to Northfield, where he would have sufficient lighting and no fear of being attacked.

"Hold still, would ya?" Dusty griped at Geoff as she cleaned his wound.

"Well, stop stabbing me with your fingers and maybe I won't flinch so much," Geoff replied.

"Waa, waa, waa," Dusty said, her voice dripping in sarcasm. "It's just a flesh wound, you wuss," she added as she reached down and picked up a small glass vial. "Put a couple of drops of this on both the entrance and exit wound." She handed Geoff the bottle that consisted of a concoction of Melaleuca, Lavender, and a few other essential oils commonly used to prevent infection. Since pharmaceutical antibiotics were pretty much extinct, Megan had become a walking library on the topic of essential oils. At first, Clay didn't buy into the whole healing potion jargon. He knew that there was some medicinal value to them, but he viewed them more as a supplement rather than a legitimate first line of defense. He quickly backpedaled on his criticisms, however, when he observed firsthand just how effective they could be. In some cases, he felt they were more effective than anything he would be lucky enough to find in a pharmacy. Since Dusty had become something of a field medic, she kept a few bottles of Megan's various concoctions in her pack—much to the benefit of Clay and Geoff, her usual travel companions. "Let that crap soak in for a little bit and then I'll bandage you up, okay? That is, if you promise not to cry so much."

"You're such a warm person, Dusty," Geoff said with a snark in his words, but quickly followed it up with a genuine, "Thanks." After following Dusty's directions, Geoff walked over to Clay, who was in the middle of reassembling the rifle. "You okay, man? You get it figured out?"

"Nope," Clay said, frustration permeating his voice. "Will have to look into it further when we get home," he said before letting out an exasperated sigh.

Geoff knew that gun was important to Clay, for sentimental reasons as much as practical. "I'm sure it's something simple, you'll figure it out. And even if you don't, I am sure Vlad or somebody else will be able to help out," he said, unsure if there was truth in his words but attempting to give Clay some hope.

"It's not just about the gun," Clay replied with an edge in his voice. "In fact, I don't even care about the stupid thing right now. What's got me pissed off is what happened this morning."

Clay fumed about the setup earlier. He had barely spoken a word the entire day. Geoff was not thrilled with the events, either, but they came out on the other side relatively unscathed, and that's all that mattered to him.

"Look on the bright side, man, we got a cow and some horses. That's gonna be a *huge* help for us," Geoff said.

"We should have never been there," Clay barked, but quickly calmed himself. Shouting, especially after nightfall, was never a good idea. "We should have never gone," Clay reiterated himself in a much more subdued tone. He turned around and walked out of the room. He hoped that Geoff had caught the hint that he wanted to be alone. He took a quick glance over his shoulder and saw his friend walk the opposite direction. Point made.

He wasn't mad at Geoff, which is why he just wanted to be alone. He was angry with the situation, irritated with Megan, and he didn't want to dish that wrath out on his best friend just because he happened to be the closest punching bag around. Clay knew that Geoff was right—the cow and horses were a monumental gain for the group. And even had he known ahead of time that it was going to cost six treacherous bandits their lives, he probably still would have done it. The three of them likely saved future victims a lot of pain and suffering by taking the thieves out, and Northfield benefited from the outcome, but the trap was only a small part of Clay's frustration. The real issue was his complacency.

Clay scratched the scruff on his neck as he looked through a cloudy window out into the floor of a large factory. He stood inside a manager's office or something of the sort, overlooking a massive room filled with degenerate machinery that once provided a living for hundreds of people. Judging from papers, signage and scraps lying around, it was some sort of plastics company. *G-A-C Manufacturers*.

Clay heard one of the horses neigh. The sound bounced around the cavernous room, adding to his fears that someone passing through the area might get curious if they heard the livestock. A horse might not be enough incentive to draw in a random traveler—after all, many armed bandits traveled by horseback—but a lowing cow would be a different story. Fortunately, Rudy—the name Dusty gave to the cow—had not been particularly vocal thus far. Clay hoped she would stay that way.

The weight of the day had taken its toll, and Clay's eyes became heavy. With his legs hiked up on the old steel desk, he fell asleep sitting in the factory manager's lumpy office chair. He woke up around 3:30A.M. to a torrential assault on the aluminum roof that spanned the entire building. It was loud, like someone dumping a bag of rice over a snare drum. The jarring noise was too obnoxious for him to fall back to sleep so he pulled out his map and began charting their path back home. With livestock in tow, they wouldn't be able to just wing it—traveling as far as they could, then seeking shelter at the last minute. Clay circled potential areas for shelter every five to ten miles. He had no idea what kind of distance a cow could cover in a given day, but with the constant rain and a potential ambush always looming, he didn't want to push his luck. He was going to be careful; he was going to get everyone back home.

No more mistakes.

****

The last mile home was always the longest for Clay. He could see the farm up ahead, but it felt as if he was walking on a treadmill—his legs moved, but nothing got closer, especially after longer trips out. Mesquite had been the longest trip Clay had ever been on. It had been nearly six weeks since they departed Northfield and the joy that filled Clay when he saw his house was almost euphoric.

It had barely rained over the last week—an answered prayer—which vastly improved their traveling experience as the ground started to dry out. It was a gorgeous evening; Clay could actually see a few stars in the sky if he looked at just the right spots. Clearer nights like this were still few and far between, making them even more stunning when they did arrive. The sky was lavishly painted with beautiful shades of purple and orange, creating the perfect backdrop for the picturesque farm. The sight tonight was surreal, like something from a painting.

Ruth's older brother, Michael, and their cousin, Levi, urgently walked toward the gate, guns in hand, as they saw horses approaching the property. They expected a cow, not four colts *and* a cow. But it didn't take long for them to recognize Dusty's almost iconic hat and they waved and cheered on the returning party.

Levi turned and jogged back to the houses to alert everyone of the news, while Michael—who suffered a severe leg injury a few years back—kept walking toward the gate.

"Welcome home," Michael said as he unlocked the gate and pulled it open. "Gotta admit, we were starting to get a tad worried about y'all." He looked over at Geoff and saw the blood stains on his jacket. "Looks like you guys ran into a bit of trouble, huh?"

"Something like that," Clay said absent-mindedly. His eyes glued to the front door of his house. He got down from the horse and handed the reins to Michael.

"If you want, I'll take them over to the workshop. We can keep them there until we figure out a long-term solution," Michael said.

"Yeah, that sounds fine," Clay said, barely paying attention.

Geoff and Dusty dismounted, too, and led the horses over to Michael. Though they were excited to have a speedier means of transportation, both were eager to stretch their legs—something they hadn't done much of since acquiring the steeds.

The door on Geoff's house nearly flew off the hinges as Ruth stormed out and came running toward Geoff. Wyatt ran behind her, doing his best to keep up. They passed Clay, barely acknowledging him as they kept their focus on who was ahead—just as Clay's did.

"Daddy!" Dakota shrieked as she leapt off the front porch and sprinted toward Clay.

She quickly closed the gap between them as she ran straight into Clay's arms. He picked her up and spun her around, throwing her in the air before giving her a tight hug. "Koty-bear! I missed you so much!" He kissed her cheek and asked, "Were you good for Mama?"

"Of course," she said with a smirk that told Clay she withheld a bit of information.

Clay put Dakota down when he saw Kelsey standing on the porch, leaning against one of the columns. She held Charles, who was doing his best to break free from his mother's grip to go greet his father. Kelsey finally put him down and he clumsily ran across the field to Clay. Several stumbles and a full face-plant later, the toddler was comfortably in his father's loving arms. Following closely behind her unsteady toddler, Kelsey grabbed Clay and kissed him passionately. Her touch on his lips was heavenly. Kelsey began to cry and wrenched him even closer. She didn't want to let go. And for the first time in nearly a month and a half, Clay finally exhaled.

Before the moment with his wife had fully passed, Clay, Geoff and Dusty were surrounded by the rest of the kids on the farm. Excited to see their family return, the children chattered noisily, recounting their own tales of the past six weeks. The screams and laughter were deafening, and Clay was being pulled in a different direction by each one of the kids. It was frenzied. It was loud. It was...perfect. He was home.

Megan and Bethany came out from behind one of the houses. Megan hauled a sack of laundry over her shoulder, Bethany doing her part by carrying a basket of clothespins. When Bethany spotted Clay, she dropped the basket and ran to greet him. By that time he, Kelsey, and a few other kids approached the porch. Clay knelt down and absorbed Bethany's affectionate impact as she squealed in delight. "Daddy! I love you so much!" she said as she squeezed her arms around his neck. Clay looked down and saw Julie, the stuffed giraffe Charlie had given to her for her second birthday, peeking over the top of her overalls. Bethany cherished that faded yellow animal. And even though she was so young when Charlie had died, Clay suspected some of her affection toward Julie was her way of embracing his memory.

When Clay stood back up, Bethany's death grip around his neck did not loosen, so he transitioned to carrying his adopted daughter toward the porch.

"Hey!" Megan said as she caught up. "Don't I get a hello?"

Clay turned and saw her overjoyed smile as she celebrated the return of her little brother with even more than he sought out to get. Clay felt viciously conflicted about how to respond. His anger toward Megan had dwindled during the long journey home, but seeing her stirred up an ire that still resided in him. "Hey," he said coldly before walking up the porch steps and on into the house.

Megan stared blankly in disbelief, unsure of what she had done or said to merit such an icy response. Clay had never been so hurtful to her before. At first, she wanted to cry, but the hurt feelings quickly evolved into bitterness. "Be that way, jerk!" she said to the front of the house before storming off to finish her chores for the night.

After a bath and a shave with his straight edge, Clay started to feel human again. The effort that went into drawing a hot bath that always ended up being lukewarm—or colder—was something Clay dreaded. But after five weeks of mud, blood, and grit on the road, a good scrub was a requirement before Kelsey would grant him entry into their bed for the night.

Clay was in the middle of the bed with his arms and legs spread out; he could feel every muscle in his body start to relax. The bed was soft and fluffy, and compared to the makeshift beds he had slept in over the last month, it felt as if he was just floating on air.

Rain started to lightly pelt the window next to his bed and a soft clap of thunder rumbled in the distance. In a matter of minutes, Clay was on the verge of sleep until he heard the bedroom door latch shut. His eyes sprang open and he saw Kelsey walking toward him.

She playfully smacked his leg. "Scootch," she said before hopping into bed next to him. She gave him a kiss that ejected him out of his drowsy state. She pulled away and smiled brightly. Clay still found himself captivated by her eyes after nearly four years. "I missed you so much, Clay."

"I missed you too, Kels..." Clay's sigh satisfied his exhaustion and joy. "You have no idea."

It was the longest Clay and Kelsey had been apart since the winter after they met, when they were forced to spend nearly six months apart, separated by a little less than fifteen miles. This trip, however, felt much longer than that first winter.

Clay moved in to kiss Kelsey again, but her touch was not quite as inviting as previous contacts. She eased back and gave him a look that said "I need to get things off my mind before *that* train leaves the station."

Clay groaned with acceptance.

"You've been gone for weeks; is it asking too much to just talk to my husband for a few minutes?" she asked playfully, but not without a dash of sarcasm.

Clay gestured for her to speak her mind.

She buried her face into his chest and held him tight. "I always get so scared when you head out on any trip, but this one was even harder than the others," she said. She rolled over and looked at him. "And it seemed like so much happened while you were gone."

"Like what?" Clay asked.

"I'm not even sure I can remember it all," she paused. "Well, for one, Charles almost drowned in one of the wash tubs that had filled up with rain."

Clay felt sick to his stomach with the thought. "How'd that happen? Where were you?" he asked, sounding more accusatory than he had intended.

"What you went through earlier—being pulled fifty different directions at once—is my life on a daily basis, Clay," she said while giving him a glare.

"I'm sorry, Kels, I didn't mean it that way."

"I had to run over to get something from Megan's and asked Dakota to keep an eye on him, but she got distracted herself."

"With what?"

"A butterfly."

Clay tried not to smirk, as the lapse in judgment could have been devastating to the family, but she was six going on seven, and was enthralled with the flying insects that had only just made an appearance again this past Summer. Her passion for the pretty winged creatures was adorable, poor babysitting skills notwithstanding.

"I know you have been home a lot more than you used to, but..." she trailed off, trying to push the stressful previous month out of her mind, and focus on the future. "Just try not to leave us for such a long time again, okay?" she said with tears in her eyes.

As the storm rolled in, Clay and Kelsey continued talking, catching each other up on the events of the past five weeks. Clay reluctantly told Kelsey what happened with the trade—the setup— as well as the voyage back. Kelsey's expression was wrought with fear as Clay told her the details, as if she was reading a fiction and didn't know whether or not the three of them were going to make it home. Even though he still wrestled with his frustration with Megan—a detail he neglected to share with Kelsey—he found that recounting the trip to Kelsey had been cathartic. He hadn't realized just how much he needed to vent.

"Did you see the sky tonight?" Kelsey asked, redirecting the conversation in a more positive direction. "Wasn't it just beautiful?" Clay just stared at her in the dim, flickering candlelight barely illuminating the room. She became bashful. "What?" she asked as she pulled the blanket up to her eyes, all the while giggling.

"Yeah, I saw it," Clay said, "but once I saw you, I was distracted by an even more breathtaking sight."

Clay meant what he said in a most sincere way, but he figured the almost cliché line would also have a positive impact on her romantic mood—a theory that was confirmed when Kelsey grabbed his face and kissed him intensely. "You think that's gonna work on me?" she asked with a wide grin.

Clay emphatically nodded.

"Well, you're right," she said followed with laughter. She leaned in and kissed him again.

As quickly as the moment heated up, the flame was extinguished with a frantic knock on the door.

"Mommy!" Dakota cried from the other side.

Kelsey whispered an apology to Clay and got out of bed to let Dakota inside. With another clap of thunder, Dakota promptly dove into the bed and hid under the blankets.

Clay was reminded that Dakota's fear was deeper than the thunder itself. Over time, her nightmares had become less frequent, but sudden, sharp cracks of thunder in the middle of the night still pulled her out of Northfield and dropped her back inside Silas's cabin to a night filled with lightning and thunder, gunshots and death.

Dakota's trembling shook the entire bed. Clay reached down to scratch her head, but she pulled away. *The poor girl.* Clay pushed his own frustrations out of his mind and tried to comfort the frightened child. He couldn't imagine the terror she was experiencing. Even though Clay was right there in the cabin with her, even though it was *he* who killed Silas on that stormy night three years ago, to witness the horrific events from the eyes of a toddler had to be far more traumatic than anything Clay experienced.

"It's okay, Koty-bear," Kelsey said as she climbed back into bed. Dakota scrambled to Kelsey's leg and latched on. Her shuddering weakened as she clutched to her mother.

Kelsey looked up at Clay, giving him a sympathetic look. It was a tough spot to be in as a wife...as a mother. But Clay made no attempt to guilt her; sometimes things just happened and there was nothing he could do about it, so why stress over it? It was one of those moments. "It's fine," he said quietly. Then spoke a little louder, "I love you, Koty. Mommy and Daddy won't let anything bad happen, okay?"

"I love you," a muffled, sniffling voice said from beneath the blanket.

Chapter 3

Clay stepped onto the porch and looked out into the large field. He loved his home. Being there gave him a sense of peace that he hadn't experienced anywhere else and any time he had to sleep in another bed other than his own, he was reminded of just how much the place meant to him.

Northfield used to be one of the most successful farms in the county, but the heavy commercialization of agriculture eventually took a toll on small, local farmers. Facing stacks of past-due bills and an unstoppable competition, Ruth's grandfather started a welding company to offset the losses. Over time, he planted fewer and fewer crops and took on more and more welding jobs. By the time the property was passed down to Cliff—Ruth's father—most of the land was leased out to the big companies. He kept farming a couple of acres next to the house, growing various plants for his own family and his booth at a local farmer's market. However, for all intents and purposes, the long line of family farmers had ended with Cliff.

Stepping off the porch, Clay headed over to the large workshop just a couple hundred yards away. The decent sized aluminum building—once the very lifeline for the family business—was now where all repairs for the homestead occurred. It also housed the community's armory.

The oversized bay door had allowed Cliff to work on anything from a small green tractor to a 500-horsepower semi. That same mechanic's bay now acted as temporary housing for the animals until a proper stable could be built. The smell was nauseating—so much so that Clay planned on making it well known to the others that the livestock's permanent home needed to be at the very top of the priority list.

He unlocked the door and walked inside, the stench assaulting his senses. The translucent, plastic ceiling provided a reasonable amount of light, even when the sun was hidden—which was still most days—and the solar panels on the roof provided enough juice for a few fluorescents at night. The nicest feature about the workshop, Clay thought, was the wood burning stove that provided heat once the freezing temps rolled in; which occurred in the middle of October last year. He contemplated throwing a couple of logs into the stove to fight off the crisp morning air, but decided it wouldn't be worth the effort. It wasn't even cold enough to see his breath, and by the time he got a hot enough fire going, the outside temperature would be on the rise. Plus, he knew it only felt cold compared to the toasty-warm bed he had climbed out of just minutes before; his body would adjust after a few more minutes.

The supply closet had already been converted into something of an armory before Clay and his family arrived. Like the server room he had transformed back at the tower, the long closet was set up with shelves, multiple rifle safes, and a workbench. Buckets of brass and a few other reloading components were strewn about, but they still lacked a reloading press and dies—something Clay was forced to leave behind when they abruptly abandoned the tower a little over three years ago. By the time he and Geoff were able to return to retrieve the crucial survival gear, the place had been thoroughly scavenged, presumably by Watson's men.

Clay placed his rifle on the bench and quickly disassembled it. After his initial exam of his weapon, he was not optimistic about his ability to fix it, but he was unwilling to retire the firearm until he had the opportunity to investigate the problem in a safe and well-lit environment. With a wealth of gunsmith tools and books nearby, Clay held onto a sliver of hope that he may be able to do the repairs himself, but it didn't take long for him to realize the tip of his firing pin had broken. It was easy to spot after he disassembled the bolt carrier group—something he decided not to do when he first examined the rifle back at the factory. However, he should have noticed it then, even without breaking it down. The stress and anxiety from the shootout in the parking lot that morning must have impaired his observation skills.

The sight of the broken pin deflated him. He glared at the tiny piece of metal that literally made the difference between having a highly tuned precision rifle and an unsophisticated club. Without it, the rifle was useless. There was no repairing the pin, and making a new one was far outside Clay's abilities—due to his lack of expertise and necessary tools.

Clay was startled by the sound of the door opening behind him.

"Hey, jerk," Megan said, unsure whether she was joking or being honest with the salutation. Likely a bit of both.

He looked at her over his shoulder and said, "Hey," before turning back to the bench.

"Why are you mad at me?" Megan snapped, getting straight to the point.

Clay sighed, his shoulders slumping. He placed his palms on the bench and leaned forward. "Megan...I'm not mad at you," he said as he shook his head.

"So, last night was what, some new type of greeting you were trying out?" Megan twirled her hair with her fingers—something she was finally able to do again after years of keeping her hair cut short.

"Okay, so I *was* mad at you..."

"Why?" she asked as she shifted her stance and crossed her arms tightly across her body. She pursed her lips and tapped her toe as she waited to hear his response—like an angry mother waiting for an explanation of how her favorite vase had become dozens of shards on the floor.

"I was mad at you for pushing us to go on that trip. I was mad that you convinced Geoff, and that he convinced me. It was a stupid idea, regardless of the outcome."

Megan was surprised by his response—she hadn't expected that reasoning—her frustration morphed into guilt. She had been the biggest advocate for the idea while everyone else was, at best, feeling tepid. But once she got Ruth on board,

Geoff quickly caved, and he was the final domino in convincing Clay.

She walked up to him and put her hand on his shoulder. "I honestly don't know why I got so amped up about that stupid cow. Normally, I would be the first one to veto such a risky decision, but sometimes..." she trailed off, trying to think of a good response. "I guess the hope for a better life gets the best of me sometimes, and I am sorry for that. I should have never talked—"

"It's all right," Clay said. "It's not your fault."

Megan was again stunned by the direction of the conversation.

"It's mine," he said as he turned around to finally face her. "Living here is great, but it has made me way too complacent. I'm careless when I go out scavenging or hunting. I'm sloppy with my security detail—it's as if I've completely forgotten that the whole world has fallen apart. As if I should be *shocked* that someone would actually try to kill me just so they could take my stuff. If I had been *half* as lazy back when we lived at the tower, I would have been dead years ago."

Megan struggled to follow Clay's train of thought. "Yeah, but I pushed you into this. That's not your fault, it's mine."

"But back then if you, Geoff, or even Kelsey had asked me to do something as insane as that, I would have called you all nuts and not even entertained the idea. And it's not like I haven't been noticing this trend, but every time I convinced myself to get my act together, a few weeks of boredom puts me right back where I was before. I am just glad that nothing catastrophic happened—this time."

"Me, too," Megan said. She reached out and gave her brother a hug. "It's good to have you back, Clayton. I love ya. Even when you act like a butthead."

"Love ya, too, Megs."

Megan punched his arm. "Stop calling me that!" she said before looking down at the guts of his rifle on the bench. "Something wrong with your gun?"

"Yep," Clay said, his voice thick with frustration as he turned back around to look at his LaRue. "And I have no idea where I am going to get the part I need to fix it."

Megan was empathetic, but guns were not her thing. Her knowledge of firearms was limited; she could load and shoot most guns and clean her own pistol, but that was about it. "Maybe somebody in Liberty can help you out?"

"Yeah, that's what I am hoping."

"Well, I need to get going," Megan said as she turned and walked away, stopping just short of the door. "Dinner's at seven."

"Dinner?" Clay asked curiously. The families only got together for the big community dinners at the main house on special occasions—holidays, mostly. But Megan enjoyed any opportunity to have company. It was a big house, and it was just her, Hawthorne, and the kids staying there. Except for Bethany, who had been informally adopted by Clay and Kelsey, all of the kids from the tower, including Dusty, stayed with Megan. "What's the occasion?"

Megan nearly rolled her eyes, as if Clay was expected to already know. "Hi, welcome back," she replied.

Clay enjoyed the community gatherings, but the amount of food consumed was borderline irresponsible—especially this year with their winter provisions lacking the quantity needed for survival.

With deer sightings becoming rarer and successful harvests unreliable—especially with the overabundance of rain they'd had this year coupled with the lack of sunshine—it could prove reckless to have a big feast merely to welcome the three of them home.

"I don't know, Megan. We've still got a long way to go on getting our food stores in order. Should we really be splurging on a big dinner right now?"

"I know, I know," Megan said, "but Levi and Michael had several successful hunts while you guys were gone. No, we're not where we need to be just yet, but we're not doing too bad—and leaps and bounds better from where we were when you guys left. So, on that note..." Megan said, her emphasis shutting down further conversation, "dinner is at seven."

"Okay, okay," Clay replied, acting as if he was upset. The food was something to worry about, but after spending the last month and a half living off scraps, his arm didn't need to be twisted to have a good, home cooked meal.

Deciding against extensive physical labor around the ranch, Clay spent most of his time creating and prioritizing a laundry list of chores that required his attention. The worst part about long trips was the endless honey-do list that greeted him on his return—a list unfortunately made a little longer by their newly acquired livestock.

As promised, Clay arrived at the main house around seven. Kelsey greeted him with a kiss; she looked exhausted—her hair was disheveled, her clothes a mess, flour and other ingredients lightly adorned her shirt and face. Her unkempt look was a rare sight for Clay's wife. Since leaving Watson's farm, Kelsey abandoned her morning routine to quickly pull a brush through her hair to face the day and made a real effort to always be presentable and put together. She decided she didn't want her "old" self to be part of her new life. At first, her time spent in front of a mirror was merely for Clay's benefit, but after a while, she came to cherish the time spent preparing for the day—even without the luxuries of make-up and hair spray, just washing her face and braiding her hair were enough to make her feel beautiful.

Kelsey rushed out the door to try and pull herself together before the dinner plates hit the table. No sooner than the door latching, Clay heard a stampede of footsteps running down the stairs.

"Clay!" multiple voices shouted as several of the kids ran down the steps.

In seconds, the children he hadn't visited with after returning home last night swarmed Clay. Tyler, especially, was excited to hear about the adventures Clay, Geoff, and Dusty had had during their travels, but was disappointed with the lack of details Clay offered. Tyler planned to pester him for more specifics throughout the evening.

The kids quickly dispersed, except for Erica, who stayed behind to give Clay a long hug. "I'm so glad you made it home safely, Clay," she said with a warm smile.

Clay hugged her back. It felt like just yesterday Erica sulked about eating a cute, fluffy bunny for dinner, but now she was maturing into a young woman that was almost nothing like the little girl he had found inside the rusted-out husk of a car so many years ago. It was a bittersweet transition—one Clay had gone through with Lona not all that long ago.

Erica was quickly summoned to the kitchen to help Paige set the tables—there were two large tables and a collapsible card table crammed into the formal dining room to accommodate so many people. It was a bit cozy—uncomfortably so at times—but it was a worthwhile sacrifice to have everyone together for a nice, hot meal.

Clay wandered into the study to look for a good book to read. Since moving to Northfield, even during the winter, Clay found it impossible to find the time for such a leisure. He felt a painful pit in his stomach when he realized the last "book" he read was the short story Charlie had written.

He missed that kid.

Clay picked out his next literary adventure and stuffed it into a cargo pocket on his pant leg. He was determined to get through it before winter hit. He wasn't optimistic about the chances of that happening, though.

A family portrait beautifully preserved in a large, simplistic frame hung on the wall opposite the bookshelf. He didn't know why, but Clay always gazed at it when he was in the study. It was grounding to see a large family, dressed in their Sunday best, smiling as the photographer permanently chronicled the moment of history. Ruth looked to be about eight or nine years old at the time, but her dimples were as prevalent then as they were today. Cliff stood tall in the center of the photo. Melissa, his wife of more than twenty years, sat on a chair just in front of him. Flanked on either side of them were their six children. Once upon a time, they were a happy family, but of all the people in the photograph, only Ruth and her brother, Michael, still survived, an agonizing reality that mirrored Clay's life almost perfectly.

When Cliff passed away back in March, Ruth was devastated, but it was Michael who almost lost it. It took Geoff and Ruth over a week to get him to eat. And it was the better part of a month before he exited his small cottage near the center of the farm, finally speaking to another soul again. As far as Clay could tell, Michael was over the depression, but Clay was concerned with what he might do should anything happen to Ruth, the last of his kin. Clay could relate to the worry.

As Megan's call to dinner rang throughout the house, Clay snapped out of his thoughts and left the study. As he walked to the dining room, he glanced into the living room to see Lona setting up the kiddie table for Charles, Wyatt, and Elizabeth. Lona looked his way and gave him a quick wave before her reflexes prevented a spill as the kids sat down to eat.

Clay continued to the dining room where the masses shuffled in to claim a seat. The drifting aroma of the venison made Clay's mouth water. It would be his first hearty meal in six weeks. Since moving to Northfield, Megan had graduated from "just a cook" status—she was now a chef. Ruth was a culinary genius and Megan was a great student—so it was only a matter of time before the culinary arts were second nature for her.

Sitting down next to an empty chair, Clay looked over at Geoff, who gave a quick blessing over the meal before the room was filled with the melody of forks and knives clinking on the plates. Moments later, Kelsey returned, looking more like her usual self. She was ready to dig in to the meal she spent all afternoon helping to prepare.

The food was great and the company was better. Clay sat back in silence and just enjoyed listening to the families swap stories while they ate in the candlelight. It was moments like these that brought a sense of normalcy to the world again, moments that were far more common in Northfield than they had ever been since the quakes first rattled the earth. If it weren't for the bitter winters they still faced each year, Clay would have thought that this was just what life was like in Texas a hundred or so years ago.

Once dinner was over, Megan and Hawthorne retrieved a couple of pies from the kitchen and cut into them. Geoff used this opportunity to stand up to make an announcement. "I just wanted to say that I am so glad we're all here, together, having this delicious meal that these lovely ladies prepared for us tonight," he said as he reached down and squeezed Ruth's hand. She gave him a smile in return. He continued. "But tonight, we celebrate more than just our return. Ruth and I also wanted to tell you all that we are expecting again."

Cheers and fanfare erupted from around the room—Megan leading the charge as she ran around the table to give Geoff and Ruth hugs.

As the applause quieted down, a sole voice was heard above the rest. "What are you guys, rabbits?" Dusty chortled.

"Sydney!" Megan scolded Dusty—breaking a promise never to call her by her birth name in front of the others.

Dusty shot Megan a deadly look before rolling her eyes. She regretted ever mentioning her name to Megan.

As the night drew on, Michael had been the first to leave, which came as no surprise to the family— they were just happy he made the effort to join them. Geoff and Ruth left soon after him to put Wyatt and Elizabeth to bed. Levi stuck around and helped clean up after dinner. He was a bit sweet on Megan and despite everyone else figuring that out, she seemed completely oblivious to the fact. Clay, Geoff, and

Dusty even had a little wager on when—if—he would ever get the nerve to tell her how he felt.

As Clay headed out, he saw Blake walk by. "Hey, Blake." Clay's tone let him know what was coming next. "Hand it over," he said.

Blake withdrew his Sig 225—Clay's old pistol—dropped the magazine and cleared the chamber before handing it to Clay. As Blake picked up the ejected cartridge from the floor, Clay examined the gun. He held it up to a light and looked through the bore. He inspected a few areas for dirt and debris, but it looked good. Part of having his own gun was keeping it clean and fully functional. So, Clay made sure to hold Blake accountable for ever having a dirty firearm. He scolded him once or twice about it in the past and Blake quickly learned his lesson.

"Good job, Blake," Clay said as he handed the pistol back. "Couldn't have cleaned it any better myself," he added.

"Thanks," Blake said as he slammed the magazine back in and returned it to the holster.

"You got a sec?" Clay asked, nodding toward the door.

"Sure," Blake replied.

Clay stepped outside and Blake trailed closely behind. At first neither of them said anything as they walked to Clay's house, but the silence quickly grew awkward for Blake and he spoke up. "Is everything okay? Did I do something wrong?"

"Huh?" Clay responded. "Oh, no, you didn't do anything wrong, Blake. I just wanted to chat with you a bit about some things that have been on my mind, is all."

Blake's relief was audible.

"Actually, I just wanted to say thank you for stepping up around here, especially since I've been gone a lot lately," Clay said. His eyes got misty as he remembered saying a very similar thing to Charlie back at the tower. Though, unlike Charlie, Blake was almost sixteen, and both he and Clay knew the days of being a kid were already behind him. Clay continued. "Kelsey and Megan have been telling me what an immense help you've been. I've even heard good reports from Michael and Levi as well."

Blake was quiet at first. "Just doing my part," he said confidently. "Everyone around here works so hard, it seems like it's the least I can do."

Clay appreciated Blake's work ethic and his willingness to put his family's needs before his own. The brief time Charlie had been part of Blake's life had a lasting impact. Even though Clay was proud of the young man Blake was becoming, he couldn't help but feel guilty that he hadn't been around much lately. The trip to Mesquite was just the most recent journey Clay had been on and would certainly not be the last. Clay was going to make an effort to spend more one-on-one time with Blake and Tyler. Clay's priorities had been all over the place, causing him to shirk his responsibility to both boys over the past few months.

Clay went inside the house and grabbed his KSG-12 shotgun, a thermos of tea, and some food Kelsey had packed before he headed toward the gate. It was Clay's night for guard duty, and every guard needed those three things to make it through the night.

As they walked down the long driveway, Clay continued. "So, how are things going with Lona?" His question was intended to provoke a conversation about their relationship. It was unsuccessful.

"It's good," Blake said with a shrug.

"That's it?" Clay asked. "Just good?"

"Yup," Blake said awkwardly, clearly lacking desire to have this conversation with Clay.

"Well...All right then," Clay replied.

Though Clay wanted to have that talk about as much as Blake did, he knew it was something that needed to happen. Forcing the conversation wouldn't do any good though, and might even make things worse, so Clay dropped it. Blake quickly regained his willingness to talk when the conversation steered toward less uncomfortable topics.

As the rain began to fall, Blake excused himself and headed indoors for the night. The rain was cold and Clay could already feel the slimy film building up on his skin. It was going to be a long night.

Chapter 4

Clay and Geoff could just barely make out Liberty Township up ahead. A heavy fog rolled in just after sunrise, prompting both of them to grip their rifles a little tighter. Not even an hour earlier, a lone gunshot echoed through the trees on the opposite side of the highway they were crossing. Likely just a hunter fortunate enough to find some game, the gunfire coupled with poor visibility stiffened the hair on their necks, adding to their resolve to get to town.

Overall, though, the journey had been easy enough. What used to take four or five days on foot now took a little over two with the horses. The animals also provided them the ability to bring more goods to trade. And once Michael and Levi finished fixing up an old wagon they claimed from a vacant, neighboring farm, Clay planned for some serious commerce between the two communities.

The clopping sound of horse hooves reverberated off the stone walls that flanked either side to the long driveway leading into Liberty. The asphalt was riddled with cracks and divots, looking more like dried mud than steamrolled pavement. Despite the dilapidated appearance, the entrance to town was a welcomed sight.

As soon as the guards recognized the approaching strangers as Clay and Geoff, one of the men unlatched the gate and tugged it open, allowing both horses to enter without stopping. Clay and Geoff said a quick hello as they passed by, heading straight into town. Leaving their horses in some empty stable stalls, Clay and Geoff headed over to Mary Anne's— the only "restaurant" in town. Though many of the businesses in Liberty carried food, Mary Anne prepared it as well. Besides making a mean breakfast, the woman crafted the best iced tea Clay had ever tasted—even before the collapse. To top it all off, she was one of the sweetest old ladies he had ever met. Clay was certain that if you put Mary Anne and Hawthorne in a room together, you'd get a cavity just by walking in.

It was a little after two, but Clay and Geoff ordered the same thing they always did: wild boar omelet covered with goat cheese and a side of fresh picked blackberries. Apart from the salty goat cheese, the dish was practically identical to one Clay would get at a diner near his house when he was a kid. Though, the sausage this afternoon had a pretty strong gamey taste to it—the boar must have been enormous—Clay wasn't about to complain. It still tasted great.

After squaring up with Mary Anne for the food, Clay and Geoff headed over to Vlad's. They hadn't visited the town since the thaw, so Clay was eager to see his old friend again. Before Clay pushed the door open wide enough to walk in, the Russian spoke.

"Clay! Geoff! My friends, it is good to see you!" the lively man said from behind the counter.

"Howdy, Vlad. Long time, no see," Clay said. He looked over at the pretty young woman standing next to him. "How are you, Olesya?" he asked politely.

"I am well, thank you," she said with a slight accent—nowhere near as heavy as her father's.

While the three men spent a few minutes catching up, Olesya busied herself displaying recent trades on the shelves. Clay stopped her as she walked by with a stack of books. Preparing for the coming winter season and determined to improve his reading habits, he removed three of the fiction novels from the heap and set them on the counter.

As the conversation wound down, Vlad asked, "Are you preparing to go to war, my friend?" pointing to the rifles over each one of Clay's shoulders.

Since Clay's LaRue was not currently functional, he had to resort to a Chinese knockoff of the classic Soviet rifle—the SKS. It was far from ideal, but it was a better option than his Scout rifle—he still hadn't found a magazine replacement.

"So, about that...you wouldn't happen to have any spare AR firing pins lying around, would you?" Clay asked jokingly but with a tinge of hope in his voice.

"Ha!" Vlad let out a single, gravely chortle that originated deep in his gut. "You are very funny man, Clay." He gestured to his store, which was emptier than Clay had ever seen it. "Sure, I have hundreds in back room, let me go grab you one," he said with a chuckle in his voice. "And while I am back there, would you like brand new flat screen television?"

"Ha-ha, *Boris,* no need to be a wise guy," Clay jabbed back. "I figured it was a long shot."

"I think Lenin has better chance of rising from dead," the Russian added.

"Well, how about someone to fix my current one?" Clay asked.

Vlad's chuckle faded as he racked his brain for a name. "I used to do business with man from Lufkin, but have not seen him in years," Vlad's expression indicating that he assumed the man had left the area or was dead. "There is other man—never met him—but others have told me much."

"Well, who is he? Where does he live?" Clay asked, a spark of optimism in his voice.

"They call him Smith, I do not know if that is real name. He is said to be north of here in FEMA camp. I am afraid that is all I know."

Clay was torn. If he didn't find someone to repair the rifle, he might as well melt it down and turn it into nails. However, traveling into an unknown area always came with risks. He wasn't about to ask Geoff to come, which meant Clay would be going alone—only adding to the danger. And with all the epidemics that had occurred in the various FEMA camps since their installation, Clay could very well expose himself to something that had been lying dormant for several years—a germ without a victim. Despite his better judgment, he decided to go.

Clay and Geoff conducted some smaller trades with Vlad and then headed to a few other shops around town. Unfortunately, most of them had the same ominous look as Vlad's—empty shelves. Fresh food now took up more shelf space than manufactured goods from the past. Though Clay was always on the lookout for food, the farm back home kept every mouth fed, even if it ran a bit lean at times. What they were running out of, however, were essentials like fabrics, functional tools, and other mass-produced items that were becoming harder to find. Clay imagined there were pockets across America—little towns and country houses—that were filled with undisturbed goods, but those places were out of reach without modern—rather, historical—means of transportation.

"So, I'm leaving for the FEMA camp first thing in the morning," Clay said as the pair walked back to Vlad's.

"What? You're crazy. You don't even know where it is, let alone who or what might live up there." Geoff shook his head, "After what happened up in Mesquite, do you think it's smart for us to go venturing into the unknown again—especially without Dusty watching our six?"

"You're right," Clay replied quickly, "it isn't smart for *us* to go."

"Okay, you're not crazy. You're downright freakin' insane. There's no way I am letting you go alone."

Clay appreciated the concern, but it would carry no weight in his decision. "What are you, my mother?" Clay asked sarcastically followed by a grin. "Besides, you need to get back home to Ruth. Megan already told me the mornings have not been too kind to her. Plus, I need you to tell Kelsey that I am going to be gone for a few extra days. If neither of us come back, they're going to start to worry."

"Then don't go yet. We'll go back home, get Dusty, and leave in a few days."

"No," Clay replied, "there is too much we need to do to prepare for winter. Having you, me, *and* Dusty gone again for another week or so isn't something we can afford right now. Remember last year? We started preparing for winter in July and we had a pretty comfortable ride. We're nearly at the end of August and we *still* haven't really started preparing."

Clay had that bullheaded tone in his voice that warned Geoff of his stubbornness and because Geoff was too exhausted to try and argue, he relented. "Fine, I'll head back in the morning. But here," he said as he slid his sling over his head. "You take the AK."

"All right. Thanks," Clay said as they swapped rifles. Geoff's rifle had a thirty-round magazine and several loaded spares to go with it. It was a much better option for Clay than the ten-round fixed magazine the SKS sported. Though not entirely without risks, the path between Liberty and Northfield was a relatively safe one, so Clay's need for the AK-47 was greater than Geoff's.

"Just don't be stupid, and get back home in one piece," Geoff said.

"You know me; careful is what I do."

"Yeah," Geoff replied sharply, "sure it is."

After claiming their room for the night, Geoff took the opportunity to rest—sleep did not come easily for him out on the road and his exhaustion had overcome him. Clay, having slept on many a hard bed since the eruptions, was wide awake and wasn't about to turn in at four in the afternoon, so he meandered around town.

The blue-haired Rose had a bottle of oil she wanted Clay to take back to Megan. It was a special blend that the two had talked about the last time Megan visited town. It was amazing that the contents inside were so potent that the tiny fifteen-milliliter bottle could last months, if not more, when diluted properly.

As he left Rose's shop, Clay heard someone call his name. He turned around and was greeted by Mayor Shelton, who already had his hand extended.

"It's good to see you, Clay. How are you and that lovely bride of yours?" Shelton asked.

"We're good, Barry, thanks. How are things here?"

"Oh, we're doin' good, too. I'm sure you noticed that supplies are a little skimpier than they were the last time you visited, but we'll get by. I suppose it's just time for us to start getting more creative with how we use—or reuse—materials and such."

Shelton's optimism was a rare character trait to witness these days and one that Clay greatly admired, even if he had little chance of learning from it.

"Hey, what are you doin' right now?" Shelton asked.

Clay shrugged and shook his head. "Nothing, really. Just killing time. We're heading out in the morning."

"Interested in joining me for a hunt? We've been havin' a bit of luck over the past few weeks in a pretty secluded place a few miles from here."

"That sounds great."

"All right then, follow me," Shelton said as they headed for the stables.

Shelton pointed to a black spotted horse toward the end of the row and said, "Saleen here hasn't been out on a good long ride in a while, so you can take her if you'd like."

Stopping short of Saleen's stall, Clay said, "No thanks, brought my own ride today."

Shelton nodded in approval. "Good looking horse you got there. I thought y'all didn't have any on the farm?"

"We...unexpectedly acquired some recently."

Noticing the grim expression on Clay's face, Shelton abandoned the discussion. "Well, all right then. Let's get going," he said, climbing up onto the saddle.

As they trotted through town, Clay asked, "Do you know how to get to the FEMA camp north of here?"

"I do not," Shelton said, "However, Scott Adams and his wife came from there before they found their way here. I'm sure they could tell you where it is."

Clay had heard the name before, but couldn't put a face to it. "Scott is..."

"He's got the furniture shop on the other side of town," Shelton responded.

"Oh yeah!" Clay said, remembering the man. "He has some incredible pieces in there. He's a gifted carpenter." Clay looked forward to trading for a few of his masterpieces once they got the wagon operational.

"That he is," Shelton said.

Their horses came to a stop at the gate while Shelton talked with the guards for a couple of minutes.

"Keep an eye out for us," he said, "if the gettin' is good, we might be out past sunset."

Normally, this would be cause for concern; traveling at night was ill-advised, even for a group of well-armed men. But the Screamer activity near Liberty was virtually nonexistent. Clay had found himself on more than one occasion strolling into Liberty long after dusk without ever bumping into the nocturnal monsters.

"Will do, Mr. Shelton; have a safe trip," the guard said as he opened the gate.

As they reached the end of the driveway, Shelton slowed his horse to a complete stop and locked his gaze toward the east. Clay watched as Shelton strained his eyes—he was focused on a very specific location. "Now, what is going on here?" he muttered to himself as he retrieved the hunting rifle hanging from his back and raised the scope up to his eye.

"What is it?" Clay asked, detecting the disconcerting tone in Shelton's voice.

"There's someone up in the second story of that house over there," Shelton said pointing toward a small cluster of brick homes about a quarter mile away on the other side of the road.

It wasn't uncommon to run into other people on the road, so Clay was confused as to why Shelton seemed so concerned. "Should we just go wide; try and avoid them?" Clay asked.

Shelton, still staring through his rifle optics, finally said, "I'm not really worried about that. I'm more concerned with finding out why he has a pair of binoculars sighted in on my town."

Now Clay was as unsettled as Shelton. He also retrieved his rifle—Geoff's SLR-95—from his back and ensured it was chambered.

"The deer can wait," Shelton said before smacking his horse on the rear, tearing off for the house up ahead. Clay did the same and together they stormed the houses.

As they approached the house harboring the stranger, Clay jumped down from his horse and had his rifle at the ready. Shelton also dismounted and pulled out his Browning Hi Power in lieu of his scoped 30-30. Clay took point with his AK-47; Shelton covered. They were greeted by the back door swaying in the light breeze as they rounded the corner of the house.

Clay entered first, doing his best impression of a ghost. Although he was swift and quiet on his feet, his anxious breathing—which was exacerbated from the pounding in his chest—was the loudest sound in the abandoned house. Even though he didn't want to give away his exact location, Clay figured the stampeding horses racing up the house had already ruined any element of surprise, and the creaky stairs only further spoiled their efforts.

Keeping the rifle stock pressed firmly into his shoulder, Clay kept one eye glued to the sight while the other attempted to spot any movement other than the dust carelessly passing in front of the arch window. He swung the rifle from left to right as more of the second floor came into view. Finally reaching the top step, they stopped and listened.

Clay's fingers strangled the grip on his rifle as he sat in total silence. The lack of sound meant one of two things: either the men were already gone or they were waiting, guns raised, and ready to shoot anyone who walked through the door. After checking the two bedrooms to the right, all that was left was the master on the opposite end of the hall. Turning to look back at Shelton, Clay gestured toward the door.

Clay crept down the hallway, pressing his back up against the wall when he approached the door. He took a deep breath and exhaled slowly, quietly. He looked at Shelton again, giving a quick nod, then spun around the doorframe and into the bedroom.

"Don't move!" Clay shouted as he dropped down to one knee and took aim, Shelton coming in just behind him.

The room was empty.

Clay immediately felt relief, but that feeling was quickly chased away by the realization that somebody was nearby. And Clay had no idea if he was armed or what his intentions were.

The rest of the house was more of the same—trashed, but empty rooms. Except for the back door being ajar—which wasn't an uncommon sight on an abandoned house like the one they were in—there was no tangible evidence that anybody had been inside in a long time.

They expanded their search outside and through a few neighboring houses. Nearly a half hour after Shelton first saw the binoculars in the window, the men quit and returned to their horses. It didn't sit well with Shelton to just give up searching and leave after seeing something as suspicious as a man watching his town from afar, but he found comfort in how well defended Liberty was. And if the small town could successfully fend off hordes of Screamers over the years, then a curious bandit or two wouldn't likely pose much of a threat.

Still, there was something disconcerting about it all, so Shelton decided to head back to town, abandoning the afternoon hunt. He wanted to alert security to the threat, and if something *was* going to go down, he needed to be there for it. Since Clay was uneasy with the stranger himself, he was not opposed to returning to town.

After securing his horse for the evening, Clay stopped by Scott Adams's store to get a general idea of where the FEMA camp was before heading back to his room for the night. Since he was leaving for the camp first thing in the morning, Clay hoped he would calm down enough to get a few hours of sleep.

Chapter 5

Finally. The end of the ocean of trees Clay had waded through for the past six hours had come into sight. Despite his compass being glued to his hand the entire time, he was convinced that he was lost. Following the road around the forest would have cost him at least an extra day, but punching right through wasn't without risks. Risks, Clay realized, that were all too real when the sun began to set just beyond the silhouetted foliage in front of him. Another hour in the former nature preserve and Clay would have been forced to camp out for the night. Small drop-offs and creeks, among other natural hazards, would make traversing the woods nearly impossible without a strong light. And someone walking in the middle of a dark forest with a bright light might as well be holding up a neon sign that read, *COME KILL ME!*

The tightness in Clay's chest subsided when he saw the weak sun glinting off a guardrail up ahead. It never dawned on him that someone could be claustrophobic while walking outside. Yet, when he lost sight of the tree line behind him as he delved deeper into the forest, finding himself completely engulfed by wooden skyscrapers, it felt as if he was receiving a loving hug from a Burmese python. The suffocating sensation forced him to stop to catch his breath on more than one occasion.

Because so much about the trip was unknown, Clay decided to leave his horse back at Liberty and make the journey on foot. It was about a thirty-mile hike, and he was on the tail end of day two. Clay was not looking forward to night camped out under the proverbial stars, but he had no idea how close he was to the campsite. If his navigation was true, then he should be a mile or two from the gates when he reached the road. If he had veered off course, however, there was no telling.

Clay took a deep breath as he stepped out from the wall of trees and left the forest behind him. As he approached the rural highway, he immediately saw a faded sign with an arrow pointing to the left that read:

FEMA 2A Regional Campsite

He was close, but how close? There were no signs except for those indicating the direction to the entrance. Though Clay would have no problem finding the camp now, the sun's already stifled brightness was quickly fading.

Keeping low in a drainage ditch just off the pavement, Clay followed the road while searching for a street sign or mile marker that would help him get his bearings. He used the line of stalled out cars—presumably abandoned by those waiting to get inside the camp—as cover from anyone that might be creeping in the forest across the street.

At last, a mile marker. Clay knelt down and unfolded his map. It didn't take long to find out that he had strayed off course—about twice as far as he had expected. The entrance looked to be another four to five miles away—out of reach before nightfall—so Clay played it safe. His unfamiliarity with the area, plus his own fragile state of mind after nearly going mad in the forest, was exhausting and distracting. He quickly decided to seek out shelter, and took up residence in a recreational vehicle.

He quietly stepped into the RV and, using what little light was left, confirmed it was vacant. The bedroom was, as expected, cramped. The bed, which took up most of the room, was lumpy and reeked of a terrible odor. It took a little while to get comfortable, but it beat sleeping outside in the rain—which had started pummeling the camper shortly after Clay walked inside.

Once he fell asleep, however, Clay slept soundly.

Morning came quickly, as it always did on nights he slept well. He sat on the edge of the bed and ate a couple of sticks of jerky, allowing his body time to wake up. Because it was only a couple minutes after eight and the entrance just a few miles up the road, Clay took his time getting ready. It was a rare incident for him to be able to wake up and prepare for the day with such leisure—especially while out on the road. After a ferocious yawn, accompanied with a series of stretches, Clay rose to his feet, picked up the two rifles—slinging the AR-15 on his back—and walked out of the bedroom.

As Clay searched through the RV for anything useful, he was distracted by a series of pictures decorating the refrigerator door. Most of the pictures consisted of the same two retirees in front of different landmarks around the country—each dated and labeled. The last one showed the couple posing with some penguins with the caption "Dallas World Aquarium!"

Looks like fun, Clay thought to himself. He had always wanted to go there.

The RV search turned up nothing. A successful scavenge was becoming rarer with each passing day. People had become so desperate that they would turn entire buildings upside down just to find that can of tuna that fell behind the fridge. It wasn't uncommon for Clay to find a small item here and there, but long gone were the days of finding a big score that would fetch a hefty price with traders.

Clay cautiously exited the RV and continued following the signs. He had to stop twice when he came across corpses lying face down on the side of the road. The first looked to have been there for quite some time, the decomposed body was enough to cause trouble with what little Clay had eaten for breakfast. The second was more recent—within the last couple of days—and the mutilation, along with the crude markings around the body, stirred up a deep-seated hatred Clay had for the group responsible for the killing. Though it had been several months since his last encounter with a Screamer, Clay's anger toward the murderous lunatics had not diminished.

The entrance to the camp finally came into view. A large, open gate, blocked by a deuce and a half and several Humvees let Clay know he was in the right spot. He carefully made his way to the front, keeping low and sprinting from car to car to reach the gate without being seen. Though he still held out hope that Smith would be there and as hospitable as the folks in Liberty, Clay knew that the odds were not in his favor. The reality of the matter was that the campsite was more likely to be vacant or occupied by a gang or bandit group. Even so, Clay pressed forward because the risks were still worth the potential reward.

Once Clay walked through the gate and got past the dozens of small buildings used as processing centers, he was overwhelmed with the sheer size of the camp. It felt like hundreds, if not thousands of acres. There were prefabricated housing units as far as the eye could see—small buildings that looked more like a set from a sci-fi movie rather than actual homes. It was the best the government had to offer, though, and most people didn't complain once they were able to taste their first hot meal in months. But as Clay stared at the seemingly infinite rows of pre-manufactured dormitories, he knew that his and Megan's decision to survive on their own had been the right call. This camp was empty, and it was empty for a reason. Something bad had happened, and of the 30,000 or more people that lived here, it appeared, at that moment, that not even one of them remained.

A strong, abrupt gust of wind drew Clay's attention back to the trees across the road. A storm was coming in—no surprise. He returned his attention to the expansive field in front of him—truly a scavenger's paradise—and started walking forward. Clay could spend months going through the structures with a fine-tooth comb, but it wasn't why he was there, and he didn't have the time to be distracted.

The field was relatively flat, so it was pretty easy to spot the two-story cement construction toward the center of the camp—like a giant, black ink stain on a wedding dress. As Clay walked by the first of the camp homes, he noticed the quality of construction was even worse than it appeared from the entrance.

The homes were far from secure—which was one of the biggest complaints Clay had heard from people who had left the camps. Theft and sexual assaults had become rampant, and unless a nearby soldier happened to catch a suspect in the act or the victims had *very* reliable witnesses, little was ever done to reprimand offenders. These structures were not secure then and would be a deathtrap now. Clay knew that if there was any chance of Smith still being alive, he would find him closer to the large building ahead.

Though the rain had started to fall and the wind picked up, there was almost an ominous silence filling the air. There was something creepy about standing in the middle of the popup ghost town.

As Clay got closer to the building, he could see that there was a concrete perimeter surrounding it. The wall—which easily towered fifteen feet into the air and was covered with razor wire—going over was not an option. Straight ahead was an opening in the wall; a heavy duty, wrought iron gate filling the void, and from where he was standing, it was locked up tight.

As he approached the gate, Clay's mind began to speculate about what had caused the camp to empty. Was this one of the camps that got hit with rioting after the first winter? *No,* Clay thought to himself, *not enough destruction for that.* It was possible that maybe they just ran out of supplies and were forced to disband. He tried to convince himself that was the likely reason, but his worries kept taking him back to a very real and more frightening possibility—an epidemic.

The faint sound of a dog's bark snapped Clay from his momentary lapse of attention and caused him to spin around with his rifle raised. He knew he had heard the dog, but it was so muffled he couldn't tell where it had come from. He stopped to listen again, but all he heard was the deep rolling grumble of the imminent storm.

He reached the gate and, as he suspected, it was locked. The gate was magnetically latched with a ten-digit keypad next to the handle. Clay let out an ironic laugh. He hadn't traveled all that way to just turn around and leave because of a locked gate. He wasn't exactly thrilled to have to find some way over the wall, but now it was the only choice. *Oh well,* Clay thought to himself as he playfully pressed the zero button on the keypad.

BEEP

Clay jumped back when he heard the audible sound. There was power running to the gate. With curiosity now firmly in control, Clay pushed a few more buttons. The beeps continued, followed by a substantial buzz that was accompanied by a small, blinking red light. Clay reached out to press the buttons again when he felt more than he heard someone walk up behind him.

"That'll do, kid," a man said from behind.

Clay didn't have to turn around to know that he was on the losing end of a gun.

****

"What's wrong, dear?" Hawthorne asked, seeing the worry on Kelsey's face as she walked inside.

Kelsey let out a deep sigh as she sat down next to the woman who was basically her mother. Kelsey only sat for a moment before standing back up to pace around the room. "Geoff just got back and Clay wasn't with him," she said with a shaky voice from a mixture of irritation and worry. "He said that Clay was going up north to see a man about fixing his gun…"

"Boys and their guns," Hawthorne said jokingly while shaking her head, trying to lighten the mood.

Kelsey smiled for a moment before twisting back to a frown. "I mean, Bev, he *just* got back less than two weeks ago, and then he goes off and does this?" Kelsey's worry was losing the battle to her frustration. "And from the sounds of it, this is a pretty dangerous trip…"

"Well, what trip isn't dangerous these days, Kelsey?" Hawthorne replied.

"I know…" she conceded, returning to her seat next to the aging woman. "I just…I just don't know what I would do if something ever happened to him. And these trips are almost always for non-essential things anymore." Kelsey fell back into the cushion of the chair and sighed again. "It was different when it was a matter of survival. When there wasn't enough food to go around or that time Sarah got sick and needed medicine. I get that. But going after a cow? Or finding a replacement part for a stupid gun? *That*, I don't understand," Kelsey said as she rested her elbows on her knees and buried her face into her hands.

Hawthorne, being the observant woman she was, knew that Kelsey wasn't upset about the cow or the gun, but because she wasn't able to see her husband. That and the extraordinary pressures that came with each day in the world they lived in pushed Kelsey to her limits. Hawthorne recalled the early days of her own marriage, back in a time when America was the flourishing economic giant of the world. Even then, married life for newlyweds was stressful, and it took a lot of hard work to get through. But now? The stresses were exacerbated by the dire circumstances all around them.

"Well, dear, I don't know exactly what it's like to be in your shoes, but I *can* tell you that I do have some experience with the constant worry of whether or not your husband would come back home each time he walked out the door."

"What do you mean?"

"My David was a police officer up in Tulsa before we moved down to Texas."

"Really?" Kelsey asked, the tone in her voice lightened. "You never told me your husband was a cop."

Hawthorne nodded. "Seventeen years up there. For the first five years of our marriage he worked the graveyard shift. I never could sleep while he was on duty, so I ended up staying up all night and sleeping during the day—that way we shared the same schedule. It made everyday things like grocery shopping a bit more of a challenge, but I made it work."

Kelsey found the story endearing—a true display of love. "That's so sweet," she said.

"Well," Hawthorne continued, "I won't lie, I didn't always do it with a smile on my face. Whenever I would hear on the radio or television about an armed criminal on the run, I would just sit at home and read a book—it was the only thing that distracted my mind enough to not have a full-blown panic attack.

"Then, one day, a man twice his size broke David's arm while he was trying to arrest him. The first thing I told him when I walked into the hospital room was that he had to quit his job. I even..." Hawthorne's eyes became glassy as she uttered such terrible words. "I even told him if he didn't quit that I was going to leave him." Hawthorne reached for a handkerchief and dabbed at the moisture collecting around her eyes.

"I'm guessing since he worked there seventeen years he never quit?"

Hawthorne shook her head. "No. He told me he would if that was what I wanted, but then he told me why he did it—his reasons for being a cop. I started to see it the way he did—that getting even just one criminal off the street made the world safer for me. In a strange, roundabout way, David being a policeman was one of his ways of protecting me."

Kelsey nodded and could see where Hawthorne was going with her story.

"You may not always get why Clay goes out on these trips, but he has his reasons. Even a blind man could see how much he loves you just by the way he looks at you. That boy adores you, Kelsey. I'm certain that you and the kids are always at the center of his mind whenever he makes those decisions."

Kelsey's frustration melted away as she listened to Hawthorne's encouraging words. Though Kelsey was always a mess while Clay was away, especially when he was out on his own, she *did* know that he did it because he thought it was what was best for his family. That didn't mean his choices were always smart, but his intentions were good, and being reminded of that brought Kelsey relief.

Both women fell silent as they sat in the living room, listening to the soft rain through an open window. The soothing sound took Kelsey back to the summer rains she fell asleep to as a child and caused her to relax.

The rain combined with the rhythmic sound of Hawthorne's knitting needles clicking together caused Kelsey's eyes to grow heavy. Within moments of dozing, she awoke to a jarring scream from upstairs.

"Give it back, Sarah!" Dakota cried from upstairs.

Kelsey's eyes exploded open as she startled awake. Her body was tense as she snapped out of that semi-conscious state. She looked over at Hawthorne and gave a sarcastic smile. "Well, that nap was good while it lasted," she said as she clumsily pushed herself out of the chair and headed toward the stairs.

Chapter 6

As Clay became aware of his environment, he was first assaulted by the faint droning sound that seemed to surround him. It was constant, almost like a central air conditioner—something he hadn't heard since the grid went down. Intermittent clicking that seemed to move around him from one side to the other interrupted the steady droning. As he concentrated on identifying the source of the clicking sound, the pain that crept into his head overcame all his senses.

The throbbing inside his skull was nauseating. He felt each pulsating beat of his heart with such intensity that he wondered if the organ was actually inside his head. The pain was so intense; he squeezed his eyes shut tight as he grimaced. The clicking sounds had gotten further away, but quickly returned as Clay began to stir. Then he felt something wet brush against his hand. *A tongue? Did something lick me?*

Clay's eyes briefly cracked open before snapping shut. The dim light bulb hanging from the ceiling might as well have been an unobstructed view of the sun it was so bright against his pounding headache. Though his mind raced to form countless questions, Clay struggled to find the energy to care about anything in that moment—that is, until he heard the man speak.

"Good morning, sunshine!" The man's booming voice echoed off the concrete walls, further antagonizing the pain in Clay's head.

Clay forced his eyes open again; this time they stayed open. A burly figure stood a few feet in front of him, blocking the sixty-watt nuclear blast that had blinded Clay moments before. Though the man was merely an unfocused silhouette, the profile of the semi-auto pistol in his hand seemed razor sharp—a sobering sight that immediately expelled Clay from the lingering daze he had been stuck in.

"So, what are you doing snooping around my neighborhood, kid?" the man asked as he fidgeted with the pistol in his hand, a subtle gesture that told Clay he needed to choose his words carefully.

Clay tried to speak, but his words—if you could call them that—were a jumbled mess of nonsense that even Clay couldn't understand. As his eyes began to focus, he could see the puzzled look on the man's face.

"Say what?" the man said as he scratched his chin buried beneath a beard that was equally as thick as his frame.

Clay shook his head and cleared his throat. "Uhm..." he said as he concentrated on each of the words he wanted to say, but all he got out was, "Vladimir."

"Vladimir? Who's that?" the man replied. "I don't know anyone by that name." The man took a step closer to Clay.

Clay looked up at the giant towering over him. He felt lightheaded. "Vladimir," Clay said as he feebly gestured with his hand, as if he was having a casual conversation. "Vlad...broken rifle...repair." His eyes shut.

When he woke up again, his head—though still aching—was faring much better than before. He was still alive, so the answer he provided the man must have been at least somewhat sufficient. Clay heard the clicking sound again and could locate a small dog as the source of the noise. He cautiously stuck his hand out, and the dog licked his fingers. Besides a pair of German Shepherds in Liberty, Clay couldn't remember the last time he had seen a domesticated canine.

Clay moved his hand to the top of the dog's head and began scratching. The dog sat down and happily accepted the stranger's offering. At first, Clay thought it was just his vision still regaining focus, but after a while, he recognized that the dog had only one eye. *It's even a tough life for man's best friend,* Clay thought.

The dog did an about face and made his way across the room toward an open doorway, his tail swinging with much more youth than the rest of his body displayed. The dog's master had returned with a plate in one hand and a cup in the other. He set the plate down on a table in the middle of the room and then walked over to Clay. Each step in his awkward gait was accompanied with a brief whooshing sound.

"Here," the man said as he reached down, placing the cup in front of Clay's face.

Clay reached up and took the cup from the lumberjack. He gave it a quick sniff before gulping down the contents. Following a satisfied sigh, Clay said, "Thanks."

"Don't have any pain meds I'm willing to spare, so that's the best I'm gonna be able to do for ya."

"I've got some in my pack, I think," Clay said just above a whisper.

The man walked across the room and then came back with the bag. He dropped it down next to Clay, returning to a table in the middle of the room to eat whatever was on the plate. Clay fished through his pack only to find an empty bottle—an unfortunate time to remember he needed a resupply from Megan.

Clay looked around the room—an oblong concrete box lacking any sort of character except for the table in the middle, a stack of bagged dog food in the corner, and some sort of map hanging on the wall. "Where are we?" he asked, his voice slightly stronger than before.

"Well, right now we're sitting in the middle of my dining room."

Clay wanted to roll his eyes, but between the pain and the fact that he knew nothing about the man he would be mocking caused him to think better of it. "And where is your dining room located exactly?"

The man finished chewing a bite of food before continuing. "We're underneath the building on the other side of that gate you were trying to break into," the man said with an accusatory tone.

"I wasn't trying to break in," Clay said, but had to clear his throat before he continued. "A friend of mine—"

"Vladimir or something, right?" the man interjected.

"Yes, *Vladimir* told me about a man named Smith up this way who worked on guns."

"Well," the man said as he picked a piece of gristle out of his teeth, "you found him." Smith walked back over to Clay and crouched down in front of him. His pant legs hiked up just enough to reveal both prosthetics, something Clay couldn't help but notice. His eyes eventually met with Smith's. "So, tell me, uh...Sorry, didn't catch your name."

"Clay."

"So, tell me, Clay, why should I help you? I've made it a habit to only work with people who have already helped me out in the past. I keep a tight circle of friends, and I don't really care much for strangers."

"I'm a good friend to have," Clay said, trying to sell his argument. "I can get you fresh produce, venison, hog...Heck, I can even get you some milk," Clay said, trying to suppress his grin. As dangerous as the trip to Mesquite had been, he liked that he would have that ace up the sleeve to use from time to time. But the man's response did not instill a lot of confidence in him.

Smith faked a yawn and waved his hand toward his mouth. "Got plenty of people I can get all those things from. And just because I can't walk very fast doesn't mean I can't go out and hunt. Come on, *Clay*, you're going to have to do better than that."

"Well, I've got a few things in my pack that might—"

"I've been through your pack already, nothing in there worth me making you a new firing pin. Unless you want to trade me that Arsenal."

Clay's head spun from that response. He wasn't sure whether he was angry that the man had gone through his things or confused with how he knew the firing pin needed to be replaced. "How did you know?" Clay asked before adding, "And no, the AK is not for sale."

Smith chuckled as he stood and walked back over to the table. He leaned against the sturdy wooden construction and crossed his arms in front of his chest. "You had mentioned something about a broken rifle. I figured it was probably not the one you were carrying when I conked you on the head—sorry about that by the way, just how things go sometimes. So, I stripped that LaRue down and found the broken firing pin."

"So, you can fix it?" Clay asked, ignoring the fact that Smith didn't seem interested in anything Clay had to offer.

"I can fix just about anything, but like I said, you don't have anything I want—not anything you're willing to part with, anyway. And a job like that won't come cheap."

Clay's frustration became evident in his expression. "So, what kind of things *do* you want to cover a bill like that?"

Smith let out a heavy sigh through his nose. He removed the ball cap he wore and scratched the top of his head before putting it back on. "I'll tell you what, Clay. If you can pick something up for me and bring it back here, I'll take care of it."

Clay's rejoicing was cut short once his common sense kicked in. If this part was going to cost so much, then why would Smith allow a simple errand to satisfy the trade—unless there was nothing simple about this errand? "So what's the catch?" Clay asked.

"No catch, really," Smith said as he placed both palms on the tabletop behind him and leaned back further. "I just need you to go to my old house and retrieve an envelope for me."

"An envelope? That's it?" Clay questioned with a healthy dose of skepticism. "So, why haven't your other *friends* been willing to go get this envelope for you if it's so straight forward?"

"Well, I ain't gonna lie. It isn't exactly the nicest part of town..." Smith said with a shrug. "Plus, my friends already have things that I want...*You* don't," he said, pointing a finger at Clay.

Clay hated the idea of extending the trip any longer than he already had, but he didn't have much choice in the matter. His AR-15 wasn't just a luxury—a fun toy to take out to the range on the weekends—the battle rifle was a combat equalizer. It was what leveled the playing field for Clay when he was outnumbered. So, despite the not-so-reassuring description Smith gave the area, it was still worth the risk. Whatever was in that envelope carried a lot of value to Smith, and if Clay could deliver, perhaps Smith could become a long-term trading ally. Having access to a set of skills like his would come in handy.

"What makes you think this envelope will even be there still?" Clay asked.

"I suppose it might not be or it could be ruined, but it was pretty well safeguarded—not really a place where anyone would think to look. And since all that was in there was mostly documents and maybe a little bit of cash, anyone who *did* stumble across it wouldn't have much reason to take it."

Clay nodded. "Fair enough." He pressed off the cold concrete floor and got to his feet. As soon as he stood up, he reached out and planted his hand onto the wall behind him to keep from falling. "So, where's your place?" he asked.

"Easy there, slugger. Don't you hear that?" Smith asked as he pointed toward the ceiling. "That's the sound of a heavy downpour. Probably not smart to leave during a typhoon."

That explains the air conditioning sound.

"Besides, I hit you pretty good back there, so I doubt you're in any shape to make good on your end of the deal at the moment. Crash here tonight and head out first thing in the morning."

Smith hadn't given Clay any room for negotiation, nor would Clay have argued even if he could. "All right," Clay said with a nod. "Thanks." With Smith still leaning on the table just beneath the light, Clay could clearly see the ball cap he wore. A black cap with gold trim and the iconic logo. "You a Pittsburgh fan?"

"Yup," Smith said, still with a hint of pride. "Born and raised in the steel city. Never really left until I shipped out to Pendleton."

"I'm just glad you didn't say you were a Philly fan or we might have had ourselves a thrown down," Clay said to try and lighten the mood a little—an attempt to get to know Smith on a personal level. The same approach worked with Vlad and many other traders in the past; it was how Clay was able to learn who he could trust...and more importantly, who he couldn't.

"Is that so?" Smith said with a subtle smirk, indicating to Clay what the man thought of his intimidation.

Clay laughed. "All right, so maybe you would have done the throwing part, but still..."

The man laughed with Clay's response, showing a true smile for the first time since they met. "Something tells me you're a fan of the 'Big D.'"

"Yep. My dad had the game on every Sunday—I even saw them play live once. Whipped the tar out of the G-Men, though that was like your guys playing against Cleveland."

Smith laughed again. "Well, Dallas was the last ones to win the trophy before all this crap happened, so I guess that's reason enough to dig 'em." Smith said. He had a content look on his face as he reminisced about fonder times.

Their conversation was interrupted by a faint but rapid beeping sound. Clay looked over at Smith as he growled with frustration and pushed away from the table. Without a word, Smith walked out of the room.

Clay trailed behind, following him through a few narrow corridors that were equally as drab as the room he woke up in. Smith hobbled down another hallway and on through a door into a room that was illuminated by several monitors displaying live feeds from around the entire campsite. Clay was in awe of the setup. No wonder Smith was able to ambush him—he knew Clay was coming from a mile away—literally.

Smith sat down at the desk and tapped a few buttons on a keyboard that looked dated from even before the eruptions. After smacking the *ENTER* key, the center screen—the biggest of the six monitors—brought up a feed from just outside the gates where Clay first met Smith. The rain made it difficult to see much, so Smith typed away on the keyboard again and suddenly the screen went dark with the letters *IR* at the top right corner of the display. Clay saw a few splotches of gray—with one bigger blob of white nearly centered.

Smith shook his head and grunted. "That stupid thing is always tripping my sensors," he said as he turned around and looked down at the little pooch that had followed them to the security room. "Chip, looks like you're gettin' fried pussycat for dinner tonight."

The dog's tail spun up as his master spoke.

As Smith left his chair, he grabbed his Faxon ARAK-21. Clay had been so enthralled with the functioning security screens that he had overlooked the sleek-looking rifle leaning up against the desk. He had never seen one in person before, certainly not one sporting a suppressor.

Unreal, Clay thought to himself. He was still staring at the rifle. Smith pushed him aside to exit the closet-sized security room and made his way down the hall. Clay followed, and Chip, with as much hatred for the cat as Smith, tagged along.

They arrived at a set of elevator doors and Smith rapidly pressed a button just off to the side. Clay's eyes widened when he saw the button illuminate. "How are you getting all this power?" he asked in shock.

The doors opened almost immediately and Smith walked inside. Clay noticed the buttons: *SB2*, *B1*, *1* and *2*. Smith pressed the *2* button and the doors slid shut moments before the elevator jolted into motion.

"The military loaded this place up with some new type of batteries and some crazy-efficient solar arrays. They were testing them out while I was stationed in Syria, but I never got to see it in action. Somehow, the panels are able to take even the smallest amount of sunlight and convert it into energy." A red light at the top of the elevator flicked on and a flat, distorted tone rang out as the ascending room reached the second floor; the doors separated. "Some fancy sci-fi type of crap, ain't it?" Smith said as he stormed out.

The second floor was one giant room with windows on all sides—an observation post of sorts. Desks, computers and other communication equipment were still in place, sitting beneath a quarter inch of grime. Because the entire campsite was relatively flat, on a sunlit day, Clay would have been able to see every acre from where he stood.

Smith headed straight for an outer door and walked out onto a covered catwalk that bordered the entire building. There was an agitation in Smith's demeanor that made Clay nervous, but it all seemed to be directed toward the cat snooping around the gate. Clay stood back and watched as Smith leaned to and fro, trying to get a visual on the target.

"There you are," Smith said as he raised his rifle. He looked through his low zoom optics and had to reacquire his target. "Got you," he whispered before squeezing the trigger.

A cracking sound spewed out from the end of the suppressor, and Clay heard the cat scream, but could tell from Smith's body language that the bullet had merely scared the feline, nothing more. The rifle's blast was much louder than Clay expected—it was nothing like the movies made it out to be—but despite being just a few feet away, he realized that his ears weren't even ringing; a little further out and it probably wouldn't have even sounded like a gunshot. Much further out and it wouldn't have even been audible.

Smith grumbled with frustration and walked back to the door. Clay, who had been standing in the doorway, stepped aside to allow enough room for Smith to walk through. He didn't say anything; he just headed straight for the elevator. Chip came over and sniffed around Smith's feet.

"Sorry boy. We'll get that stupid thing someday," he said as he bent over to scoop up the little terrier.

Clay thought it was amusing to see such a big man carrying around a tiny lapdog. Clay used to hate smaller dogs, but now, he was envious of such a creature comfort.

Clay and Smith returned to the elevator and descended back to the basement. Due to the late afternoon hour, they decided to kill some time by playing cards. It didn't take long before they got settled into a game of poker—five card draw, deuces wild. Ammunition was the currency. Clay had his bag of bullets he always brought with him, as well as three full magazines for his AR-15. He wasn't willing to gamble any of the 7.62x39 away, not when the AK was his only functioning rifle.

"So…" Clay said with hesitation in his voice, "What happened to your, uhm…?"

Smith looked up from his cards and gave Clay a brief glare. He laid two of his cards down and took two more from the deck. "Same story, different Marine," he said, almost nonchalantly. "IED."

Clay lowered his head and stared blankly at his cards. "That sucks, man. Sorry," he said as he discarded two of his own for a fresh pair.

"Just how it goes sometimes. Some people leave their wallets at fancy restaurants, others leave their limbs in a part of the world that were no worse off than before the apocalypse came," Smith said.

Clay felt awkward for asking the question, but his approach was working. Smith was talking and Clay listened. In the event Clay was unsuccessful in finding Smith's envelope, he needed a backup plan—an alternative way into Smith's little circle of friends.

Smith tossed out fifteen cartridges in the middle of the table. Clay looked down at his hand, then up at Smith's face. The same stone-cold expression was present as when Clay first saw the man. He was impossible to read, but Clay had a full house, so he had this one in the bag. Clay put a full magazine down. "I see your fifteen and raise ya fifteen more."

"Hmmm," Smith grunted. After contemplating for a moment, he dropped another fifteen rounds. "Call."

Clay laid his hand down on the table, a satisfied grin pasted across his face. "Full house."

"Good hand," Smith agreed. "It's been a while since I've played, so correct me if I'm wrong, but I *think* this hand is better," he said as he laid out a royal flush. "Thanks for the extra magazine, Cowboy."

Clay's sigh gave way to a guttural growl—not just for the thirty rounds lost but that Smith took his magazine, too. A complimentary prize that Clay had not intended to part with, but decided not to argue over. He had already decided that even if he lost all the ammo he brought, it was a good investment to get on Smith's good side. And as the evening wore on, Clay's strategy paid off. It wasn't long before Smith brought out some food and homebrew to share. Clay nearly gagged after the first shot, but managed to swallow the homemade alcohol and keep his "man card."

"Got any family?" Smith asked, starting to warm up to Clay.

"Just me and my older sister." Clay said, purposefully leaving Kelsey and his kids out of the picture. He was fine sharing a little bit about himself with Smith, but he wasn't about to put it all out there. "You?" Clay asked.

"Nope. None," the man said as his body visibly tensed.

"So, what'd you do after being discharged?" Clay asked.

Smith knocked back another shot and then began dealing out the next hand. "I opened up a gun shop. Took two years to get all the paperwork approved, but it finally came through," he said with a sharp solitary laugh while he shook his head.

"I imagine business wasn't nearly as good once all you could sell were hunting rifles and 'smart guns', huh?" Clay asked.

Smith's expression shifted to a wry smile, "Oh, business was booming, just not the kind of business I listed on my tax forms." Smith laughed and filled his shot glass.

Clay's confusion was written on his face. "What do you mean?"

Smith's laugh faded as he realized that chapter of his life was over ten years ago. The man in front of him would have just been a boy at the time, meaning his subtle comment of his illicit firearm business went right over his head. "Let's just say that Uncle Sam told me I wasn't allowed to sell certain guns," he said before leaning across the table to whisper. "But Clay, do I look like the type of guy who likes being told what he can and can't do?"

Clay was visibly uncomfortable, but managed to shake his head and say, "No."

"That's right," Smith said as he sat back in his chair, his laugh transitioned to a cough. "How do you think I ended up with a rifle like this?" he asked as he gestured to the ARAK-21. "I conducted legitimate business, sure. I sold the same crappy, sissy guns that they wanted me to sell and I repaired just about anything that came through my door. But there was never a shortage of people looking for the classics—the type of rifles that didn't require Wi-Fi. If they had the money, I got them what they were looking for."

Clay nodded along as the man proudly shared his story of Federal defiance.

"All right," Smith said as he leaned back in his chair and stretched. "It's getting late and you should head out first thing in the morning if you want to make it to the house before nightfall." Smith got out of his chair and picked up his rifle. "Allow me to show you to your accommodations for the night."

Clay got up and followed Smith to the elevator where he pressed the button next to the text *SB2*. Clay's optimism bolted as the elevator doors split apart. The dimly lit hallways and moldy walls made the floor above feel like a beach resort by comparison. And the smell...it was all Clay could do to keep from throwing up on Smith's shoes.

Smith led Clay to a holding cell at the end of the hall and gestured inside. The tiny room had a wafer-thin cot mattress, an overflowing toilet-sink combination, and a small metal tray table mounted to the wall.

Clay looked over at Smith. "You're kidding, right?" he asked, trying not to gag over the smell.

"Sorry, Cowboy, but I just met ya. You seem like you're on the level and all, but I don't know you from Adam, and I'm not the type to just let a stranger wander around my house while I sleep. I'll be back in the morning with your gear to send you on your way," Smith said before handing Clay a bottle of water.

Clay stepped inside and looked around the depressing five-by-eight cell. The stench was life threatening. Of all the stupid choices Clay had made since the ash had fallen, hunting down Smith was fast-tracking its way to the top. He turned back around to face Smith standing just outside the door. "Cozy."

Smith chuckled as he spun a key ring around his finger. "Sweet dreams."

The door latched shut, engaging the lock.

Chapter 7

The trek had taken longer than Clay had expected. He wasn't sure if the house was further away than Smith had said or if his own physical state was to blame for the long day. His head still ached, and the lump Smith left from the rifle butt to his skull was tender—even more so than the day before. On top of that, his food intake was minimal at best. He had carefully rationed the food when he left Liberty, but it was simply not enough to sustain the calories he was burning each day. He was tired, wounded, underfed and sopping wet; it was a lousy time to be trudging through another swampy forest in the rain. But, at this point, Clay was too invested to stop.

The fading light brought with it the callous shrieks in the distance. The sound always put him on edge, but it was even worse when accompanied by the howling wind tearing through the trees all around him. On more than one occasion, Clay squeezed his eyes shut, praying that he was just dreaming. Yet, as always, when he opened his eyes, the ten-yearlong nightmare continued.

A loud snap echoed through the woods, causing Clay to drop to one knee and swing his rifle toward the sound. He watched as a deer pranced off, gracefully navigating around the various obstacles on the forest floor. Under different circumstances Clay would have pursued the beast in hopes of a nice dinner, but his priority was to find Smith's home before night chased the sun away; not his grumbling stomach.

Clay exited the woods with the same relief as he had the other night. *Still not out of the woods yet, though,* Clay thought to himself, then rolled his eyes. All puns aside, his plan to reach the house before nightfall was not looking good. He had little idea where he was—and more importantly, who was nearby—causing him to quicken his pace despite his body's protest.

To Clay's much needed relief, the rain started to ease. Though he was already thoroughly soaked, the frigid rain always added an extra layer of discomfort to an already weary traveler.   As he often was, Clay was surprised with how quickly darkness took over the sky. The setting sun, while a gradual process, still provided enough light to navigate his surroundings. But then, as if a candle was suddenly extinguished, the world succumbed to blackness.

A nearby street sign confirmed that Clay had made it to Smith's street, but the *611* adorning a nearby doorpost indicated he had a long way to go before reaching Smith's *2409*.   And Clay could no longer see the house numbers. Every few minutes he ran up to a random porch and would briefly turn on his light to see the numbers. *1983. Almost there.* He felt confident he would be able to stumble his way through the night and eventually end up at Smith's place, but then he heard the murderous cries—it was time to find shelter. The screams came from no more than a hundred yards away, making the Screamers far too close for comfort—a discomfort made worse by the begging cries for mercy from the victim. There was nothing Clay could do—even if he ran as fast as he could, the poor soul would be dead before Clay could get halfway to him. Not to mention the lack of light gave the sadistic night dwellers the upper hand. He tried to block out the cries for help, but it didn't work. Fortunately, both for Clay and the prey, the ritual was not dragged out.

Circling back behind the nearest house, Clay found shelter in a house with an unlocked door. As he carefully checked each room on the first floor, he could still hear muffled screeches from outside, but the sounds faded as the group moved further away. Clay moved up the stairs as quietly as he could; all clear. There were four bedrooms, three of which were the same size. Clay was not happy with the arrangement. It was an older home and lacked the modern amenities he was used to seeing. There was no giant master closet—not even a master bath. The only bathroom on the floor was at the top of the stairs, equidistant from the bedrooms on either side of the steps. He picked the bathroom as his overnight accommodation, inside the tub—which thankfully still had a shower curtain hanging up—and cozied up for the night.

Sitting on the edge of the tub, Clay unlaced his boots. Each one seemed to hold a cup or more of water that spilled onto the peeling linoleum floor as he yanked them off his feet. After pulling off his socks and hanging them from a towel rack, Clay unzipped his pack and untied the plastic bag inside. Anything that had to stay dry needed to be tied up in a plastic bag. While Clay's backpack was water resistant, years of abuse combined with the relentless rain meant that the contents inside were equally as soaked as the outside of the bag. He reached into the plastic bag and retrieved a pair of socks that had been rolled into a ball—it was one of a half-dozen pairs. Besides food and water, there was no greater preparation for Clay than to ensure he kept his feet dry. He always had at least three extra pairs of socks on him whenever he left Northfield; he had heard far too many horror stories about "jungle rot," a term often used by soldiers in Vietnam.

With dry, albeit wrinkly feet, Clay got settled into the tub. Since he had acquired the necessary skill to fall asleep almost anywhere, he anticipated his slumber to come quickly. It did not. His mind was far too focused on the slaughter he heard earlier—the desperate and departing cries of an innocent soul. Thinking about it made him shudder.

"When's this going to end?" he said quietly to himself as he leaned his head back and let out a soft sigh. The years of traveling, gunfights, hunger, and loss had taken a devastating toll on Clay, particularly with his spirit. He recalled the words Shelton had assuredly told him a few years back, "So long as there is hope, there's a will to carry on." It was not that Clay disagreed with the sentiment; the problem was that Clay's hope was fading. His family, for now, kept him motivated enough to keep pressing on when he didn't have anything left, but as Clay found himself away from home—and his family—more and more, the despair in his heart grew darker. He wanted to cry uncle, but who would hear him? It seemed as if God had pushed the mute button a long time ago and complaining to his family would only add to their ever-growing angst. There was no other choice but to suffer in silence and just find a way to endure.

The night dragged on; Clay didn't sleep a wink. When the fading glow on his watch hands indicated it was approaching *4:45,* Clay determined there was little point in trying to sleep. He decided to rest another thirty minutes then head out, but around five o'clock he heard footsteps downstairs followed by crude banter.

Oh, crap!

Clay got out of the tub as fast as he was able to without making much noise. He quickly slipped his boots on, but didn't bother tying them; he just gave the laces a few tugs and tucked them into the boot. He pushed the door closed, stopping just short of the latch, and backed away as far as he could.

Footsteps climbed the stairs; voices became clearer. Clay took slow, deep breaths to prevent his heart from pounding its way out of his chest. The only thing separating him from the ruffians on the other side was a rotting piece of wood feebly hanging from a few hinges. It would likely only be a matter of time before one of them popped into the bathroom, forcing Clay to fire the first shot in what would become his final fight.

His knuckles turned white as he ferociously squeezed the AK's pistol grip. He curled his finger around the trigger and waited to fire.

"What?" a man's voice yelled just outside the door.

Clay's finger pressed on the trigger, but did not complete the transaction. He waited. Suddenly, the footsteps on the other side of the bathroom door moved down the stairs and more voices began chattering. He heard laughing and mocking screams followed by more laughing. Clay's eyes widened as a horrible pit dug into his stomach. These weren't bandits or scavengers searching a random house…

Screamers.

Being paralyzed with fear made figuring out his next move difficult. And after a few minutes, Clay concluded that there wasn't one. The psychos were roaming around the house, gabbing away with each other like they were drinking at the pub. Clay was trapped. The bathroom had a small window looking out to the back yard, but it was small—too small for an adult to climb through. There was nowhere to go.

Clay listened in horror as the group recounted their inhuman activities from the night. One man touted about a family of four he found sleeping off the highway. He spared no detail of the gruesome ordeal, and it took a lot of effort for Clay to keep his meager dinner from making an unexpected appearance all over the floor. They all talked about their "hunts" for the night, chatting casually as if talking about just another day at the office.

Clay found that all his fear and anxiety had transformed into rage. He fantasized about brutally and viciously murdering every last soul in the house—dispatching each one mercilessly, making them cry for their mothers as their last breaths departed from their lips. He considered the satisfaction of watching their blood pool around their lifeless bodies—seeing them as the center of carnage instead of the creators of it. But killing them wouldn't bring back those they had slaughtered throughout the night. And attacking them certainly would not end well for Clay, either.

He started to tremble again, not because of the Screamers so much as his own thoughts. Though he had never even considered such atrocities before, he was frightened with how easily they entered his head. Clay eventually shook off the troubling thoughts. *Anyone who spends enough time in this world will think that way from time to time,* he convinced himself, though he still found himself disturbed by the brief episode of psychosis.

Nearly an hour passed before the last of the voices hushed—Clay assumed the men had gone to sleep. He was now faced with a decision: sneak out while they slept or wait for nightfall and make an escape after they leave. If he waited until they left, then Clay would be outside, once again, while the Screamers looked for their next victim; that didn't sound too appealing. But then again, attempting to sneak through a house that creaked and groaned under the weight of a mouse while a group of sadists slept next to bloodied machetes and baseball bats didn't seem like a smart idea either.

Time to go, Clay finally decided. He questioned his ability to stay cooped up in that bathroom for the rest of the day without losing his mind. Leaving right away felt like the better of the two choices. He press checked his rifle, ensuring it was chambered before stepping into the viper's pit. Slowly pulling the door back, Clay tiptoed out into the hall.

He couldn't see much—it was still fairly dark outside, though he could see evidence that the sun was about to crest the horizon through a window in one of the bedrooms. He stayed motionless for a moment while he listened carefully for the slightest sounds. Nothing. It was completely silent save a few snores coming from around the house. Clay was terrified to walk through a dark house with sleeping Screamers scattered about. It was like being asked to walk through a minefield with a blindfold.

Clay managed to get down three steps before the groaning lumber became an issue. He wasn't sure if his heightened senses made the sound seem more profound than it was or if the stress Clay put on the stair actually caused a sound akin to that of a Redwood falling over. Either way, he didn't want to push his luck.

Clay tried to shake the banister and was pleased to find it quite sturdy, which gave him an idea. He grabbed on to the bannister with both hands and carefully hiked his leg up and then as delicately as a mother laying her newborn down into the bassinet, Clay eased his weight onto the railing, making sure it could support him. With just a slight whimper from the aging wood, Clay began to ease his grip and gravity took over from there. As if he was repelling down a cliff face, Clay controlled the speed of his descent with his hands. Slow and steady. It probably took him more than five minutes to reach the bottom, but the effort was without sound.

Clay eased himself off the railing and onto the hardwood floor again. The snoring and breathing from the living room to his left was unsettling. The front door was inches in front of him, but having gone through the back door the night before, Clay had no idea what state the front door was in. Was it locked? Was it nailed shut? If he opened it would it just fall off the hinges? The unknown potential to wake the slumbering sociopaths was too great. And, as best as he could recall, the back door in the kitchen was not particularly noisy—it was his exit.

After inching his way into the carpeted dining room to his right, Clay headed for the kitchen. The kitchen had a nice grouted tile that seemed to be as quiet to walk on as the day it was installed. But then, as he was just a few feet away from the door, Clay's foot found a glass bottle on the floor. The loud clanking sound as the bottled skidded across the tile made every muscle in Clay's body tense so tightly that his back began to spasm. As he tried to work out the painful twinge, Clay heard a grumble come from the living room.

"I will hang and gut the next person who wakes me up!" a voice shouted with a sinister wrath from the next room over.

Relief washed over Clay when it became apparent that the threat was verbal only and no one was coming to investigate the source of the sound. He stayed put for a few minutes to allow the Screamers to fall back to sleep and to let his nerves settle. He was *so* close, yet he just could not seem to get out of this house of horrors! The dull, muted sunlight crept in through the kitchen window, providing a dim light throughout the house. He could barely make him out, but Clay noticed that one of the men was sleeping in the dining room; sprawled out on the floor no more than three feet away from the path Clay had walked just minutes before. The close call was nauseating.

It had been long enough since Clay had bumped into the bottle. *Time to leave this hellhole,* Clay thought as he reached for the doorknob. The tightness in his chest started to ease as he swung the door open and walked outside. He moved his gun to the left and right, looking for threats.

Nothing.

He quickly made his way back to the road, and as soon as he felt he had put enough distance between himself and the house, Clay tore into a full-on sprint. With his adrenaline spiked high into the stratosphere and dawn finally arriving, Clay felt as if he could keep the pace for miles. Fortunately, seconds later, he found himself hunched over, puffing for oxygen in front of *2409*. His watch showed that it was a hair past six, which meant rush hour was over for the Screamers.

Clay made his way inside Smith's house and was discouraged with the mess he saw in front of him. Though there was no activity inside—and he triple checked just to be sure—the cluttered mess of a thoroughly searched house was not what he wanted to see, especially after what he just went through.

His first objective was to find the envelope. After that he would do a brief scavenge of the house, but he was not feeling optimistic that his efforts would yield much. The search would have to be quick, though; Clay didn't want to stay in the area a minute longer than necessary. He now understood why nobody had ever taken on this job before. It was well beyond going behind enemy lines; it was diving headfirst into the belly of the beast. Had Clay known what he was walking into beforehand, he wouldn't have taken the job, either.

At the back of the house, Clay found the master bedroom. Except for its first floor location, it was almost identical to the master bedroom in the other house: small and no bathroom. Clay walked in and located the safe off to his left next to the bed. Smith told him the envelope was in a hidden compartment beneath the floor of the safe. It didn't take long for Clay to discover the false floor and unveil a stack of papers beneath. He pulled everything out and skimmed through the various papers. He found the only envelope—a large manila envelope with a metal prong on the back—and stuffed it into his backpack. Just to be thorough, Clay glanced at the other documents in case anything stood out. It was mostly tax forms or legal papers with FFL and LLC on them—he assumed those weren't what Smith was after.

After doing a quick search of the room, Clay checked the rest of the first floor without finding anything. The first bedroom he checked had been converted into an office. He snatched a few pens and a couple of legal pads that he found in one of the desk drawers, but nothing else. The next bedroom was mostly empty, just clothes—or what appeared to be clothes—and broken furniture lying around the room in a thousand pieces. Nothing worth grabbing. But, as Clay walked into the bedroom at the end of the hall, he was struck by an overwhelming grief. With his eyes locked onto the pair of toddler beds on either end of the back wall, it clicked that the furniture in the other bedroom at one point in time had been a crib.

Clay rested his hands on his head and sighed. He was no stranger to loss. The eerie sight of the children's beds reminded him of that crippling pain he had experienced more than a few times. It was indescribable. But now that Clay had a son—his own flesh and blood—he couldn't comprehend what he would do if something were to happen to him. He knew that if someone *ever* tried to harm his son, though, that the visions of torment he had in his head earlier would pale in comparison. Somehow, Smith found a way to make it through to the other side, but Clay doubted his ability to do the same.

Between the emotional thrashing triggered by the twin beds and his adrenaline finally wearing off, Clay's fatigue hit back hard. But there was no time to rest. He needed to get back to the campsite so Smith could make the new firing pin, and Clay could finally head home.

Clay had to grasp to the railing to support his weight as he walked down the stairs. He had no idea how he was going to find the energy he needed to make it through the rest of the day. He was starting his journey with the gas tank already on "E."

As Clay approached the front door, he saw the handle twist. His eyes widened and, like a floodgate opening, his adrenaline levels were immediately replenished. The door swung open, and a man started to walk through. The shaven head...the horrific tattoos...the Kevlar vest.

Not again!

By the time the man noticed Clay standing in the living room, Clay had his rifle raised. Both stopped dead in their tracks as they quickly sized up their opponent. The man was armed, but his pistol was nestled inside a holster hanging from his belt.

"Don't move," Clay said with a hushed voice and a piercing stare.

The Screamer remained still for only a moment longer before his hand flinched toward his sidearm.

The silent morning was disrupted by the explosive power of Clay's rifle being fired rapidly. The full metal jacket bullets did what they were designed to do and tore through the man's light body armor. He stumbled back out onto the porch and dropped to the ground.

Clay wasn't sure how many times he pulled the trigger, but one shot was more than enough to draw some very-much unwanted attention. Operating on instincts, Clay grabbed the man's pistol, stuck it in his waistband, and bolted out of the house, making a run for it. As expected, shrieks quickly filled the air.

As Clay ran down an alley, he spotted movement in the corner of his eye. The man coming toward him fit the profile of a Screamer, so Clay fired several shots in his direction as he continued to run. He hadn't hit anything except for maybe the house the man was standing next to, but Clay was confident the suppressive fire bought him precious seconds.

Playing cat and mouse with his pursuers, Clay evaded the Screamers long enough to seek shelter in a rusted-out aluminum tool shed. He peeked through one of the many holes in the side of the shed and kept an eye on the search party. Surprisingly, they gave up quite quickly. As a few of Clay's hunters walked back to a nearby house, somebody shouted from down the block, "It was Slater!"

"Slater?" one of the nearby men said. "I'm not going to lose my sleep chasing down the guy responsible for killing *him*," he scoffed. "If anything, they just saved me the trouble of doing it myself," he said callously before turning to walk back with the others.

It was unfathomable to hear how little these men valued another human life. Admittedly, killing was becoming easier for Clay to do, but at least to this point, it did not come without a dose of guilt, regardless if the kill was justified. But the Screamers? They were as indifferent to the slaying of one of their *own* as a duck is to rain.

After waiting another hour, Clay was finally able to escape the neighborhood and return to the forest from which he came. He found comfort when the claustrophobia of the trees overcame him.

It was dark by the time he reached the FEMA camp gates. He had contemplated crashing in the same RV he had stayed in a few nights before, but pressed on. Clay suspected he had triggered more than a few of Smith's motion sensors, making his presence known to the Marine. He imagined Smith watched him stumble his way across the field through the infrared lens of the camera. He just hoped Smith wouldn't mistake him for a zombie and open fire before he had a chance to deliver the package.

Clay hobbled up to the locked gate and looked toward one of the cameras mounted to the building. A few seconds later Clay heard a buzzing sound followed by a loud click—the magnetic lock had disengaged. Clay pushed the gate open then snapped it shut. The lock promptly reengaged.

The door at the base of the building swung open before Clay had even reached it. His feet, along with every other part of his body, ached relentlessly.

"Sometime this week would be nice, Cowboy," Smith said impatiently.

Clay had a few choice phrases he wanted to respond with, but couldn't find the energy or nerve to reply.

"Did you find it?" Smith asked as he held the door open for Clay.

"I think so," Clay weakly said as he limped inside.

As they took the elevator down to the basement, Clay retrieved the envelope and handed it to Smith. As soon as the doors opened, Smith took a hard right from the elevators and proceeded down the hall. Clay had trouble keeping up. About halfway down, Smith walked into a room. By the time Clay got there, he saw what remained of the envelope and scattered papers lying across the bed. Smith sat on the edge of the bed, his back to the door, holding a Micro SD card in one hand and a tablet in the other. He stared at the tiny flash card for several seconds, trying to convince himself that it was damaged; that he shouldn't waste his time trying to get it to work.

"Screw it," he said under his breath as he slid the card into a slot on the side of the tablet and waited for the operating system to recognize the device.

Several long seconds later, a folder finally popped up with dozens of icons inside. He hesitated again, this time only briefly, before he tapped on one and a video player popped up.

The first thing Clay heard was the sound of two young boys shouting in unison...

"Happy birthday, Daddy!"

Chapter 8

Clay watched helplessly as Smith stared at the tablet screen with his hand over his mouth. As soon as one video ended, the next one popped up, each more unbearable to watch than the last.

Glancing down at the bed, Clay noticed a pink Post-it note stuck to one of the papers with a note scribbled on it:

Here are the videos you wanted. Now would you please sign the papers so we can both get on with our lives?

The papers scattered around the bed were divorce papers. Smith—or Justin Akers as the legal documents declared—had never signed them. Clay could only speculate why, but judging from his body language whenever the woman showed up on camera, he still loved her.

A video of twin boys chasing the family puppy around the yard ended and the screen quickly snapped to a new scene: a serene moment of peaceful bliss and the miracle of life. The same woman held a newborn baby on her chest. She smiled contently; the baby was asleep. But as Smith's body began to bounce up and down from the weeping he could no longer suppress, Clay realized these joyful moments from his past had become the very nightmares that would terrorize him for the rest of his life. And even though these people had never been alive to him— merely pixels on a screen—Clay couldn't help but share in the sobbing man's heartache in his agonizing despair.

"Hello Jola," a softer-spoken Smith said on the video as a hand appeared on screen and gently rubbed the baby's back. "Welcome to the family," he said, which prompted a glowing smile from the exhausted mother.

The media player went black as the notch on the timeline found its end and displayed the folder of files again. Smith didn't bring up another video, he just stared at the blank screen until the inactivity dimmer kicked in, snapping him out of his trance. Clay subtly cleared his throat, which startled Smith, causing him to turn around. His bloodshot eyes screamed of pain and the grim look on his face further supported that claim. Tears streaming down his cheeks glistened from the subtle glow of the tablet screen. He didn't say anything; he just stared at Clay with that unmistakable expression of loss and remorse.

He turned back around and looked at the tablet. He raised his hand to tap another video, but couldn't bear to subject himself to anymore tonight. He started shaking again, an audible whimper this time. Ten minutes ago, Smith was a rock that instilled fear into Clay, and despite his prosthetic legs, Clay suspected that he would have been an intimidating sight even to the toughest of Screamers. Yet, here he was, broken, crushed, defeated; brought to his knees by videos on a computer—like digital terrorism, striking horror and pain into the brawny man's very soul.

Clay wanted to say something, but he knew the last thing Smith would want to hear was some obligatory condolences or the unfounded optimistic pep talk. So, Clay waited for Smith to speak first; silently mourning with the man he had just met, yet somehow felt as if he already knew better than some of his closest friends.

"You always think there's going to be a tomorrow," Smith spoke with a broken voice. "'I'm busy today, we'll play tomorrow'…or, 'Daddy can't take you out for ice cream, he has work to do— maybe tomorrow.'" At this point the screen on the tablet had turned off completely; the drab hallway light spilling in from the doorway prevented the small bedroom from falling into total darkness. "There's always a tomorrow," Smith repeated, "until there's not."

Clay shifted awkwardly as he tried to find the right wording for his question. It was never easy asking someone how they lost their family, but somehow, after witnessing the desolation Smith had just been put through, Clay found this particular instance even more difficult. "How'd it happen?" he finally asked.

Smith looked as if he was wrestling with numerous thoughts. He rubbed at his eyes as he let out a weary sigh. "I happened."

It was not the response Clay had expected—it was almost unsettling.

"Running your own store is a tall order. Even though business was great, it didn't mean I could just sit back and count the money. There were always more things to get done and keeping customers happy was a fulltime job in itself. I finally convinced my brother, Phil, to move down from Pittsburgh to help me run the place. He was smart, always got good grades, good with numbers and all that, so I wanted him to handle the business side of things while I dealt with the inventory, customers, and repairs.

"It wasn't long before we were one of the biggest, private owned shops in the state. We had a three thousand square foot store, and that's not including the 'invite only' section of the shop, which is where we sold the big, scary guns that had been banned. Usually, just one transaction a day in that room kept the lights on for a week."

"Sounds like you had a pretty good thing going," Clay said, reaffirming the man's own words.

"We did," he said as he absent-mindedly rubbed his hands together. "But success doesn't come without sacrifice. Some people give up sleep, others give up hobbies...some give up their family...I did all the above," he said as he lowered his head, shaking it with regret. "The average day for me was at least sixteen hours. Everyone was asleep by the time I got home unless Amanda made the effort to stay awake so she could let me know just how bad things were between us." Smith took off his cap and threw it on the bed so he could run his hands through his hair. He interlocked his fingers and rested them on top of his head. "I used to get so mad at her for the lectures she would give me—about how I worked too much, that I needed to spend more time with the kids...that I needed to spend more time with her. My response was always the same, 'Gotta pay the bills,' or something stupid like that. But she was right... She was right," Smith said with a quivering voice that matched the shudder in his body as painful memories from the past resurfaced. "Things got better for a while. Phil and I hired a buddy of ours from Austin to help out. So, I started trying to be everything again. Faithful husband, loving father, successful business owner...

"Then Jola was born. It was early August and I even managed to take a few weeks off to spend with the family. They were...they were the best weeks of my life," he said with a genuine, albeit momentary joy. "But, by the end of the month, business picked up again and, despite the hired help, I was forced to return to my old ways. Work all day, sleep a couple of hours, rinse and repeat."

Clay knew where the story went. Though his own father had not been absent to the same degree, his line of work, both as a police officer and a paramedic, caused for long shifts where the family would see very little of him for days at a time. And even though his father was still very much dedicated to his family, the strain on everyone during those weeks was still significant. It wasn't an uncommon sight for his parents to have some heated discussions on the matter.

Smith continued, "I was working so hard to create a successful business so that I could give my wife and kids the great life I thought they deserved. I hadn't even noticed that my marriage had fallen apart. Amanda had come to me more than once about working things out, about us going to get some help. Every time she brought it up, though, I was in the middle of fixing this or inventorying that. 'We'll do that soon, Amanda. Just give me some time for things to slow down,' I always told her." Smith paused and let out a single, ironic laugh. "I was always telling her 'tomorrow,'" he said as he wiped his forearm across his face.

"One day, after staying at the shop for three days straight, I came home to an empty house. No wife, no kids, no note. And I didn't hear from her again until Jola's first birthday. She was *kind* enough to do a video chat so I could say happy birthday to my only daughter." Smith was barely able to finish the sentence before his emotions took over.

Clay stood in silence as the man fought with the agony of his past.

After a few minutes, Smith collected himself enough to continue. "And that...that was the last time I spoke to my baby girl."

The eruptions, Clay thought at first...but no. Somehow, he knew it was worse.

"A few months later, out of nowhere, Amanda calls me. She was so frantic I could barely understand her, but when I heard her tell me that Jola was sick and that I needed to get out to California right away, I knew it was bad. It took her eight months to finally tell me where they lived, and it was only because my daughter was dying." Smith's face was twisted with a mixture of sorrow and rage—it was unclear if it was directed at his wife or himself, and Clay wasn't sure if Smith even knew. He stared at the wall in front of him as he went on. "By the time I got to the hospital, Jola had already died. Meningitis or something like that. The doctor assured us that there was nothing that could have been done, that it hit too quickly. But it didn't stop me from blaming Amanda.

"I wanted Jola buried back in Texas, but Amanda wouldn't have it. And since her new boyfriend was some big-shot lawyer, she made it *very* clear that that was a battle I would never win. I hated her for that," he said, a dark contempt in his voice. "But, rather than put my boys and myself through that ugly situation, I let her have her way. I stayed in California for a few weeks after the funeral—spending time with my boys was the only thing that mattered to me. And after getting back to Texas, I decided to sell the company off and was already making the arrangements to move out to California to spend more time with Kyle and Marcus. I offered my half of the company to my brother, but he didn't want to run the product side of the business. It took less than a week to find a buyer—one of those big chain sporting goods stores that you could find every fifteen miles."

"So, you sold?" Clay asked.

"Yep. Big money, too. Phil and I split it down the middle, and each gave some of the profit to the people who had been helping us over the years. The house was already under contract, and we were just a few days from closing when I got the Presidential alert on my phone."

Being reminded of that moment sent shivers down Clay's spine; a moment when the world—his world—would forever be changed. Clay had watched silently as his mom gasped while reading the emergency alert on her phone before running to turn on the TV. It was just minutes after it had occurred, so the information was only just starting to trickle in. All that they could confirm was that the USGS reported a 9.6 earthquake had just struck off the coast of Washington state. The live feeds came online just minutes before the tsunami delivered a devastating blow to the west coast. Then, San Andreas went. It was only a paltry 7.5 in comparison to the Cascadian quake early that morning, but it was more than enough to ravage the major cities along the faultline—many of which were already battling the floods from the tsunami. That night there had been dozens of earthquakes greater than 7.0 around the world, and all eyes were on New Madrid, which had already started to rumble. Clay remembered the intense shaking he felt when the New Madrid roared to life. He had never felt an earthquake before and the only thing he felt at that moment was fear.

Clay's family had been glued to the TV all day, watching as *new* footage of catastrophic destruction around the world surfaced every couple of minutes. It was terrifying for the thirteen-year-old boy to watch. And then, airing on live TV, Clay and his family witnessed the Memphis-Arkansas bridge collapse, plummeting down to the Mississippi and taking with it hundreds of souls. It was in that horrifying moment that the pit in Clay's stomach told him this was not going to be a disaster the world would recover from. A feeling that was reaffirmed when Yellowstone began to clear her throat.

"I tried calling her," Smith continued, "but I could never get through. So, I grabbed all the food, supplies, and guns I could fit into my Jeep, and drove west as fast as I could." Smith paused for a moment as he continued to battle against his quivering body. "I was about a hundred miles from Vegas when the roads started to become impossible to drive on. I kicked in the four-by-four and went off-roading, but after a while even that was no longer traversable."

The anguish radiated from the man like a furnace. Clay could only imagine the torment Smith had been through in his life. Before *and* after the eruptions. It was far more than any one man deserved.

"I'm so sorry, Smith," Clay said with heartfelt sincerity. "Two days after the quakes hit, my dad was one of the thousands of people who volunteered to fly out to the coast for relief efforts. Being a paramedic as well as fifteen years with the police, he felt convicted to go help out any way he could. He told us he'd be gone at least two weeks, maybe a month. But then he decided to stay an extra couple of weeks as things were just starting to settle down there." Clay's own eyes started to water up as he told his own depressing tale. "Yellowstone erupted a few days later and he, uh..."

Smith looked up at Clay and simply nodded. There was no need for further explanation.

An uncomfortable silence filled the room, which prompted Smith to stand from the bed. "Well," he said as he walked toward Clay, sniffling away the last of his emotions, "let me set you up with a room for the night."

Another night in the bathtub at the Screamer house sounded almost as appealing as the awful smelling concrete coffin Clay slept in last time. But much to Clay's surprise, Smith turned right out of the door, heading *away* from the elevator. Clay followed him and they ended up in another bedroom like the one Smith stayed in.

"I imagine this will be a bit more comfortable than the piss-box downstairs," he said with an unenthusiastic grin.

There was an actual bed, dry blankets, no chilly draft, and best of all, no toilet next to his head. Clay looked around and then over at Smith. "Yeah, this is great. Thanks." Clay stepped inside and dropped his pack on the bed and sat down.

Smith turned around to leave, but came back to the door. "Please let yourself out in the morning. The code to open the gate is *513972*."

Clay was taken aback. "Why would you give that to me?" he asked, realizing Smith was making himself vulnerable by offering it to someone he barely knew.

Smith opened his mouth, but couldn't speak. He tried again, but no success. Finally, he managed to spit out, "You earned it, Cowboy."

"Thanks."

"Thank you, Clay," he said solemnly. "I, uh..." he trailed off for a moment then cleared his throat, changing the subject. "Uhm, anyway, if you come back toward the end of the month, I'll have your firing pin ready. It would be sooner, but I have a lot of things to take care of before then."

Nearly a month without his rifle did not sit well with Clay, but he wasn't about to berate the man for the long turnaround time—especially after the thrashing he took tonight. Clay was just happy to have a solution to the problem. "All right, that sounds good. I'll be back at the end of the month, then."

Smith turned and walked away with Chip loyally following behind, and a few seconds later Smith's whooshing steps and Chip's clacking nails faded into silence. Clay fell back on the bed with his knees bent over the edge. He looked up at the peeling paint on the ceiling and wondered how life might have been different had his dad returned home when he said he would. Would they have still been forced out of their home? It seemed unlikely they would have ever ended up in the tower, and even less likely they would have ended up in Northfield. But the most curious thought of all was whether he would have ever met Kelsey. The answers to all his speculative questions was an obvious no. No, they wouldn't have been forced from their home; his dad would have stood his ground. No, they wouldn't have ended up in the tower or at Northfield. And no, Clay never would have met Kelsey. And as much as Clay's heart ached from recounting the stories from his past—which forced him to remember *all* the losses he had experienced—he wondered if he would have changed anything. Kelsey was his wife and he loved her more than any other woman on earth—past, present, and future. So, he wasn't surprised when he realized that, no, he wouldn't have changed a thing about the past if it meant he would have never been around to hear Kelsey's cries for help on that road three years ago.

Chapter 9

"I hope you have something for me, Arlo," the well-dressed man said before striking a match and lighting up a cigar. Taking a seat on a bench just next to the back entrance of the office building he had temporarily claimed as his own, the man took a heavy drag on the tightly rolled tobacco, enjoying the temporary euphoric sensation as the smoke gently slipped back out of his mouth. "Because," he continued, "we're runnin' short on time here."

Arlo's eyes locked to the cigar in the man's hand; he wondered how he continued to acquire such luxuries so many years after society collapsed. It was both impressive and bothersome that he had the resources to waste on trivial things like bad habits, but such was the vanity of the man sitting in front of him. Suppressing his contempt, Arlo feigned a smile. "Yes, sir. I've had a team of scouts in the field for several weeks now collecting data on the location—everything is still looking good."

"So why *this* town? From the sounds of it, it's pretty well defended, and I imagine there are other places nearby that would put up less of a fight," he said before placing the cigar back into his mouth to await Arlo's reply.

"Liberty is an ideal location for our groups. It's large enough to house our people, there is a well-established agricultural scene, and the perimeter is already fortified. It is considered 'move-in ready' in most regards, which is imperative this late in the year," Arlo replied with a strong, confident voice.

"Hmmm," the man said, clearly not sold on the idea just yet. "So, this has nothing to do with your history with the town?" he questioned with a sneer. "Don't get me wrong, Arlo, I am always in the mood for a good ol' fashioned revenge story, but I don't typically offer up my own resources to settle someone else's score." His stone-like expression offered up more warning than any of his words.

"I assure you, my personal experience with the town has not, and will not, play a factor in this decision. I chose Liberty because it meets the necessary requirements for our people—more so, actually. If we play our cards right, this will be an incredible asset for our group."

"*Our group*," the man mocked. "You keep saying that as if somehow we're equals. It would do you good to remember that this is *my* operation and I've been kind enough to let you tag along for the ride. Or have you forgotten that when you came knocking on my door you had just twenty-five men with you, most of whom were circling the drain from starvation."

"No, sir, I have not forgotten your overwhelming generosity, which is why I am doing my best to find a place that is fitting for a man of your importance to call home," Arlo replied. He wanted to vomit as soon as the words left his lips.

"Well, I am not denying that this place sounds like its worthy to be on a postcard, but that border you talked about, that's going to complicate matters a fair bit."

Arlo nodded. "Ordinarily, yes. But I know the leader of this town—quite well actually—and I am confident that after I make my opening statement as to why it would be in his and his town's best interest to leave, he will comply. The structures within the town would be well preserved."

"And you believe your 'opening statement'," the man said doing air quotes, his now-stubby cigar cradled between two of his fingers, "will be effective enough to persuade him that sticking around is a bad idea?"

"The men I sent out have been making detailed notes on everything from shift changes to traders who come and go from the town. We won't have any problems, I assure you."

The man took one final drag on the cigar before dropping it to the ground and smashing it with a twist of his foot. "And if your friend doesn't leave?" he asked, now resting his folded hands on his hefty abdomen. "What then? I don't imagine this town will be of much use to us if it's destroyed in the process..."

"In the event the town decides to go to war with us, we will take great care to minimize the collateral damage. We will patiently, but strategically, wear their defenses down. We have numbers on our side," Arlo said.

"Yeah," the man said with an ironic chuckle, "it's always easier when it's someone else's money being spent. Arlo, you surely would have made a great politician back in the day."

Arlo ignored the backhanded compliment and reassured the man of his plan. "That is all hypothetical. As I said, I am confident the town will quickly surrender and we will be fully relocated by the end of October."

After a contemplative moment of silence, the man spoke again. "Okay. I'll bite," the man stood up off the bench, a throaty grunt coming out of his mouth. "If I were to agree to this plan, how many of *my* men would you need?" he asked, making it perfectly clear that Arlo's men were automatically enlisted.

Arlo paused for a moment, he already knew the number, but he also knew what the response would be. "Two hundred."

The man laughed. "Well, let me put this as politely as I can for ya. You've got two chances: slim and none, and I have a bit of bad news for ya—slim just left town."

"What would you be willing to offer?"

The man immediately fired back with, "Seventy-five. That puts you close to a hundred with your men."

"I implore you to reconsider. I am confident that they will leave, but *only* if our initial strike has the necessary impact. We need to hit them hard and hit them fast. We want them to know that this attack is just a taste of what's to come if they decide to stay and fight."

"And you can give me your word—regardless of whether or not this town fights back—that we will be ready to relocate by the end of October."

Arlo looked into the man's eyes, "It shouldn't be a problem," he said confidently.

The man weighed Arlo's request. His current situation was not critical just yet, but they were fast approaching that cliff. Realizing that he would likely lose twice as many men as Arlo was asking for this coming winter, he started to lean in favor of taking over the town.

Smiling as a crisp breeze swept between the corporate office buildings, the man said, "Boy, it's a gorgeous day today, isn't it? Why couldn't they all be like this?"

"Yes, sir, it is."

After a lengthy sigh, the man finally agreed. "All right, you have your two hundred men, Arlo. When will you be moving out?"

"I'll be sending another scout team out in the morning to find us suitable housing during this campaign. Once that is decided, I expect it to take a week or two for us to get situated there. After that, I will draw up the final plans based on the most recent reports from the scouts. We will strike soon thereafter."

The man was still skeptical, but he, too, knew Arlo well and knew that he was as cunning as he was determined. "Well, if you are half as good on the battlefield as you were in the courtroom..."

Arlo nodded. "I will not disappoint."

"You better not," the man shot back. "You know what I am capable of, Arlo. And disappointment is not something I tolerate."

Arlo took a moment to revel in his victory. He often daydreamed about the fear on the man's face as he begged for his life with a gun held to his head. That day would come eventually, but not now...Not until they were comfortably set up in their new village. Continuing his Oscar-worthy performance, Arlo gave a slight bow toward the man. "Yes, your honor."

Chapter 10

Clay had come up with dozens of excuses for why he had been gone a week longer than he was supposed to, but he knew none would be good enough to get him out of the very deep hole he had dug. Kelsey was very understanding when it came to Clay's absences in the past, but in the last year, she had grown more irritable by trips longer than a few days. Even though most times she would bite her tongue, the looks and cold shoulders she gave revealed more than any words she could have spoken. They were the same kind of looks Megan gave him back at the tower—almost as if Megan had passed that torch to Kelsey as a wedding gift.

The sun rose just as the farm came into sight. Clay felt a sense of relief even greater than he had felt when he returned home from Mesquite. Though the trip to Smith's was not terribly long, the physical, mental, and emotional toll Clay had endured over the last week and a half had been nothing short of shattering.

Unlike last time, there wasn't fanfare or screams of excitement when Clay arrived at the gate. Just a weary Geoff who had manned the gate all night, waiting for his shift to end.

"Welcome back," Geoff said casually. "Was starting worry a bit."

"That makes two of us," Clay replied jokingly.

"Went that well, huh?"

"It was...exhausting," was all Clay could say—he wasn't in the mood to discuss all he had experienced.

Geoff quickly brought Clay up to speed on the happenings around the farm while he had been gone. Wasn't much to report—just the way Clay liked it. The biggest news was that Michael and Levi had finished repairing the wagon and had started building a new one from scratch since they had found another set of wheels to salvage.

The rain started to fall just as Clay left the stables, making him even more thankful to be home. He hadn't been caught outside in the rain since leaving Smith's compound. It drizzled a bit after he left Liberty, but even then, it was barely enough to get the ground wet. It made for a more pleasant journey home than what he had prepared for.

Clay walked inside his home and dropped his pack on the floor. The house was eerily quiet and had Geoff not forewarned him about the stomach bug making its way around the children, he would have been worried about the lack of a joyous, childhood commotion. Before he crossed the living room, Lona descended the stairs.

"Oh!" she said, startled. "Hi, Clay," She gave him a genuine smile—a sight that never got old. "Welcome home."

"Thanks, Lona."

The bags under her eyes and the medical kit slung over her shoulder spoke to the long night the medic-in-training endured. Having been inspired by Megan's knowledge, Lona had gradually become Megan's protégé and served as the community's nurse. The extra help gave Megan some much needed respite from the day-to-day injuries and allowed her to be more readily prepared for the bigger mishaps—like when Tyler nearly lost his thumb playing with a hatchet he found in the toolshed. However, when mini-pandemics such as the flu or stomach viruses struck the farm, it meant little rest for either woman.

"How's everyone doing?" Clay asked.

She stepped off the last stair and gave Clay a quick hug. "They're all okay, I think, but Dakota is still having trouble keeping hydrated, so we need to keep an eye on that. Fortunately, her fever broke last night and it hasn't come back; hopefully the worst is behind her and she'll be back to normal in another day or two." Exhaustion was thick in her voice.

Clay gave her a warm smile. "Thanks, Lona. You're going to make a great doctor someday."

She returned the smile as she headed for the door. Clay thought about his words while he quietly climbed the stairs. Lona demonstrated the knowledge, skill, and discipline to become a fantastic doctor, but would the world ever offer her a chance to formally earn that title in the future? Doubtful.

As he reached the top of the stairs, Clay heard soft murmurs coming from down the hall. He glanced in the first bedroom as he passed by. Empty. He went down to the next door and saw Charles conked out in his bed. After the last discussion he and Smith had, Clay wanted to go scoop his son out of bed and squeeze him tightly. He resisted, though—for

Charles's sake. Clay looked on the other side of the room and saw Dakota's bed was stripped down to the mattress. *That's not good,* he thought.

He reached the end of the hall and walked into his own bedroom. Dakota was resting in the queen-sized bed and Kelsey stroked her hair as she read the little girl's favorite book about animals wearing pajamas. Sitting on the bed was a small plastic bin within arm's reach. Even though Dakota's eyes were heavy, they opened wide when Clay walked in.

"Daddy," she tried to exclaim, but could only manage an excited whisper.

Kelsey spun her head around and saw Clay standing at the door. She smiled at him and lowered her shoulders before turning back to finish reading Dakota the story with much greater enthusiasm than before. He walked over and sat down on the bed next to Dakota. Clay rubbed Dakota's hand while Kelsey finished the final few pages of the book. Having managed to keep the water down for the past two hours and content with her parents flanking either side of her, Dakota's exhaustion bested her and sleep overcame her.

"You hungry? Want some breakfast?" Kelsey asked as she and Clay made their way downstairs.

"Starving!" Clay quickly replied.

Kelsey fetched some eggs from the refrigerator before grabbing a cast iron pan from a cabinet. The wood burning stove was already lit to fight the frigid morning temperatures, so Kelsey removed one of the lids on the stovetop and placed the pan down. She cracked the eggs open and within seconds they sizzled over the intense heat.

Clay loved that stove—a beautifully crafted appliance that Ruth's oldest brother, Peter, had purchased for a hundred dollars a year or two before the quakes. It was apparently in pretty rough shape when he bought it, but the skilled contractor was able to restore it perfectly. What was once used to offset heating costs during Texas's mild winters was now a life-saving tool for Clay and his family. All the houses and cabins on the farm were equipped with such devices from before the ash fell, but none were as elegant or practical as the one currently cooking Clay's breakfast.

"Where's Blake?" Clay asked.

"Feeding the chickens and milking Rudy," Kelsey said as she reached for a wooden spoon. "I think it would be good if—" she stopped mid-sentence when she burned her hand on the blazing hot pan. Her reflex to withdraw her hand from such pain caused her to knock the pan off the stove. She jumped back as it crashed to the floor, narrowly missing her bare feet. Kelsey immediately grabbed her finger and sucked in air with clenched teeth.

Clay darted over and grabbed her arm. "Are you okay?" he asked with a concerned look on his face. "Let me see."

"I'm fine," Kelsey said, but didn't resist when Clay pulled her hand away from the burned finger.

It was a pretty nasty burn, but Clay had seen much worse. He walked over to the refrigerator and opened the top door, grabbing a plastic tray and dumping the few cubes of ice left into a towel. He wrapped it up before gently placing it on Kelsey's finger.

Their eyes locked as Clay held the cold towel on her hand. To Clay, Kelsey's gaze was still captivating and he found himself quite often getting lost in her green eyes. It was as if everything in the world was right—it was normal—when he looked at her. His body, for the first time in more than a week, started to relax.

Kelsey slowly pulled away. "Thank you," she said as she walked over to the pan, but Clay insisted she sit down; he would take care of the mess. Kelsey sat down at the table in the middle of the kitchen and peeled the towel away; a small blister had already developed. "Listen, Clay…"

Here it comes, Clay thought. Even though he had been bracing for it ever since he left Liberty, he hated that the moment had finally arrived.

Kelsey was visibly frustrated, but the soft-spoken voice did not match her expression. "I was so mad at you when Geoff told me that you had run off on your own—"

Clay cut her off, immediately going on the defense. "I know, Kelsey, but it was *really* important that I find someone to fix the gun." Kelsey's pursed lips and icy glare was an unpleasant reminder that he had cut her off—a bad habit she hated and something Clay struggled to break. "I'm sorry, Kels," he said as he gestured for her to continue.

Her stare lingered a moment longer before she fluttered her eyes and recalled her thoughts. "As I was *saying,* it really frustrated me that you ran off like that without help and without coming home first to talk about…" she trailed off, but Clay knew she wasn't done so he remained silent. "But I trust you, Clay."

Clay physically felt his eyebrows raise by the unexpected comment. He tried to mask it, as to not look too shocked, but Kelsey noticed the gesture and cracked a smiled. Kelsey did her best to not add to Clay's stress, so she constantly found herself biting her tongue when he did things she disagreed with—such as a several-hundred mile journey to trade with a stranger. But she could at least see the logic and benefit of that trip. However, when she struggled to understand how the reward would outweigh the risk—like walking into uncharted territory to find someone to repair a gun that wasn't essential to living—she was not typically too quiet about it.

"I may never understand why you take some of the risks you do. I may not ever agree with certain decisions, but someone helped me understand that everything you have done has been for the good of your family." She stood up from the table and knelt down next to Clay as he picked up remnants of egg off the floor. She gave him that loving, hypnotic look. "And you've never given me any reason to believe otherwise. So," she said before leaning in to give him a kiss, "I trust you."

Clay was stunned. His mouth hung open as he tried to process what had just happened. He went into the conversation expecting a lion and found a kitten instead. Though he avoided the verbal thrashing, the pang of guilt hit him as he realized just how much he had been gone over the last two months. He needed to make it a point to be home more, *especially* with the winter months closing in. He also knew that he and Kelsey needed some time together, to have a moment where they could just focus on each other instead of one of the many thousands of things that needed to be done around the homestead. Fortunately, the perfect opportunity to do such a thing had just been presented to him.

Clay stood up from the floor and helped Kelsey to her feet. He put the pan in the sink and turned around to look at her. He leaned back into the counter and had a smile on his face. "So, Barry caught me as I was heading out the other day. He has invited us—all of us—to some sort of fall festival early next month. It's a week-long event with lots of food, crafts, games and such. Sounds like a lot of fun, and apparently, a lot of activities with the kids that would allow us to have some time to ourselves," Clay said.

Kelsey's face lit up as she recalled the last event she went to in Liberty—the night Clay proposed. "A whole week?" she asked nearly in disbelief. "That sounds incredible! But next month? What if it starts to snow?" she asked.

"It might get a bit cold, but if last year is any indication, I think we'll be okay. Besides, Barry said they had some alternative plans if that happens." Clay walked over to Kelsey and rubbed her arms and kissed the top of her head. "It'll be fun," he added.

Kelsey sunk into Clay's chest and let out a sigh of contentment. The very thought of spending some time alone with Clay—where they could have a quiet conversation over dinner or take a walk through the quaint neighborhood in Liberty—seemed like a dream. Kelsey hugged Clay tightly. "That sounds so incredible." She looked up at him and smiled. "I love you, Clay."

Clay smiled. "Love you, too." He looked down at her hand and saw the blister forming. "I'm going to go run over to Megan's; see if she has some oil or something to help with that."

"Okay," Kelsey said as she walked over to the fridge and fetched a few more eggs. "*Hopefully* I'll actually be able to have your breakfast ready by the time you get back," she said with a renewed joy in her voice.

Clay made his way to the door, but paused as he reached for the handle. He turned around and looked at Kelsey. "I know I've been gone a lot lately," he started, "and I'm sorry for that. I still have a few things I'll need to take care of later this month—none of which should be more than a few days at a time—I promise, Kels, I'm going to be home a lot more from now on."

Kelsey smiled at the sincerity in Clay's voice. "Well, I certainly wouldn't complain about that," she said with a flirtatious voice. "I do like having my husband around from time to time."

"All right," Clay said as he waved a lazy goodbye, "back in a few," he said and walked out the door.

Clay walked to the main house and upon entering, was greeted by Courtney, one of the only children in the house who managed to dodge the virus thus far. She was on her way out the door to hang some laundry to dry—the downside to staying healthy when everyone else was sick was the added workload; something Clay was all too familiar with.

Expecting Megan to be in the infirmary studying, Clay went to the master bedroom on the first floor, but much to his surprise, he found the room empty. Staying quiet as best as he could, Clay made his way up the creaky steps and down the hall to Megan's bedroom. He lightly knocked.

After a few seconds passed, he heard a groggy response. "Huh?"

"It's Clay."

Soon after, unsteady footsteps approached the other side of the door. The door opened and Megan flashed a smile before hugging Clay. "Good to see you little brother," she said as she stepped back and stretched.

"You look terrible," Clay said.

"You're quite the charmer, Clay. I can see why Kelsey fell for you."

If it had been anybody else, Clay might have felt bad over his choice of words, but Megan was never one to put much stock in looks—certainly not in the last ten years. She looked exhausted, though, even for a woman who constantly pushed herself harder than she should. "Sounds like it was a rough night," Clay said.

"Yeah, it was," Megan said as she fought through a yawn. "What time is it?"

Glancing at his watch, Clay answered. "Almost eight."

"Ah, yes, forty-five minutes ought to be enough sleep to get through the day," she tried to say sarcastically, but her weary tone failed to deliver.

"Well," Clay said, "Kelsey burned her finger on a pan. I just wanted to get an ointment or something from you and then I'll let you get back to sleep," he paused for a moment. "Sorry for waking you."

In the middle of another yawn, Megan waved him off. "It's fine, Clayton. I need to go check on Maya's fever anyway," she said as she headed toward the door. Clay followed her down the stairs and on into the infirmary. "Maya spiked to nearly one-oh-five last night. I actually took her outside into the rain to cool her down." Megan sifted through a box of oils and canisters with different blends. "That was about as unpleasant a fifteen minutes as I think I've spent in years."

Clay felt badly for his big sister. In the last three years, it felt as if everyone had changed, but Megan was still the same old Megan. Always giving so much of her time to others that she never had any for herself. Clay wasn't the only one worried all the stress and lack of sleep would eventually catch up to her one day, but such was the nature of Megan, and she couldn't be persuaded by anyone on the farm to care for herself from time to time. Stubbornness was the cornerstone of the Whitaker bloodline.

Frazzled and unable to find what she was looking for, Megan walked to the other side of the room and rummaged through a different box. "Here it is," she said as she pulled a small mason jar out of the box. "It's peppermint and Aloe Vera. Putting this on should help with the pain and then in a couple of hours have her apply a bit of lavender," she said.

"Got it," Clay said and thanked her for the ointment. "You going to be okay?" he asked. "You seriously look like you're about to keel over."

"Yep," she said as she grabbed her medical bag and headed out the door. "I've gotten two, maybe three good days of sleep since the world ended, what's another night going to hurt?" she said with a faint smile as she walked over to the stairs.

Back at home, Clay repeated Megan's instructions for applying the ointment and Kelsey noticed the cooling sensation take effect almost immediately. "This stuff is amazing," she said. "Hard to believe so few people relied on it back when we were growing up."

Clay shrugged.

Breakfast was cooked to perfection; a fancy bistro couldn't have prepared it any better. Clay savored each bite of egg so he could enjoy his first legitimate meal in nearly two weeks. It made him all the more aware of just how much he hated to leave home, even though it was something he did frequently. Dry clothes, a warm bed; creature comforts such as books and music—Paige was becoming quite the pianist—tending to the crops and livestock—all things Clay missed while he was out for days or weeks at a time. But all those things paled in comparison to what he missed most: his family. In Clay's mind, there was no better way to start a day than waking up to Kelsey's beautiful smile. But the dwindling supply of goods and necessities on the farm demanded he and the others continued on their expeditions from time to time. Even if it meant sleeping in a bathtub inside a Screamer lair.

Chapter 11

"Hand me that wrench, would ya?" Levi asked.

Clay grabbed the rusty tool sitting on top of a toolbox and handed it to Levi, who promptly put it to use. Clay was helping Levi with the second wagon, which was on the verge of being road-worthy. Clay was not much of a handyman so he appreciated the opportunity to learn a few things. Back when they lived in the tower, he was forced to repair critical items whenever they broke, but his lack of skill was always evident in the hack-job type repairs. He was a bit more competent fixing electronics, or to a lesser extent, firearms, but Clay was a novice when it came to carpentry and general construction. Since he was away while the first wagon had been restored, he volunteered to help with the second.

It was nearly noon, but the heavy clouds blanketing the sky provided little light for them to work. The interior lights helped, but Clay found himself bouncing between the three dynamo lanterns to keep the work area bright enough for them to see what they were doing.

"Okay," Levi said as he crouched down next to the rear axle and applied some grease. "You really wanna slather this stuff on there—keep everything moving smoothly."

"Makes sense," Clay acknowledged. Levi used fat they had rendered from a hog they ate for dinner last week. The smell wasn't particularly pleasant, but finding a commercially made grease was not a simple task anymore—improvising was just a way of life and the pig fat seemed to work quite well.

Clay and Levi picked up the heavy wagon wheel and slid it onto the axel. Clay then secured the second wheel to the wagon, applying what he had learned from Levi's example with the first one. Grabbing one of the spokes, Clay gave it a good spin.

"Like butter," Levi commented as he observed the wheel's rotation. Everything was working perfectly. "Okay, two down, two more to go. After that, just a few more odds and ends and she'll be ready for the Oregon Trail."

Clay smiled at the historical reference; he enjoyed having a few older guys on the farm. Not just so he could learn from them, but also so he could talk to them about life before the eruptions—something most of the kids could barely remember, if they were even alive at the time. The men contributed much more than just conversation, as well. Levi, Michael, and Geoff's input, knowledge, and experience alleviated much of the burden that Clay had been forced to bear for so many years. Even though Clay was still viewed as the unofficial leader of the community, it helped that most of the of the time they were all on the same page—disagreements were few and far between. It was nice that he didn't always have to shoulder the entire weight of the responsibility anymore. Clay was free to have a sick day occasionally, and he wasn't the one who had to make every little decision for the group. As he helped Levi finish up the wagon, Clay realized just how much he appreciated the other men on the farm with him.

Clay and Levi turned as they heard the shop door open. Megan headed toward them with a plate of food: ham and egg on wheat. "I thought you boys might be hungry," she said as she put the plate in front of them.

"Oh, yeah!" Levi said excitedly, reaching for the sandwich. "Thanks! Been out here since sunrise, didn't get a chance to eat breakfast."

Clay looked down at the plate then up at Megan. "Thanks, sis," he said as he grabbed his.

"You're welcome." She looked over at Levi, who was already scarfing the sandwich down. She chuckled at the piece of egg dangling out of the corner of his mouth. "You have a little something..." she said as she scratched the corner of her lip.

"Oh," Levi said with an embarrassed look on his face before pushing the leftover bite into his mouth. "Mmmmm. This really hit the spot," he added, giving her an adoring look that was not as subtle as he might have hoped.

Clay swallowed his bite and added, "Eh, could've used some mayo."

Megan let Clay know what she thought of his comment with a slug to the shoulder. "Tell you what, little brother, next time you can make your own lunch," she said while giving him a sarcastic glare. "Speaking of making food," she said as she held out a small cloth, "Bev and I took a stab at some cheese last night. It's not exactly a sharp cheddar, but I think it turned out pretty well."

In shock, Clay snatched the bag from Megan and opened it up. Like two kids wrestling over Halloween candy, Levi's hand ended up inside the bag while Clay was still trying to fish out his own piece. Moments later, both men were chewing. The last time Clay had eaten cheese—or a bucket full of chemicals claiming to be—was from an MRE several years past its prime.

"Okay, well don't kill each other over it. We're still figuring things out, but there will be plenty more where that came from," Megan said. She looked up at the wagon, seeing the progress for the first time and added, "It's starting to look like a wagon." She turned her attention to Clay. "Will it be ready in time for us to go to Liberty's festival?"

Clay deferred to Levi, who nodded and mumbled through a mouth full of cheese. "Mmmm-hmmm."

"Yay!" Megan exclaimed.

Getting everyone to the Liberty in a single trip with just one wagon would have been impossible, but the second wagon solved that problem, allowing everyone to go. Michael and Hawthorne elected to stay behind to take care of chores around the farm while everyone else was gone. No one was surprised by that news; Michael didn't care to be surrounded by a bunch of people he had never met and Hawthorne preferred the comfort of her own bed— traveling two or more days there and then back didn't sound all that appealing.

"I can't wait to go; it's going to be so much fun!" Megan added, smiling toward Levi. "All right, I'll let you guys get back to it. Great job on the wagons, Levi."

Levi's cheeks reddened as he smiled at the compliment. His eyes remained fixed on Megan until the door closed behind her, a gesture that did not go unnoticed by Clay.

"So, when are you going to tell her?" Clay asked.

"Tell her what?" Levi replied, his voice cracked.

"Tell her what?" Clay said mockingly as he took another bite of his sandwich. "Tell Megan you're in love with her." Bread crumbs flew from his mouth.

"Uhm, what? I don't..." Levi stammered before conceding. "Is it that obvious?"

Clay's eyes got big and he made a funny face while he nodded.

"Oh," Levi said as he took a sip of water.

"And, if you haven't noticed, Megan seems to enjoy being around you, too. I mean she pretty much never brings me food anymore unless we're working on something together."

Levi blushed even more, not just because of what Clay said, but the fact that Clay was the one who said it. Talking to *anyone* about his feelings for Megan would have been uncomfortable, but talking to her protective, albeit younger, brother made Levi feel queasy. "I-I-I don't know, Clay."

Clay started to feel awkward for his friend. He was a very outgoing, social guy, but when it came to Megan, he adopted a shy, nervous demeanor. "Just saying, man. I'm not in the business of finding boyfriends for my sister, but the way you two stare at each other... the way you're always doing things for each other... seems like you guys are already a couple. It's just that neither one of you are aware of it."

Levi didn't respond and there was an uncomfortable silence as both men finished their meals.

"Uhm, well, would you mind?" Levi asked Clay.

Even though he was embarrassed for Levi, Clay couldn't pass up the chance to make Levi spell it out. "Would I mind what?"

"Would you mind if I, uh, pursued Megan?"

Clay made a funny face with the archaic word choice. "Uhm, if by 'pursue' you mean ask her out then no, I don't mind. Megan is a big girl, she can make her own decisions. Just know that the brotherly rules still apply. If you break her heart, I am contractually obligated to inflict a substantial amount of pain on you," Clay said with a grin.

Levi returned the smile. Though he was thirty-one, he had never really been involved in a relationship before. He had met a girl in college that he was interested in, but Yellowstone erupted during summer break. Levi lived in Bryan, Texas at the time, and Abigail lived just outside of Pocatello, Idaho—a short drive from the heart of the volcanic crater. Though he hoped he was wrong, Levi knew she didn't survive the eruption. And even if she was still alive, he figured he had a better shot of going surfing down in Rockport next week than seeing her ever again.

After his parents died during a home invasion at the apex of the civil unrest, Levi packed up his old Ford pickup with everything he could cram inside it and headed for Northfield to stay with his Uncle Cliff and Aunt Melissa. No sooner than when he pulled into the Metzger's long, gravely driveway, did Levi's truck run out of gas. Cliff, Michael, and Luke had to help Levi push it the rest of the way to the house so they could unload what he had brought. Since then, his mind had been too preoccupied with surviving than to chase after a girl. However, once Megan and the family arrived on the farm a little over three years ago, he constantly found himself thinking of her, but lacked the courage to tell her about his feelings. Even after asking for Clay's permission, he was still unsure if he would say anything. "I was thinking about talking to her during the fall festival."

Clay crouched down and started winding up the lanterns again. "That's several weeks away, why wait?"

Because I'm a chicken, Levi thought, but he delivered a better line to Clay. "I think it will be more romantic to do it there. Plus, hopefully with all the activities they have planned for the kids, she might actually have a few minutes free for me to talk to her alone," he said.

Clay shrugged. "That's fair enough. The ball's in your court," he said as he folded his hands and gave a slight bow toward Levi. "You officially have my blessing."

"Thanks," Levi replied. "All right, enough chit-chat," Levi said, confidence restored in his voice. "Time to get back to work."

Clay and Levi put in a few more hours on the wagon before exhaustion set in. Accomplishing more than he had expected, Levi called it a day. They worked quickly to put the tools away and clean up the mess they had made. As Clay put the last of the tools away, Levi flipped the lights off and waited by the door.

"You go on," Clay said, "I have to grab a few things from the armory, so I'll lock up when I'm done."

"All right," Levi said, "have a safe trip."

Clay unlocked the door to the armory and walked inside. He opened the safe closest to the door and grabbed his Scout as well as a .270. He opened a cabinet near the reloading bench and fished out what was left of the .308 ammo—just a box and a half. It had been almost two years since Clay had acquired a bullet in that caliber, so he usually only used it to hunt bigger game like black bear or the moose that had started showing up a few years after the eruptions. Clay thought he was hallucinating the first time he saw a moose that far south, but after thinking about it a little bit, it made sense. Texas, post-eruption, was probably not all that different than pre-eruption Wyoming—as far as weather went anyway. Though he had only seen a handful of moose over the years—and only killed just the one—the Scout was the most suitable rifle for the job.

Clay reached into a bucket and grabbed a handful of .270 cartridges. Except for 7.62x39, they had more .270 than any other cartridge, sitting just a hair under 800 rounds—the benefits of living in a state with a lot of hunters.

Clay quickly went through a mental checklist to make sure he didn't need anything else before he locked up. Nothing came to mind, so he picked up the rifles and headed out.

Once back home, Clay packed for the hunting trip he and Blake were leaving for in the morning. As was the ritual before heading out for more than a couple of days, Clay emptied his backpack onto the table and inspected every item; this time he remembered to check *inside* his med kit to see what was needed. The only thing lacking was the ibuprofen. He quickly remedied that, but noticed his reserves were getting a bit low.

After resupplying the medicine and adding some additional items that were essential for longer journeys, Clay zipped up his pack and headed back outside. It was getting late, and he had every intention of leaving before dawn. Waking up before the sun was not a new concept for Clay—Blake on the other hand...

After a quick scan outside, Clay headed to Megan's place. As expected, Blake was with Lona in the den—one of the only rooms that was off limits to the younger children.

"All right, Romeo, it's time to go," Clay blurted out as he walked into the den.

Blake and Lona both looked perplexed.

"Romeo?" Blake asked.

"I suppose they didn't teach you Shakespeare in first grade...Never mind," Clay sighed. "Anyway, I'm not sure you're aware just how early four-thirty comes, so I think we should probably get home and hit the sack soon," Clay said.

"I'll be there in a few minutes," Blake replied.

Clay debated whether he should give Blake enough rope to hang himself. He knew "a few minutes" really meant "I'll be there in three or four more hours." Being dog-tired on a long trip could be a valuable teaching moment for the teenager. If they were staying on the farm or close by, Clay would have just walked away, but he needed Blake to be prepared for the day-long hike ahead of them. Without saying a word, Clay folded his arms and leaned up against the doorway, which sparked a glare from Blake.

"What are you doing?" Blake asked.

"Nothing," Clay said with a wry smile before adding, "Oh, don't pay any attention to me...I'm not here."

"Fine!" Blake sighed with frustration. "Can you give me a minute to say bye? We're going to be gone for a while, right?"

"Make it quick," Clay ordered before turning to leave the room.

As he walked into the hallway, Clay heard Kelsey, Megan, and Hawthorne talking in the living room. Hawthorne, as always, was knitting while Kelsey and

Megan had their feet propped up on the coffee table, recovering from a long day.

"Hey, baby," Kelsey said as Clay walked into the room. "You all packed up?"

"Yeah. Just gotta drag Justin Bieber out of the den and then we'll be heading to bed."

Kelsey chuckled, Megan rolled her eyes, and Hawthorne looked nearly as confused as Blake and Lona had been with the Romeo comment. Clay was on a roll.

Kelsey groaned as she got off the couch and walked over to Clay. She gave him a quick kiss and she wrapped her arms around him. "You two be safe out there. I hate that you're going to be gone *again*," she paused for a moment and looked into his eyes, "but I think it's really good that you're doing this with him," she said.

"I'm excited about it, too, actually. It'll be nice to do some hunting without the never-ending pissing match between Dusty and Geoff."

"I heard that," Dusty yelled dryly from upstairs.

"I figured as much, ya blonde-haired bat," Clay replied.

"Yeah, that was a good one," Dusty fired back sarcastically.

Clay turned around as he heard footsteps approach the living room. Blake stood at the threshold between the kitchen and living room, sulking. "All right, I'm ready," he said.

"About time," Clay said with a smirk. He turned and looked over at Kelsey. "Love you, Kels," he said before he kissed her again.

"Love you, too. Be safe."

On their way back to the house, Clay said goodnight to Charles, Dakota, and Bethany, who were playing with Paige and Courtney.

"Be good for Mama," Clay said as he hoisted Charles up for a hug.

Charles gave his typical response. "Mmmmhmmmm."

Clay and Blake grabbed a quick meal, then got the rest of their gear together, placing it all by the front door.

"Why do we have to leave so early?" Blake asked dreadfully.

"Because there's really no good place to camp between here and there. Honestly, we should *probably* leave even earlier to make sure we get there with enough light left to settle in. In case you were wondering, it really sucks to be caught outside after dark," Clay said sternly.

"Okay, okay...I get it," Blake replied in typical teenaged form.

Clay put the last of their gear down by the door and looked it over—everything seemed to be there. "Okay," he said as he turned to Blake. "There's a blanket on the couch..." Clay said, pointing across the room.

"Why can't I sleep in my own bed tonight?

"It's just easier this way..." Clay said. "I'll see you in a few hours." He slapped Blake on the shoulder as he headed for the stairs.

Chapter 12

"How much further?" Blake asked with a whine in his voice.

Clay looked down at his watch and did some math. Because they were walking through a large, open expanse of land, Clay used the time to approximate how far they had traveled in lieu of landmarks. "Should only be another hour or so."

A long-winded sigh came from the teenager who lagged behind. Blake was no stranger to physical activity—he worked as hard around the farm as anyone else—but his body wasn't conditioned to handle a twenty-mile hike in a single day. The march was brutal even for an experienced traveler such as Clay, let alone for Blake. However, the fertile hunting grounds made the long journey worth every step, especially since wild game activity around Northfield had significantly diminished over the last year. Though his family probably wouldn't starve with what they already had set aside for winter, Clay's food stores were still on the light side. With the unexpected travels over the past few months and another lost week or so from the upcoming family trip to Liberty, Clay's open window to fill his freezer was closing. He would have been on this trip regardless, but was happy to turn the necessary journey into an opportunity to spend some time with Blake.

Of course, Clay had ulterior motives for the trip—teaching Blake the importance of having survival skills. Though it was far from an easy life, living on the farm provided a sense of security that Clay never felt back when they lived in the tower. The additional people and the remote location of the property always gave Clay an excuse to shirk his responsibility to teach such things to the boys. But now, for all intents and purposes, Blake had become a man. The world they lived in was no less dangerous than before. In fact, it was quite the opposite as food and supplies became increasingly more difficult to find. It was naïve to think they were untouchable on the farm. At a moment's notice, the family could be forced to flee, becoming sojourners once again, looking for a place to call home. Any given day might also be Clay's last—especially with the number of close calls he had experienced as of late. If that day ever came, Clay wanted Blake to be prepared to step up in his absence. More importantly, Blake needed to learn how to be a provider for his own family. Though he had not been very forthcoming about his feelings toward Lona, Clay saw the same twinkle in his eye that he had had when he met Kelsey—the boy was in love. And even though everyone on the farm helped one another out, it's up to each household to provide for its own people. So, it was time to ensure Blake knew how to do such a thing. Yes, this trip was about bringing home some food, but it was going to be so much more—or that was Clay's hope, anyway.

"Why didn't we take the horses again?" Blake asked, winded.

"A little bit of walking won't hurt us," Clay said. Walking was just the beginning to Blake's training. Clay had gone the first ten years of this disaster without a horse. After the gas ran out in his dad's old pickup, Clay did all his traveling on foot. The horses were a nice luxury, but they were just that—a luxury. And such extravagances, especially now, didn't last forever. "Besides," Clay followed up. "I know Michael and Levi were planning to hit up a couple of neighboring towns for some scrap materials, so they need the horses more than us."

The hazy gray sky had darkened by the time they reached the little cul-de-sac. Though Clay had never encountered another soul there—never even heard a distant Screamer—as soon as they entered the neighborhood, he became much more alert and had his SKS slightly raised. Blake held the KSG-12, though a bit more relaxed than Clay. And each one had a hunting rifle slung over their backs.

The neighborhood was nestled away from the main road, obscured by the hills and trees. The years of weather abuse combined with overgrowth made the turn-off nearly unnoticeable from the main road. It was an urban oasis, and should the day ever come when the family would be forced to leave Northfield, this would be at the top of a very brief list of alternatives.

At the very end of the cul-de-sac was a nice two-story home. Towering trees that went on for miles provided a beautiful backdrop for the modern brick construction. Clay pointed toward the house. "That's our home for the next few days," he said quietly.

Blake, excited to finally have the long journey behind him, smiled brightly. "Yes!"

Clay didn't want to stifle the young man's excitement, but he held his finger up to his lips. "Shhhhh. We still need to clear the house," Clay whispered.

"Oh, right. Sorry," Blake replied softly, reigning in his joy.

"When you're out in the wild, never let your guard down," Clay said, nonchalantly sprinkling in survival tips where appropriate. He thought about the words he just spoke, realizing that *he* needed to be following his own advice more often than he was.

They went around to the back of the house and walked beneath a second-floor deck that overlooked a steep grade of trees that eventually bottomed out at a creek about two hundred yards away.

"Whoa," Blake murmured as he took the sight in. Though there were hills and trees in Northfield, the young man had not seen anything quite like this before—not since the ash fell, anyway.

Clay walked up to a sliding door—the glass pane was still intact. It had been unlocked when he found the place, so there was never a need to break the window. He looked over at Blake and signaled for him to get his shotgun ready. Blake complied. Wrenching the door to the side, Clay and Blake walked in and began clearing the house. Clay was confident nobody occupied the residence. The undisturbed decoy cans of food he had placed on the counter told him as much. Nevertheless, for the sake of due diligence as well as to teach Blake thoroughness, they cleared each room together.

Once Clay was satisfied the house was empty, Blake immediately plopped himself down on a couch in the living room, causing a blast of dust to erupt in every direction. After a few coughs, he let out a sigh of relief. Rest at last.

"Oh no," Clay said sternly. "We've still got some work to do."

"Seriously?" Blake complained.

"Yep. Drop your pack and follow me. Just because the house is empty doesn't mean it's secure."

Blake shadowed Clay around the house as Clay showed him different techniques for noise alarms around entry points. The first was various Christmas ornaments and lightbulbs beneath all of the first-floor windows. The loud popping sounds from ornaments being crushed would provide sufficient sound to alert Clay of any intruders. It was an unintuitive, if not cliché, trap, but effective nonetheless. After that, they set up a few different rigs with tin cans and string around the house. They also made sure the wedge was still snugly nestled beneath the front door. It was.

Upstairs, Clay showed Blake the room they would sleep in. Having been at the house numerous times in the past, Clay had nailed some boards over the windows so he could run a lantern at night without fear of being spotted from afar. Clay turned on his lantern and set it down in the middle of the floor.

By that time, Clay could see Blake's face was consumed with exhaustion. "All right, we're done for the night," Clay said.

"Thank God," Blake said as he fell back onto one of the twin-sized beds in the room and lay down. Clay did the same and both of them began to drift to sleep. A grumble from Clay's stomach punched through the silence of the room, reminding them that they hadn't eaten much all day—certainly not enough to make up for the thousands of calories they burned on the hike.

Clay reluctantly got out of bed and reached into his pack. "So, I have something I need to tell you," he said as he continued to rifle through the contents inside. He pulled out a small bag of food and held it up. "This is all the food we have with us."

"What!?" Blake said as his eyes widened. "That's not going to last us!"

"Nope," Clay agreed. "It's our dinner tonight, and with a little luck, maybe some breakfast in the morning."

"Okay, so how do we not starve to death?" Blake asked.

"We hunt, fish, scavenge, forage..." Clay said, tapping a finger with each word. "We do whatever it takes to survive."

Blake shook his head, his mouth still slack as he stared at the measly helpings inside the bag. "Why didn't you just bring more food?"

Clay answered with another question. "Let me ask you something, Blake. What would you do if all the sudden you were on your own?" Clay paused for a moment, "Heck, let's make things more complicated. How would *you* feed a family if it was just you providing for them? Forget about me, or Megan, or Geoff, or Kelsey, okay? We're out of the picture. Could you provide for a wife? For kids?"

The weight of the question quickly sank in as Blake's eyes locked onto one of the countless stains decorating the carpet; he was silent. The prospect of being on his own—or as Clay suggested, having others rely on him for their safety and wellbeing, was not a scenario he had given much thought about since joining Clay and Megan's group—even less so after they arrived on the farm.

Blake looked up as Clay stared at him, waiting for a response. Blake gave the slightest of shrugs, then shook his head. "I don't know," he said quietly.

"And that's okay, Blake, I don't expect you to know how. There's no reason to be upset or ashamed of it. You're not prepared because *I* dropped the ball." Clay leaned back on the bed, eventually finding the wall. He sighed and rubbed his eyes with his palms. "When Charlie asked me to show him the ropes, I thought he was too young—that he still needed to just be a kid. With you, it was the opposite problem."

Blake looked offended.

"Don't get me wrong, Blake. I'm not calling you immature—far from it. Like I told you a couple weeks ago, your contributions back home have been nothing short of amazing. You work hard, you're responsible enough to have your own gun, and I know you wouldn't hesitate to put yourself in harm's way to keep the family safe..." Clay paused for a moment before he smiled, "I see a lot of Charlie in you."

Blake smiled as fond memories of Charlie, who worked very hard to make Blake and Courtney feel welcomed when they first arrived at the tower, came rushing to his mind. He took Clay's comment as a compliment. As an honor.

Clay continued. "You're willing to do whatever it takes and that's a good deal of the battle already. But now it's time to get the knowledge to back up the willingness...to be a provider, to be a protector," Clay paused, his expression was serious. "Blake, I pray you don't find yourself in that situation anytime soon— alone and providing for your family—but if you do, I want you to be as ready as you can be.

Blake's body stiffened as he speculated what the next few days had in store. What had originally started as a camping/hunting trip to celebrate his upcoming sixteenth birthday had just morphed into Survival 101 and that scared him. It was certainly not what he was expecting, and though he wanted—he *needed*—to learn how to survive in this harsh world, he had grown so accustomed to the comfortable life on the farm that he wasn't looking forward to the crash course ahead of him.

As Clay's question, again, entered Blake's mind, he got queasy as he thought about the prospect of stepping into Clay's shoes someday. He wondered if he could ever do it as well as Clay does. "Do you ever get scared?" Blake asked, feeling ashamed to continue. "Because...well, I do, and I know if I am going to take care of my family like you, then I can't let myself be."

Clay reached into the bag then handed Blake some food before responding. "My mom died a few days after my fourteenth birthday. It was that exact moment—when I heard her take her last breath—that I felt like the weight of the world had crashed down on my shoulders. Even though Megan was older than me, I still knew it was my responsibility to take care of the family; that others relied on me to provide for them. The fact is I was already doing that before my mom died, but it just seemed more...," Clay hesitated as he searched for the right word, "*official* once she had passed away. Since then, I've lost three of my sisters and more than a dozen others that came to stay with us over the years. Those kids trusted me to provide for them; to protect them from the evils of the world..." Clay trailed off for a moment, his eyes became glassy. "To this day, I *still* feel like I failed each and every one of them. And every morning, when I wake up, the first thought through my head is, 'Will I fail someone else today?'" Clay looked directly into Blake's eyes. "Do I ever get scared?" Clay asked, a heavy breath escaping from between his lips. "Blake, there's not a day that goes by where I'm not."

Blake was surprised with his answer; Clay always seemed calm to him. "But you never seem scared of anything."

"I've learned to hide it well," Clay said as he took a bite of smoked bass. "For the first couple of years, I was terrible at it. And each day I came home empty handed or when one of the kids would get sick, the others saw how scared I was. Fear is contagious; even worse, it's destructive." Clay took a sip of water and swished it around his mouth before swallowing. Dried fish was never his first choice, but it was still precious calories and protein. He continued. "After we were forced to leave our house and set out to find a new home—which eventually was the tower—Megan pointed out to me just how much the others looked to me for hope, and whether I was scared or not, I needed to find a way to act like I wasn't worried about a thing. It was on that day that I found out that Megan, the one who was always cool and calm, was just as terrified as I was. But I had never known it because she kept those worries to herself. Somehow, knowing that I wasn't alone with my fears made it easier to act stronger than I felt. If only to bring comfort and peace to those around me. Does that make sense?"

Blake nodded along. It *did* make sense and he immediately understood the relief Clay felt when Megan told him that she, too, was afraid. Blake saw all the adults around him as strong, brave, unwavering individuals. He didn't feel like any of those things, but knowing he didn't actually have to *be* those things—at least not all of the time—eased his mind.

Clay handed Blake another piece of food and looked down in the bag. "You want to eat the rest tonight? Or start tomorrow with a little food in our stomachs?" Clay asked, giving Blake the choice.

He thought about it for a moment. Even though his stomach was not satisfied after the small portion, Blake knew they would fare much better with some fuel in the morning. "Save the rest for the morning," Blake said.

"A wise choice," Clay said as he tied the bag.

Clay turned off the lantern and they both lay down in their beds. A loud slapping sound from across the room broke Clay from his drifting slumber. "Stupid mosquitoes!" Blake said with a hushed voice. After another moment of silence, Blake added, "You still awake?"

"Yeah," Clay replied groggily.

A silent minute passed. Clay started to wonder if there was a reason Blake had asked, but then he finally spoke. "You remember what happened to my mom before you found me and Courtney?" Blake asked.

He remembered. They were on the brink of starvation and their mother had gone out to find some food. She came back with a fresh-baked loaf of bread and a bullet in her stomach. After handing the bread to Blake, she told them both how much she loved them, then decided to take a nap.

She never woke up.

It was a heartbreaking story—one that was way too common. Clay cleared his throat. "Yeah, I remember."

"Well," Blake said, "that was only half the story. I never told you this, but until about a month before my mom died, my dad was with us."

Clay wasn't optimistic with where this was going.

"Even though things were hard, I always felt safe knowing both my parents were there for us; that they would protect us. But one night, after Courtney and I had fallen asleep, I woke up to hearing them arguing. I heard my dad say, 'We'll have much better odds if we aren't having to worry about them every day,' and that's when I saw Mom burst into tears. I could barely understand what she said, but the more I repeated it to myself, the clearer it became. 'How could you say that about your own children?' I ran back to bed after that, and the next morning my dad was gone. Mom told me that he went out to try and find some food, and when he never came back she said that he must have died trying to provide for us or something like that." A loud sniffle came from Blake's bed as he battled through the painful memories. "I knew she was lying to protect us more than him, which is why I never said anything about it—to my mom or Courtney."

Clay was horrified. Tyler had been abandoned, but it was by his aunt, not his parents. After Clay became a "dad" to these kids, he couldn't fathom how a parent could do such a thing. But especially after Charles was born, Clay would rather face off against a legion of Screamers than leave his children to fend for themselves. "I'm sorry, Blake." It was all he could say. He wanted to comment on Blake's father's cowardice behavior, but regardless of how Blake felt about his own father, it wasn't Clay's place to say such things.

"I do love her, Clay," Blake said. "Lona, I mean. I love her and she loves me, too. I plan on marrying her someday, but I want you to know something first..." Blake's voice trailed off, then suddenly, a bolder, stronger—if not angry—voice broke the silence of the room. "I *will* be a better man than my father. I will never abandon her *or* our kids."

"I know that, Blake," Clay responded immediately. "Circumstances reveal the true character of an individual," he said, a subtle jab at Blake's father while also acting as a compliment to Blake. "You have already shown me what kind of man you're going to be and I have no doubt in my mind that you will make a great husband and father someday."

The room went silent and Clay drifted to sleep. Several minutes later Blake whispered, "Thanks, Clay."

Chapter 13

Clay departed Northfield a day earlier than he had originally planned so that he could go around the wildlife preserve in lieu of going through it. He justified his decision by identifying several promising spots on the map along the wide path around. He was confident he would have some good luck searching the area, but he knew that was a copout. He just wanted the reason to avoid the eerie forest again. As creepy as the forest was, however, punching straight through was on track to save eight to ten hours of travel time, which had to be factored into Clay's decision-making on future trips.

Though, this morning, Clay had timed his departure from the pit stop well, a heavy afternoon storm mucked up almost two hours of the day. He considered pushing through the rest of the way, but images of the two bodies he found on the side of the same road earlier that month forced him to abandon the idea.

Approaching a semi he had spotted just off the road, Clay hopped up onto the aluminum frame step and opened the door. After pulling himself inside and locking the doors, Clay climbed into the sleeper area and yanked the privacy curtain shut. The cramped space was efficiently designed to maximize every millimeter of space. After a quick search, Clay settled in for the evening. Reaching into his bag, he pulled out his dinner—smoked rabbit and a chunk of cheese—which was the last of the food he had brought with him. As he popped the morsels of food into his mouth, Clay wondered if he had enough bartering goods to make a deal with Smith for some food. He would be leaving straight from the camp to head to Liberty, since it didn't make sense to walk all the way back to Northfield only to get on a wagon and head straight back out for the festival. And since Liberty was barely a three-day hike from where he was—if he went around the forest—Clay only needed a little bit of food to sustain him for the trip. Looking through the items he had brought, especially the ten stripper clips of 7.62x39 ready to feed into the SKS, Clay was optimistic they would work something out.

After getting to know him, Clay realized that as intimidating as he looked, Smith was just another man. Someone who had suffered greatly over the last decade and found the strength to power through. Smith was a fighter, which is why Clay planned on extending an invite for the man to join the Northfield clan. Smith had a nice little fortress setup—there was no doubting that—but what good was a fortress if there wasn't anything worth protecting? Being isolated out in the sticks wasn't doing the man any good and, based on their last exchange, he could benefit from some time around a few friendly people.

Of course, the added muscle to Northfield's roster wouldn't hurt, either.

Amidst the rush to get everything prepared for his journey, Clay had forgotten to pack any form of entertainment; namely, a book to read. He found two paranormal romance novels beneath the bed—an odd find in a trucker's cab—but had no interest in opening them. However, since Lona *was* a fan of such fiction, he stashed them in his backpack anyway. He would have to take extra precautions to prevent Smith from seeing them in his possession or the man would rib him relentlessly.

As Clay lay in bed, he began to reflect on the week he and Blake had spent out in the woods. It was astounding how seriously Blake took the opportunity and how fast he picked up on everything Clay had to teach. The boy exceled so much so that about halfway through the week Clay had run out of things to go over—the things he had planned for, anyway—and became more of a spectator. He merely observed the young man in action, only offering corrections or tips as issues crept up.

More than just developing survival skills, Clay witnessed a maturing in Blake's attitude as well. He suspected that that had more to do with the conversation they had on the night of their arrival than anything Clay had taught him out in the field.

The trip had gone as planned except for one aspect: hunting. Though they had had some luck fishing and a few successful rabbit snares, Clay was discouraged when they failed to spot a single deer the entire week. The spontaneous drop in the deer population was worrisome, and it made Clay even more concerned with their food situation for the coming year. But then, about halfway through their journey back to the farm, they spotted a doe traveling through the field they were in. Clay had pointed it out to Blake, who slowly took the rifle off his shoulder and raised the scope up to his eye. Blake was no stranger to taking down a deer, but the doe was at least 200 yards out, which easily doubled Blake's longest shot to date. Following Clay's tips and advice, Blake brought the deer down with a single shot.

After waiting the typical fifteen minutes, the two made their way over to the kill. Once they arrived, Clay wasted no time getting to work, pulling everything he would need out of his pack and laying it on a small plastic tarp next to the body. The field, pockmarked with trees and overflowing with tall grass, provided decent protection from being spotted while they field dressed the animal. Though Blake was familiar with shooting deer, he had never been too involved with the butchering process, so Clay took his time explaining each step. Clay grabbed a heavy cotton sack and soaked it with his bottle of drinking water. Knowing they were only about six hours from home, he was willing to risk losing precious water. With each cut of meat he removed from the carcass, Clay placed it in the wet sack. The sack, or a game bag as it was called in the past, would keep the meat protected from flies and other insects that would quickly ruin the food given an opportunity. And the water-soaked cotton, along with the small amount of blood from the cuts, would act as a sort of fabric refrigerator to keep the meat from spoiling during the rest of the trip. Clay suspected it wasn't quite warm enough to spoil the meat in that amount of time, but he didn't want to take any chances. In the past, a few hours of walking could quickly turn into a couple of days for any number of reasons. Having the meat in a bag like this would keep it reasonably safe to eat for a few days as long as it stayed wet. It might be difficult to convince a health inspector to eat meat stored in such a way, but Clay was more concerned with keeping his family fed over the winter months. The cloth bag was worth its weight in gold, a gift he had received from Shelton a few years back.

All in all, the trip had been positive and Clay was already looking forward to doing the same thing with Tyler when the time came. He felt sixteen was too late, but Charlie had been a bit too young. Maybe fourteen would be the sweet spot. In any event, Clay still had a little time to decide with Tyler, and in the meantime, he would start to slowly introduce some of the same skills to the energetic boy from within the safe confines of the farm.

Clay's thoughts then shifted to Liberty's festival. If it was half as nice as the celebration he and Kelsey had attended three years ago, they were all in for a treat. Mayor Shelton seemed quite excited for the event, which was infectious. Clay imagined another night out with Kelsey: tasty food, a romantic setting, and no kids...

In the darkness of the stale semi cab, Clay smiled brightly. A "vacation" from his day-to-day life was long overdue.

****

"Smith!" Clay shouted toward the gates as he looked up at the security camera. "Smith? It's Clay, open up!"

No response.

Clay waited a while before shouting again. He waved his arms in front of the camera as if he was stranded on an island and saw a low-flying plane passing nearby. But once again, nothing.

The sun had only been up about an hour, so Clay started to wonder if Smith had left before dawn to go hunt. The FEMA campsite was massive, so even if Smith had stayed on the property, it could take hours to find him.

Resigned to the idea that he could be waiting all day, Clay decided to use the gate code Smith had given him on his last visit. Being inside the walls would at least offer Clay protection from a wandering bandit. He would just need to be careful with how he announced his presence to Smith.

"Five-one-three-nine-seven-two," Clay said aloud as he punched in the code onto the panel.

After three solid beeps, a buzzing sound erupted from the gate's lock, startling Clay. Then, there was a loud clanking sound. The gate cried out with a hideous screech as it swung open, grating on his already tense nerves. Upon closing the gate Clay heard another, quieter clanking sound. The lock was re-engaged and Clay was safe—as safe as one could be these days.

There were several large, plastic crates lying around the concrete courtyard. Even if there had been anything of value in the crates when the place was abandoned, Clay was certain they were empty now. But he checked them anyway.

Though the concrete walls cut down on the bulk of the wind, the slight breeze that managed to get inside was intensified by the chill of the morning air. After dragging some of the crates over to the wall of the bunker, Clay stacked them two-high and created a little horseshoe fortress. Concealed by the bunker wall and crates, Clay sat down and waited for Smith to return. Boredom struck fast and hard. Clay even considered grabbing one of the paranormal romances in his pack, but the thought of Smith finding him deep in a romance novel kept the book safely hidden away.

Hours went by and Smith was still gone. When Clay had decided he would wait all day, he didn't actually believe he would need to, but that prospect looked more and more likely with each passing minute. As the afternoon crept closer to the evening, the silence and boredom was shattered by a distant rumble.

With a frustrated sigh, Clay grabbed onto one of the crates and pulled himself up to locate the source of the sound. Pins and needles terrorized his foot as the feeling crept back into his toes. He scanned the horizon, quickly zeroing in on the dark clouds a few miles away. They were headed straight toward the camp.

At first, Clay was worried about the approaching storm, but he figured Smith would have heard it, too, and would be rushing back to avoid the downpour. Being out in the rain is never fun and it is particularly dangerous this time of year. Hypothermia from the icy rain would claim its victim faster than being naked in a blizzard. *Smith will be back soon*, Clay reasoned as he waited.

Clay held out as long as he could, but it only took twenty minutes of rain before he gave in. His shivering had become so violent that he started to feel lightheaded. Of course, not eating in nearly eighteen hours played a significant role in his involuntary shudder, but his body's natural response to warm itself only made matters worse.

If he was going to survive the night, Clay needed to get out of the freezing rain. With what little energy he had left, Clay repositioned the plastic bins to create makeshift steps up the wall. Once standing on the highest crate, he could grab ahold of the metal railing of the catwalk Smith had used when shooting at the cat.

His biceps felt like they were being fed into a paper shredder as he struggled to pull himself up and over the railing. After several attempts, Clay managed to swing his leg up high enough to hook around the lower bar running along the railing. It gave him the leverage he needed to hoist himself up onto the walkway. He fell onto the catwalk and lay face down on the cold diamond-plated steel. Though the catwalk was covered, the damage from the storm was already done—Clay was soaked and the mercury was still falling. It was a situation Clay had found himself in more times than he cared to remember and each time his saving grace was finding a dry place and getting out of the wet clothes.

Growling through the exhaustion, Clay pushed himself off the catwalk and stumbled over to the door leading to the observation room. He immediately felt relief—albeit just a little—from the protection the room provided from the wind and the rain. The temperature inside, however, was negligibly different from outside. The basement was his only option.

As Clay pressed on the call button, he was both relieved and terrified as the button's light activated. He kept asking himself *What if Smith is down there?* It wasn't unrealistic to think that the security system had malfunctioned and was offline, cutting all video feed and deactivating the motion sensors around the camp. And the sound of the elevator suddenly ascending to the second floor would be cause for more than a little concern for the occupant below.

"Crap," Clay mumbled between his heavy breaths. There was no turning back now.

The elevator's pitiful tone sounded and the doors parted. Clay took a deep, painful breath as his lungs started to warm before stepping inside. As if he was venturing a bit too close to a bear's den, Clay began shouting as loud as his body would allow.

"Smith! It's Clay! Don't shoot!"

The elevator wrenched to a stop, and Clay cut himself off midsentence and held his breath. As the doors opened, he squeezed his eyes shut and prepared for the worse.

Silence.

Clay kept his eyes shut until the doors automatically closed. At last, the relief from being inside the compound boxed out the fear and anxiety of breaking into an ex-Marine's stronghold. If Smith were here, he would have already announced his presence via multiple .30 caliber bullets.

He reached up and pushed the open button on the panel and the doors parted once more. This time he heard something. CLICK CLACK CLICK CLACK.

Chip!

The half-blind dog rounded a corner and darted toward Clay, barking insanely all the while wagging his tail. The high-pitched, almost shrill bark of the little dog made Clay keenly aware of the headache he had developed. *What is it with this place and headaches,* he thought as he left the elevator.

Despite his body aching, Clay made the effort to kneel down next to the excited dog who only stilled his body once he was scratched behind his ear. The dog seemed eager for attention and was satisfied to get it.

Clay groaned as he stood back up to his feet and stretched his back. The effort had little impact on his tightening muscles. After watching Clay stretch with his head cocked to one side, Chip took off the way he had come, continuing his awful bark—as if inviting Clay to follow.

Clay stumbled down the dimly lit corridor wondering when Smith would be back. It felt wrong to just let himself inside; Clay *was* breaking and entering. But he had no choice in the matter and once he explained the whole thing to Smith, he knew the burly man wouldn't fault him for the decision.

Chip darted into Smith's dining room. As Clay followed him, he felt pebbles under his feet and after studying them as he walked, he realized it was little piles of dog food. Clay started to joke with Chip about his eating habits as he turned the corner into the dining room and had the wind knocked out of him. He gasped for air and his body trembled as the sight in front of him sank in.

Smith was on the floor, his lifeless body leaning up against the wall in the corner of the room. With a pistol in his right hand and blood splattered on the wall behind him, it didn't take a forensic scientist to figure out what had happened.

The trembles turned into uncontrollable shaking as Clay stared at the catastrophic aftermath the .357 hollow point had left behind. Like a helpless bystander watching a devastating crash, Clay couldn't seem to look away. He just stared at the slouched body in front of him, almost as if he was waiting for the corpse to spring to life and yell "Gotchya!" But the gray tone in his skin and the vacant eyes reassured Clay that the scene before him was no prank.

A dark aura began to smother Clay as he recalled the times he had contemplated the same end Smith had chosen; to escape the frozen hell on earth once and for all. To be released from the stress and burden that fell with the ash ten years ago could be an appealing alternative during Clay's darker days, but it was always his family, both blood and adopted, that pulled him away from that obscure abyss. Had he lost that reason...like Smith had...

The thought shook Clay to his core.

Though he had only just met Smith earlier in the month, Clay felt as if he already knew the man quite well. Smith, whether he intended to or not, revealed more about himself to Clay in a single night than most people had over the course of several years. Most folks, including Clay, were not quick to divulge details about their past to people they had just met. Far too often, such information was viewed as vulnerabilities and was used as weapons. But, as it would seem, Smith wasn't concerned about that since he had nothing left to lose at that point.

As Clay looked down at the body, he wrestled with what words to say. Not that it mattered much—the only ones to hear him would be the All Mighty and the dog. But still, it felt wrong not to say *something*.

"Some wars are just too big for one man to fight..." Clay said with a wavering voice—he could no longer determine if his trembling was from low core temperature or from the loss of his new friend. "I hope you found the peace you were looking for, brother."

Unable to stay in the room any longer, Clay headed to the bedroom he had slept in on his last visit. He took his wet clothes off and wringed them out as best as he could in the corner before draping them over a chair. He grabbed a blanket off the bed and pulled it around his shoulders. Feeling warmer, but still battling violent shivers, Clay explored the rest of the compound to try and get the blood flowing, eventually finding himself in Smith's workshop.

Toward the back of the room was a work bench sitting beneath a hanging light—the only one in the room. Tools and hardware were strewn about the bench, but right in the middle was a small, polished metal cylinder sitting on top of a piece of paper. It was Clay's new firing pin.

Clay battled whether he should be mourning the loss of Smith or rejoicing over the regained functionality of his rifle. But his internal struggle was eclipsed by the gut-wrenching message scrawled across the piece of paper previously holding the firing pin.

Thanks for the closure, Cowboy.

"Damn this world," Clay said through a clenched jaw.

Chapter 14

Morning came too quickly. But as the sunlight slipped through the blinds, Clay's natural response was to get moving. If the sun was up, there was work to be done, or so his mind always convinced him, regardless of his body's wishes.

But not today. Over the past few days, Clay had been hard at work helping the town of Liberty prepare for the festival. Far more went into pulling off such a large event than Clay had ever realized, and he had not been ready for the task list awaiting him. However, except for a few odds and ends, everything was ready for the festivities to kick off later in the evening. So Clay lay in bed, alone with his thoughts—a dangerous situation.

Still drowsy, his eyes closed once more, immediately greeting Clay with images of his discovery at the bunker four days earlier: the pool of blood collecting around Smith's body, the pain and sorrow still lingering in his hollow stare, his hand still clutching the revolver as if it was a life raft amidst choppy seas. The images relentlessly invaded Clay's mind like a mental Blitzkrieg, snuffing out any chance of respite from the nightmares that had plagued him since leaving the camp. Because moments of idleness quickly turned to terror, Clay had made it a point to work sun up to sun down since he arrived at Liberty, allowing himself to be blissfully distracted throughout the day.

He tried to roll over and force himself back to sleep, but the muscle he had pulled while moving Smith's body outside still nagged him. Clay arched his back and applied pressure to the spasm with his hand, which brought some relief. Although the strain felt better than it had all week, he would have given anything for some truly potent pain meds.

Along with the pain came the memory of standing in front of the pile of dirt that was covering Smith's body. When he arrived at the camp that morning, the last thing Clay had expected was to bury his new friend. But such was life in the frozen wastelands of Texas. Nothing should be taken for granted, especially life.

As he towered over the shallow grave, Clay thought back to his great-grandfather's funeral a few years before the eruptions. Because he valiantly served in World War II, there was a large military funeral held for him in Fredericksburg where he had lived most his 104 years of life. Chills still crept through Clay as he recalled the officer ordering the twenty-one-gun salute and the sounds of the rifle shots echoing throughout the cemetery. It was the most unforgettable moment of the entire ceremony.

At Smith's grave, Clay charged his AR-15—with Smith's new firing pin securely in place—and shouldered his rifle. Smith had served his country and Clay was determined to honor him for his sacrifice, despite the risk posed by the successive shots. He fired his first three shots into the air, timing each trigger pull about one second apart. As the final gunshot echoed across the massive field of decayed, temporary housing, Clay heard in his head a brilliant rendition of *Taps* being played.

"So long, Justin."

The "funeral" was hardly fitting for a man who had fought and nearly died for his country, but it was better than just letting his corpse rot in the dank basement of the bunker. And though it seemed cold-hearted to think about while he dug the man's grave, Clay had every intention of utilizing most of the bunker in the future. The dining room, however, would forever be off limits.

A barely audible yawn and high pitch squeak emanated from the foot of the bed, pulling Clay from his wandering thoughts. He looked down and saw the little dog stretching as he roused from his slumber.

"Morning, Chip," Clay said.

Chip crawled toward Clay, expecting the quick attention he felt entitled to. As Clay scratched Chip's head with one hand, he used the other to tilt the dog's red, bone-shaped tag on his collar. The inscription made him laugh.

Devil Dog

Glancing over at his watch sitting on the bedside table, he decided it was time to get up. Kelsey and the others were supposed to arrive sometime after lunch. It was almost two weeks since he left Northfield, so once he realized that he was finally going to see his family in the afternoon, it was as if all became right with his world again. Even the haunting memories that previously consumed his thoughts struggled to compete for his attention.

After a few groans and grumbles, Clay managed to climb out of bed and get dressed before heading down to Vlad's store. The house was mostly empty, save a few out-of-towners that had also received one of the limited invites from Shelton. It truly was an honor to be on that list.

"Good morning, Clay, how are you?" Vlad asked.

"Better than yesterday," Clay replied.

Vlad nodded. Clay had told him about Smith. He wanted Vlad to know so he didn't send anyone else to the camp just to be stopped by locked gates outside an empty bunker. But what started as a simple "for your information" turned into a night of venting and vodka drinking—both of which helped dissipate some of the darkness that had been lingering in Clay's heart since discovering his friend. And as hard as the last couple of nights had been, Clay could only imagine how much worse it would have been if he hadn't been able to talk to someone about it.

"Oh!" Vlad suddenly shouted. "I have surprise for you," he said as he walked over to a metal cabinet and unlocked it.

"What is it?" Clay asked, his curiosity piqued.

Vlad looked back with a smile as he unlatched the lock. "You will see, my friend." He opened the door and retrieved a wooden box that he then set down on the counter. "Have look inside," he said, gesturing to the small crate.

Clay walked over and stared at the box for a minute, like a kid staring at a Christmas gift, speculating as to what was inside. With curiosity now running rampant, Clay placed his hand on the box and lifted the lid.

He gasped.

"Is that?"

"It is," Vlad said with assurance.

"How...How did you get it? Did he sell it to you?"

Vlad shook his head. "He had bad poker face."

Clay's eyes were still as wide as they were when he first lifted the lid. He started to reach in when he quickly stopped himself. "Oh, sorry...may I?"

Vlad laughed. "Of course, it is why I show you."

With a mixture of eagerness and respect, Clay pulled the pistol out of the box. The old gun demanded admiration. Even in the post-apocalyptic day, it was an incredible design, and in his mind, was visually nothing short of perfection. He ran his fingertips along the slide, feeling the etched words *Model of 1911. U.S. Army* along the side. He was still in disbelief as he held his grandfather's Colt 1911 in his hand again.

Every scratch, every scuff, every stain on the beautiful pistol had a story with it—some dating back to the 1940's, while others more recent. The old .45 had had a tough life, but she was still ready for more.

Managing to tear his gaze away from the gun, Clay glanced inside the box and saw two spare magazines and a handful of rounds—twenty to thirty at most. His eyes shifted between the gun and Vlad. "What do you want for it?" Clay asked, but the tone in his voice came across more as a demand.

Vlad was still smiling as he watched Clay admire the piece of Americana, a piece of Clay's heritage. "You have been good friend for many years. I know that gun means a lot to you; I cannot ask you to pay. It is a gift."

"Wow," Clay said, stunned by Vlad's generosity. "But I can't do that, Vlad. Something like this has a *very* high price tag these days." Clay put the gun back down in the box and looked at Vlad again. "How about a swap?"

Within a minute Clay was back in his room, rifling through his pack. He found the Glock 17 first, but he was long overdue for an upgrade from his current pistol, and he planned to keep it. He kept digging and grabbed on to the suppressor for the ARAK-21. *Definitely* not. As he continued rummaging through a hefty amount of PMags and boxes of ammo, Clay started tossing things out in a frantic effort to find what he was looking for.

"Crap! Did it fall out?" he asked himself. Then, finally, he sighed in relief as his fingers wrapped around the barrel of the Ruger R8.

Revolvers never felt right in Clay's hand, but oddly enough, this one felt amazing. He had planned on keeping it for himself—something he could actually use to bring down a deer if he found himself in the right situation. And since he had quite a few boxes of .357 back home—most of which were factory—he thought the unique revolver could find a place in his arsenal. Vlad's recent acquisition, however, changed his mind on that.

The 1911 wasn't just a gun or even just his great-grandfather's gun. Except for a family photo, the World War II relic was the last thing connecting Clay to his family's past. It was important to him and he was going to get it, but not at the expense of an unfair trade with his friend.

Clay stuffed the revolver into his waistband. He quickly grabbed the box and a half of shells he had also taken and rushed back to Vlad's store. He set down the R8 next to the 1911 box.

Vlad looked the gun over and grinned. "Yes, this is good trade," he said.

Getting a quality trade out of the deal enhanced the Russian's joy from the transaction. He was insistent on returning the family heirloom to its rightful owner, but Clay could have brought him a broken Derringer and Vlad still would have called it a good trade. He just wanted to make sure that Clay left with his great-grandfather's gun in his possession.

Vlad popped open the cylinder of his newest acquisition, revealing some dried blood Clay hadn't noticed when he cleaned the gun. Bile crept up Clay's throat from the sight, but it, thankfully, didn't have the gut-punching effect he expected.

Clay's expression didn't go unnoticed. "I am very sorry, Clay," Vlad said.

Clay swallowed hard and forced a smile. "Nothing to be sorry for, Vlad. Honestly, I am not sure why this is bugging me so much," he lied. Being responsible, even indirectly, for the death of a good man was not something to get used to.

Vlad loaded up the revolver with some of the shells Clay had given him and stashed it beneath the counter—a clear indication that the trader had no intentions of making it available to his customers. Following suit, Clay started sliding cartridges into each of the 1911 magazines. He was one round shy of having three loaded magazines—twenty-three bullets in all.

After helping Vlad and Olesya rearrange the store to accommodate more of their homemade inventory, Clay headed out to go check the newly updated bulletin boards to see if anything notable had been reported. Clay never made it there, because, as he walked down the main street, he spotted the two wagons in the distance approaching Liberty's gate.

****

"Just about done," the man said as he looked down through his glasses, watching carefully as he made the finishing touches.

"Good," Clay said, "I am not sure how much longer I can sit here."

"And there...we...are," the man said as he sat back in his chair and observed his work. "This is one of my finest, if I do say so myself," he said as he stroked the gray stubble on his chin. His balding forehead was wrought with wrinkles as he studied the drawing. The man picked up the easel and twisted it toward the couple sitting in front of him. "Sorry it's a little...exaggerated. It was kind of my thing back in the day."

Clay immediately chuckled with the caricature illustration in front of him. The resemblance was spot on. A quiet sniffle from Kelsey surprised Clay. He looked over and saw tears welling up in her eyes.

"What's wrong?" Clay asked, alarmed by her response and wondering if maybe the artist had embellished on one of her insecurities.

The old man also looked at her, worry filling his eyes as he grew concerned that he might have offended her somehow. As the tears slid down Kelsey's cheeks, she smiled brightly. "It's beautiful," she whispered.

Clay looked around as if he had missed something. "Then, why all the, uh..." he said, gesturing toward her eyes.

The man handed Kelsey a handkerchief and she immediately dabbed at her eyes. This life—*her* life, had been anything but easy. And even though things vastly improved once she and Clay arrived in Northfield, Kelsey still struggled with the heavy burdens that had been heaped upon her shoulders—

AJ POWERS

a weight that became increasingly difficult to bear as she watched her husband slay his own demons. Her fading optimism over the last year and a half did little to help Clay and vice versa. Though artificial smiles and vague answers did a good enough job at hiding her growing depression, Kelsey's difficulty in finding hope each morning had been weighing her down. Seeing Clay for the first time in nearly two weeks—a short span of absence compared to some recent trips—had done her spirit good. The picture showed the woman Kelsey pretended to be, the person just that morning she decided she *would* be. "This drawing..." she said, wiping away at more tears, "Clay, this is our first portrait together." The tears continued to stream, but her smile grew wider. "Solomon, it's just wonderful. You are a truly gifted artist."

"Thank you, young lady," Solomon said, giving a subtle bow with his head. "I must say, of all the folks to come by so far, you two have been the most enjoyable to work with."

Kelsey smiled warmly.

Though all the games and booths were free of charge, Clay handed the man a few rifle bullets. Vlad would give him a fair price for them—that is, if Solomon didn't want to keep them for himself.

"Thank you very much, good sir," Solomon said as he took the post-apocalyptic gratuity from Clay. He carefully tore the paper off the easel and rolled it up before tying a string around it. He handed it to Kelsey, "Here you go, my beautiful lady," he said, before playfully kissing her hand.

"Talented *and* a charmer," Kelsey said with a giggle. "You better watch out, Clay," she added.

"I've got my eye on you, old man," Clay said through a chuckle before reaching his hand out.

"You're a lucky man, Clay. You take good care of this one," Solomon added before grasping Clay's hand for a firm shake.

As Clay and Kelsey left the small booth—one of dozens along the road leading to the center of the little town—Clay felt a sense of peace fall upon him. The last couple of months had been hell—among the hardest since Charlie's death—and it was not something a good night's sleep or a hot meal could fix. He needed an escape from the demanding reality that enveloped him every day, even if just for a little while. And finally, such an opportunity had arrived. For the next five days, Clay wasn't going to worry about whether the freezers were stocked with enough food for the winter or how much longer the dwindling supply of medicine would last. He wasn't going to think about the joyful torments he saw on Smith's tablet or the losses he had experienced over the last ten years. While he stayed in Liberty, Clay would not live in the past, nor fret over the future. He would live in the now and savor every moment of it until he was dragged, kicking and screaming, back to reality.

Chapter 15

Clay tightened his grip on the club as he waited patiently for his time to act. He attempted to block out the shouting and screaming crowd surrounding him and focus on the person standing in front of him—more importantly, focus on what the man held. Clay drew a deep breath and slowly exhaled...Timing would be everything.

Come on, already, he thought.

As if reading Clay's mind, the man hiked his leg up, pulled his arm back and threw the object at Clay.

No, this no good, Clay thought to himself—his gut was wrong.

"Steeeee-rike!" Shelton yelled as he enthusiastically signaled the call.

"Full count, wuss," Dusty said as she tossed the baseball back to the pitcher. "I'm betting you'll whiff on this next one."

Clay ignored her insults as he stepped back and took a few practice swings. He looked around at the makeshift baseball diamond and admired the effort it took to construct the playing field in such a short amount of time. It had turned out to be a beautiful afternoon—the perfect way to close out an incredible week in Liberty. But as the sun inched closer to the horizon, threatening clouds from the southwest had already started to move in. The rain looked to be at least an hour or two off, and seeing as it was already the top of the seventh, the game would be finished and cleaned up before the first drops hit the ground.

Stepping back into the batter's box, Clay tapped the bat on each shoe and prepared himself for the next pitch. Two outs, full count and down by four, time was running out for a comeback rally.

"Come on, Kohler! Bring the heat!" Dusty shouted to the man on the mound.

Clay locked his eyes onto the ball as the pitcher made his throwing motion.

CRACK!

Clay connected with the ball and it popped up just out of the centerfielder's reach and on into left field. As Clay closed in on first base, he was being waved on—he arrived at second base with time to spare. The crowd roared with applause for the big play, but that happened with *any* big play regardless of which team was responsible. The mere act of witnessing this classic American pastime was in and of itself thrilling, and none of the spectators cared who had the most points on the board after the ninth inning.

Even though nearly two hundred people had gathered to watch the event, Clay was only playing for one person in the stands. And when he spotted her in the crowd, he fell in love all over again. He could see the pride she had for her husband as she clapped her hands and cheered him on. It was that moment, for the first time in a decade, Clay had *completely* forgotten about the world they lived in. It was pure bliss.

Geoff was now at bat, and Clay could see that Dusty wasted no time ramping up the smack talk. No batter was exempt from the onslaught, but Clay saw Geoff turn around and say something back to her that made her shut up immediately.

What on earth did he say, Clay wondered. It had to be pretty epic to get Dusty to stop running her mouth.

Clay led off second base as the pitcher wound up. As soon as he heard the crack of the bat, Clay took off running. He saw the ball skim along the foul line past third base, but it stayed in play. The third base coach signaled Clay home. Quickly tagging third, Clay aligned his body with home plate and kicked it into overdrive.

Doing her best to intimidate the charging runner, Dusty readied herself to stop Clay at all costs. Halfway home, Clay saw the ball fly over his head toward home plate. It also flew over Dusty's head and hit the fence behind her. As she scrambled to pick up the ball and return to the plate, Clay made his dive.

"Yer out!" Shelton yelled, throwing his thumb over his shoulder.

Clay immediately stood up and started shouting. "Are you blind? She wasn't even close!"

"Now, who do you think was in a better position to see that? You or me?" Shelton fired back.

"Back off, crybaby!" Dusty chimed in, smacking Clay in the chest with her catcher's mitt. "I could have killed and skinned a rabbit in the time it took for you to get here."

Clay gave Dusty a nasty look before reengaging Shelton. "Get your eyes checked, old man! I was safe by a mile!" By this point, Clay was standing up tall and in the mayor's face.

The hushed crowd watched in shock as the beginning stages of a brouhaha unfolded right in front of them. Unable to continue, the rage on Clay's face transformed and he began to laugh. Shelton joined in and put his hand on Clay's shoulder. The ruse was up and the crowd broke out in laughter. After all, how could they relive an American pastime like baseball without a shouting match between a salty runner and a stubborn umpire? Though Clay and Shelton were in on the scheme from the very beginning, Dusty's involvement was an added, albeit unexpected, dose of believability.

Clay and Shelton shook hands as Clay headed back to his team's bench to an off-key rendition of *Take Me Out to the Ballgame*. Clay bypassed the bench and found Kelsey among the spectators. After a quick kiss, he picked up Charles and sang with the rest of the crowd. The toddler's perplexed look was priceless—why would people be playing a game, then suddenly break out in song? If only Clay had a camera.

"Buy me some peanuts and cracker jack, I don't care if I never get back!" Clay shouted, but then lost his voice as he heard a popping sound in the distance. The crowd continued to sing as Clay leaned toward Kelsey. "Did you hear that?" he asked. She shrugged and shook her head.

Another series of popping faintly echoed across the field.

Clay looked over at Geoff, who was on the mound warming up to pitch. He had a startled look on his face. As did Dusty and Shelton.

The crowd's singing trailed off and the sounds became all too clear; all too familiar.

Gunfire.

For a brief instant, everyone remained motionless, each person thinking the same thing. *Did I really just hear that?*

The collective question was answered when another volley of gunfire erupted from the center of town. The laughing and cheering quickly turned to panic and screams. The confusion in the crowd upgraded the panic to hysteria. There was nothing but fields around them, providing them little in the way of protection. But scrambling to their homes—directly toward the imminent threat—was also out of the question. The spectators didn't know what to do.

Shelton and Kohler both sprang into action as if they'd prepared for this scenario before. "You, you, and you," Shelton said as he pointed at Geoff and two other men in the crowd, "get the women and children out toward the creek and wait for the all clear."

Each one hesitantly agreed. Clay wasn't sure if it was because they wanted to help the others fight off the attackers or if it was the fact that nobody in the field was armed—it didn't make much sense to strap an AR-15 to your back when trying to hit a homerun.

"Stay close to Ruth and the kids," Clay said, yelling to be heard over the frantic crowd.

Kelsey squeezed Clay's hand. She didn't want to leave him—more than that she didn't want him running toward the gunfire—but the look of worry he had for her safety spoke louder than any words could. "I love you," she mouthed out, as trying to speak over the commotion would have been fruitless.

Clay kissed Charles on the forehead and then handed him to Kelsey. He then knelt down and looked at Dakota, who was latched on to Kelsey's leg. "Koty, I need you to go with Mama and Charles. Tyler and Uncle Geoff are going to make sure you guys are safe, okay?" Clay spoke loudly.

Dakota gave a nod and squeezed Kelsey even tighter. Clay stood up and saw Tyler fighting through the crowd. Clay waved at him and then pointed at Kelsey. Tyler nodded his acknowledgement of Clay's expectations.

As the three men ushered the rest of the crowd toward the stream at the back of the property, Shelton turned to those who remained. "I have no idea what's going on, but everyone needs to get ahold of a gun right away. If you don't have one, Daniel Kohler and I have some extras." Shelton, eager to come to his town's aid, had nothing more to say. He turned around and ran toward town; toward the continual clusters of gunfire.

Clay and the others followed closely together. Gunfire continued as they approached the center of town, and when they were within a few hundred yards of the first street, they began to split up, each man going their own separate way to retrieve their guns.

Within moments, Clay found himself on his own. Most of the population lived on the eastern side of the community with shops and businesses— including Vlad's—on the western half. Clay had expected Dusty to travel with him, but she opted to get a more appropriate rifle from Shelton. With his mind in such a frenzy, Clay didn't think to tell her to grab Geoff's AK-47.

Clay's heart pounded harder with each round of gunfire that sounded closer by the minute. He was alone, unarmed, and surrounded by unknown hostiles. It was a tactical textbook case of being screwed. But, with no other viable options, Clay kept running toward his weapon.

He was a block away from Vlad's when he heard two shooters engage each other. First was the shotgun blast followed by four quick shots from a pistol. The exchange was followed by a frantic cry for help.

Clay darted across the street and rounded the corner of Short Stop Grocery when he saw a body lying dead, face-first, in the dirt. The man still grasped the double barrel shotgun, and was properly dressed for the violent occasion. Clay let out a sigh of relief when he realized the deceased man was not someone from Liberty. Two people toward the back of the house caught his attention, a young woman pressing down on a man's arm. Her crimson-colored hands shook as she tried to maintain pressure. As the woman searched her surroundings for help, she locked eyes with Clay.

"Lona!" he screamed as he sprinted toward her.

Before he could see the young man's face, Clay knew it was Blake. Clay came to Blake's side and assessed his wounds. It looked as if a few of the buckshot pellets had caught his left bicep. It wasn't a fatal injury, but Clay knew all too well the pain of being hit in the arm with shotgun pellets.

Clay saw the P225 in Blake's right hand; he was still prepared to defend his and Lona's life if anyone else surprised them.

"Blake," Clay said, stealing a glance at the corpse before returning his attention to Blake. "You did good. But we need to get you somewhere safe until this all blows—" Clay was interrupted by rifle fire.

RAT-A-TAT-TAT!

There was no way to know if the shots came from the good guys or the bad guys, but it was close. Clay looked at Lona and said, "Help me get him up."

With little struggle, they helped Blake to his feet and moved to the back of the house.

A door swung open and a man said as loud as he dared, "This way!" He motioned them inside. Clay recognized Simon, the owner of the store, as he passed.

Simon locked up behind them. His wife took over for Clay and helped Blake over to the couch. She then turned and ran down the hall to find some towels.

"What's going on out there?" Simon asked.

"I don't have a clue. Are you armed?" Clay responded.

"I've got my twelve gauge and a Colt .38."

"Good. If someone you don't know tries to get in here, *don't* hesitate," Clay said sternly to the older man who might have been offended with the life-lesson under different circumstances.

Clay looked over at Blake as a weeping Lona continued to hold pressure on his arm. "You're gonna be fine, Blake. Just a flesh wound," Clay said and headed toward the back door.

"Please be safe, Clay," Lona said, struggling to keep her voice steady. "Get to the others."

Clay heard her, but didn't acknowledge. He was focused on getting back to Vlad's and getting his guns. Once outside, he ran around to the side of the house and commandeered the dead man's shotgun. He took the bandolier of shells off the man and slung it over his own shoulder before replacing the two spent shells with fresh ones. He snapped the barrel shut and started running.

Clay reached the front of the house and looked down the street both ways. Though the gunfire was still heavy, it seemed to be more concentrated toward the center of town. Feeling confident it was clear, Clay quietly but quickly made his way down the road.

A minute later he could see Vlad's place. He was almost there.

As he cut through the back yard of one of the shops, Clay heard a shot from across the yard. He ducked his head and swung the shotgun around. He dumped both barrels toward the shooter. The gunman was nearly twenty yards away, but the spread from both shells was still tight enough to drop the man. Clay barely broke his stride as he cut across the yard, giving little thought to the man he had just killed. He stopped only to reload the shotgun behind a tool shed and take a few seconds to catch his breath, before sprinting to Vlad's.

Clay was running toward the back of Vlad's house when the side door on the garage exploded open and an armed man jumped out. Clay raised the shotgun and prepared to fire.

"No shoot!" A voice yelled out with a thick Russian accent.

Clay dropped his arms and shook his head. "Vlad, you can't be doing that to me," he said as he puffed for air. "I almost turned you into Swiss cheese, man."

Vlad held an M44 Mosin Nagant, the Ruger R8 tucked away in his waistband. There was a grim look on his face, one that Clay had never seen before, and it scared him.

"Olesya was in town, I must go find her." Vlad's words pleaded for help.

"I need to grab my stuff and find Megan and the kids first, but then..." Clay trailed off and took a deep breath. "Vlad, we'll find her."

"Thank you, Clay," Vlad said.

"Godspeed, Vlad."

Vlad headed toward the road and Clay ran to the back of the house. He practically knocked the door off its hinges as he stormed inside and up the stairs. He grabbed his AR-15, Glock 17, and every spare magazine he had. The thought of taking the ARAK-21 crossed his mind, but he couldn't spare the time to load the magazines with .300 blackout. He also didn't know the rifle like he knew his LaRue.

Certain he had everything he needed, Clay was finally combat ready. Hoping he wasn't too late, he ran back down the hallway, practically skiing down the stairs. He planted his feet on the bottom landing and bounced off the wall, using the impact to help change direction. Barely a minute after entering the house, Clay was back outside running toward the center of town; running toward the threat.

Clay slowed his pace as he approached the town square—his rifle at the ready. Brief flashbacks to the gunfight in Mesquite made him worry about a rifle malfunction again. But he trusted Smith's work was as good as his word and pushed the thoughts out of his mind. *No distraction*, he told himself as he focused only on the battle around him.

The closing feast—the big dinner everyone looked forward to all week—had been ready to start immediately following the ballgame. Tables, chairs, centerpieces, glasses of water and plates were already placed. It had looked similar to the night that Clay proposed to Kelsey three years ago, except now tables were flipped over, broken glass littered the ground, and several bodies lay lifeless—each appeared to be shot in the back as they fled from the attackers. The scene was disturbing.

More gunshots rang out, causing Clay to spin toward the sound. There was nobody there, and the town hall—the repurposed community club house—blocked most of the view in that direction. Clay's senses were heightened to levels he could only assume were superhuman; he was ready to fight.

Just up ahead was the Robinson's House. Once the community gym and pool, it was now the town's daycare and where Megan had volunteered to help watch the kids during the game. Levi chose to stay, too, making Clay feel slightly better. But as more gunfire erupted through the town, Clay began to fear the worst. Neither Megan nor Levi had their guns—a pitfall of feeling safe. Clay scolded himself for knowing better. To think any town could be outside the grasp of evil men was naïve, but he let his guard down again—a habit that was proving difficult to break.

The pools hadn't been filled in years and the large gated area out back was now jammed with playscapes and jungle gyms. Every time Clay passed the building, he saw no fewer than a dozen kids outside, swinging and climbing, jumping and sliding. But now, with barking gunfire coming from every direction, the kid's paradise was a ghost town. The only movement was from a few swings swaying in the wind as the storm drew nearer.

Clay jogged toward the building when he heard gunfire and breaking glass. This time, he saw where the shots came from; he also saw dirt and mud kick up just feet in front of him. The shooters were in the daycare and Clay was in their sights.

Taking cover behind a wall, Clay press checked his rifle to ensure he had chambered a round. Incredibly enough, he *hadn't*. In the scramble to collect his gear and get into the fight, he had neglected to charge his rifle. Had he contacted a hostile beforehand, Clay would have certainly ended up on the losing end of that exchange.

"You're an idiot, Clay!" he said as he tore the charging handle back in frustration. His weapon was now hot.

Unlike the movies, the men didn't waste ammo peppering a wall they could never hope to shoot through. Clay had sought shelter behind good cover, and they weren't going to shoot until they had a target to aim at. Clay was at a major disadvantage until he saw a man approaching from across the street out of sight from the shooters pinning Clay down. Unknown to Clay, the man was also there seeking the safety of his three daughters.

Clay immediately recognized the man as one of the shop owners in town. Clay had never learned his name, but he was a tailor or something to that effect. The man saw Clay leaning up against the wall. The two made eye contact and Clay nodded toward the building. The man held up one finger indicating that Clay wait a minute. Clay was unsure what the man was going to do, but got the feeling he would know when it was his time to act.

Time slowed to a standstill as Clay waited. He started to wonder if the man had abandoned the plan and gone elsewhere. Though the gunfire had decreased significantly, the peaceful town of Liberty still sounded like a bad neighborhood in Baghdad. Clay was calculating his next move when he finally heard several gunshots close by. The men started shouting from inside the daycare followed by more gunshots. *That's my cue,* Clay thought to himself. He spun around the corner and headed toward the building.

For the moment, the gunmen inside had diverted their attention to the man across the street. This afforded Clay the opportunity to move undetected. He managed to get himself pressed up against the wall of the childcare without notice. He slid along the wall toward the broken window and readied himself. Clay took a deep breath then pressed off the wall, whipping himself around. Taking aim through the window, Clay lined up his shot.

"He's done," one of the shooters yelled just before Clay squeezed the trigger.

The first man dropped immediately. Clay fired three more rounds as he transitioned to the next man. His aim was off, but the explosive reverberation that bounced around the room stunned the other man long enough for Clay to adjust.

Success.

The second man crumpled to the floor and Clay cleared the small lobby area of the daycare from outside the window. He ran around to the front of the building and stopped just to the side of the door. Clay looked over to where he thought he saw the man last and quietly yelled, "It's clear!"

Unsurprisingly, there was no response.

Clay went inside alone and confirmed the two hostiles he shot were neutralized. As Clay reached the gym, which had been converted to something of an arts and crafts area, gruesome images of a massacre began to creep into his head. Clay reached out and turned the door handle; his gut told him everyone inside was dead. He pushed the door open and raised his rifle looking to the left and the right. There were no bodies; no blood. Instead, he found a vacant room that smelled of glue and paint. And as Clay searched the rest of the building, he found more of the same thing—none of the rooms showed any sign of life.

"Megan!" Clay shouted.

There was a faint, unintelligible cry in response.

Clay kept calling for Megan as he carefully tore through every room, slowly zeroing in on the sound. He found himself in the swimming pool maintenance room. Shelves stocked with blankets, towels, and toys lined both sides of the narrow room. Straight ahead

Clay faced a shut door with a faded chemical warning sign.

"Megan?" Clay said again, this time a little quieter.

"Clay!" A muffled shout erupted from the other side. The door burst open and out came far too many people to fit in such a small room.

Megan ran over to her brother and embraced him. "What's going on?" she asked, her cheeks and eyes both red and wet.

As some of the other adults helped the rest of the kids from the small room, Levi ushered Courtney and Erica over to Clay. They were all relieved to see him.

"I don't know, Megs, but there are still more of them out there."

Megan visibly shook and looked as if she was going to pass out. The adrenaline from the shooting coupled with thirty-plus bodies crammed into a small room wreaked havoc on her.

"Levi, take this," Clay said as he handed him the Glock and a spare magazine. Noticing there wasn't a dry shirt in the entire room, Clay realized Megan wasn't the only one suffocating in that closet. "Stay in this room until you get the all clear. But if you hear someone coming, you get *everyone* back in that closet and lock the door, understood?"

"Yeah, okay," Megan said as she wiped a combination of sweat, tears, and dirt off of her cheek.

"You take care of them, Levi," Clay said.

"With my life," he responded.

Other than Geoff, Dusty, or himself, Clay wouldn't want anyone else there protecting his sister. There was no doubt that Levi would put himself between any one of the people in that room and a bullet. That was just the kind of man he was.

"I'll be back in a bit; I need to go help the others."

Clay promptly turned and left the room, heading to the front of the building. He carefully made his way east keeping an eye out for Vlad—or more accurately, Olesya. Along the way, he clashed with three other groups of hostiles. Clay's participation in their downfall was minimal as the citizens of Liberty had now armed up and were effectively fighting off the invaders.

As Clay reached the end of the neighborhood, there was still no sign of Vlad or Olesya. The gunshots were gradually replaced with screams for help as citizens found their loved ones dead or dying. It was truly a horrific thing to witness—another nightmare to haunt Clay for the remainder of his days.

Standing at the end of the street, Clay just looked around searching for any clue of where his Russian friend might be. Movement caught his eye; someone walking nonchalantly toward Shelton's house. It wasn't the significant distance that made him impossible for Clay to identify; it was the ski mask covering his face.

Clay took off running toward the assailant.

Chapter 16

The tremors in Shelton's hands turned the simple task of loading his Ruger Mini-14 magazines into a frustrating chore. He had handed out every other rifle that he owned to those who needed more effective means to fight off the attackers. Having also given out the extra boxes of ammo he kept in the safe, Shelton was forced to crack into one of the spam cans of .223 he kept in a coat closet.

He had nearly topped off the first magazine when he heard the front door open. Before he could insert the steel mag, the intruder's VEPR-12 was aimed right at him. The intruder's face was obscured by a black ski mask with a white, demonic-looking face painted on. Shelton raised his left hand slowly as he lowered the rifle to the floor with his right.

"All right," Shelton said calmly, still kneeling on the living room floor, "let's not get stupid here. There's far more of us than there is of you. You'll never make it out of here alive if you kill me."

The man remained silent. His eyes squinted from the smile his mask obscured, his finger curled around the trigger. His orders were simple: deliver a message to Mayor Shelton. But as he stood there with his semi-automatic shotgun trained on the old man's chest, he became consumed with retribution.

"Listen, son, just put the gun down and we can work this out," Shelton said quietly. "Nobody else needs to die tonight."

The man let out a sarcastic laugh. "It's always the people who have no options left that say stupid crap like that."

Shelton swallowed heavily as he looked up into the man's eyes; there was no mercy, no empathy. And if he felt it was advantageous that Shelton not take another breath, there would be nothing to stop him from squeezing the trigger. "All right then, what do you want?" Shelton questioned.

The man briefly wrestled with the decision literally kneeling in front of him, follow his orders or enact vengeance. Finally, deciding to follow his orders, he lowered the gun slightly, but keeping it plenty ready to fire if Shelton decided to be a hero. "I've got a message to deliver."

"A message?" Shelton repeated, nearly in shock. "Son, you don't blast your way into a community, killing God knows how many people, just to bring a message," he said, struggling to keep his anger in check.

"You don't understand, old-timer..." the man said as he stepped closer, "the killing is part of the message," he said with a sly grin.

Shelton was sick to his stomach. "Then what is the other part of this message?" he asked.

"Yeah, I'm rather interested to hear it myself," Clay said as he stepped into the room with his rifle raised, the intruder's body inside his optics.

In a gesture of good faith, the assailant eased his stance as he contemplated his next move. He quickly deduced he had none—at least none that had him leaving the house upright, anyway.

"Feel free to go ahead and drop that gun any time," Clay said.

The man complied with Clay's request and placed the AK-style shotgun onto the floor. As soon as his hand left the grip, Shelton stood up and shoved the man down onto a couch across the room. Clay stepped into the living room, keeping his AR-15 on the assailant while Shelton picked up the VEPR-12.

"I really like this couch, so don't make me ruin it by turning your head inside out," Shelton said as he moved the muzzle of the twelve gauge to within an inch of the attacker's face.

The man had a satisfied smirk on his face—he had gotten under Shelton's skin. His smug grin morphed into mocking laughter. "You know, you're really terrible at the whole 'tough guy' act, *Barry*."

Without saying a word, Shelton reached down and pulled the ski mask off the man's head. Shelton squinted his eyes as he tried to identify the familiar face in the dim light of the house. Then it hit him.

"What are you doing here?" Shelton roared with anger, a tinge of fear flashing across his face.

"Like I said...I'm here to deliver a message."

Clay shifted his aim to the front door as numerous boots stomped up the porch steps; Shelton kept the shotgun on the attacker.

"Mayor Shelton!" one of the voices yelled as the group came in through the front door.

Recognizing the men, Clay immediately lowered his rifle.

"How bad is it?" Shelton asked, never breaking eye contact with the man in front of him.

"It's really bad, sir."

****

The piercing screams from the woman was almost too much for Clay to handle. The buckshot had made her thigh all but unrecognizable as part of a leg. Her face was a ghostly white and her eyes filled with despair. "Please! It hurts so much!" she cried in vain as Clay and another man lifted her onto a homemade stretcher—one of only three the town had. As a result, only the most severe injuries utilized the archaic means of transporting wounded.

"One...two...three," the man said as he and Clay lifted the woman off the ground.

This action was met with a blood-curdling shriek.

The three-hundred-yard walk to the infirmary went at a snail's pace. The woman had already been through enough—adding to her agony by bumping and jostling her around wasn't going to do any good. There was no saving her, anyhow. Clay glanced down again at the destruction to her leg and recalled the last time he saw so much blood pouring out of a person. *I'm so sorry,* Clay thought to himself, not wanting to be the one to give her the grim news. Her cries ceased before they reached the infirmary, but as Clay and the man approached the door, countless others' agony covered the silence.

Chaos was the only word to describe the activity inside the ill-equipped, makeshift hospital. The wounded cried out in pain as volunteers scrambled to meet the needs of each patient. The reassuring lies being spoken to loved ones—that everything was going to be okay—was a punch in the gut to Clay.

"What do we have?" an older woman asked as she came up to Clay. The woman, who went by the name of Jackie, was Doctor Sowell's assistant. A quick glance down at the leg evoked a "Dear God," out of the middle-aged woman. Jackie had been a nurse practitioner for eighteen years before the eruptions, but she had seen more devastating injuries in that night than she had her entire career up to this point. "Follow me," she said as she turned and walked briskly to the other side of the room to try and find some space.

She stopped near the back wall and pointed to an empty spot on the ground. Clay and the other man gently set the stretcher down, and with the aid of Jackie and another volunteer, they slid the woman over onto several stacked blankets on the floor.

"I'll make sure that Doctor Sowell sees her next," the woman said as she walked back to triage another person who had just been carried through the door— someone she might be able to help.

Clay sighed deeply as he ran his fingers through his hair. *Why did this happen,* he asked himself. Though he didn't say anything, it was obvious that Shelton knew the man in his house. Clay wanted to ask him about it, but there were more pressing matters to tend to. Shelton threw the man into one of the town's two jail cells under *heavy* guard while they fought off the remaining attackers. The whole thing was disturbing, but the mystery behind the whos and whys of the attack were almost as unsettling as the attack itself. *Almost.*

A tall, slender black man walked up to Clay. Without saying a word, he knelt and checked the woman on the ground for a pulse. Still silent, the man grabbed a blanket on the ground next to the body and draped it over her. "She's gone," he said with a deep, weary voice.

Doctor Sowell was a great surgeon and an even better man. He had been a rising star at one of the top hospitals in Houston for many years before he got bogged down with the bureaucratic lunacy that consumed the healthcare system. Having made a decent amount of wealth in the first half of his career, he left that life behind and went into medical mission's work both at home and abroad.

The man always seemed to be in good spirits, even during some of the harshest winter months the town had ever faced. He was an optimist through and through and had a way of making his positivity contagious. But as Clay looked at the blood-soaked clothing, the overwhelmed expression, and the slumped shoulders, it was easy to see that the doctor's high spirits had been conquered.

"There's nothing you guys could have done. There's nothing *I* could have done," he said while shaking his head.

Clay nodded; he'd suspected that prognosis before they even walked inside.

It had been more than two hours since the last shots had been fired, and since then, Clay had been transporting the wounded to the infirmary. Exhaustion exuded from both Clay and the other man, and the surgeon took notice.

"You guys are looking pretty drained. Please, go get some water and sit down for a few minutes before going back out," he said, gesturing to a small break room through a doorway.

Clay slowly got to his feet and then both he and Doctor Sowell helped the other man up. Clay looked toward the door and noticed that the inflow of wounded had finally slowed. Clay couldn't help but feel badly that his night was ending, but *anyone* with even a hint of medical experience would continue to work through the night.

Clay saw Lona working feverishly across the room—he had never seen her look so flustered. She tried to calm a toddler with a gash across his forehead. Clay's fists began to shake and his knuckles turned white as he imagined the kind of monster that would take a shot at a young child trying to flee from danger.

Following the doctor's orders, Clay found himself slouched over a collapsing table with a red, plastic cup of water in his hand. While the wall separating the tiny break area from the triage/exam/operating room blocked out the gruesome sights on the other side, it did little to muffle the sounds of agony that callously burrowed into Clay's head. Even so, Clay's body managed to relax just a little bit.

Although he ached all over, Clay felt compelled to find some way to help—and sitting at a table drinking water wasn't accomplishing that. But, as he considered his next task, Clay's desire to get back to Kelsey and the kids overcame his willingness to assist in the infirmary. He needed to ensure their safety from another wave of barbarians that everyone feared was coming soon.

Dusty was currently perched in the decorative clock tower with her .270 just off the town's main entrance. The moonless night would make it virtually impossible to spot potential attackers, but if anyone could tag an enemy on a stormy night, Dusty could. And she would make them pay for it. If nothing else, her position offered her the ability to alert the town of a coming attack.

Clay tilted his head back as he threw back the last few ounces of water in his cup. He looked across the room and saw the man he had spent the evening with drifting in and out of consciousness. Clay hadn't even caught his name. *Helluva way to be introduced,* he thought.

Resigned to the fact that there probably wasn't much more he could do at the infirmary, Clay decided to head back to the hotel for the night. Before he could get out of his chair, the dwindling commotion on the other side of the wall roared back to life, Megan's voice rising above the rest of the noise.

Clay startled the other man when he jumped out of his chair and raced for the door. Megan was already briefing Doctor Sowell on the condition of the patient that Levi and Kohler carried across the room without a stretcher. Clay's stomach sank when he realized who it was.

"Vlad!"

Clay's vision blurred as he walked toward his longtime friend. The world around him started to move in slow motion, causing Clay to wonder—to hope—that this was all just a bad dream—a terrible nightmare he would eventually wake from and return to the slightly less horrific one he had been living for the past decade.

Megan looked over at Clay. Her grim face told him everything he needed to know—it was time to come say goodbye.

Clay staggered past the scurrying people and over to Vlad's bed as Megan, Doctor Sowell, and Jackie prepped Vlad for surgery. He approached slowly, as if he was walking up the edge of a cliff, fearful that he might slip and fall into the abyss. He didn't want to look his friend in the eyes as he departed this life for the next. *I can't do this anymore,* Clay thought. *I am so tired of saying goodbye.*

It took all the energy Clay had to take those daunting final steps up to the bed. Though the amount of blood on the sheets and his clothes was inconceivable, Vlad did not seem to be in a lot of pain. He looked up at Clay, a look of hope flashed through his eyes at the sight of his friend.

"Clay, please," he said through labored breath. "Olesya..." His eyes closed.

"I promise..." Clay said, his lip quivering. "We'll take care of her." Clay swiped his hand across his face as he fought back the tears.

"His vitals are dropping," Doctor Sowell said. "We need to do this now."

Clay took the hint and backed away to give the surgical team some space. He walked over to Lona and embraced her. She buried her face into his chest while she sobbed quietly. An evening that started out as close to heaven as possible had quickly plummeted into the depths of hell.

Watching the brilliant surgeon work across the room, Clay felt a pang of guilt in his stomach. Being caught up in the moment at Shelton's house with the masked assailant and then being recruited to help transport the wounded, Clay not only failed to keep his promise to help Vlad, but he had forgotten all about him until he was carried inside.

The door opened and Shelton stepped inside. He stood in silence as he witnessed the destruction that had been left in the wake of the attack.

After talking to one of the volunteers for a few minutes, he approached Clay. "Do you have a minute?" he asked discreetly.

"Yeah, sure," Clay responded as he released his hold of Lona.

The house was about fifteen yards behind them before Shelton started to talk. "Clay, uhm..." the usually clear-spoken Shelton stammered over his words.

"What's going on, Barry?" Clay asked.

"There are at least twenty-two unaccounted for—and as far as we can tell, almost all of them are children."

Clay's eyes widened. Shelton's words only fanned the rage growing hotter with each bloodied victim Clay picked up.

"We're forming search parties now," Shelton said. "Clay, I hate to ask you, but we're really stretched thin, and—"

"Just let me go get a few things," Clay interrupted.

Shelton nodded, grateful for Clay's willingness. "Thank you, Clay. Meet back at my house as soon as possible."

Clay turned around and jogged back to Vlad's hotel. His thoughts were in complete disarray, like two radio frequencies competing to be heard, but mostly coming through as static. He slowed his jog down to a walk to try to clear his mind. He would need to be sharp if he was going to leave the town in the middle of the night.

As he approached the hotel, he heard Vlad's voice echo in his head.

"Olesya." His distressing voice made Clay feel weak. He prayed that his daughter's name would not be Vlad's final word.

As Clay slowly shook off the events from the evening and prepared for the challenge still ahead, it dawned on him what Vlad was *actually* telling him just before he passed out. He didn't ask Clay to look after his daughter...

Vlad begged that Clay find her.

Chapter 17

It was cold, wet, and dark. Ordinarily, going out into the wild under such conditions was a recipe for a gruesome death. The extraordinary circumstances, however, cared not for the time or the weather.

Clay and Geoff walked in silence as they searched for any signs of life. Each search party consisted of three men that would head out as far as they could manage in a pre-determined direction. There were twenty-three men in all, which meant one group would be down a man. Clay and Geoff volunteered to be the two-man team. Having worked together for years, the pair operated more like a single entity than two individuals. Apart from Dusty, throwing a third person into the mix would have only hampered their effectiveness.

It had been hours since they left town, and it appeared they had gone the wrong direction. Between the pounding rain and the lack of light, any trail left by the abductors was long gone. Clay and Geoff merely headed out in the direction assigned to them, looking for the slightest clue that a group of people might have passed through over the past few hours.

"Check path," Geoff said quietly.

Clay lifted his heavy, oversized poncho off his body and on top of both him and Geoff. Geoff pulled out a compass and clicked on a flashlight.

"Still southeast," Clay said. "Good."

Geoff killed the light and Clay pulled the poncho back onto himself—not that it was doing much good anymore.

"So, what do you think?" Geoff asked. "Keep going?"

Clay didn't have any way of telling time, but he guessed it was closer to dawn than not. He had long burned through his energy reserves and was down to fumes. With the daunting trip back still ahead, Clay wanted to call it off. But with Vlad's desperate plea for help still echoing in his mind, he forbade himself from quitting just yet.

"Let's push a little further."

Geoff walked forward, offering his nonverbal agreement; Clay trailed behind.

About twenty minutes later, they found what they were looking for—a dim light in a window several hundred yards away. The jolt of adrenaline brought a renewed bank of energy. Clay and Geoff quickly moved closer, hoping to get a better look at the target. It was too dark to know for sure, but Clay's gut told him they found what they were looking for.

Clay and Geoff crouched down and formulated some strategies. With visibility piss-poor at best, their options were limited. Every plan they came up with, however, relied on the element of surprise, and Clay's suppressed .300 blackout was going to play a crucial role. He just hoped it was sighted in properly—his mind kept thinking back to Smith missing the cat.

They decided to wait until dawn before making their move and found cover in a patch of trees. Even though most of the leaves had already fallen to the ground, the scraggly branches would provide them with some level of concealment and slight relief from the rain.

Clay and Geoff had already staged their ambush minutes before sunrise. It was still too dark to make out details, but the ever-so-subtle hint of light creeping over the horizon allowed them to get a better idea of the building's layout. It was a farmhouse with a barn around fifty yards off to the side.

They refined their plans based on that information, then moved in closer. With each minute that passed, the scene in front of them brightened. Geoff used the binoculars to do a quick scan; all quiet.

The sun finally crested the horizon, bringing everything into much clearer view. They waited patiently for some indication that they had found who they were looking for. And within minutes, their suspicions had been confirmed.

Geoff watched as a man holding a rifle walked out of the house and over to the barn. As he approached the barn, he shouted and another armed man walked out. They chatted for a moment and the one man had pointed back to the house he had just come from. They then went their separate ways, each going to the opposite building from which they came.

"Looks like shift change," Geoff said, "but if I had to guess, they're not going to be here all that much longer."

"Yeah," Clay agreed as he observed through his ACOG scope. "I think you're right."

Clay and Geoff solidified their plan of attack and prepared for the assault. Clay ensured he had his subsonic ammo loaded. He only brought two mags worth, but to make the suppressor as effective as possible, he needed to use it. If all went well, he'd only burn through a couple of rounds.

Ditching their packs behind some shrubs, Clay and Geoff followed the tree line for as long as they could. They were about a hundred yards from the barn when they ran out of woods. At that point, Geoff knelt down, pulled a few magazines out of his pouch, and placed them on the ground next to a tree for quick retrieval.

Geoff nodded toward Clay. "Good luck."

"You just make sure none of those SOBs sneak up on me."

"You know I got your back."

He did.

Staying low and moving fast, Clay quickly closed the gap between the trees and the barn. The sounds of whimpers and cries crept into existence as he reached the rotting, wooden structure. All doubt that they might be attacking an innocent family was gone.

For the most part, Clay was no longer visible from the house. Making sure he kept it that way, he hugged the wall of the barn and move toward the back. About half way down the building, one of the wooden planks was popped out enough that he could get a glimpse inside.

There were two guards inside; both armed with SKS rifles. His field of view was limited, but Clay saw three kids sitting on the ground, huddled together under a filthy blanket. Their bodies shivered from the frosty morning air. It sounded as if there were more hostages inside, but he couldn't be sure.

Clay weighed his options. At that moment, the best approach he had was to pop in from the front door and take both guards out. He felt confident enough in his ability to shoot both men before they could react, especially since one of them had his rifle slung over his shoulder. The problem with that idea was that it would mean Clay would have to expose himself to the farmhouse. If one of the guards managed to get a shot off or even shout, Clay's position would leave him vulnerable, ruining their plans to silently extract the children. They, of course, had a fallback plan, but it came with a much higher risk for collateral damage, which was unacceptable to both Clay and Geoff.

Moving to the rear of the barn, Clay leaned around the corner and saw there was a back entrance. He had no idea what he would be walking into, but Clay immediately decided it was the most viable option.

About halfway to the door Clay froze at the sound of boot soles walking across a concrete floor. He pressed up against the wall and crouched down just as one of the guards walked out of the door and headed straight toward a heap of rusted metal and cracking rubber that was once called a tractor. When the guard reached the old farm vehicle, he widened his stance and unzipped his pants. Clay inched past the door while the man relieved himself on the deflated tractor tire. As the man finished, Clay stood up and aimed the rifle center mast.

"Don't move and don't make a sound," Clay said with a hushed voice.

The man raised his hands and slowly turned around, a coldblooded grin smeared across his dirty face. He looked at Clay as if he was merely a child holding a water pistol, his expression daring Clay to pull the trigger.

Clay was left with a decision he didn't want to make. He had no way to subdue the man, nor did he want to risk getting any closer to him. At the same time, he didn't want to shoot a man who had, for the time being, surrendered peacefully. Fortunately, yet unfortunately, the man forced Clay's hand.

He took a deep breath and opened his mouth. Clay knew he was preparing to holler for his friend back inside the barn. The man's gamble that Clay was bluffing would be the last mistake he made. The solitary popping sound from the 208 grain A-Max bullet was quiet enough that he was confident nobody back in the farm house would have heard it, but there was little chance the man inside the barn hadn't noticed.

"What are you doing out there, Avery?" A voice from inside yelled.

Clay readied himself to fire.

"Avery!" the man yelled again. "I said, what the h—"

The man's words were cut off by the sound of gunfire coming from the woods. Geoff had engaged the enemy, which meant there were others headed toward the barn.

Jumping to his feet, Clay ran inside the back door and saw the other guard running toward the front of the barn. Clay stopped, took aim, and fired twice. Both shots were true and the man went down.

The terrorized children all screamed, frantically scrambling away from Clay. "Hey!" Clay shouted as loud as he dared. "It's okay, it's okay, I'm from Liberty. I'm not going to hurt you, I need you to trust me."

Most of them were still crying, but a few of the older ones took the time to get a good look at Clay. One of the boys recognized him. Frightened, but willing to trust him, the boy nodded. "Yeah, I've seen him there before." The boy's announcement spread a temporary relief among the group that was quickly chased away as Geoff exchanged fire with the hostiles outside the barn.

"Listen," Clay said, directing his words to the older boy who had recognized him, "I want you guys to go out that back door and straight away from the barn until you find somewhere to hide."

The boy nodded and led the group out the back door. Clay stayed inside the barn until the last child cleared the door before moving up to the front of the barn. He swapped magazines to a standard-velocity cartridge, and pocketed the magazine with the subsonic ammo.

"Here goes nothing," he said to himself as he leaned out from the doorway to take aim.

There were men in two of the second-floor windows, a man at the rear of the house, and a fourth hiding behind an old SUV just in front of the porch. From Clay's vantage, the man at the rear of the house was his clearest target.

Steadying the rifle on the barn's doorframe, Clay looked through his 4X scope and took aim. The shooter's focus was squarely on Geoff, leaving him oblivious to the danger about to blindside him. Clay fired. The quiet pop of the final-chambered subsonic bullet was no match for the other gunfire and went virtually unnoticed.

After dispatching the gunman at the back of the house, Clay exited the barn through the rear. Taking a wide path, he made his way around the house and looped around to the front, positioning himself behind the man using the SUV as cover. The attacker popped up over the hood of the rusted vehicle to take a few shots at Geoff before concealing himself from Geoff's return-fire. When the man stood up again, Clay took the shot. The bullet's initial blast was as quiet as the subsonic loads, but the loud crack of the sound barrier being broken alerted the shooters inside the house that Geoff had backup.

The two men inside shouted at each other as they tried to find a way out of their predicament. While they had the tactical advantage of owning the high ground, they were also at a major disadvantage of being contained inside the house.

The standoff lasted the better part of a half hour before both men suddenly stormed out the front door. They had their guns raised, one aiming in Geoff's direction, the other in Clay's. The men had foolishly put themselves right in the middle of a crossfire.

Neither stood a chance.

After waiting a few minutes, Clay and Geoff cautiously regrouped in front of the porch.

"Thank God for Plan Bs," Geoff said as he approached Clay.

"No kidding," Clay replied as he wiped sweat from his face. "I sent the kids back behind the barn. Do you want to go track them down while I check inside?"

"You sure you don't need help?" Geoff asked as he looked at the open front door.

Clay glanced over at the house before looking back at Geoff. "If anyone was still in there, I think they'd be shooting by now."

"That's a fair assessment," Geoff replied. "All right, I'll go catch up with the kids. Meet you back that way in a few minutes?"

Clay nodded before turning toward the porch.

The steps groaned in protest as Clay carefully walked onto the porch and into the house. Though he was confident nobody was left inside, he still exercised due diligence. His lack of focus in the past couple of months had nearly killed him on multiple occasions; sloppy tactics and poor discipline was unacceptable. He cleared each room on the first floor as if someone waited to ambush him inside. Thankfully, it was empty.

As he made his way to the second floor, he expected to find more of the same; nothing. But as he reached the top of the stairs, a loud thud from down the hall shattered his assumption. Clay let his rifle hang from his sling and reached for his Glock. The old, picturesque farmhouse had a long, narrow hallway leading to the bedrooms. Though the AR-15 was an SBR—the barrel just ten and a half inches— the added length of the suppressor brought the length closer to eighteen, which was not all that great in such tight spaces.

Keeping his 9MM close to his chest, Clay inched his way down the hallway, listening for the sound again. It was quiet. He started in the bedroom at the end of the hall at the back of the house. There was a dead body clutching to an old hunting rifle—a result of Geoff's solid aim. The amount of blood soaking into the carpet was a strong indicator that the man had died immediately and wasn't the source of the sound.

Directly across the hall was another bedroom. Clay stepped across the hallway and entered the room; quiet noises came from inside the closet. Stepping back and raising his pistol, Clay spoke sternly. "Come out now! Slowly," he ordered.

The sliding closet door shimmied open a few inches before long, slender fingers wrapped around the edge of the door, sliding it the rest of the way. A young woman stepped out; she was fifteen, maybe sixteen. Her eyes were blood shot and her cheeks streaked with tears. She wore an oversized shirt, but no pants. She twisted her body so that her shoulder was toward Clay, a passive attempt to shield herself from the armed man in front of her. Her stare was hollow, her expression haunted.

Clay slowly put his hand up and eased his pistol back into its holster. He didn't recognize her. "I'm not going to hurt you," he spoke with a soft voice. "Were you...Did you come with the others out in the barn?"

The girl's blank stare was unfazed by the question, but after a moment she gave a subtle nod.

Clay picked up a blanket off the floor and walked over to her. She flinched as he swung it around her shoulders. "It's okay," he said. "You're safe now."

The girl looked up at him, revealing a spark of life in her eyes for the first time since she stumbled out of the closet. She didn't say anything, but Clay understood the question she wanted to ask.

"They're all dead," he said with an almost satisfied tone in his voice.

The girl looked out the bedroom door and saw the corpse in the room across the hall. Her expression remained unchanged. With her eyes still fixed on the corpse in the next room, she said, "Please take me home." Her voice was all but gone.

Chapter 18

It had been two days since the attack, and there were far more questions than answers—at least for Clay. Shelton had been in and out of meetings since Clay and Geoff had returned with the kids, and there still was still no official word of what had happened and what Liberty's response—if any—would be.

The entire town was on edge, including the visitors. No one knew if the attack was isolated or if they should expect more bloodshed. And getting Shelton to comment on the matter had proven quite difficult. Earlier in the morning, a group of people showed up outside the town hall demanding answers. Shelton told them that the town officials were still putting the pieces together, and that the security teams had been doubled and were more than prepared to repel future attacks. His words brought relief to some but did little to bring comfort to the distraught parents whose children were still missing. They insisted the town leadership come up with a plan to bring their kids home. Shelton graciously took their misdirected anger and finger-pointing, willingly allowing himself to be their punching bag.

The jubilant little settlement that always seemed to be bustling with excitement was now eerily quiet. Despair filled the air like a thick smog, suffocating those who lived within. It was a disturbing sensation that was magnified with the wails of mourning families as they laid loved ones to rest. As Clay looked down at the small grave he had just finished digging—the final resting place for a seven-year-old boy—the war inside his head raged on. It was sorrow pitted against fury, and which was winning changed by the minute.

Clay saw a young man and his wife walking toward him. The woman sobbed inconsolably as she embraced a frightened toddler. Her husband struggled to find the will to keep walking forward as he carried the small body in his arms. The stained, white sheet draped over his son flapped in the breeze, which grated at Clay's nerves. Walking next to them, Pastor Rosario prepared for his fourteenth funeral of the day, with still more to come. The sight filled Clay with both grief and gratitude. Grief for those having to say goodbye to their loved ones, a pain Clay knew all too well. Gratitude for the fact that none of *his* loved ones were among those going into the ground this chilly evening.

Hearing footsteps approach from behind, Clay turned and spotted Megan walking up to him. She didn't say anything; she just put her arm around her brother and rested her head on his shoulder. Watching as the family approached, Megan's stomach twisted like a pretzel as she recalled what that long, dreaded walk to a small grave felt like. She said a silent prayer for them and their departed child. There were few feelings worse than what this family was going through.

Megan let go of Clay and stepped back, swiping at her eyes before the tears had a chance to slide down her cheeks. "Uhm," she said in a gravely, exhausted voice, "he's starting to wake up, if you want to come say hi."

Clay looked down at the grave before looking back at Megan, "Yeah, okay," he said. "I still have to finish up here first, but I'll come after that."

Megan mustered up a supportive smile and put her hand on Clay's shoulder. "You want me to stay?"

Clay wrestled with his response. He wanted her to stay, but there was no reason she needed to subject herself to the emotional toil of witnessing a mother and father burying their little boy. That was not a burden Clay was willing to hoist onto Megan's shoulders. He looked at his sister and replied, "No, that's okay. I'll meet you over at the infirmary in a few minutes."

Megan nodded. "Okay," she said before stepping closer to her little brother, answering the call to his unspoken request. She stood up tall and brushed away another tear. Standing shoulder to shoulder, Clay and Megan silently watched on as the memorial commenced.

As with every other burial Clay had attended that day, he found himself fighting back tears as Pastor Rosario read the same passages from the Bible that he had probably long since memorized. However, unlike the others, Clay knew the boy being buried. He and Tyler had become friends over the past week, which made this service even more difficult to witness.

When Clay and the boy's father lowered the body into the grave, the woman started screaming. She dropped to her knees and clutched on to her only living son as if he were life itself. Pastor Rosario's attempts to comfort her went unnoticed by the lamenting mother. As Clay and the boy's father stood up, Rosario immediately went into prayer to end the service.

Afterwards, Rosario escorted the family back to their home, and Clay got to work carefully covering the body with soil. Megan picked up a nearby shovel and helped him finish the unbearable task. He welcomed the help.

The walk to the infirmary was cold and breezy. The sweat from the day's work might have chilled him to the bone had his mind not been so utterly consumed with other matters. It was as if his brain couldn't process everything that was going on, so it stopped registering physical needs like hunger and shivering.

Clay knew Megan was speaking, but he didn't hear a word she said—she might as well have been speaking Swahili. He tried to force himself to pay attention, but quickly gave up on the matter. His thoughts were galaxies away, obsessing on what he was going to tell Vlad...how he was going to tell his friend that his daughter was still missing.

Megan was still talking as they reached the door to the infirmary. She stepped in front of Clay and swung around. "Clay, are you hearing me?" she said, knowing full well that he wasn't.

"Huh?" Clay said with a confused look on his face. He blinked his eyes a few times and cleared his throat. "Uh, yeah, I'm listening."

"Clay," she said with a grim face, "it's a miracle that we were even able to save him, but you should know that he's never going to walk again."

"Uhm...Wow, okay..." Clay said, still a bit consumed with his own thoughts. "Does Vlad know yet?"

Megan shrugged. "If Doctor Sowell hasn't already told him, then I'm sure he's figured it out for himself," she said, almost heartlessly. She made a face and sighed. "Sorry, Clay, I didn't mean to—"

"It's okay, Megs," he said with a weak smile. Clay wasn't mad at her for being a bit insensitive about Vlad's injuries. Being a doctor in a well-equipped, sterile hospital was a brutal job that required a thick skin. Being a "doctor" in the apocalypse where a minor injury could lead to death faster than Clay ever thought possible had to be monumentally worse. It was only human for her to find ways to disconnect herself from her obliged occupation. What was amazing, though, was that Megan's cold response, in fact, *wasn't* normal for her. How she could care so much, even after losing so many loved ones, and continue pushing forward was nothing short of remarkable.

Megan, knowing what Clay was about to do, gave him another hug. "Good luck."

"Thanks."

Clay hesitated for a moment before he pulled the door open and walked inside. The room was still packed with wounded people, though not as bad as the night of the attack. Most of the room was open, rows of beds lined up against the wall with about a foot and a half of space between each one. Toward the back of the room, several sheets had been hung from the ceiling to create some privacy for the more critical patients.

Standing near the back, Clay heard Doctor Sowell talking to Vlad on the other side of the curtain, so he waited outside for the doctor to finish up.

"Olesya?" Vlad whispered.

Vlad's first words after waking up were the same as the last ones he uttered before passing out, and it sent a nauseating concoction of emotions through Clay.

"I'm sorry, Vlad, but I've not left this building much in the past two days. I'm not up to speed on everything going on," Doctor Sowell replied sympathetically.

A single cough from behind the adjacent curtain distracted Clay from the depressing conversation currently in progress at Vlad's bedside. He leaned around the edge of the sheet to see the girl he had found in the closet at the farmhouse sitting up in her bed, a look of hopelessness in her eyes. He wanted to say something to her, maybe ask her how she was doing. Before the words reached his lips, Vlad's curtain was tossed to the side and Doctor Sowell came out, nodding at Clay as he walked into the girl's room.

"How are we feeling, Madeline?" the fatigued doctor asked, trying to sound as upbeat as he could.

Clay remained outside as he struggled to figure out the best way to tell Vlad the news—as if there was an easy way to tell a father that he might never see his daughter again.

"This sucks," Clay said quietly through a deep sigh before pulling the sheet back and stepping inside. Vlad lied on a rickety old bed that was more akin to a cot found inside an Army barracks rather than a hospital, but it beat sleeping on the floor. Barely.

Vlad looked over at his visitor, and after a severe coughing fit, he finally gathered enough energy to speak. "It is good to see you again, my friend."

Clay forced a smile. "Good to see you, Vlad."

There was a painful silence in the room as Vlad fought to keep his eyes open. Despite his heavy eyelids, the man managed to give a look that pleaded with Clay to tell him some good news. The piercing gaze forced Clay's vision down, and he stared at his feet while he struggled to find the right words.

"Clay," Vlad spoke, his hoarse voice fading with exhaustion, "just tell me."

Clay's vision remained fixed on his boots. The dreaded moment had arrived and there was no fleeing from it now. He finally looked up, his glossy eyes gave Vlad the answer before his voice could. "I'm sorry, Vlad, but...I...we," Clay cleared his throat, "we haven't found her yet."

Vlad pressed into his pillow and began to weep as much as his shattered body would allow. The pain he was in—both physical and emotional—was a dreadful sight for Clay. Before long, the weeping turned to howling sobs loud enough that everyone in the infirmary grieved with the poor soul.

Clay knelt next to the bed and grabbed Vlad's hand. His eyes seemed to scream for deliverance from his hell on earth—as if he preferred Megan left him to die in the field she found him in.

After a few minutes, the cries waned, and Vlad lay lifelessly in bed. His eyes glazed over as he looked up at the ceiling. He began to speak in his native tongue, repeating the same couple of sentences over and over. Clay didn't need translation to know he was begging God for just one more day with his beloved daughter, one more minute to relish in her presence.

The curtain behind him swung open, causing Clay to jump. Jackie walked in with a pill and a glass of water. "Here you go," the middle-aged nurse said as she handed the cup to Vlad. "Take this."

Vlad remained motionless.

"Doctor Sowell asked me to give you this," she said. Seeing no reaction from the man, she lowered her voice, "Please...it's going to help."

Vlad slowly turned his head to look at what she offered. Reluctantly, he took the pill and tossed it in his mouth; he didn't bother with the water. He returned to his staring contest with the ceiling and a short time later, as both the physical and emotional pain started to numb, Vlad drifted to sleep.

Clay stood to his feet and looked down at his friend peacefully resting—or so he hoped. He wasn't sure how much time had passed since he walked into the room, but it felt like days. Though he had a heavy heart for Vlad's loss, Clay also felt a weight lifted from his shoulders since the dreadful task of telling his friend Olesya was still missing. "Hang in there, Boris," Clay said as he turned to leave.

On his way out, Jackie glanced over at Clay. "He's out."

"Good," she said with a compassionate voice.

"What was that?" Clay asked.

"Vicodin."

"Really?" Clay asked, stunned with the response.

"Yes. We only have seven of them left—well, six now—for the whole town. It's not something we give out lightly, but Doctor Sowell was, in this case, quite insistent."

"Thank you..."

Jackie smiled before returning to her patient.

Feeling utterly exhausted, Clay stepped outside to see darkness had fallen over the town of Liberty. It was oddly comforting to the weary young man.

Chapter 19

The day of interrogation culminated with Shelton's fist through his living room wall. For the last six hours, he and two others from the security team questioned Brendan—the man in the mask. After an hour of silence, Barnes wanted to move on from questioning to more persuasive means of interrogation. Shelton was quick to shoot the idea down. "That is *not* how we do things," Shelton said before kicking Barnes out of the room, leaving him and Kohler to get the man to talk. But as Shelton stared at the damaged drywall next to a picture of his wife Sarah, he found himself a little more open to Barnes's line of thinking.

The throbbing in his knuckles was intense. It was not often that Barry Shelton let emotions get the best of him—especially anger—but after what happened to his beloved town, he noticed his fuse was not nearly as long as it used to be.

He walked into the kitchen and opened the cabinet above his refrigerator, retrieving a half-full bottle of scotch. Shelton rarely drank alcohol—and when he did it was always in private. The bottle of Chivas Regal only came out under extreme duress. The last time he reached for it was five years ago, immediately following Sarah's burial. The time before that was when he and Sarah had laid Anna, their only child, to rest. The liquor, as far as he could remember, had always been used for somber occasions. But as Shelton tipped the bottle and filled the small glass on his counter, he hoped that the drink would quell his rage.

It did not.

Slouching in his brown Chesterfield chair, the wheels continued to turn in Shelton's head. Why did Brendan say he had a message to deliver, then suddenly become a mute after capture? That perplexing turn of events didn't sit well with Shelton. Something wasn't adding up—and that thought paralyzed him with fear.

An exasperated sigh passed through Shelton's lips as he remained slumped in his chair, his hand cradling the nearly empty glass. Despite being ineffective against his indignation, the alcohol *had* helped with the tension. His neck and shoulder muscles had felt as if they were ratchet straps tying down an oversized load on a flatbed. Thanks to the alcohol, Shelton felt somewhat physically relaxed for the first time since the attack two nights ago.

With nineteen dead, thirteen missing, uncooperative prisoners, and no idea what was coming next, Shelton was at a loss as to what he should do next.

A loud thumping on the front door ejected the jumpy mayor from his thoughts. Setting the glass of scotch down on a coaster as Sarah had taught him in their first year of marriage, Shelton stood from his chair despite his popping knees and walked to the door. Kohler was on the other side of the door, the chill in the air evident from his visible breath.

"What is it, Daniel? Did you get the little brat to talk?" he asked.

"No," Kohler replied immediately, "but...his father is here to post bail."

Shelton felt as if he'd just been kicked in the stomach by an angry mule.

Arlo.

It was time to get some answers.

****

"Have a seat," Barnes said as he pushed Arlo into the chair sitting across Shelton's desk.

Arlo let out a derisive laugh. "Now, now, Timothy, there's no need for such aggressive behavior. After all, I am unarmed and of no threat to you."

"No threat to me, huh?" Barnes scoffed.

Arlo had a wry smile plastered across his face as he fixed his disheveled hair. "I am merely here to negotiate the release of my men."

Barnes rested his hands on his hips and stroked his holster as he stared down the man in the chair. He looked around the room before looking back at Arlo. "Well, in case you were wonderin', this ain't America no more. That whole 'innocent until proven guilty' malarkey don't fly—even for a big shot *has-been* like you."

"I see," Arlo responded softly as he sat back in the chair. "Timothy, I do apologize, it seems we have gotten off on the wrong foot after all these years..." he said with a malicious grin before adding, "So, tell me, what's new with you? How is Chloe these days?"

Arlo had gotten the reaction he wanted when Barnes furrowed his brows and clenched his jaw. Barnes pushed Arlo, causing him—along with the chair—to tip backwards and crash to the ground. He jumped on top of the former prosecutor and wrapped his hand around Arlo's neck. Barnes panted with rage while Arlo seemed almost apathetic to the assault.

Barnes tightened his grip, cutting off Arlo's air. "If you so much as speak her name again, I swear to God I will put a bullet right through that big head of yours, drag your corpse over to the jail so that daddy's lifeless body is the last thing your son sees before I slit his throat," Barnes said through a menacing whisper before finally releasing his grip on Arlo's throat.

After a few small gasps, Arlo responded, "Oh, Timothy, it would seem I've struck a nerve with you. I apologize again. Did something happen to your dear wife?"

Barnes's eyes flashed hot white with rage. "See you in hell, Arlo," he said as he stood up and reached for his gun. Just as he removed the pistol from his holster and pointed it down at Arlo's head, Shelton and two others stormed through the door.

"Tim, put that gun down right now!" Shelton ordered.

Barnes kept his sights between Arlo's eyes and put his finger on the trigger.

"Why?" Barnes asked with a frail voice, an about-face from seconds earlier. "Why?" The gun was heavy in his hands, as if he held a dumbbell.

"Tim...please," Shelton pleaded. "You are a better man than him."

After several tense seconds passed, Barnes slid the gun back into his holster and walked out of the room. The other two men followed and closed the door behind them.

Arlo nonchalantly got up off the floor, corrected his chair and returned to his seat. He removed a handkerchief from his jacket pocket and dabbed at the spit Barnes had sprayed during the attack. He looked up at Shelton, who leaned on the edge of his desk. "Thank you, Barry, for putting the hound on the leash. I much prefer dealing with sophistication inste—"

Shelton interrupted Arlo with a vicious right hook to the jaw, catching the man completely off guard. The audacity of the violent gesture, not the pain, was what surprised him the most. Arlo shifted his jaw side to side as he said, "Well, I do believe that was quite unnecessary, *Mr. Mayor*."

"Oh, I beg to differ," Shelton shot back, his fist still tightened. "In fact, it was *real* necessary." He tried to relax his knuckles, but the pain was excruciating. If he didn't already break a knuckle or two on the wall earlier, Arlo's face certainly had.

Shelton walked around to his desk and sat down. Hundreds of questions plagued him and he wanted answers. "Why did you attack us?" Shelton asked, getting straight to the point.

"Barry, it's been, what, eight... nine years since we last saw each other? Nine years since you threw me and my boy to the wolves...*exiling* us from this little 'utopia' of yours," Arlo said with disdain.

In all the years Shelton had known Arlo, he never once remembered the man being offended or hurt by anyone. In fact, he had been dubbed 'The Thing' by many of his professional acquaintances—both attorney and criminal alike—for his ice-cold demeanor and ferocity in the courtroom. Nothing seemed to get under his skin. But Shelton knew, as Arlo sat there in front of him nearly a decade later, he *had* gotten to him. He had shaken the unshakeable and despite everything they had been through over the past few days, the realization filled Shelton with remorse.

"I'll admit," Arlo continued, "it was touch and go there for a little while. Being out there was far worse than either of us ever imagined." He paused for a moment as he dabbed at the cut on his lip with the handkerchief. His eyes narrowed on Shelton as the memories snapped to the front of his mind. "It was so, *so* much worse."

Shelton's mind was suddenly plagued with images of the victims of Arlo's attack, causing him to shrug off the guilt trip Arlo had been attempting to generate. Under different circumstances, he might have offered a heart-felt apology for the tough choice that he and the rest of the council made ten years ago, but the chance of an apology had washed away with the blood of the town. "We did what we had to do, Arlo."

"Ah, yes. The mighty and noble Barry Shelton...*Mayor* of Liberty Township. The last bastion of hope for humanity," Arlo said mockingly. "Do tell me, Barry, is it noble to sentence a nine-year-old to death for the sins of his father?"

"I did no such thing, Arlo. I gave you every opportunity to leave the boy here; we would've cared for him."

Arlo let out a scathing laugh. "So, I was supposed to just abandon my only son, then? Let some other man raise him while his father wandered off to die in the frozen hell out there?"

"Yes," Shelton responded immediately. "If you loved him, that's *exactly* what you should have done. Instead, you dragged him into hell right alongside you."

Arlo shot him a glare. His jaw tightened and he took a deep breath through his nose. Shelton got under his skin again. "You have *no* idea what it's like to have to make that choice, Barry," he said through gritted teeth. His pursed lips softened, briefly flashing a menacing grin before he continued, "But, I must say, it wasn't *all* bad. Being out there, I mean." He gestured out the window toward the fence. "I always thought of myself as a strong man—a leader—but being cast out into that world with just a hunting rifle and a week's worth of food will quickly humble a man."

Shelton suppressed a laugh at the thought of Arlo being humbled by anything.

"And over the years," Arlo continued, "I was refined by fire and became every bit of the leader I always thought myself to be. And it's why I, my son, and countless others are alive to tell that tale today. I realized that a good leader must act, not speak."

"And a good leader must think before he acts," Shelton interjected.

"Oh, I always think before I act," Arlo responded immediately, his eyes piercing like two daggers into Shelton's soul. "You and I are two very different people, Barry. You follow a sort of 'code' that dictates every decision you make, but I...well, I am far less rigid. Every day is different and some days our choices are easy. Other days, however, they are life and death." Arlo leaned back into the chair and relaxed his body. "I already know that you are willing to die for the people of this town, Barry, but the real question is, are you willing to kill—or even *murder*—for them?"

"You're right, Arlo," Barry said, nodding along. "We *are* two very different people."

Arlo laughed. "Yes, that's right, old friend, we are. You know, Barry, you and I complement each other quite well. It's a shame we couldn't have given things more time to balance out. This town could have been great."

"It *is* great," Shelton shot back.

"We'll see," Arlo replied with a twisted grin.

Arlo's response sent chills down Shelton's spine. One thing he knew well about Arlo Paxton was how to read between the lines. Shelton attempted to mask his concern by shifting in his seat and placing his hands down on the desk, interlocking his fingers. He sat up straight and asked, "So, give me a reason why I shouldn't throw you into a cell next to your boy and put you both on trial for terrorism?"

"Oh, come on, Barry, you ought to know me better than that. Did you really think I would just walk into the lion's den without some leverage?"

Shelton immediately knew he was talking about the missing children. "A prisoner exchange?"

Arlo smiled. "I do believe that would be the wise move on both of our parts, yes."

Shelton slowly slouched back into the chair. He couldn't risk playing hardball with Arlo, using innocent children as pawns. The man was a sociopath—a Screamer with a more sophisticated wardrobe—and couldn't be reasoned with. Shelton had no other choice.

After a long, deflating sigh, Shelton looked at Arlo. "When and where?"

"St. Clair Park, tomorrow at noon. You may bring no more than six men and we will do the same. You have my word."

After a moment of silence between the two, Shelton replied, "Noon it is."

Chapter 20

Shelton led the pack on his horse. About twenty yards behind him Stevens and Horton guided the wagon full of prisoners. Clay, along with Adams and Blair, brought up the rear.

They were a few miles from St. Clair Park, an area Clay knew fairly well. In fact, with a halfway decent pair of binoculars, he could see it from his old room in the tower. There was never much reason to visit when Clay and Megan resided in the office building, but on occasion, he found himself stopping there to take a rest during his trips to Liberty. There were several smaller buildings with few points of entry that Clay would shelter in when such a need would arise. It had been years since he last visited, but he imagined it looked the same as it did back then. As with most places in the world, it quickly reached a deep level of decay and then became frozen in time.

Clay clicked his tongue and squeezed his legs around the horse, causing her to quicken her trot. When he caught up with the wagon, Clay saw Brendan out of the corner of his eye, a smirk on his face that Clay was more than eager to wipe off. It was as if he knew what was coming next. He probably did, Clay surmised, which added to the angst.

Clay's horse overtook the wagon and crept up on Shelton. Shelton turned around to see Clay approaching.

"How you holding up?" Clay asked.

After a lengthy sigh, Shelton spoke. "I've been better, but I'm hanging in there the best I can," Shelton said with a weak voice as he kept his eyes forward. "Thanks again for coming along."

"No problem."

"Folks are still pretty shaken up from the attack. Some people are afraid to leave their homes, but others are out for blood," he said, Barnes coming to mind. "We're already so shorthanded on security detail back home and the last thing we need is someone flying off their hinges during this exchange. So, you being here is very appreciated."

Clay nodded. "Like I said, not a problem, Barry."

Shelton felt comforted with Clay's response. Clay had become a good friend—a loyal friend—over the years. After what he and his family had been through the past few days, tagging along for a risky prisoner swap was a slightly bigger favor to ask than borrowing a cup of sugar. Shelton's face went grim as he spoke, "For several years, I feared this day would come," he spoke quietly, as if to make sure he wasn't heard by those behind him. "I even sent people out to look for them."

"I'm sorry?" Clay replied.

Shelton realized his out-loud thinking would be confusing to anyone who didn't know the story.

"So you know these people?" Clay asked.

After a moment, Shelton nodded. "I do," he said. "Well, Arlo and Brendan, anyway."

Clay glanced over his shoulder at the wagon, the sneer still on Brendan's face. "What happened?" Clay asked as he returned his focus to the path ahead.

"Arlo and Brendan used to live in Liberty, even back before the eruptions," Shelton replied.

"I'm going to go out on a limb here and say their departure from town was not of their own volition," Clay said.

"That's a pretty accurate assessment," Shelton said before briefly getting lost in his thoughts, replaying history in fast forward to come up with an appropriate summary of the past. "It was about three months after Yellowstone. Things weren't totally upside down just yet, but everyone knew those days were ahead. Food and supplies were already slowing, and first responders sometimes took up to twelve hours to arrive, if they came at all."

Clay nodded along. "I still remember those days. Even though I didn't believe it, I was hopeful that things would eventually return to normal," Clay said, followed by a dry laugh.

"Some folks back in town held out hope, too, but those of us on the town's security council had to plan for the worst-case scenario—we were on our own. For good."

"It's a good thing you did, because obviously, you *were* on your own," Clay responded. "But how do Arlo and Brendan play into this?"

"As I mentioned before, we formed a town security council shortly after the eruptions. We had several other men and women involved—including

Arlo. Arlo had been a district attorney in the next county over. The man was a brilliant attorney but as shrewd as they came. Our paths didn't cross much before the collapse—I probably knew more about him from newspapers and internet headlines than personal conversations—but once things started to go south, we all knew he would be a valuable member to our community," Shelton said.

"How so?" Clay responded.

"He made significant contributions to our town's defensive measures. He had an insight into criminal behavior that most of us couldn't comprehend and that intuition saved the people of Liberty a lot of grief on more than a few occasions.

"Arlo was a rising star and had made many friends with local police and government officials over the years. Those connections gave us access to some critical resources, while there were some left, anyway."

"Wow," Clay said, annoyed with the hint of admiration in his voice.

"I can't say that I really ever cared for Arlo all that much as a person, but his contributions to the foundation of our town's self-reliant state were invaluable. To be perfectly honest, if it weren't for him, we might not have made it through that first winter."

Clay's natural response was to have respect for the man who played such a crucial role in Liberty's establishment, but after personally digging a half-dozen graves the other day, Clay still visualized a bloody death for the man. "So, what happened?" Clay asked.

"It was greed!" Shelton said, his words wrought with anger. His body stiffened and his hands shook. There was a twitch in his cheek as he clenched his jaw. He took a deep breath before continuing. "That first winter had been rough. Food and supplies were already stretched thin and we had no choice but to get creative on how to make the remaining supplies go even further. We had established a community food bank, which we heavily regulated—only so much food per person per week. And, if you were able-bodied, you were expected to work for those rations."

"That seems fair," Clay said. "I assume Arlo disagreed?"

"No, he was fine with it, but what he *wasn't* okay with was people keeping their own food and supplies from before the eruptions. He didn't agree that the citizens should have undistributed food caches in their home. So, he proposed we go door to door and confiscate all food and medical supplies that had not been issued by the town." Shelton took another deep breath to try and calm himself. He had had maybe twelve hours of restless sleep since the attacks and many more still to come. Finally, he continued, "What's worse, Clay, is that most of the people that already had food stored in their house *rarely* took food from the community pool. Only some perishables, like milk and eggs. And they often donated some of their own stock to the community as supplies dipped. It was more than reasonable that they hang on to what was theirs from before."

"So, the people who had the good sense to prepare ahead of time were told to *donate* their food...or else?"

"Pretty much, although Arlo felt it was only fair to take a quarter of the confiscated items and distribute it amongst the newly formed town government—of which he was part of."

AJ POWERS

The true motives were revealed. It wasn't about the greater good of the town; it was an opportunity to proliferate his own personal fortune. Once the ash fell, a man's true character surfaced.

"I assume that idea didn't fly with the rest of you?" Clay said.

"It didn't, but just barely. The vote shouldn't have even been close, yet it was seven to six. I had a good mind to smack each one of the 'yes' votes upside the head. When I vented about it to Sarah, she reminded me that everyone is just scared and that it's easier to rationalize questionable decision under such pressure. I still detested their votes, but her words helped me to see things from their view.

"Fortunately, the idea quickly faded away for everyone who voted in favor of the motion. Except for one person."

The pieces started to fit together now.

"Almost immediately following the vote, Arlo started swindling people out of their personal reserves. He told them that if they didn't cooperate, he would personally see to it they never got food from the community pool."

"That's sick!" Clay commented.

"It was. But what were the people to do? Everyone in town was already terrified about the unknown and having their names scratched off the supply list was threatening enough to get most people to cave."

"How long did he get away with it?"

"It went on for about six months. He walked around from house to house in the middle of the night, demanding payment like he was part of the mafia or something. But once we found out about his little racket, he was kicked off the council and warned of the *steep* consequences that would occur if he continued harassing people.

"About a week later, Jasper, the man who first came to us about Arlo's scheme, was found beaten half to death in a field just outside town. That was strike three for Arlo."

"Good Lord," Clay gasped. Ever since finding Liberty years ago, he just assumed that the town's bright, optimistic manner had always been, as if they jumped into the apocalypse head first, ready to be a beacon of hope in the world. But, as is all too familiar to Clay, most stories of hope are peppered with darkness. "Were you sure it was him before you kicked them out?"

Shelton sighed again. "Not entirely, no. And I'll be the first to admit that we *should* have been certain before coming to such a serious conclusion. However, we were vindicated when Jasper finally regained consciousness and confirmed our suspicions."

Clay shook his head. "I had no idea," he said, stunned from it all.

Shelton pressed his lips together and nodded. It was obvious that, regardless of the justification behind the decision, banishing the man and his son from the community still gnawed at the mayor's conscience. Sending a man out into the wild was not far off from signing his death warrant.

"For years, I expected him to retaliate, but after five years had gone by, I figured if they hadn't already died, that they were settled in well enough elsewhere to just let sleeping dogs lie." Shelton released his grasp on the reins and cleaned his glasses with the cuff of his shirt. "Guess I was wrong."

Shelton battled a myriad of emotions and with the group closing in on the park, Clay stopped prodding so they could be prepared for the exchange.

The roads became more chaotic as they got closer to the park, making it difficult for the convoy to traverse. While the others helped maneuver the wagon around obstacles, or push decaying car husks off to the side of the road, Clay kept his eyes peeled in every direction. Distractions, such as clearing a path on a road, made for an opportunistic ambush. With one hand on the reins and the other firmly attached to his LaRue, Clay covered the group as they plowed through the last mile.

The park was in even worse shape than Clay expected. Nature had once again reclaimed what it felt entitled to. As the group closed in on the meeting location, they saw a body hanging from a tree. The ominous sight of rotting flesh and exposed bone suggested it had been there for weeks, if not months. The body hung like a puppet, swaying ever so slightly in the gentle breeze that was persuading the last of the leaves to let go of the branches. The corpse was an appropriate decoration for the mood in the air.

Shelton held up his hand and the party came to a stop. Both Clay and Shelton climbed off their horses and walked about thirty yards over to a pavilion next to a kid's water playground. Shortly after reaching the decaying structure, Arlo and another man rounded the corner of the park's rec center. Good to his word, it was just Arlo and one other man approaching. As the men advanced, Clay felt a familiar spike of adrenaline and anxiety. It was a feeling he never got used to; he hated the tightness in his chest that came with it, but the heightened senses kept his focus razor sharp.

Clay heard a waver in his breath that was in sync with the thump in his chest. He looked over at Shelton for some words of encouragement, but felt like he was looking into a magic mirror that projected the future—Shelton was as apprehensive as he was.

"Barry, so glad you could make it," Arlo said as he stepped onto the poured concrete platform. "I do hope your travels were smooth."

"Where are they?" Shelton asked gruffly, brushing past Arlo's greeting.

"Come on, Barry, there's no reason why we can't keep this civil," Arlo replied. The look on Shelton's face suggested otherwise. "But, I suppose in the interest of time we can get right down to business." Arlo looked past Clay and Shelton to the wagon of prisoners. "I assume my boys are all in good health, yes?"

"They're still breathing," Shelton replied, trying to sound as cold-hearted as his counterpart standing in front of him. Sounding scared and defeated would only add to Arlo's already over-inflated confidence.

"Hmm. Well, I suppose an exchange is in order then." Arlo looked over at the man he was with and nodded.

The man took one of his hands off his CZ Scorpion and made a hand signal back toward the rec center. Shortly after, several armed men rounded the corner with a little less than a dozen kids and a few older prisoners. Shelton turned around and whistled, prompting Stevens and Horton to jump off the wagon.

"So, how did you get your hands on that?" Shelton asked, nodding toward the armed man's short-barreled carbine.

Arlo smiled. "There are benefits to being me," he replied with a leer.

The sound of whimpering and soft cries was the first indication that the kids were near. They walked in a line, tied together at their wrists. Clay looked at each face as they passed.

"Son!" Arlo said, his face lighting up with a genuine smile as Stevens and Horton escorted their prisoners to the exchange point.

Brendan walked up and gave Arlo a hug. "Good to see you, Dad."

Arlo put his hand on Brendan's shoulder and gave him a squeeze. "I trust that our old friend, Mayor Shelton, treated you well?"

Brendan made a sour face. "Not exactly a five-star hotel," he said as he glared at Shelton, "but I suppose it could have been worse."

Just then, Clay caught a glimpse of her face—Olesya. Both Clay and Shelton immediately noticed the bruising and swelling around her eye.

Arlo turned to see what they were staring at. "Ahh, yes," he said, "that one is a bit feisty. She nearly killed one of my men with a broken bottle." He turned back to look Shelton in the eye. "Not very lady-like of her, huh?"

Shelton was seething, but refused to let his anger take control—at least not while Arlo could still harm the kids. After fighting the urge to give Arlo an up close and personal introduction with the business end of his Browning Hi Power, Shelton was finally able to calm himself enough to speak. "Arlo, if you so much as touch a hair on another person in my town..."

Arlo was unconcerned with Shelton's vague threat. He looked at the last of the children walking by then back at Shelton. "Whether any more of your people get hurt or not is not up to me—it's entirely up to you."

"What's that supposed to mean?" Shelton replied.

"Ten years ago, you gave me an impossible choice to make. Now, my dear friend, I am returning the favor."

Brendan revealed that sinister grin that caused Clay to cringe.

"You and your people have seven days to vacate the town," Arlo said.

Shelton felt as if he had just been punched in the gut by a gorilla. The rage boiling in his blood had gone stone cold with Arlo's words. His demeanor transformed from an angry, protective father to that of a little boy being bullied on the playground. "Why are you doing this?" he asked, his words disrupted by a tremble. "Is this how you're getting back at us?"

Arlo scoffed. "Do you *really* think I am that petty, Barry? I assure you, the history between us is just that—history. This is not personal; it's just business."

"Just business?" Shelton responded. "How is this 'just business?'"

"It took me a while to find my footing out here, but once I did, things have been going quite well. As you can see," Arlo gestured toward the men standing guard behind him, "And, as luck would have it, a few months ago I ran into an old friend who, like me, had taken a sizeable group under his wing. We decided it would be in our best interests to combine arms—to work together and build something great!" Arlo's lips slowly bent into a belligerent smile. "Unfortunately, for your precious town anyway, we've outgrown our current accommodations and need a more suitable location. It just so happens that Liberty is the perfect fit. Like I said, just business."

Shelton's silence was music to Arlo's ears. "And if we don't leave?" Shelton asked, almost timidly.

Arlo took a comb out of his pocket and ran it through his greasy, black hair. The grin on his face faded and his malevolent eyes narrowed. "Well," he said as he leaned in toward Shelton's ear, "I do believe that's a bridge you don't want to cross."

Chapter 21

Bed...It was only twenty feet away, yet might as well have been in El Paso. Since returning late last night with Shelton and the kids, Clay had been unable to find more than five consecutive minutes to sleep. After observing the tearful reunion between Vlad and Olesya, Clay was pulled into meeting after meeting with Shelton and the other town leaders to discuss the situation with Arlo.

Clay hadn't been expecting a thirty-six-hour day to cap off the hellish week he had been through. Though he was grateful to be on the right side of the soil, he felt like death. Ignoring the call of the comfortable, over-sized mattress upstairs, Clay still had one last matter to address before bed and he dreaded it.

Clay checked his watch as he tapped his feet on the hardwood floor of Vlad's living room. A brew of exhaustion and frustration came out in the form of a sigh while he waited for everyone to arrive. He felt a soft, reassuring hand on his arm, gently stroking his bicep. Ordinarily, Kelsey's touch brought immediate relief to any angst-filled situation, but not tonight. In fact, her caress seemed to make him feel worse.

Geoff and Ruth came downstairs about the time Megan and Lona walked in, fresh off their shift at the infirmary, which was evident by the bags under their eyes and the stains on their clothes. A few minutes later, Blake had returned with Levi and Dusty; everyone was present.

Every eye in the room was fixed on Clay, expecting an update on what had happened—except for Kelsey, who sat on the couch, staring at the floor; she already knew what Clay was about to say and it took her every ounce of strength to keep her composure.

"So, what's going on?" Megan asked.

"Well," Clay said before pausing for a moment. He racked his brain to find the right words, but all that managed to come out was, "Liberty is preparing for war."

Clay's words hung heavy in the air like storm clouds on the horizon. A rogue sniffle from Kelsey was the only thing that broke the palpable silence.

"The men who attacked us last week...that wasn't just some random strike by a bunch of bandits. It was carried out by someone who knows this town very well..." Clay shut his eyes for a minute as the room began to spin a little. "Listen, I don't have it in me to go into all the details right now, but the man made it abundantly clear: in seven days, he and his crew will be back to take over this town," Clay said. He took a deep breath before adding, "One way or another."

Megan and Ruth both had the same response— putting their hands over their mouths as they gasped in horror—while murmurs began to fill the room from the others. Lona found herself clinging to Blake's uninjured arm, pulling herself close to him.

"So, what do we do?" Geoff asked.

"Well, that's why I called for this meeting. After a *long* night of discussions and planning with Shelton and some other people in town, it was decided that the town leaders, along with volunteers, would stay and defend Liberty."

"Hell yeah!" Dusty shouted. "Bring it on!"

"Easy, Dust," Clay said, trying to get the teenaged girl to understand the gravity of the situation. "Also," Clay followed up, "those who will not be staying behind to defend will need a place to go. Ruth, I know I really should have talked to you first, but I told the mayor that everyone was welcome to return to Northfield and stay on the farm until this all blows over."

Ruth looked at Clay with glassy eyes, "Of course, that's okay," she said, as if there was no other possible answer.

Clay was relieved with her response. It wasn't his place to volunteer her family's land to house the refugees from Liberty, but there was no other option. "It's not going to be easy and things are going to be cramped, but the folks need a place to stay, especially once winter hits."

"Winter?" Geoff asked. "How long do you think this will last?"

Clay shook his head. "I have no idea." He shrugged his shoulders before continuing, "Ideally, this man, Arlo, is bluffing and has a much weaker force than he claims. If that's the case, this will be over in a hurry."

"And if we don't live in a perfect world?" Megan asked, immediately catching the irony of her question.

Clay's eyes looked past the group of people in front of him and he found himself lost in thought. The weight of everyone expecting him to have a plan became crushing. "Weeks? Months?" he said as he once again shook his head. He blinked his eyes a few times, snapping himself out of his self-induced trance. He then met every eye in the room with his own before saying, "We hope for the best, but plan as if Arlo *isn't* lying about the strength of his force."

The room was shrouded in darkness as Clay's statement burrowed into their souls. Right then, they all knew that it was a strong possibility that within a few weeks, the beloved town of Liberty Township would cease to exist.

"I have already volunteered to stay and fight," Clay said. He saw Kelsey out of the corner of his eye trying to stifle her emotions. "The people of this town were there for me in my darkest hours; I couldn't call myself their friend if I wasn't willing to do the same for them. So..." Clay gave a quick glance around the room. "This is *absolutely* voluntary; nobody should feel ashamed if they decide to leave..."

Dusty practically scoffed at Clay. "You know I'm in," she said, a little too enthusiastically.

Megan, who was fighting off tears, nodded. "I'll stay."

Megan's words evoked a confident "Me, too," out of Levi, which came as no surprise.

Geoff looked over at Ruth—she was terrified. He took a breath to speak, but Clay looked him in the eye and shook his head. Geoff closed his mouth, furrowed his brows and grunted.

"I'll stay," a young voice said.

Clay couldn't help but respect his willingness, but there was no way he was going to allow it. "Blake, I appreciate the offer, but you need to give that arm time to heal." Clay then looked over at Lona and said, "And I need you to see to it that he follows those orders."

Relief flashed across Lona's face as she realized she would be returning home to Northfield with Blake and the others.

"Are there any questions?" Clay asked, looking around the room.

"When do we leave?" Ruth asked.

"Two days...Three, max. Mayor Shelton wants everyone out of here by then so we can have time to stage the defense. We have our two wagons and Liberty is sending all five of theirs. There won't be enough room to carry everyone on the wagons, so the wounded and children get precedence. Be ready to do some walking," Clay said glumly.

With no other questions, Clay adjourned the meeting and the room quickly emptied as they prepared for the coming departure.

Geoff walked up to Clay, "What gives, man? You know I can help out here," he said.

Clay put his hands up to try and calm his irritated friend. "Do you really think I would doubt that?" Clay asked, almost offended. "I want someone that I trust—someone I trust with my life—to keep things safe back home. Shelton is sending a few of his guys to help out, but I *need* to know my family is safe. If I can't be there to do it, then I don't want anyone else to but you. Besides, I imagine Ruth wouldn't mind having you around to help out during her morning sickness..."

The frustration in Geoff's eyes subsided. He was honored with Clay's reason to bench him for the game.

"All right," Geoff said, conceding to Clay's request. "I'll make sure things run smoothly until you get back."

"Thanks," Clay said before his shoulders dropped and his expression twisted into solemn anguish. "Geoff...just in case I don't—"

"Shut your mouth, fool," Geoff interrupted. "Don't you finish that sentence or so help me, you'll be limping your way over to the wagons with the other wounded," Geoff said with a half-smile.

Clay wanted to laugh at Geoff's response, but the words that never left his lips were still bouncing around his head. He looked Geoff in the eye and said, "Take care of them."

"As if they are my own, brother," Geoff said.

****

Clay walked into Shelton's office. The mayor's face was buried in inventory sheets, maps, and an alphabetical list of the residents—several names had been scratched off.

Shelton looked up at Clay. "How ya holdin' up, Clay?"

"Exhausted."

"It's been a long day; go get some sleep," Shelton said.

"I will, but I needed to stop by and let you know that Megan, Dusty and Levi are also staying here to help out."

"Are you sure? Are *they* sure?" Shelton asked. "Clay, this isn't your fight. You don't need to do this."

Clay mustered up a smile. "Your fight is my fight, Barry."

Shelton was overcome with gratitude. "Clay, I don't even know what to say…"

"Just tell us how we can be of most use to you."

Shelton glanced down at the mountain of papers on his desk. To say he was overwhelmed would have been a gross understatement. How, in ten short years, did he go from a maintenance manager for a small cable company to mayor, and now military commander, of a post-society town? It was beyond believable to the aging man, but in a world where crazy is the new normal, it almost started to make sense.

After a lengthy sigh, Shelton looked back up at Clay. "Go get some rest, Clay. I'll have Captain Kohler sync up with you in the morning and we'll get y'all started on some things."

Clay nodded before giving a feigned salute. "Aye, aye," he said, giving Shelton a much-needed laugh. As Clay reached the door, he turned back around and looked at Shelton, a serious look on his face. "We'll win this, Barry…We will."

"Yeah…I know we will," he lied.

Chapter 22

It was a ghost town, or it certainly felt that way. In the nearly nine years Clay had visited Liberty, he had never seen the place so still; so hushed. Only the frosty breeze in the air kept the sound of silence at bay. Many of the town's buildings had been repurposed into war rooms, armories, and barracks, while others had been sacrificed entirely for materials to harden the defenses around the perimeter. The few dozen vehicles that remained inside the gates had been strategically positioned around town, most of which were placed near the main gate, creating a choke point for the attackers if they were to break through. Drums—both steel and plastic, filled with sand and water—haphazardly pockmarked the streets and grassy fields separating the homes. The three-story clock tower—which had been erected just six months before the ash fell—had been fortified with steel plates, sandbags, and an enormous amount of lumber. The tower, which was located at the center of a roundabout near the front gate, would be a crucial asset for Liberty. With a sharpshooter and a spotter stationed there around the clock, the once-iconic structure would be the eyes for the town—about as close to satellite feed as one could get anymore.

Most of the northern and eastern boundaries took advantage of a steep drop-off down to a stream, giving it a nice geographical border. The sharp natural grade of the landscape coupled with a reasonably sturdy fence erected shortly after the first winter made that entire area an unlikely point of attack. While some efforts were made to strengthen the northern property line, reinforcements were focused to just a few vulnerable locations, most of which were on the western side.

Though unlikely to be breached, Captain Kohler wouldn't allow for such a large section of perimeter to go unmanned, so he stationed three small groups to cover the entire back border. With baseball fresh on the mind, the entire northern most half of town was known as "outfield" since only three "players" would be covering such a large swath of land.

As he sat in one of the dozens of foxholes dug on Captain Kohler's orders, Clay marveled at just how much the peaceful city had transformed over the past week. The quaint town of Liberty Township now looked like it belonged next to the Alamo rather than part of an HOA. It went from Mayberry, USA to Camp Mabry overnight. The sight was both ominous and awe-inspiring, truly something to behold.

The seventh day looked to exit the same way it had entered: with a whimper. As the sun dipped behind the horizon, the warriors who stayed behind to defend the town sat anxiously at their assigned posts, waiting for an enemy that had already struck fear and terror into their souls.

Clay started to wonder if Arlo had been bluffing after all. But then he recalled the look on Arlo's face—the sincerity in his eyes. His gaze was filled with determination, but lacked deceit. No, Arlo and his men *were* coming and thinking otherwise would be a dangerous lie to tell himself.

Clay looked up at the clock tower and wondered what was going through Dusty's head as she kept her scope glued to the tree line in the distance. Clay and Dusty had been through their fair share of battles in the past, but this was different; this was war. Over the years, Clay had seen the flash of fear in her eyes on a few occasions, and though she'd never admit it, Dusty got scared like everyone else—she just happened to be better at masking it than everyone else.

Nevertheless, Clay wasn't terribly worried about Dusty. She was tougher than most guys he had met in the wastelands, and regardless of what cruel situations the world slung at her, the teenager would grit through and emerge victorious.

Megan, on the other hand...

Clay was worried about his sister—the last of his kin from the old world. As with everyone in this new world, Megan had not been exempt from facing violence. But, apart from that fateful night in their childhood home many years ago, she had never even pulled her gun on another man, much less squeezed the trigger. It wasn't that he doubted her toughness—Megan had always risen to whatever challenge that came her way—but there was no telling how she would handle this kind of stress. For that matter, there was no way to tell how *Clay* would handle the stress. The unknowns terrified him, but there was no turning back now. The wheels were already in motion and there were only two ways to get off this ride: victory or defeat—the latter likely meaning death.

Though he fought against it, Clay couldn't help but think about Kelsey. It was not the time or place to worry about the look she had on her face when he decided to stay behind, but every moment that his mind wasn't already occupied with another thought, there she was.

He hated disappointing her. More than that, he hated hurting her, and there was no doubt that, with his complete lack of presence over the past few months, he had been doing it a lot lately. He didn't blame her for the cold shoulder she gave him before leaving for Northfield. But with no way to make things right between them, Clay was not only frustrated; he was distracted. And that was the last thing he needed as he prepared for the upcoming battle. He just prayed that he would have another opportunity to right his wrongs with her.

As if dealing with the psychological stress wasn't bad enough, sitting in the frigid, rock-hard dirt all day added insult to injury. After a brief, but chest-rattling cough, Clay realized just how sore his body had become. He stretched his back the best he could inside the shallow trench, but was no more satisfied than before. Then, without warning, a ferocious Charlie horse struck Clay's leg, causing him to shuffle back and forth as he frantically searched for a position that would bring relief to his throbbing calf.

He let out a violent growl as the tightened muscles in his leg began to release, then a relieved sigh as he leaned back into the rear wall of the trench. Another barrage of coughs rattled the foxhole, triggering a nagging headache. He looked down at his watch—still four more hours until shift change. Before he even finished his calculation, Clay felt a droplet hit his head. Then another. Within minutes, he sat in a half-inch of muddy water.

"Fan-freakin-tastic," Clay grumbled.

Chapter 23

Clay startled himself awake with a deep, raspy cough. Though the cough had significantly improved, the pain in his muscles was agonizing. Even a small hiccup felt as if someone jammed a shiv between his ribs. That pain, however, was more tolerable than the aching lungs he still battled with.

He was far from being completely well, but Clay felt better than he had since the wet, frigid night in the foxhole the previous week. At one point, while Megan checked in on him, Clay told her he felt like he was going to die. This slightly melodramatic comment resulted in a swift smack to the back of his head from his sister. Ordinarily, Megan had as much of a sense of humor as one could have these days, but joking about death was a crossed line too far. "Not now. Not ever," she said adamantly, pointing her finger sternly in his face, leaving no room for negotiations. Throughout the years, far too many loved ones died under the care of Clay and Megan.

And even though the news was always gut-wrenching for Clay, his constant outings often spared him from witnessing the last moments of their short, precious lives...

The same could not be said for Megan.

Megan was *always* there, sitting right beside their beds, squeezing their little hands until their palms went cold. She watched helplessly as their frightened eyes begged her to do something...but there was nothing she could do. Just thinking about it made Clay's stomach churn with grief. Whenever he thought about just how much Megan had been through over the past ten years, it was surprising that she never ended up on the roof of the tower, walking carelessly along the edge as she waited for a strong gust of wind to finish what she couldn't.

For his own sanity, Clay forced the thoughts out of his mind. The lives lost during the attack, the grisly scene he discovered at the FEMA camp, and the memories of all his departed loved ones over the years made it difficult to find the necessary motivation to get out of his comfortable bed and return to his post, to wait for an enemy that may never show. It was sixteen days and counting—nine past the deadline Arlo had given to Shelton. Though he had been convinced that Arlo wasn't bluffing, Clay started to have his own doubts.

The entire week that he was bedridden, Clay relied on Dusty to keep him up to date with the latest happenings around town before starting her shift each day. His spirit was filled with hope when she mentioned overhearing a conversation between Kohler and Shelton. If Arlo failed to make a move by the end of the month, then they would call back all citizens from Northfield and scramble to prepare for winter. Even if they made that decision today, it would be an uphill battle at best. But waiting until November, after the lakes started to freeze and the already scarce deer population thinned even further, the struggle would be like trying to shave a porcupine with a spoon. Still, preparing for winter late in the year was a more preferred alternative than fighting a war—especially when that alternative would have Clay sleeping in his own bed, in his own house, next to his beautiful wife.

After managing to break out of his toasty cocoon, Clay climbed out of bed. The waves of dizziness that had been pestering him the last forty-eight hours went nuclear as soon as he planted his feet on the ground, causing him to fall back into bed. After a few slow, deep breaths, Clay *slowly* got back to his feet and gingerly made his way across the room to get dressed. His legs shook and buckled as his muscles got used to supporting weight again. It was a disconcerting sensation that he hoped would go away soon.

Once dressed, Clay picked up his ARAK-21 and did a quick visual inspection to make sure everything was in working order. Though he had given it a pretty thorough cleaning after the rainy night at the farmhouse, he wanted to make sure there was no rust or nasty film from the rain. It was good to go. Clay threw on his chest rig and double-checked his magazine pouches. He had nine spare mags and one already in the rifle. Sliding his Glock 17 securely into his holster, Clay picked up a small backpack—a more compact version of the one he usually carried—before leaving his room.

It was still early, and with sleep being a precious commodity, Clay made every attempt to stay silent as he walked down the stairs. As he tiptoed through the living room, he saw four men and two women sleeping on anything that was softer than the hardwood floor, their weapons within arm's reach. Due to material harvesting and location to the perimeter, many houses were deemed uninhabitable for the duration of the war. As a result, the houses deeper inside the once-elegant subdivision all got a bit cozier.

As Clay pulled the front door open, it only took seconds for him to feel the effects of the arctic blast piercing through his tattered clothing, inducing a violent chatter from his teeth. A dusting of snow quickly piled up around his feet. The accumulation was minimal, but the statement from Mother Nature was all the same—winter was nigh, and it wasn't even Halloween.

It was a dreary day outside, the skies grayer and hazier than he could remember seeing in recent months. A little voice in Clay's head tempted him with another day's rest. After all, he *was* still sick. But after being out of commission for so long, he refused to allow another man to double his shift just because he didn't want to be out in the snow. So, against his body's protest, Clay continued his hike to the foxhole.

Though much of the perimeter fence was well over eight feet tall and reinforced with wood and metal panels to obscure the enemy's sight, Captain Kohler insisted that everyone move swiftly and tactically when traveling between posts. However, Clay, like most of the other soldiers, quickly viewed this rule as optional so long as Kohler wasn't within eyeshot. The aches plaguing Clay's body made it even more enticing to ignore that particular rule; Clay did, however, move with a bit more urgency as he passed by a few of the larger gaps in the fence.

Fighting the wind was a simple task made difficult by fatigue and lightheadedness. *What I would give for some cold medicine,* he thought to himself. A wish he usually had at least once a year. Finally, about fifteen minutes after leaving the warmth of his bed, Clay had arrived at his "office" for the day. The barely-passable foxhole was a welcomed sight, if for no other reason than to shelter him from the wind.

"Clay!" a voice shouted from inside the foxhole. "So, you *are* alive," the man joked—it was Simpson.

Clay sat down near the edge of the foxhole and warily lowered himself inside. "Tommy, good to see you again," Clay grunted as he settled into the rock-hard dirt.

"How ya feeling?" Simpson asked. "You look like crap."

"And I feel even worse," Clay said as he adjusted himself in a feeble attempt to get comfortable, "but at least I am on this side of the dirt..." Clay looked around at the mud walls that encompassed him before adding, "Well, sort of."

Simpson laughed. "I hear that, buddy. Though, I've been so bored the past couple of days, I'm starting to wonder if the alternative really would be all that much worse."

Don't joke about that, Clay thought to himself—Megan's policy was rubbing off on him.

"Anyway," Simpson continued, "as you can see, there's not much going on. Been almost no sign of anyone."

"Almost?" Clay asked.

"A few days ago, a scout team found a smoldering fire about two klicks to the east, but there was nothing to suggest that it was anything more than a couple of travelers avoiding frostbite."

"Gotcha," Clay said. "I'm really starting to think nobody's gonna show."

Simpson nodded in agreement.

Clay opened his backpack and pulled out a bit of food. "I still have no appetite, but I know my sister will kill me if I don't at least eat *something*. You want the rest?" Clay asked as he held the food out.

Simpson's eyes went wide. Though they weren't starving yet, food rationing was one of the first rules to be enforced. Apart from the few non-combatants that stayed behind to deal with things like food and laundry, there was no one else to prepare it, and as such, the town was going to have to survive mostly off of the stores that had already been set aside for winter. With some extra nourishment staring him in the face, Simpson enthusiastically snatched the food out of Clay's hand. "Thanks, bud!" he said as he crammed an entire granola bar into his mouth.

Clay nibbled on a few crackers as Simpson devoured the bulk of the meal. While the pair ate, Simpson relayed everything he had heard over the last week, most of which Dusty had already covered.

Simpson licked every one of his fingers twice, then let out a sigh of contentment. "Never thought I would say this about pink salmon...but that was some good grub. Thanks again, Clay," he said as he began to stuff his things into a bag. "I am going to go try and catch a few Zs. Martinez also came down with something, so I'm at the tail end of a double."

"Ouch. That sucks," Clay replied.

"You know it."

"All right, go get some rest, Tommy. See you back here around eight tonight?"

"Unless I score myself a hot date before then, I'll be here," Simpson said as he pulled himself out of the ditch onto the topsoil. "Think Megan's free tonight?" he replied with a chuckle.

"Doubt it, but I heard Estelle is," Clay fired back.

"Bah!" Simpson waved off the comment. "I'd rather sleep in a cold ditch next to your ugly mug," Simpson retorted with a laugh. "All right, stay warm," he said as he stretched his back for a moment before walking off.

Without wasting any time, Clay fished through his pack again to set up for his shift. His Griffin Armament suppressor was right at the top, along with two sub-sonic magazines. He didn't want to waste the bullets or cause unnecessary wear and tear on the can during an all-out gunfight, but he also didn't want to find himself in a situation to need muffled shots and have nothing nearby.

After rummaging around for a few seconds, he pulled out his binoculars, a few bottles of water, a Sterno can, and a book of matches. Canned fuel was not a common discovery anymore, so he would only run it for a few minutes at a time every half hour or so, just to keep the edge off. And since the painful tingles were already creeping into his fingertips, it wouldn't be long before he fired it up.

Clay was reaching into his pack to get a notebook and pencil when he heard a loud cracking sound.

Then he heard shouting.

"Who was that?" one man yelled.

"Where'd it come from?" another shouted.

Clay sat up and peeked over the shallow ridge of dirt. He had done nearly a full three-sixty before he finally saw Simpson lying on the ground, motionless, surrounded by red snow. The shouting in the distance continued, but Clay could no longer make out what was being said. His mind was paralyzed. He tuned out the noises from around the world, leaving just the sound of his thumping heart and heavy breathing to fill the silence.

Simpson's arm moved—he was still alive.

"MEDIC!" Clay shouted furiously.

Moments later, the medic appeared from around one of the houses and headed straight toward Simpson. It was Megan. And why that surprised Clay, he was unsure. She was one of three medics on rotation, but was the only one considered experienced enough to be a field surgeon. Doctor Sowell, though was an incredible surgeon himself, was long past his battlefield expiration date, as was his assistant Jackie. That left Megan as the most senior medic in the field.

As Clay watched Megan move toward Simpson, he was hopeful that she would be able to perform a miracle and save his life until he noticed that Simpson's body was directly in front of one of the exposed sections of fence, which would put Megan at high risk of catching a bullet from the same shooter.

Clay leapt out of the foxhole. "Stop!" he screamed at Megan as he frantically waved his hands. Megan reluctantly complied, just mere feet from exposing herself to the sniper's lane of fire. Clay cautiously jogged the rest of the way over to Simpson, staying on the opposite side of the opening as Megan with Simpson splitting the difference.

The sounds coming from Simpson as he struggled to breath were haunting. Clay looked in horror as the steam rising from the devastating bullet wound in his chest dissipated into the cold, morning air—as if it was life itself fleeing the man's body.

"Clayton, I need to get to him *right* now or he is going to die!" Megan shouted, knowing full well his death was likely anyway.

"And what happens when you get shot, too?" Clay shouted back. "Who's going to save *your* life?"

Megan clenched her jaw. "Well, we have to do something! We can't just let him bleed out," she said.

By then, Clay noticed a couple of men circling around the houses on Megan's side. He waved them over, and the pair knelt next to Megan.

"I'm going to lay down some fire, you guys get him out of there, okay?" Clay said, panic flowing through his voice.

Both men nodded and waited for Clay's go.

With precious seconds wasting away, Clay took a quick, deep breath before swinging out of cover, firing rapidly toward the tree line. When his rifle had spit out its last shell, he dove back to cover to reload. By the time he dropped the empty magazine from the rifle, the two men had successfully dragged Simpson out of the line of fire; Megan was already hard at work. However, her speed and body language did not give Clay a lot of confidence that there would be a happy ending for his new friend.

Clay's grief was disrupted with the ringing of a bell from the clock tower.

"South-southeast!" he heard Dusty scream from above.

With adrenaline tearing through his veins like an unstoppable virus, Clay grabbed a fresh magazine from his chest rig and slapped it home. Standing back up to his feet, he sprinted toward the main entrance where the first wave was headed. He jumped as he heard a single gunshot. Then another. And another. Before long it sounded like the grand finale on the Fourth of July.

As soon as the decision was made to take a stand, Shelton, Kohler, and several others started planning in great detail how the town's defenses would be setup, the responsibilities of each individual, and numerous ways to minimize loss. Yet, as the first shots of the war were exchanged, Liberty was already down a man, and everyone else seemed to be scrambling around, unsure of what to do. Even Clay, who had more experience in "battle" than most of the citizens in town, had forgotten his orders to stay at his post in the foxhole. Instinct trumped his training, and he found himself running toward the gate to join the effort keeping the crowd out.

As Clay neared the entrance, he stopped at a section of fence with several small gaps between panels, allowing him to target the enemy while keeping himself relatively shielded. His stomach sank when he saw no less than fifty bodies running toward the town, and the random shots he heard off to the north told him this was not their only point of attack either.

Resting on one knee, Clay looked through the gap in the wall with his ACOG scope. Lining up a solid shot proved to be difficult as his targets moved erratically and used any means of cover they could find. After setting his sights on a hefty-sized man, Clay squeezed the trigger a few times. A mixture of snow and dirt kicked up around his target, who went to the ground in a hurry. Unfortunately, the attacker got back up and dove behind a decorative cobblestone sign near the road where he proceeded to return fire. Clay backed away as a myriad of bullets pummeled the wall with deafening impacts.

That looked like an AK-47, Clay thought to himself—a terrifying thought. There was little doubt that Arlo had numbers on his side, but the notion that Liberty had more sophisticated firepower gave Liberty an edge. Fighting off hordes of barbarians carrying SKSs, double barrel shotguns, and hunting rifles made everyone feel a little more confident about winning. But that theory was, at least for the moment, proving to be untrue.

Clay dared another look through his optics and saw several men and women with the kind of weaponry he had expected—one man was even using an old Enfield No. 4. But for every three or four of those guns, Clay saw a modern battle rifle of some sort—something equivalent to an AK-47 or AR-15.

This is not good, he thought to himself.

Just then, he heard a shout come from the clock tower—a man's voice this time. "They're breaching the corridor!"

The corridor was the nearly eighth of a mile stretch of driveway that led up to the gates of Liberty. Cars, trucks, and anything else weighing more than a hundred pounds that could be pushed, dragged or carried outside of town was placed in the driveway to create a funnel for the enemy as they negotiated through the last patch of ground separating Liberty from the wild.

The short stretch of debris and cracked asphalt would prove to be very costly to Arlo's troops.

Chapter 24

Miraculously, Simpson was the only loss Liberty experienced during the first encounter between the two groups. Though seven others had been wounded, six of them never even left the battlefield before Arlo's men retreated. The seventh, a young man named Victor, was still being tended to by Doctor Sowell. Though the man fought the good fight against death, the final decision would ultimately come down to whether death called heads or tails.

All in all, the first encounter had not been as costly to Liberty as expected. The same could not be said about Arlo's fighters; *at least* eighteen men and women lay lifeless along the Deadly Eighth, a nickname the long driveway had quickly received after the battle had ended. Kohler ordered a team to head out at nightfall to retrieve weapons and supplies from the bodies consumed in the Deadly Eighth. The team, however, was under strict orders to leave the bodies.

"Let their fallen comrades be a horrible reminder of what's at stake; that they cannot, and *will not* just walk in here and take our homes," Kohler said in a post-battle speech.

While most people understood that the tactic was nothing more than psychological warfare in its most pitiless form, others were disappointed, if not disgusted, with the decision.

"They are still people!" one man shouted.

"They deserve a proper burial, regardless of what they did in life," another said.

Kohler was empathetic, but firm in his decision. "When this war is behind us, I assure you that each of them will be dealt with respectfully, but until that day comes..." he said. There was no need to repeat his order.

Clay wasn't bothered with Kohler's directive. In fact, he was impressed with the move. He had recently concluded that sometimes the only way to defeat your enemy is to play by *their* rules. Diplomacy had its place in the world, but the world had changed. If you didn't play for all four quarters, if you weren't as ruthless and hardhearted as the enemy, you were dead. It was that simple. And the voice in Clay's conscience that often protested such ideas became quieter with each passing day.

As darkness overpowered the sky, the small team of five prepared for their excursion into the driveway. Clay attached his suppressor to his rifle and put in a magazine of subsonic rounds. There wasn't much anticipation for gunfire, but as his dad always said, *If you're not always prepared, you're never prepared.*

Besides a rifle and a few spare magazines, the only other thing each member of the squad could bring was an empty duffle bag. The objective was straightforward: fill up the bags with supplies—ideally with guns and ammo.

The team consisted of Clay, Robert, Morgan, Hicks, and Warren. With the exception of Robert, who was the centerfielder on his baseball team, Clay had just been introduced to the others as the recovery team was assembled. Robert used to be a librarian; Warren had been a butcher at HEB. Hicks...well, nobody really knew about him. He was a quiet man and the oldest of the group. Rumor was—according to Robert—he used to work for the NSA back in the day. Warren had heard he was an author. Nobody was sure what he had done before the ash blanketed the planet and the confusion only seemed to please the mysterious man. However, one thing was for certain, he was a good shot and a trustworthy brother-in-arms; the type of man you wanted by your side when the chips were down.

Then there was Morgan. Last year, Morgan's father and brother went out on a hunt and never came back—their mutilated bodies were discovered a few miles away a month later. Then her mother— the last living relative she had—was killed during Arlo's surprise attack at the beginning of the month. Though Morgan had been encouraged to go back to Northfield with the others, she insisted that she stay and fight. With the number of volunteers as skimpy as they already were, nobody tried to talk her out of it.

The team approached the gate, each one fighting waves of trepidation. The stigma of exiting the gates at night was heavy enough as it was, let alone after the kind of day they had had. In addition to the inherent dangers of walking around at night, there was no telling if any of Arlo's men had stuck around, waiting to pounce on some easy prey.

"I'll take the front of the driveway," Hicks said, taking charge of the operation. "I'll cover from the box truck to the road. Robert and Warren, you guys cover the space between the dumpster and the box truck. Clay and Morgan, you two will have everything between that dumpster and the gate," he said as he pointed to the large wrought iron gate in front of them. "And there is to be *no* talking, understood?" he added.

There was unanimous agreement.

The three guards on duty yanked the gate to the side as the group stared out into the dark abyss ahead of them. Though Clay had been up and down the driveway many times over the years, never had it felt so unsettling, so haunting.

Without saying a word, Hicks walked past the gate and into the driveway. Robert and Warren, standing shoulder to shoulder, went next. Clay glanced over at Morgan, who was struck with fear.

"Just stay close to the gate," Clay said.

The nervous teenager nodded as she swallowed. "Yeah, okay."

Clay walked out the gates, Morgan closely behind. The guards closed the gate, but kept it unlatched.

It didn't take long to find the first body; Clay and Morgan both tripped over it. With it being so close to the gate, Clay suggested Morgan start there and he would venture a little further out. He decided to work from the front of his zone back, so he walked out to the dumpster to begin his search. A few moments later he had found another body—a heavyset man from the feel of it. Clay knelt beside the unfortunate soul and patted around, searching for useful items. Between the near-black conditions and the growing numbness in his fingertips, Clay struggled to determine what was junk and what was valuable. His solution was to stuff every single item into his bag.

Clay's attempts to find a rifle came up empty. During the chaos of the retreat, some of Arlo's men retrieved the guns from the dead. It was unknown how strong their armory was—and as Clay discovered today, it was already stronger than they had anticipated—but leaving any gun behind for your enemy to use was something that Clay would avoid at all costs, so it was no surprise that Arlo's men had the same thoughts.

Rolling the heavy man over required more energy than Clay had to spare. Settling for half way, Clay used his leg to prop up the body while he searched. The efforts were not in vain, however, as Clay discovered a pistol from the man's holster. Finding nothing else, Clay grunted as he pulled his leg away from the body, causing it to stiffly roll back over onto the asphalt with an eerie sound. With the area around the dumpster clear, Clay started moving back toward the gate as he expanded his search.

Having found three more bodies along the way, two of which carried revolvers, Clay finally started to feel better about being assigned this task. It wasn't that he didn't see the value in trying to scavenge as many resources as possible; he just wasn't thrilled about being the one to do it—especially at night. But, as the search continued, so did the silence. There were no gunshots ringing out or screams of agony. There were no orders being barked or cries for medics. Only the soft, almost soothing sound of a cold evening breeze rolling across the area...

And the whimpers of a dying soul.

With his almost-relaxed state once again replaced with an adrenaline-fueled preparedness,

Clay darted toward the sound of the stifled cries, his rifle at the ready.

"Please," a woman's voice cried, so softly Clay could just barely hear her.

The cries grew louder as he got closer to a small SUV off to the side of the Deadly Eighth. With each step, fear's grip on Clay's breathing tightened. He could feel the perspiration building on his forehead. He wanted to flick on his rifle's flashlight, but knew that decision could be costly to him as well as the others. He resisted.

"Please, help me," the invisible person pleaded once more.

Clay finally found the source of the cries. His stomach twisted in knots as his brain processed the information repeatedly, as if hoping it would eventually come to a different conclusion. Though it was dark outside, Clay's vision had adjusted well enough to know what lay there in front of him.

Having no recollection of the prior few seconds, Clay found himself running toward the gate, a limp body in his arms. "Open the gate!" Clay yelled at a whisper as he saw Morgan crouched down next to a body.

"What? Why?" she replied, trying to keep her voice quiet.

"Just do it!" Clay repeated, without explanation.

Morgan hurried back to the gate and passed Clay's request off to the guards.

By the time the guards realized what was going on, Clay was already running through the gate. "No bodies!" one of the guards stated firmly.

Clay ignored the rebuke and went straight to the infirmary.

****

"So, tell me what happened," Shelton asked Clay from across his desk.

Captain Kohler stood on the other side of the room awaiting Clay's response as well. He had been emphatic that none of the bodies be moved, but even he couldn't blame Clay for his decision.

Clay's eyelids drooped as he noticed the sun rising through the window. What started as a lengthy yawn ended in an exhausted sigh. "Uhm," Clay said as he tried to organize his thoughts from the events a few hours ago. "While searching the bodies in the driveway, I heard someone nearby crying. At first, I thought maybe it was a woman, but when I reached the source of the sound, I saw it was a boy."

Kohler clenched his fists and shook his head. *What kind of monster would send a little boy into battle?*

"Do we know how old?" Shelton asked.

"Doctor Sowell's best guess was ten or eleven," Clay replied.

"Is he still alive?" Shelton asked. "Unfortunately, I've not yet had a chance to speak with Doctor Sowell myself."

Clay nodded. "Yes. Well, he still was when I left the infirmary. I'm no doctor, but he wasn't looking too hot, though."

Shelton took off his glasses and rubbed his temples with his fingers. Although Shelton and Kohler didn't see eye to eye on everything, Shelton respected the man's combat experience in Iraq and Syria and did not wish to question every decision he made. And though it was evident that Kohler was just as bothered by this situation as he was, Shelton wanted the responsible party reprimanded.

"Daniel, you need to figure out who pulled that trigger and set them straight," Shelton said, anger creeping into his voice.

"Sir?" Kohler responded.

"You heard me, Captain. We will *not* win this war over the dead bodies of countless children."

Kohler understood the point Shelton tried to make—and he didn't disagree with it—but Shelton's request was not going to undo the damage done to the boy's body, nor would it prevent another child from being shot if Arlo were to heartlessly send more into battle. "Have you ever been to war, Barry?" Kohler asked, throwing formality out the window. "And I mean *actual* war." It was a question Kohler already knew the answer to, so he didn't wait for a response. "When the bullets start flying and the adrenaline is pumping, your mind tends to operate on instinct and reflexes. There isn't always time to figure out who is trying to kill you; if you get shot at, you shoot back. It's just the way it works."

"I understand that, but we need our guys to be better..."

"It could've been me," Clay blurted out, yielding a strange look from Shelton. "I was right there, Barry, shooting down that same corridor as everyone else. I took shots at dozens of different people over that hour, several of which I know I hit, and not once did I think I was shooting at a kid. Not once did I look through my scope and think there was even a remote possibility of that. So," Clay paused for a moment as the reality of his words sunk in, "I could have been the one to shoot that kid. I may very well end up being responsible for his death."

Shelton sighed again—Clay's distressing words supporting Kohler's defense.

"I killed a little boy, once," Kohler said. The room fell eerily silent. Kohler's eyes glazed over as he stared at the wall across the room, looking into a past nightmare he wished he could forget. "It was in Syria, in the closing days of the war. My platoon was sweeping an ISIS-controlled neighborhood near Aleppo. Predators had already flattened half the neighborhood by the time we got there, so we expected resistance to be minimal. After clearing the first block without issue we moved on to the next. And right as we stepped into an intersection, one of them ran out into the street and opened up on us, shooting my staff sergeant. We dropped him immediately, but right as two of my men ran out to try and save Sergeant Foster, I saw movement out of the corner of my eye..." Kohler's expression went grim, his voice filled with a sorrow-filled rage. "My reflexes trumped my training and I engaged the target without processing all the facts. My three-round-burst clipped the kid in the neck and he died just a few feet away from the gunman that had taken out Foster."

The pain in Kohler's word cut deep.

"Experience told me the boy was headed straight for his dad's Kalashnikov, ready to pick up where his old man had left off. But, then again, it's also possible the boy was just running to embrace his dying father; just doing what any loving son would do." Kohler cleared his throat before continuing. "I'll forever be haunted by the decision to take that kid's life—to let instinct overpower humanity. But that debilitating thought is always countered by a single what-if question: what if the boy *was* going for his dad's gun? Or worse, what if he was attempting to flip that switch on his dad's suicide vest filled to the brim with washers, nails, and ball bearings? What if the boy had taken out my entire squad because I hesitated to pull the trigger? Most of the agony is that I'll never know what his motives were, because I never gave him a chance to show me. And I will have to go to my grave not knowing. But, I will say this," he said as his dazed eyes narrowed and locked onto Shelton's eyes, "after years of training and experience, if *I* made that mistake, or perhaps life-saving choice, solely on instinct, what do you expect from a bunch of traders and farmers just trying to survive?"

Shelton's shoulders slumped as he stared down at his desk. Kohler's point was on the mark.

"War is...well, it's just about the only thing that hasn't changed over the last ten years. It's still just as ugly, just as brutal, and just as evil as it ever was. The only difference is that, now, *nobody* is exempt from living it." Kohler ran his hand over his face, his palm pausing over his mouth as he once again stared at the wall across the room. "It's never pretty and is seldom fair. And all we can do is try...try to do what is right and good. But gentleman, sometimes the enemy takes those choices away from us," Kohler said, the grief dropping from his expression and leaving just anger. "And may God damn him when he does."

War was hell.

Chapter 25

When the dust had settled and smoke had cleared, Thomas Simpson was *still* the only fatality Liberty had suffered.

That was the good—miraculous—news.

The bad news, however, was that even though the recovery team managed to scrounge together a decent haul of guns and ammo from the Deadly Eighth, the income was far less than the outgoing. The level of consumption from that single battle would be unsustainable. Kohler reminded everyone of the importance of making each shot count. It wasn't that he expected each pull of the trigger to result in a notch on the side of the rifle, but he *did* expect each trigger pull to have a purpose—a positive one for Liberty and a negative one for the enemy.

Kohler's words echoed in Clay's head as he sat at the round breakfast table, staring at his disassembled ARAK-21. He had taken stock of his own ammunition after the first encounter: 117 subsonic rounds, 233 supersonic. Because of the *very* finite amount of ammo he had left for the .300 blackout, Clay would, once again, put his LaRue to work. He still had more than 400 rounds of 5.56MM of his personal ammo, and after that was gone, he could resupply from the town's armory. He also knew there was at least a case and a half back at Smith's bunker that he could retrieve if supplies *really* thinned out. However, since nobody in town used the .300 blackout cartridge, when Clay ran out, he was out. So, he would save the suppressed rifle for a rainy day—figuratively speaking.

Clay grabbed a rag lying on the table and wiped the excess solvent and oil off the rifle. He quickly reassembled it and inspected his efforts. The candlelight glistened off the liberally applied lubricant just inside the ejection port, letting Clay know it was ready for storage up in his room until a need should arise.

Setting the rifle down, Clay reached across the table and picked up a cup and put it to his lips. He hesitated for a moment before taking a sip. Though he was down to the last gulp inside the Styrofoam cup, he made the exact same wrinkly face he had made after the first sip. Unfortunately, Clay had never developed a sophisticated enough palate to enjoy the taste of black coffee. To him, it might as well have been 10W30. The lack of bean juice ingestion over the years, however, meant that it was a particularly effective way to keep him going long after his body hit its limit. Although supplies were very limited and most of the grounds were reused three and even four times before being discarded, Shelton agreed that it was a necessary resource to consume for a group that would only grow more exhausted by the day.

Clay clenched his teeth as he swallowed the last swig. *Disgusting,* he thought. *Why on earth people used to willingly pay seven bucks for a cup of this is beyond me.*

As he sat alone in silence, Clay's mind began to digest the past thirty-six hours. He couldn't help but go to an alternate reality; one that had him dragging his feet to get out of bed that morning. One that had him crossing that small clearing in the fence *after* the sharpshooter had set up for the opening statement of the war. On that fateful morning, it wasn't a bullet that had a name on it—it was time. And, unfortunately, it was Simpson's name that was pulled out of the hat.

The front door in the living room opened and Megan, along with Dusty and Morgan, tromped in from the snow. Clay looked over and noticed Morgan looking a little worse for wear. Megan handed her some pills and a bottle of water, while giving her some instructions. Dusty made a joke, causing her new friend to chuckle and Megan to roll her eyes. "Drink *lots* of fluids," Clay could barely hear Megan say before the girls headed upstairs.

Megan lightly knocked on the doorframe as she came in. "Hey, Bub," she said as she gingerly made her way over to the table, sitting down across from Clay. A wince flashed across her face as she took her shoes off and an exhausted groan escaped her lips as she sat back in the chair. "So, how was your day?" she asked unenthusiastically.

"Well, nobody shot at me today, so that's something," he replied as he pushed a cartridge into an AR-15 magazine.

"I'll drink to that," Megan said as she reached for Clay's coffee cup, only to give a look of disappointment once she realized it was just a few grounds swimming in backwash.

"You use up your ration for the day?" Clay asked.

"Uh, yeah, that bird left the nest by nine this morning."

Clay looked down at his watch. "It's getting pretty late anyhow, you probably don't want to be drinking more."

"If only, little brudder," she said. "I'm just on my 'lunch' break right now. Gotta be back in about an hour; shift ends at midnight."

The daily eighteen-hour shifts for the medical staff was nothing short of punishing. Soldiers were on twelve-hour rotations, but there were about twenty times as many people filling that role. With only one doctor, a nurse practitioner, and four medical apprentices, there was no other choice but to assign ungodly hours to the weary souls. And poor Doctor Sowell...he had taken up residence in the supply closet of the infirmary.

"That sucks," Clay said. "Sorry."

Megan's cheeks puffed up before letting the air squeeze out between her lips. "Yes, it does. *But,*" she said with a hint of optimism in her voice. "Doctor Sowell convinced Shelton that we in fact *do* need some more help in the infirmary, so I'm actually going to start training one of them tonight."

"You're taking some of our fighters away?" Clay asked.

"Kind of have to," she said with a crooked smile. "The resumes aren't exactly flying in," she added.

"Who are you taking?"

"Samuelson and..." she struggled to remember the other name. "Oh! McCreary. We're also working with Estelle at the mess hall to get some assistance from a few of the ladies there—at least for a couple hours a day to help with things like changing bed sheets and dressings."

"McCreary?" Clay asked, giving Megan a disapproving scowl. "He's Dusty's spotter. He's kind of important."

Megan blew a few rogue strands of hair out of her face before snapping back. "Don't get mad at me, Clayton, I didn't pick 'em. Doctor Sowell made his request and that's who showed up on our doorstep."

Clay wanted to have a few words with Kohler and Shelton about the choice in personnel, but both men had far more important things to worry about than his complaints and Clay knew that. Rather than beating the horse to death, Clay changed the subject. "So, how's the boy doing?"

"He's still not awake," Megan said, hopelessness clinging to her words.

"How long can he survive like that?"

Megan shrugged. "Really all depends. Back when the grid was up, he could be kept alive for years without waking up. But, the world we're in now..." she trailed off, holding up her hands and shaking her head. "Thank God Doctor Sowell had spent so much time in Haiti," she continued, "the man's *pretty* creative when it comes to improvising. Because of that, we have been able to give the kid some IV fluids, but it's not like we have a warehouse full of that stuff to spare. And even if we did, it would only help for so long. If he doesn't wake up soon, he never will."

"Poor kid," Clay said under his breath.

As the flame continued to consume the final inches of wick on the candles, Clay and Megan both sat quietly in their own thoughts. The weight of the world grew heavier by the day, and Clay started to realize that he was fast approaching his breaking point. And his foot was either unable or unwilling to let off the gas.

Kelsey and the kids invaded his thoughts as he wondered if staying to fight for Liberty had been the right choice. *Of course, it was,* he told himself. But, as he sat in the kitchen in a town that might as well be on the other side of the world, Clay couldn't seem to snuff out images of bandits overrunning the farm or one of the kids getting sick while he was away. And if that happened—if anything happened to his family while he was off fighting a war that wasn't his to fight—he knew that that was a spiral he'd never pull out of.

"Well, Clayton," Megan said as she stood from her chair, interrupting Clay's thoughts, "since you're out of coffee, you're no longer of use to me," she said along with a warm smile—the first in several weeks. A drawn-out yawn took control of her mouth as she stretched her back. "I'm going to go try and get a quick catnap before heading back in." She ruffled Clay's hair as she walked by. "Love ya, Bub."

No sooner did Megan step out of the kitchen than the sound of muffled shouting come from outside. Clay and Megan both held their breath as they tried to determine if they were hearing things.

More shouting. Then a gunshot.

Megan darted back into the kitchen, grabbing her coat off the back of the chair. With a look of defeat on her face, she looked him in the eyes and said, "Be safe, Clayton."

****

By the time Clay had reached the gate, the battle was already over. He did manage to squeeze off a few shots in the direction of a retreating attacker. This time his target hit the ground and didn't get back up. Clay struggled with his emotions, or lack thereof, after realizing his aim had been true. It was getting far too easy to cope with taking another man's life, and it was unsettling that it seemed to comfort him.

As the gunfire tapered off, Clay saw four dead bodies on Liberty's side of the gate, and numerous wounded. Though the skirmish lasted just a few minutes, the length of the battle was not congruent with its ferocity. With seven confirmed dead on *their* side of the gate, the kill-death ratio was still in favor of Liberty, but much less so than the first battle.

With no technological enhancements like night vision or infrared, it was expected that most of the fighting would occur during the daylight hours, so the surprise attack just after dusk had caught everyone off guard. *That won't happen again. It* can't *happen again*, Clay thought.

Clay helped carry the wounded back to the infirmary. Warren had been hit in the leg while Robert took a large-bore rifle bullet to the arm.

"I'll just learn to shoot with my off hand," Robert said through clenched teeth as Doctor Sowell evaluated the damage, lightening the otherwise grim mood.

Unfortunately, Warren wasn't as lucky. Just like the woman Clay had carried to the infirmary weeks earlier, Warren's femoral artery was chewed up, and he was gone before he could reach the operating table. Five to seven—the ratio was falling.

Clay watched as Megan calmly gave orders to the various volunteers. Doctor Sowell looked up from time to time with a tired smile on his face as he watched her take charge of the makeshift hospital. Her leadership allowed him to focus exclusively on the patients, which was what he was best at.

"Melissa, bed two needs a few sutures on his head then he's good to go," Megan said as she handed a petite young woman a Ziploc baggie with some supplies inside. "Tim, bed five needs dressing and pain management. Take this and this." She handed the middle-aged man some gauze and a nearly empty bottle of Ibuprofen. "Ashley, do follow-ups with beds three, seven, and fourteen. After that, assist Melissa and Tim. Jackie and I are assisting Doctor Sowell with an operation, so do *not* bother us unless it's absolutely critical, understood?"

A collective, "Yes, ma'am," came out of their mouths as they all went separate ways. Megan zoomed by Clay on her way to join Doctor Sowell in the operating "room" to try and save Robert's arm.

While Clay had watched Megan work before, it was remarkable to see how she was handling every train wreck that barreled her way. She was in her element, and he'd be lying if he said he wasn't impressed.

The subtle moans and groans around the room were abruptly replaced with agonizing cries from outside the infirmary.

"Someone open the door!" a booming voice shouted from outside.

Clay ran over to the door and pushed it open. Two men carrying another shuffled toward him. Still holding the door, Clay stepped out of the way to give them space.

"Over here!" Tim yelled, pointing to a vacant bed on the other side of the room.

Clay's stomach soured as the extent of the man's injuries was revealed.

"Dear God, how did this happen, DeMarcus?" Tim asked, trying to maintain his composure.

"They tried to get in from the creek," DeMarcus replied as they carefully put their friend down into the bed, which was met with more excruciating screams.

"We had everything under control," the other man started talking, "until one of those pricks lobbed a Molotov over the fence. It landed right inside Nolan's foxhole, and..." he said, his lip started to tremble. "They burned him alive, man."

Without saying a word, Tim turned around and ran back to the OR to get help.

"After that, they broke through," DeMarcus picked up where his friend left off, his booming voice bouncing around the room. "One of them actually made it inside, but me and Sean here smoked him before he got too far," he said, putting his massive hand on his friend's shoulder. "Fortunately, we was in the middle of a shift change when it all went down, so there were a few extra guns nearby. Every one of us shot until we was empty; sent those fools runnin' for the hills."

"Is the fence secured?" Clay asked worriedly.

"Still was a hole in it when me and Sean left with Nolan, but there was at least a dozen guns guardin' the place until it could get fixed up," DeMarcus replied.

Tim came back with Jackie; her clothes and gloved hands were smeared with Robert's blood. Her eyes widened when she saw the severity of the burns, but then softened when she looked more closely at him. Holding her hands in the air to avoid contamination, she looked at Tim. "Can you check his pulse, please?"

Tim flinched when his fingers touched the scaly burns on the man's neck. He pushed his fingers in, repositioning them several times. He turned around and gave a subtle shake of his head toward Jackie.

"I'm sorry guys," Jackie said to DeMarcus and Sean. Without another word, she spun around and returned to the operating room.

Sean tried to stifle his cries, but was unable to. "It's going to be a'ight, Sean," DeMarcus said as he consoled his friend.

Tim put his hands on top of his head and let out a lengthy sigh. "I didn't sign up for this. I used to be a dentist for crying out loud, not some *combat* doctor."

DeMarcus shot Tim a glare. "Man, I had six colleges offering me a full ride before all this happened. You think pulling my friend's charred body out of a hole in the ground is what I was expectin' to do ten years ago?"

Tim was silent.

"Ain't none of us doing what we thought we'd be doing, but here we are." He paused and looked over at Clay as well as Sean. "So, we can either bitch and moan about our problems or get back up, dust ourselves off, and *keep fighting.*"

After a couple of sniffles, Sean wiped his eyes and nodded. He grabbed DeMarcus's shoulder and gave it a squeeze. "Thanks, man," he said. "I needed to hear that."

Me too, thought Clay.

Chapter 26

"How much you wanna bet I could pick that guy off from here?"

Clay observed one of Arlo's men standing at the edge of the tree line through his spotting scope. "That's about a five hundred yard shot there, kid. You're good, but not *that* good."

Dusty scoffed at the insult. "Whatever. Five hundred might be a long distance for someone at *your* skill level..." she replied without taking her eye off her scope.

"*Besides*," Clay added, "you know the orders. No shooting until they cross the road or fire first."

"Yeah, yeah, yeah..."

Conversation fell away as Clay and Dusty searched the area for anything unusual—more unusual than the scouts plotting their next attack, anyway. It had been a week since the last clash and the entire town braced for more. It seemed long overdue, but both sides suffered significant losses during the last battle, so it was not terribly surprising that Arlo's men held off longer than expected.

"By the way," Dusty said, breaking the silence, "thanks for filling in for Morgan tonight. She still hasn't shaken whatever she got last week; she needed a night off."

"No problem," Clay replied. "How is she working out? Good spotter?"

"Pretty decent. She's got some things to learn, still, but I'm showing her the ropes. And with *such* a capable teacher like me, she'll be up to speed in no time."

Clay laughed with Dusty's superhuman confidence. "Good deal," he said as he watched the scouts start to fall back, disappearing into the woods. "I saw you guys hanging out at the mess hall the other day. Seems like you found yourself a new friend."

She responded with an overly dramatic sigh. "I've got enough friends, Clay. Like I said, just showing her the ropes."

Dusty was very touchy when it came to the topic of friends—as in, she never talked about having any, past or present. Though there was no denying that Clay and Geoff fit the dictionary definition of the word, she never once used the term to describe either of them. Being betrayed by a friend, especially as a young, impressionable girl, had a lasting and devastating effect.

"What do you think is going through their heads right now?" Dusty asked, changing the subject.

"Huh? Who? Arlo's guys?"

"Yeah. I mean, how could anyone just go and kill a bunch of unarmed people like that and still sleep at night?"

"I don't know," Clay responded. "Before I found you in that school a few years ago, you probably did some things you never expected to do, right?"

"Well, yeah, but I didn't kill anyone…At least not anyone that wasn't already trying to kill me, anyway."

"Yeah, but you did what you had to do to survive. Even killing someone that was trying to kill you, that's a tall order, *especially* for a little kid. But you did what was necessary to stay alive. You tried to run, that didn't work, so you had no choice but to fight."

"I guess," Dusty said as she fiddled with the zoom on her scope slightly.

"And that 'tough girl' act that you *still* put on for us every day..."

"That's no act, chump..."

"Okay, fine," Clay conceded, despite seeing through the lie. "My point is these people are probably just doing whatever it takes to survive."

"Wait a second," Dusty said, her eyes coming off the lens for the first time since the conversation started. She gave him a baffled look. "Are you actually *justifying* what these guys are doing?"

"Of course not!" Clay barked back. "I am, however, playing devil's advocate here. What Arlo and these people are doing...what they've done...it's wrong. *Wrong!* Okay? But I want you to remember that we're not all that different from them. We're not above crossing the same line they've already crossed. I'm sure these people didn't just wake up one morning and go, 'I think today I'm going to murder a bunch of people so I can take their stuff,' Dusty." Clay looked her in the eyes, "Staying on the right side of that line, especially in the world we live in now, is a choice...no, a *fight* we have to make every single day. But don't assume you'll always make the right choice. Don't even assume you'll always *want* to make the right choice. Because that's when you'll get blindsided.

"I know you've been through a lot, Dusty. More than any kid should ever have to go through, but you're not alone. In fact, there are a lot of people out there who have been through even worse. So, fight every day to stay on that right side—the good side—but never assume you aren't capable of going down that same path. Or one day you might find yourself scouting along a tree line looking to prey on some innocent victims."

Dusty remained silent. She didn't nod or acknowledge Clay's statement; she just turned her head back to the scope and continued to scan the horizon.

Clay's words were just as much for himself as they were for Dusty—perhaps even more so. With everything he'd seen, everything he'd been through—especially over the last few months—the hope that he had been clutching to all these years started to fade. Decisions he had made and the thoughts he had had indicated he flirted dangerously close with that very line he just spoke of. He might have been able to give himself a pass if this had all started after Arlo's ambush on Liberty—call it a side effect of war—but this demon had started whispering into his ear the moment Charlie died, a whisper too faint to notice until he contemplated slaughtering the Screamers in that house last month. He hoped—he prayed—that this was just a bad stretch of road that he would soon see in the rearview mirror. And hopefully, before too much destruction occurred. Until then, he would try to follow his own advice, as well as DeMarcus's.

Keep fighting—two wars at the same time.

****

Clay knocked on the door.

"Just a sec," Megan replied.

Megan was in sweatpants and a sweatshirt when she opened the door, a towel wrapped around her head.

"Hey brother, what's going on?" she asked.

"My head is killing me; I was wondering if you had brought any medicine from home with you—I don't really want to take anything away from the infirmary over a headache."

"Yeah, come on in," she said as she walked over to her bed and rummaged through her pack. She pulled out a bottle and opened it up, quickly counting what was left inside. "Are you okay with just one?" she asked.

"That's fine. I'm planning to go straight to sleep after this, so anything to help get me there would be great," he said before grabbing the pill and swallowing it without a drink. "Thanks."

"No problem. Hope it works."

"I'm sure it..." Clay trailed off as he noticed some clothes folded on the bed along with a few other items next to the backpack. "Going somewhere?" he asked.

"Uhm, yeah, kinda," she said hesitantly.

"Kinda?"

"Well..." Megan said, reluctant to tell her brother about her new assignment. "Doctor Sowell mentioned to Mayor Shelton this morning just how thin our supplies are getting. And, evidently, you guys aren't faring all that much better with ammunition, either. So, after a little impromptu meeting with me, Doctor Sowell, Shelton and Captain Kohler, it was decided that a supply run is necessary."

Clay stared at her like her hair was on fire.

"I leave just before dawn."

Clay shook his head. "No. No way! They need to find someone else. I am sure Doctor Sowell needs your help in the infirmary. Just tell one of the others what to look for and send them."

Megan was already plagued with guilt before her brother even walked into her room; his desperate pleas only made the sensation worse. She shook her head. "It's not that simple, Clay. We talked for a while about who to send and ultimately, Doctor Sowell felt I was the best option. I have the most experience with medical training; I know medicines and antibiotics better than anyone else except for him and Jackie. I also know the kind of items he's looking for when it comes to his more improvised medical creations. Plus," she said as she put her hand on Clay's shoulder and smiled, "thanks to my big-little brother, I know how to handle a gun."

"Yeah, and so does McCreary. And no offense, sis, but he's a much better shot than you are."

Megan rolled her eyes. "And, as of three days ago, McCreary didn't know the difference between ibuprofen and acetaminophen."

Clay's puzzled expression said it all.

"Thank you for proving my point, Clay," she said before turning to her bed to pack her clothes. "Look, I don't want to be going either, but we're not going to make it through winter and a war with aspirin and Band-Aids. Even if you guys had a train car full of ammunition, we can't patch you up with buckshot and hollow points. We need good medical supplies, and we need someone on this trip who can identify and prioritize what those supplies are. Without that," she stopped and turned around, revealing the fear in her eyes. She lifted her hands up before dropping them to her side. "Clay...it just has to be done," she said with a glum look on her face. "There's no way around it."

She was right and there was no denying it, no matter how much Clay tried to convince himself otherwise.

"Who is going with you?" Clay asked.

"Well, Levi volunteered, but between an ankle sprain and his overall lack of knowledge on medicine and self-defense, that idea was shot down pretty fast. So, they are sending Kelvin with me."

"I bet Levi's not too happy about that," Clay added.

"Ohhhh no," Megan replied, making a funny face. "He was even worse than you about it, actually," she said as she stuffed two boxes of 9MM into her bag.

"You know why that is, right?" Clay asked, immediately regretting the decision to open that can of worms.

"Clayton, I am a lot of things, and I am doing a lot of things, but I *am* a woman and I am not stupid. Just because I haven't thought about that kind of stuff in a long, *long* time, doesn't mean I am oblivious to it. I mean he's not exactly subtle. I've never met a man who wants to help do dishes just because he 'likes doing dishes.'"

"Well...good point. He actually brought it up with me back home...or maybe I brought it up with him, I don't remember. But, if I recall correctly, I more or less told him to just man up and talk to you about it already."

Megan whipped a sweatshirt through the air before folding it up. "Yep. That's all I am waiting for."

After an awkward moment of silence, Clay said, "Well, I think I've had enough girl talk for the night." He started to walk out of the room before stopping. He turned around and hugged his sister tight. "You be safe out there, kid," he said.

Megan's eyes were glossy. "You, too, Clay." Megan stepped back, the tears were running down her cheeks now. "I suspect we're going to be gone for a few weeks—we're going to be going out at least fifty miles, probably further. You better be here when I get back."

"I'll be here...love ya, sis."

Clay turned and walked out of Megan's bedroom and headed for his own. He lay down in his bed to try and shake the headache, but all he could think about was Megan going out for such a long trip. Clay was confident in Kelvin's ability as a soldier and knew that he would likely do a fine job at keeping Megan safe. But at the same time, to what extent would he be willing to sacrifice himself to keep her alive? Having only just met him in the past few weeks, Clay couldn't be sure that he wouldn't take off if things got too hot—at least not enough to bet his sister's life on it.

Ignoring the throbs in his head, Clay got to his feet, grabbed his coat, and left the house. After a few minutes of walking, he found himself at the doorstep of Mayor Shelton's temporary residence. Clay rapped on the door and Shelton quickly answered and invited Clay to get out of the frigid temperatures.

"Why didn't you talk to me first, Barry?" Clay said as he stomped inside, a fiery edge in his voice.

"I'm sorry, Clay. I kind of figured you'd be upset, but Captain Kohler was insistent you sit this one out. He finds you to be a valuable asset on the battlefield and didn't want to lose you for such a long period of time."

"That's not his decision to make," Clay said.

"I don't like the idea either, but I am *trying* not to let my personal feelings get in the way of him doing his job. He is the only man here who spent fifteen years in the Army; he knows what he is doing when it comes to this stuff. I don't." Shelton took off his glasses and rubbed his eyes before putting them back on. "It's hard to know where to draw that line. This isn't the Army and y'all aren't soldiers. But, I *have* been hampering Kohler's efforts far more than I should. That's why I didn't object to his plan to send someone else out with Megan." Shelton gave Clay a remorseful look. "And I apologize for not doing so."

Clay let his hot head cool down for a moment before replying. "Listen, Barry, I won't pretend to know what you're going through right now. I can't imagine being in your shoes, making the calls you have to make and then living with the consequences. I'm sorry you're in that boat, I really am...but this is nonnegotiable."

Shelton silently nodded.

"Listen, you know that I will stand by your side and defend this town as if it were my own..." Clay said, his head slowly turning to look out the window in the direction of Vlad's house where Megan was likely still packing for her journey tomorrow, "but my family comes first, and if they need me, I'm gonna be there for them."

"I sincerely appreciate everything you've done for us, Clay. And if you decided to just pack up and head home now, I wouldn't think any less of ya for it. Y'all have gone way beyond the call of duty for us, and—"

"I'm not going home, Barry. Megan and I *will* come back, and when we do, we'll be ready to fight. We will *not* let Liberty fall."

Chapter 27

Megan nearly jumped out of her skin when she opened the door and saw Clay standing just outside her room, a pack slung over his shoulder and a rifle in each hand.

She smacked his arm. "You scared the crap out of me, jerk!" she hissed. "What are you doing?"

Clay mockingly rubbed his arm where she had hit him. "Good thing you know how to use a gun, because you hit like a girl."

"That's because I *am* a girl," she grunted as she struck him again.

Clay gave a feigned yawn. "Anyway, being the nice guy that I am, I decided to relieve Kelvin of the daunting task of traveling with you for the next few weeks."

"Daunting task?" Megan replied, a snarky expression on her face.

"Don't think I forgot about those family vacations we took as kids. We had to stop every fifteen minutes so you could go to the bathroom, or get something to eat, or stretch your legs, blah blah blah..."

Megan recognized what Clay was doing and gave him a hug. "I love you too, brother. I'm glad you're coming with me," she said, her words washed in relief. "Everything is just so chaotic right now and to go out on such a long trip with someone I barely know..." She sighed and smiled as she looked at her brother. "I feel a lot better knowing you're coming with me instead."

"Me too," Clay said. "Well, shall we?" he asked as he handed Megan the LaRue.

Megan looked down at the rifle and then back at Clay, giving him a funny look. "You know I hate shooting that thing, right? I'd rather just use my pistol if it comes to it."

"That's fine, but you're still carrying it," Clay said with a grin, indicating with his hand for her to turn around.

"What am I, your donkey?" she quipped as she spun her back to him.

"Hey, you said it, not me."

Megan rolled her eyes as she took off her backpack. "Fine, whatever. I'll carry your gun since it's clearly too heavy for you," Megan said in a mocking tone.

Clay laughed as he put the sling around her neck and shoulder, adjusting for comfort.

"How's that feel?" Clay asked after he put her backpack back on.

Megan shifted her body back and forth and took a few steps. "Hardly notice it, actually."

"Good," he responded as he put his ARAK-21's sling over his neck. "All right, we need to get out of here before the sun comes up."

Clay and Megan walked downstairs and heard the sounds of hushed voices. "Guess Bravo team had watch last night, huh?" Clay said as he saw the group of men and women taking gear off in the living room.

"Yep. And it's a cold one, too, so bundle up," a man called Hopkins replied.

Hopkins wasn't kidding. When Clay first stepped outside the door, he was nearly dazed by the chilled blast of air. "For crying out loud, we were outside playing baseball only a month or so ago," Clay said as they started walking toward the command post for a quick brief with Kohler.

"Strange weather for strange times, little brother."

Clay used his breath to warm up the insides of his gloves before jamming his cold hands into them. "Well, if that ain't the understatement of the century..."

As they made their way through town, Clay appreciated the relatively clear moonlit night, gazing upon the rare sight of a crisp moon. The giant rock floating in the sky provided him with some much-needed respite from the whirlwind of anxiety battering his thoughts. The view was peaceful and calming.

As they turned onto Pecan Street, Clay spotted Captain Kohler already waiting for them on the front porch. "Come on inside, you guys. This won't take long," he said as they walked briskly toward the porch.

"Yes, sir," Clay replied as he and Megan jogged up the stairs and through the door Kohler held open.

Kohler spread out a folded map onto his dining room table. With only a few candles giving light to the room, Kohler clicked on a flashlight to illuminate the map. "This is a map marking off the areas we've picked clean over the years. Unfortunately, it's not great news for you two. As you can see, it's nothing but red X's for the first forty klicks or so.

"Since we *suspect* that Arlo's camp is to the south, we're going to have you moving north. You might find a few things here and there, but it's going to be pretty sparse until you get up to about here," he said as he motioned out a circle with his finger just south of a small town that was barely large enough to be worth the ink on the map. "I know that somewhere up here..." Kohler slid his finger a few inches north of the town, "there was a FEMA camp."

Clay pointed to a very specific spot on that map, "Actually, it's right here." Kohler gave him a strange look. "I'm familiar with the area," Clay added with a grim look on his face.

"Very well," Kohler continued. "Those camps would have been well stocked with food, ammo, and medical supplies, but I'm not holding my breath that you'll find much. However, those camps *were* pretty massive, so you might get lucky. The bad news is that you might end up spending a few days picking through scraps with nothing to show for it. So, you'll have to make that call when you're on location."

Clay nodded. "Got it," he said, knowing full well he and Megan wouldn't bother searching the grounds. Smith would have snatched up anything of value a long time ago; it would be a waste of precious time to expand on the dead man's efforts.

"Anything in particular you want me to keep an eye out for?" Clay asked.

"Well, not that you wouldn't grab it if you saw it, but our magazine situation is less than great. Any AR magazines would be a huge help. Then, obviously, some five-five-six and nine mil would do us a lot of good. But really," Kohler said as he started to fold the map up, "you know what you're doing. Anything that will give us an advantage in this war is worth bringing back." He handed the map to Clay. "Good luck, you two. Be careful, be quick, and be safe." Kohler stuck his hand out.

Clay shook Kohler's hand. "Thank you, sir," he said as he put the map in his coat pocket. "We'll be back as soon as we can."

"Oh, one more thing," Kohler said as he walked to his living room and picked up a strange looking rifle. "Take this. I know it's added weight, but it may very well come in handy."

Clay looked at the rifle—it was something he had never seen before.

"It's an M6 Scout rifle," Kohler said before showing Clay how it worked. He then folded it in half and stuck it inside Clay's pack along with a small amount of ammo.

"Thanks!" Clay said before turning around and heading for the door.

As Clay and Megan stepped out onto the porch, a shadowy figure limped toward them.

"Oh good! I'm so glad I caught you before you left—I thought I had missed you for sure," Levi said as he hobbled up the steps. "I have something for you." He held out a medium-sized thermos and tilted it toward Megan. "First round grounds."

Megan snatched the metal canister from his hand and quickly unscrewed the lid. The steamy aroma wafted into her nose as she soaked in every molecule of the heavenly scent. "Coffee!" she nearly shouted. "I could so kiss you right now, Levi."

Clay thought the comment was a bit callous considering Megan knew how Levi felt about her, but then she put her hands on Levi's face and gave him a passionate kiss. After several awkward seconds, Clay cleared his throat. "Manned up, did we?"

Levi pulled away from Megan just long enough to glare at Clay before giving Megan another kiss.

"Seriously?" Clay interrupted. "I really don't want to start this trip by ralphing up my measly breakfast."

Megan looked back at her brother, giving a much harsher glare than Levi had. "Shut up, Clay!" she said, sounding more like an embarrassed schoolgirl than his wise-beyond-her-years sister.

"*Please* be safe," Levi pleaded pulling Megan's attention back to him.

"I promise," she said.

Levi's eyes shifted over to Clay. "You too, Clay. Please take good care of her," he added.

Another sarcastic response neared the tip of his tongue, but "You know I will," was the only appropriate response to that appeal. This trip was not something to joke about. Of the thousands of journeys, big and small, that Clay had taken over the last decade, this one was by far the most dangerous, *and* the least likely to succeed. He knew it. Megan knew it. And Levi knew it.

Megan noticed a hint of light breaking across the horizon. "Well, we better get going," she said to Levi. "You stay safe, too. Remember to keep off that ankle as much as you can."

Levi nodded. "They have me stationed out in centerfield from now on; not much activity out there usually," he said as he embraced his new love one last time. "I'll see you in a few weeks."

Megan smiled as she turned and walked away, Clay joining her. Levi remained motionless and watched until their silhouettes were consumed by the fading darkness.

DeMarcus hopped out of his foxhole as he saw Clay and Megan approaching. Clay noticed Brendan's VEPR-12 slung over his back—he was happy to see the Russian shotgun was now playing for their team. "You guys all set?" the tall, muscular man asked.

"As ready as we can be," Clay said through a yawn—sleep had been evasive.

"Torrez!" DeMarcus called.

A short, stocky man jogged over, a small mesh sack in his hand. "We heard what you guys were doing, and, well, it's not much but we all set aside a few of our rations for ya," the man said as he handed the bag to Megan.

"That is so sweet, you guys...thank you so much," Megan said as she fought back tears. Small glimpses of humanity like shared rations in such cold-hearted times were what kept her going. The people of Liberty were truly remarkable, and it was a pleasant reminder of why she volunteered to stay in the first place.

"Appreciate it, fellas," Clay said as he nodded at both men. "Would love to stay and chat, but time's a bit of a factor here. Where can we sneak out?"

"Right over here," DeMarcus said as he turned and walked. "It's gonna be a tight squeeze, so I hope you didn't eat a big breakfast."

"A big breakfast?" Clay asked. "What's that?"

DeMarcus chuckled. "I hear that," he said as the three of them passed a heavily manned foxhole about forty feet from the fence. "A'ight, I think y'all gonna need to take your packs and guns off," he said as he looked at the small gap between the northern and eastern fence line. Then studying Clay before glancing back at the fence, he said, "I dunno if you gonna fit, man. We might have to find another way."

Clay walked up and inspected the gap himself. "I've been in tighter places," he said recalling Dusty's kit-bashed maze at the school gymnasium.

"Well, all right then. Let's do this," DeMarcus said as he helped Clay take his pack, rifle, and chest rig off. "Better suck in that gut."

Clay laughed at the irony of DeMarcus's statement as he turned sideways and started to shimmy through the opening. He led with his head and then his shoulder. All clear so far. His chest was where things went sour, however. By using all his strength in addition to a few solid pushes from the outside linebacker, Clay was able to get through to the other side.

"Yeah, that was a lot of fun," Clay said sarcastically as DeMarcus handed him the rifle and chest rig.

"I'll have to take your word for it," DeMarcus replied. "I think I'mma have to hand you your pack over the top, it's too big to fit through."

With the extra food, ammo, spare duffle bag, and a subzero sleeping bag crammed into his pack, it was twice as thick as Clay was. "All right, I'm ready."

DeMarcus handed the pack to Clay before turning his attention to Megan. "Your turn, cutie," he said with a smile as he took her pack and rifle.

"Don't be flirting with my sister right in front of me, dude. You may be twice my size but I'll still jack you up," Clay joked.

"Your sister?" DeMarcus said, brushing off the laughable threat. "I didn't know that. She's *way* too good lookin' to have you for a brother," he said. "Or wait, was that offensive? Maybe I should've said, you too ugly to have a sister this good lookin'," he laughed.

"Oh, haha. Got ourselves a jokester here," Clay replied.

"I do what I can."

As the banter subsided, Megan slid through the gap with little effort.

"You made that look way too easy," Clay said jealously.

Megan grabbed her rifle from DeMarcus while Clay reached up to grab her pack over the top of the fence. As Clay helped her with the rifle and pack, Megan finally replied, "Maybe it's time to cut out the Twinkies and Mountain Dew from your diet."

Clay licked his lips. "You better watch it, I'd trade my own sister for that spongy goodness right about now," he said.

"Okay, you two, give 'em hell," DeMarcus said, his face peeking between the four-by-four fence posts.

"Will do. Thanks, DeMarcus. Keep this place in one piece while we're gone," Clay replied.

The descent into the creek bed was difficult and slow. One misplaced step could have ended the trip before it began. Less than gracefully, Clay and Megan managed the hill without falling or making too much noise. As they approached the stream, ice began to crackle beneath their feet, indicating they had reached the bank.

"No...No way, Clay. I'm not joining the polar bear club this morning," Megan said adamantly.

In the interest of time, Clay had just planned on braving the ice-cold waters of the creek to get their journey underway. Megan's protest, however, was not unwarranted. In fact, it was the only logical approach. Starting their day with hypothermia due to bullheadedness was nothing short of lunacy.

The rising sun slightly improved visibility in the shallow ravine, allowing Clay to spot a downed tree a small hike away. "All right, follow me," Clay said as he headed for the tree. After buckling his ankle twice on the rough terrain, Clay reluctantly slowed his pace and carefully thought through each step.

The tree itself was not very wide, maybe six inches thick. It wasn't exactly like walking a tight rope but offered little room for mistakes, especially in pre-dawn lighting. The end of the tree was on the ground on their side of the stream, but the trunk was five or six feet up a hill on the opposite side. It would be an upward walk across the fallen timber that looked as if it had been dead for some time. Clay placed his size eleven boot on the tree and gave it several good shakes; it seemed sturdy enough. "All right, here's the deal," Clay said matter-of-factly. "I'll go first. If it holds me, it'll hold you. If it doesn't hold...well, we don't have a whole lot of time left, so we'd be getting wet either way."

"Okay," Megan acknowledged.

Clay stepped up onto the tree and inched forward. Keeping his balance while navigating around the many smaller branches proved to be challenging, but, fortunately, most of the remaining branches only jutted out a few inches. Nevertheless, stepping on one of the seemingly insignificant nubs could easily result in an icy bath. The branches trailed off as Clay neared the shore and the trunk widened slightly. The final few feet were a breeze, so Clay picked up his pace until the tree cracked—something he felt more than he heard. He immediately froze and assessed the situation. He was about four or five feet from the bank.

"What's wrong?" Megan asked as loudly as she dared.

Clay took another few steps—it was still solid. "Nothing," he said as he moved forward again, this time a bit more cautiously. He crouched down and hopped off while still grasping to the tree with one arm to soften the impact on the rocky creek bed below.

After a long sigh of relief, Clay called to Megan, "Okay, you're up."

Megan was wrought with hesitation, but as the sky grew brighter around her, she knew there was no time to hesitate. She stepped up and made her way across, nimbly traversing the craggily branches on the midsection of the tree, once again making Clay shake his head with how easy his sister made the task look. She was past the branches and almost across when a loud crack ripped through the silent morning air echoing through the shallow canyon. Megan let out a short but loud screech.

"Megan!" Clay gasped as he moved toward her.

The tree's sudden shift caused Megan to stumble forward. Destined to get a mouthful of bark, and probably some serious stitches, her instincts kicked in and she pushed her feet off the tree leaping for the shoreline. Everything happened so quickly that Clay barely prevented her from smacking her head into the rocks, but not before she banged her knees on the same jagged rocks. Megan grunted as she suppressed a painful scream.

"Are you okay?" Clay asked frantically. Megan didn't respond as she examined the damage to her knees. "Megan?"

"I'm fine, Clay," Megan said, irritation permeated her voice. "Cut and sore, but I'll be fine."

Relieved she was not seriously hurt, Clay seized the opportunity to take a shot back at his sister. "You were saying something about me and Twinkies…?"

Megan stood up and got in Clay's face, "You better watch it, bub," she said sternly letting Clay know that even the apocalypse was not an okay time to make jokes about a woman's weight. Finally, Megan let a chuckle escape. "Oh, Clay," she said with a faux whine in her voice, "Think it's too late for McCreary to go for me?" she said half-jokingly.

If only she had listened to me yesterday. Clay thought. "Brace yourself, Megs, we've got a long road ahead of us."

Chapter 28

With every strand of muscle screaming loudly, Kelsey finally climbed into bed, careful not to disturb Charles, who had already been asleep for hours. With a wobbly exhale fleeing her exhausted lungs, Kelsey attempted to clear her mind and find sleep. But, once again, sleep had no desire to be found.

Idleness at Northfield was never an option, but with the farm's population exploding to nearly three hundred overnight, the demand for productivity had never been greater. With each house filled with enough people to give a safety inspector a stroke, and a food supply that would last, at best, through the end of the month, Kelsey's thoughts, when there was enough time to have some of her own, were warped with anxiety. Throw in her concerns for her husband and sister-in-law on top of everything else, Kelsey had the perfect antidote for sleeping.

She wondered how much longer Clay would be away—if he would ever come back at all. She wondered if he did come back, would a lifeless village that had surrendered to starvation weeks before his arrival greet him? How would he cope with the loss? What if *nobody* makes it through this time? Each one leaving this life wondering if their loved ones would already be there, waiting for them on the other side. Morbidly, a part of her hoped for the latter, so that she and her family could, at last, leave this forbidding world behind.

Kelsey coughed into the crook of her arm, trying her best to stifle the sound. Each cough reminded her body of the hard day of labor she had endured. And they were now completely out of pain medication.

With a limitless sum of issues vying for Kelsey's attention, it was Mrs. Hawthorne that currently occupied her mind. Hawthorne, the closest thing she had to a mother, was not doing well. Though the stubborn lady played down the concerns, Kelsey saw through the façade. She had lost weight, had a harder time getting around, and struggled to keep her breath at times. Kelsey wasn't as medically in tune as Megan or even Lona, but she didn't need to be a doctor to recognize the signs—especially having seen it so many times in the past. And to make matters worse, due to the increase in responsibilities around the house and farm, Kelsey spent less and less time with her dear friend, as well as her own children.

She managed to shove the bleak concerns of Hawthorne's health out of her head, but those thoughts were replaced with an equally, if not grimmer issue: Madeline. Kelsey knew the agony in her eyes—she herself had seen the world through the same malevolent tinted lenses before. But the girl refused to talk about it, or anything, which was the only way Kelsey had been able to pull out of the same spiral Madeline was in. Not wanting to push her too hard while also not letting her stew in an all-consuming hatred, Kelsey did everything she could to help alleviate Madeline's suffering—Madeline just had to let her.

Over the past few weeks, Kelsey's optimism faded—both from a lack of progress with Madeline as well as her own demons terrorizing every conscious thought. At times, she just wanted to walk away. How could she sit there and tell a girl who had been through the worst kind of hell on earth that there was hope when she wasn't sure how much longer hope would be around? She was being a hypocrite.

Kelsey loved Clay; of that there was no doubt. In fact, it was Clay that had given her the hope she needed to carry on with a smile, to believe things would get better. Someday. But even Clay's optimism seemed to be getting consumed by darkness over the past few months.

I don't know how much longer I can do this, Kelsey thought as the tears splashed off her pillow. The stress of it all had become too much for the young woman to bear. As the tears continued to slide down her dirty cheeks, she forced herself to silence her sobs. It wasn't the good, hard cry she desperately needed, but for now, it would have to do.

She was startled to feel a small hand grasp her own. Charles never woke, but it was as if he knew his mother needed to experience his gentle, loving touch to remind her why she would wake up after a few restless hours of sleep and do it all over again. Why she continued to fight despite her desire to admit defeat. The serene peace brought by the touch of the toddler also carried her to sleep.

Honest to God sleep.

****

Shelton sat in his chair, his fingers drumming the flaky leather armrest as he stared down the front door. It had been two hours since he heard the last shot fire, and he was still in the dark. And he *hated* that.

The sound of boots scuffing off the front porch stirred him from his drowsy state. The door opened and Kohler walked inside, a fresh dusting of snow building up on his hat and shoulders. After a couple of stomps on the floor mat, Kohler walked into the living room.

"How bad?" Shelton asked, not bothering to stand from his chair.

Kohler walked across the room and stood at attention while warming himself by the fire. "We lost two more."

"Who?"

"Evans and McCreary."

"McCreary?" Shelton asked with surprise. "I thought we moved him to the infirmary."

"Yes sir, he was attempting to render aid to Evans when he was hit by sniper fire."

Shelton squeezed his eyes shut, but when they opened again, he was still in his living room and the news was just as bad. "How many snipers does Arlo have?" Shelton asked in frustration.

"Not many people are consistently *that* good. Nearly twenty percent of our losses have come from a sharpshooter, and I am starting to think it's just the one shooter."

Shelton looked up at Kohler, "We have to do something about him, then."

"I already have a team working on it, sir. We'll get him."

Shelton gave a weak nod. "Well, how many of them did we get?" Shelton asked, as if it really mattered. Arlo's army seemed to respawn back at base.

"As far as we can tell..." Kohler trailed off, reluctant to finish his sentence. "None, sir."

"None?" Shelton asked in disbelief.

"Yes sir, there were no *confirmed* kills tonight."

Seemingly impossible, Shelton managed to sink further down into his chair. His face twisted with a grim expression and released a heavy sigh. After several silent moments passed, Shelton finally asked, "Consumption?"

"It was estimated to be between 350 to 500 rifle and around seventy-five pistol."

"And at that rate..."

"We'll have nothing but empty boxes by December—and that's being overly optimistic. If we keep burning through our ammunition, Arlo can sit back and send in the fodder until we're left throwing rocks. Then, all he has to do is let himself in."

Kohler's SITREP was about as bad as it could get. But he wasn't finished.

"I also just got word that the boy—the one Clay carried in from the corridor—died this evening."

Shelton was both furious and guilt-ridden with the news of the boy's death. He wanted nothing more than to climb the stairs and hide in bed the rest of the night. Unfortunately, that wasn't going to be happening anytime soon.

"Permission to speak freely?" Kohler asked.

"Daniel, I'm not some high-ranking officer, and this isn't the army. You don't need to ask for permission to tell me something that I'm obviously not going to want to hear."

Kohler took his hat off, the very same one he wore around the barracks in Raqqa, and ran his thumb across the front of the bill. It had become a tick he had developed to deal with post-combat stress after his squad came back from an assignment. "Sir...Barry...even if Clay and Megan come back with as much of a resupply as they can both physically carry..." he trailed off. "Short of them driving up to the gates in a Panzer, I'm not sure there's going to be a way for us to win this. Not while we're constantly on our heels."

"What are you suggesting we do then, Captain?" Shelton asked.

"We need to come up with some contingency plans, most importantly how to evac everyone, including the wounded, at a moment's notice, and bring as much as we possibly can."

"We've already been over that."

"Call me crazy, Barry, but I don't think waving the white flag and handing Arlo the keys will do the trick anymore. I believe that ship has sailed; he's not going to let us just walk away now. Listen, when—*if*—you decide it's time for us to abandon our posts, we will need to do it in a hurry... and undetected."

Shelton stewed in a myriad of emotions. Even failure itself would come with a set of challenges to overcome. After a lengthy sigh, Shelton pulled himself out of his chair and walked over to his friend of many years. "Go ahead and come up with some contingency plans and bring them to me by the end of the week."

Kohler nodded. "Yes sir." He put his hat back on his head and looked Shelton in the eyes. "Get some rest, Barry. You look like you haven't slept in days."

"Try weeks," the weary, old man said. As Kohler headed for the door, Shelton added. "One more thing, Captain..."

"Sir?" Kohler said, returning to soldier mode.

"While you're coming up with the contingency plans, see if you can't come up with some ideas to get us off our heels."

A glimmer of fire in Shelton's eyes gave Kohler a boost of confidence. "Yes sir!" Kohler said, giving a salute before walking out of the house.

Chapter 29

With a loud crash, the butt of Clay's rifle shattered the sidelight of the front door. He reached in and felt around for the deadbolt lock. After successfully unlatching the deadbolt, but unsuccessfully opening the door, he discovered that there was a wedge jammed beneath the door—a trick he had used more than a few times. Megan stood behind him with her back to Clay, her pistol drawn and her head constantly rotating. Clay walked past her, heading toward the parking lot.

"What's up?" she asked.

"Need to find something long enough to reach behind the door on the inside," Clay said as he swiped some snow off a car window and looked inside before moving to the trunk.

Megan joined the effort and searched through the very few cars left in the rural office building's parking lot. Neither of them had high hopes of finding anything useful inside the dilapidated agriculture lawyer's office, but they did need a place to sleep for the night. And since the points of entry all seemed to be intact, Clay felt comfortable calling the place home for the next ten hours.

Finding a military thriller on the passenger seat of an old Volvo, Clay stuck it in his pack to read later. Though the paperback wouldn't help him open the front door, literature—particularly fictions—that hadn't been consumed by the elements were always a nice find.

Clay turned as he heard the snow crunching beneath Megan's feet. "Will a three-wood work?" Megan asked, holding up the dusty club.

Clay took the golf club out of her hands and extended his arm, gauging the overall length. He pressed his lips together and nodded, "Yeah, that might do the trick," he said as he headed back to the front door.

Megan kept guard while Clay maneuvered the club through the broken sidelight and pushed at the old plastic wedge. The years of grime and mud caked around it had cemented the thing to the floor, but after a few powerful and angry whacks, Clay was able to knock it loose before shoving it out of the way. A few shoulder rams later, the door was open and they walked inside. Once they were inside, Clay returned the wedge to its place beneath the door and scattered a few papers on top of it so that if someone else tried to get in the same way they had, the doorstop wouldn't be obvious.

Clay did a quick sweep of the office to ensure nobody else had taken up residence inside. Being a bit more lackadaisical with his search than usual, Clay cleared the place in record timing. If someone else *had* been inside, Clay and Megan would have heard about it as soon as he busted out the windowpane.

When the office was officially clear, Clay decided to barricade the front door; he was quite uncomfortable with the security provided by a door wedge next to a broken window. Together, Clay and Megan pushed a heavy bookshelf over to the door. With the side of the shelf blocking the sidelight *and* a portion of the door, it ensured entry would be a very difficult and noisy process. One that would afford Clay more than enough time to greet the unwanted guests with a few .30 caliber-sized warnings.

While searching the office space for anything useful, Clay came across a square, metal bar with two curved bolts sticking out of either end. After investigating it further, he discovered that it was a door lock that fit the rear fire-exit door, making it virtually impossible to open while in place. Even though the heavy gauge steel door was securely locked, a little bit of time, a prybar, and proper motivation to get inside would've popped it open. However, by dropping the door lock into place, Clay had turned the little farm attorney's office into a decent fortress. And with the only windows being smaller and high off the ground, Clay found it to be protected enough to let his guard down. A little.

"You find anything yet?" Megan asked as she opened a filing cabinet, peeking inside.

"Nothing worth writing home about," Clay replied. "You?"

"Just a couple cigar butts and an empty bottle of Jack."

Clay stood in the middle of the large office and looked around. In addition to the token degrees, attorney certifications, and various community awards hanging on the wall, there was a rather large longhorn skull mounted behind the desk with a few hog heads flanking either side. There were a few personal pictures Clay assumed were the lawyer on various hunting and fishing trips just beneath one of the room's two windows.

"You check the desk yet?" Clay asked.

"Not yet."

Clay walked over and pulled one of the drawers open. Not much. He placed a letter opener on top of the desk and moved his search to the next drawer down. It was more useless than the first. The rest of the drawers were similarly useless.

He reached for the wide, middle drawer and tugged, but it was locked. *A lock is always a good sign,* he thought. He pulled a prybar out of his pack and made light work of the old desk's latch. The drawer slid open and Clay immediately saw an orange bottle roll to the front of the drawer. He picked it up and shook it; three pills dancing around inside.

"What is that?" Megan asked cautiously optimistic.

Clay clicked on his flashlight and aimed it at the bottle. "Hydromor…uhhh," he said, struggling to read the faded label.

"Hydromorphone?" Megan replied, excitement inflating each syllable.

Clay shrugged. "Maybe, I can't really read it," he said as he tossed her the bottle.

Megan examined the label closely and then opened the top to look at the pills inside. "I'll have to check with Doctor Sowell when we get back, but this is excellent! It's not much, but if it's still potent, it could make a major difference in someone's life, at least momentarily. Good find, little brother."

A smile crept across Clay's face over the excitement in her voice. Apart from a few smaller things like bandages and a wrist splint, they hadn't found much yet. Though, the lack of supplies was not at all unexpected since they were still within the marked zones on the map. So, *any* find was a welcomed surprise; some painkillers were a post-ash jackpot.

Clay pulled the drawer open even further, revealing two plastic baggies-full of pills. He lifted one up and examined it; at least four different types of pills inside. "Well, I'm no pharmacist, but something tells me these aren't vitamins," he said as he held up the bag for Megan to see.

Megan's jaw hung open like it had detached from her skull. "Holy crap," she muttered through a gasp before rushing over to the desk.

She grabbed the bag and looked inside. "That one is Oxy, for sure," she said with a huge grin on her face as she pointed to one of the pills. "I have to imagine the others are going to be generics or similar opioids."

"Well, somehow I doubt our good friend," Clay paused and looked down at the bent, metal plague on the desk, "Donald Thurston, Esquire, was pedaling allergy meds on the side, so I imagine you're right."

"This is an amazing find, Clay! I can't believe it," Megan said as she looked at the second bag still in the drawer. "We just hit the jackpot!"

Clay gave an enthusiastic thumbs-up.

"Seriously, Clay, this is huge. And while I certainly hope this isn't the case, but if we find nothing else on this trip, medically speaking, it will still be counted a success."

Fueled from the find, Clay and Megan continued their hunt in the office.

"So, why do you think he never used the drugs?" Megan asked.

"Who? Our friendly pill-pushing lawyer friend? Who knows. Maybe he was, but then decided to take a stroll a little too late at night," Clay said, not the slightest bit bothered with the attorney's likely demise. "I wonder if he tried to plea with his murderers, promising them a nice high in exchange for his life," Clay said indifferently.

Megan gave him a strange look before he turned around and started peeking behind some of the picture frames on the wall. One in particular seemed to rest strangely against the damp drywall. It was a picture of the lawyer with another man, each one hoisting up an impressive largemouth. There was an inscription on a brass plate at the bottom of the wooden frame.

Me and Mayor Pruett
Choke Canyon – Memorial Day 2016

"Looks like those were better days for you, Mr. Thurston," Clay said under his breath as he removed the picture frame from the wall, unveiling a small wall safe with the door popped open.

Clay's hopes of another score were quickly dashed when all he found inside was stacks of cash, mostly tens and twenties, and an empty box of .380 along with some drug paraphernalia.

"Wanna buy a yacht?" Clay asked as he tossed a few thousand dollars-worth of bills over his shoulder.

Though the use of paper bills had gone out of style within the first year of the disaster, the instinct to dive across the room and snatch up the cash was still one Megan had to resist. "Anything a little more useful in our current economic climate?" she asked.

"Just an empty box of shells and a few hypodermic needles."

"Are they still in packages?"

Clay shook his head.

Megan sighed. "We're already sterilizing what few needles we have back in the infirmary, but I don't feel particularly comfortable throwing an addict's personal stash into the mix."

"Not gonna hear an argument from me," Clay noted.

The room grew darker as the sun dropped lower into the sky. Clay pulled a dynamo lantern out of his pack and gave it several dozen cranks before turning it on and placing it on the desk. It wasn't particularly bright, but would give them enough light to continue their search with the aid of their flashlights. Unfortunately, the rest of the office was not nearly as exciting as the find in the desk, yielding just a few smaller things that might end up being discarded in the event they run out of space.

Content that they had thoroughly searched the building, Clay and Megan settled in for the night. Clay groaned as he slowly made his way to the floor and leaned up against the wall. He grimaced as he leaned forward to unlace his boots. "I'm getting too old for this."

Megan plopped down in the executive chair behind the desk. She blew her bangs out of her face. "I don't know how you do this so much," she said as she leaned back in the chair, her head hanging over the back. "It's been, what, three days? And I'm already ready to be back home."

Clay pulled a sock off and examined a rather painful blister on the ball of his foot. "Well, my body's not as conditioned for it as it once was, but you'll get used to it—after a few months."

"No, thank you," Megan immediately replied. "You can give me a broken bone to set or flesh to stitch back together, but make me walk a hundred miles and I'm likely going to kill someone," she said with a chuckle.

"You'll probably do that by the end of this trip, anyway," Clay said.

"Which one?"

Clay let out a yawn as his body began to relax for the first time in nearly twelve hours. "Both."

Chapter 30

"Make sure you keep an eye out for that sniper. Captain Kohler is pretty hellbent on us finding him," Dusty said.

"Will do," Morgan replied as she scanned the horizon of trees ahead of her with a pair of binoculars.

Things had been quiet over the past couple of days. An increase in snowfall and decrease in temperature likely played a role in the lack of activity. Nobody in town was complaining over the temporary reprieve, though. Being gassed from the sustained attacks over the past few weeks, everyone needed a bit of downtime.

"So, I've got a question," Morgan spoke up.

Since becoming a spotter for her, Dusty had taught Morgan as much as she could. Everything from tactical movements to windage, field dressing a deer to starting a fire with sticks. Arriving at Liberty shortly after the collapse, Morgan had been shielded from the worst of the worst, giving her the opportunity to still focus on being a kid. It wasn't that she was incompetent when it came to fighting and surviving, but the two girls grew up in two very different worlds and Dusty was far more seasoned at survival than Morgan. But, as Dusty quickly learned, just because Morgan lacked experience did not mean she lacked the necessary grit to survive in such an unforgiving world. In that regard, Morgan gave Dusty a run for her money.

"What's up?" Dusty asked, glancing over at her friend.

"If you could choose *any* guy to date, past or present, and, you know, things weren't all war and snow and stuff...who would it be?" Morgan asked, suppressing a giggle.

Dusty let out a long, drawn out sigh. "Just tell me if you see that sniper," she said, ignoring the slumber party inquiry.

"*I will*..." Morgan said, looking back through the binoculars. "So, who would it be?"

She was relentless.

Dusty initially balked at the question. It was the type of sixteen-year-old-girl talk that Dusty typically made fun of. But she was scared to answer. Not because she didn't have an answer, but because she had never found herself in a position she felt comfortable enough to let her guard down so much. She had never had the sisterly friendship with another girl like she now had with Morgan. It felt both terrifying, yet warmly inviting.

"Come on, I know there has to be one," Morgan pressed.

Dusty tried to hide her smile as she shook her head.

"Just get it over with," Morgan said. "You're practically lighting up the room with those rosy cheeks of yours."

A quiet chuckle left Dusty's mouth. "Ugh," Dusty growled with a fake frustration. "Chris Pratt, okay? There! Are you happy now?" she said, her smile growing a little wider.

"See? That wasn't so bad. So, my next question would be, who's Chris Pratt?" Morgan asked.

Dusty shrugged. "I dunno, some actor or something. I saw a cardboard cutout of him at a movie theater a few months back."

"Wait...is he the guy in that dinosaur movie?"

"Yeah, that's him."

"Oh, yeah, I remember seeing a poster of him once. Yummy," Morgan added. "I was going to say Bradley Cooper, but I might have to change my answer to Pratt, as well."

"No way; get your own fake boyfriend!" Dusty fired back.

The clock tower erupted in hushed giggles and a volley of "shut ups" as the two carried on with conversations Dusty never dreamed she would willingly have, much less actually enjoy. It felt...nice to be a sixteen-year-old girl for once, and not just a survivor—even if it was just for a few minutes, as the conversation callously dropped them back down in reality.

"Do you still miss your parents?" Morgan asked, a grief-stricken expression plastered on her face.

The answer should have been obvious to Dusty, but the words didn't come as easily as she had hoped. "Yeah," she said, the response sounding more like a question than a statement. "I mean I guess I do. I was pretty young when they died, so it's hard to remember a whole lot about them. And it wasn't like either of them were up for parent of the year…" she trailed off as she racked her brain for some fond memories; they were few and far between, all coming before the eruption. "They tried, in their own, strange ways, to take care of me, I guess."

Dusty's strange, non-answer confused Morgan. "They sound like they were pretty…unique?"

"Yeah, that'd be putting it mildly. Let's just say, they weren't cut out for living in *this* world."

Morgan nodded solemnly. She didn't know which was worse: the heartache from losing a loving family or being almost unfazed by it. "I really miss my mom," Morgan said. "I mean I miss my dad and brother, too, but I've had time to mourn their deaths. But my mom…she and I had never been all that close, and once Dad and Ian died, all we had left was each other. Over the last year, we had gotten pretty close." Morgan looked back through the binoculars to hide her glassy eyes. As much as she had rubbed off on Dusty to be more of a girly girl, Dusty had rubbed off on her as well, and she felt embarrassed to reveal her tears to her friend. "So, yeah, I miss them…a lot," she said with a wavering whisper.

The tree line shimmered and swayed as the tears slowly drained from Morgan's eyes. She blinked rapidly to help speed the process along, but to no avail. Suddenly, a bright, yellow blob flashed brilliantly in her vision. Her mind hadn't finished asking the question, *What was that,* when she heard the shot.

"Sniper!" Dusty shouted in vain, as seconds later, she heard someone screaming for a medic; yet another soldier had fallen prey to Arlo's predator.

Dusty frantically searched for the shooter, but had to abandon her efforts as a wave of soldiers exited the trees and sprinted toward town. Working the bolt of her rifle at impossible speed, Dusty took multiple shots at a group of attackers, forcing them to seek cover behind a garbage truck on the side of the road. Morgan, equipped with a Kel-Tec SU-16, also engaged the enemy. Each pull of the trigger inside the clock tower rattled their heads as they tried to beat back the onslaught.

A close call from a barrage of bullets compelled Dusty and Morgan to move to the back of the room and keep their heads down. They were both panting as several more bullets hissed overhead, striking the back wall.

Morgan looked at Dusty, her eyes were wide and filled with hope. "I saw the flash!"

Chapter 31

Clay was struck with the same sensation walking through the forest as he had experienced the first time: suffocating anxiety. And the foggy snow only antagonized that trepidation. Megan's shaky breathing and incessant need to check over her shoulder told Clay she felt it, too. The eerie forest was like a brown and white ocean, splayed out as far as the eye could see in every direction.

A gust of wind ripped through the trees up ahead, bringing every plant to life—big and small—with a disturbing, almost demonic dance. Then came the ominous howl as the squall slithered between the trees, causing the hair on Clay's neck to stiffen. The creepy moans from the woods were sporadically disrupted with the sharp crack of a snapping limb screeching toward the ground, ending with a hollow thud as it burrowed into the accumulating snow.

"We need to get out of here, Clay," Megan said with a tremble in her voice.

AJ POWERS

Clay kept his eyes forward, scanning the entirety of the horizon up ahead, trying to distinguish the difference between the movement of the flora and that of a murder. "We can't turn back now, Megan. Just keep pressing forward; we'll be out soon enough."

Another loud crack—the hefty branch landing just feet away from Megan.

Her loud shriek caused Clay to jump. Clay's shushing morphed into a callous, "Shut up, Megan!" His angst, along with the frustration of Megan's lack of noise discipline, was getting the best of him.

"I'm sorry, Clay," she said, stricken with fear. "I am doing my best here, but I am not made for this kind of stuff."

"And you think I was?" Clay snapped back. "I had to figure out how to deal with this kind of crap before I was old enough to drive. And *I* had to do it alone. So, get it together, or we're both going to end up as corpses out here."

A solitary sniffle came from Megan. "I said I was sorry, Clay. I guess I am not as strong and brave as *you* are."

The guilt quickly sank in as he heard Megan's stifled whimpers. The woman was already terrified, so it only seemed logical that Clay took the opportunity to make his sister feel like a coward, too. "Megan, look...I'm sorry, I—"

"It's fine, Clay," Megan said, her words as chilly as the air.

"It's just this forest... something about it brings out a bad side of me..."

"Yeah, that must be it."

After Clay's unprovoked scolding, they walked in silence. Then they heard the first scream of the night carried in by a gust of wind. It was off in the distance

318

but caused both to kneel down, making themselves as invisible as possible. Clay looked down at his watch and brushed away the snow on the face. He tapped it a few times. "Oh, you've *got* to be kidding me!" he said through a clenched jaw.

"What?" Megan asked worriedly, her pistol drawn as she frantically looked in every direction. "What time is it? You said it was quarter after twelve when we first walked in. I know it hasn't been more than three or four hours since then, what time is it now?" she asked again.

Clay sighed deeply. "Quarter after twelve."

This was bad. Even though his watch couldn't have been all that far off, as he had looked at it just an hour or so before they arrived at the preserve, every second factored into the decision Clay had made to cut through the immense forest. He had debated whether 12:15 would be cutting it too close, let alone whatever time they had *actually* left.

"What do we do?"

Clay remained silent as he contemplated her question. Efforts for his eyes to pierce through the patchy fog encompassing them were snuffed out after about a hundred feet. It looked like a scene out of a horror movie—the kind of setting where the random, no-name actors fall prey to the villain so that the viewer would understand just how evil he was.

There was no other choice. "We keep moving," Clay said as calmly as he could, trying not to contribute to Megan's already bloated anxiety—any more than he already had, anyway. "If we can't see them, they can't see us. We move slowly and *quietly*. Stay alert and we'll be fine."

Megan nervously nodded her head. "Yeah, okay," she said, a shaky breath separating the two-word response.

Clay took a couple of deep breaths in a feeble attempt to calm his nerves. "Let's do this," he said under his breath, more to himself than to Megan, as he stood up and started walking. He kept low, and had his rifle's stock pressed snuggly into his shoulder, ready for the fight he knew would come.

But it didn't.

Although they managed to avoid contact with the Screamers, Clay and Megan were bombarded with the distant shrieks and screams of the sadists the rest of the time they walked through the forest. The psychological warfare, whether the Screamers were aware of it or not, wreaked havoc and caused Megan to hyperventilate on several occasions.

At one point, Clay found himself hoping that the maniacs would finally show up so that one way or another the barbarous saber-rattling would come to an end.

As the trees parted and the road came into view, Clay let out a deep breath he felt like he had held since they walked in. The sun had not quite set, offering them a little light to finish out the leg of the journey. Clay looked around as he got his bearings. The area was familiar, but they had not come out where he had expected. They were even closer to the camp's entrance, meaning they had walked a bit off path but to their advantage.

"Okay," Clay said. "The entrance is just a couple of miles down the road. I know the last thing you feel like doing is moving fast, but if we can keep a pretty quick pace, we'll be there before we lose daylight."

Megan's weary eyes were beyond blood shot. The girl had taken just about all she could handle for one day. Even so, as she wiped away a rogue tear that had managed to escape her eye, she agreed.

"You okay?" Clay asked.

"I'll be fine. Let's just get to this place so we can get out of the cold."

The snowfall had picked up, further muffling the distant screams and helped to subdue Clay's fears. They passed the pink car with the yellow, smiley face on the driver's door, something he remembered seeing the first time he visited Smith's compound. The still vibrant colors on the sedan stuck out in the drab world around them like an ink stain on a wedding dress.

"It should be just around the bend up ahead— only a few more minutes."

Just then, Clay heard shuffling footsteps in the snow behind him. He whipped around just in time to evade a devastating swing from a pickaxe head attached to the end of a baseball bat.

"Megan, watch out!" Clay screamed.

Megan also ducked out of the way, narrowly avoiding a deathly blow.

As Clay regained his balance, he raised his rifle and fired three shots into the attacker. The suppressed .300 sounded even quieter in the deteriorating weather, but the damage it inflicted on his target was no less destructive.

As soon as the man's body crashed to the ground, the shrieks began and several other Screamers came into view. Four from behind them and two ahead of them.

Standing back to back with her brother, all Megan could say was, "Clay?"

"You've got this Megan," Clay said, quietly encouraging his sister not to hesitate.

"Stay back!" Megan yelled, trying to make herself sound threatening, but her voice cracked under the stress.

Megan's audible fear caused the two men in front of her to laugh. One carried an Arabian sword and the other sported a homemade weapon fashioned from a pipe, circular saw blade and rusted nails.

All six men stood their ground while they gleefully discussed how much they were going to enjoy the next few minutes. The vile words they spoke twisted Megan's stomach, forcing her to swallow bile. The two men in front of her sneered as they observed the shaking gun in her hands.

"This is gonna be fun, boys," the one said, his dagger-like gaze piercing deep into Megan's soul.

"I have dibs on the girl," the smallest of the four in front of Clay said. "I bet she tastes as sweet as cherry pie on the fourth of July," he said with a thick, southern accent before swiping his tongue in front of his crooked, yellow teeth.

The man's revolting rhyme filled Clay with a red-hot fury. The line had been drawn, but Clay would not wait for them to cross it. Without so much as a warning, Clay slid his rifle over to the right and squeezed the trigger.

The small man's head whipped back as the suppressed, subsonic bullet allowed for everyone to hear the devastation the .300 blackout had on the man's skull. Before the shell dropped to the snow, the other three men had started running toward him. Clay fired several more shots, dropping the man on the far right before he transitioned to his next target. Megan's gunfire startled him, causing his next three shots to miss.

"Clay!" Megan shrieked.

Her plea for help fell on deafened ears as he shot again at the two barreling down on him, striking the one on the left in his stomach. Clay then spun around and sent three rounds into the only man coming for Megan; his body quickly crumpled to the ground.

"Look out!" Megan yelled just moments before Clay felt a searing pain in his shoulder blades.

The impact knocked Clay to the ground. Hard.

Recovering from the impact, Clay saw that the man was now chasing after Megan as she fired wildly in her attacker's direction. Getting to one knee, Clay pulled his rifle scope up to his eye and took a few shots at the Screamer pursuing his sister before he ran behind a car. Having both eyes open, Clay saw two more shadowy figures emerge from the trees on the other side of the road.

With the other two men running his way, Clay was forced to engage. He ignored the pain in his shoulders as he raised the rifle and lined up his shot. He pulled the trigger, but his shot was wide. He felt the bolt on his ARAK-21 lock back, and without checking, he let go of his rifle and reached for his Glock.

The vivid flash from the +p ammunition combined with the falling snow was disorienting. But the crimson red voids on the man's chest let Clay know his aim had been true. He tried to switch targets, but before he could, the other man had plowed his shoulder into Clay's chest, ramming him into the side of an SUV.

"You like that, don't'cha?" the man said as he landed several clean shots to Clay's abdomen. Clay fell to the ground, gasping for air on all fours. "Yeah, you do like it," he added. "Well, don't worry, there will be plenty of time for foreplay..."

Clay felt around for his pistol in the snow when the man grabbed the shoulder straps of his backpack and pulled him up high enough to drive his knee into Clay's stomach.

The agonizing moans coming out of Clay only seemed to excite the man. He once again picked up Clay off the ground, this time throwing him up against the SUV. He pinned Clay against the rear door of the vehicle and gave a twisted grin as he leaned in. "I'm normally a lady's man," he said into Clay's ear, "but I'll make an exception for a pretty boy like you."

The world flashed white for the man as Clay slammed his head forward, breaking the Screamer's nose. As if he was incapable of recognizing pain as a bad thing, the man laughed manically. He licked his lips as the blood began to pour out of his nostrils.

"Ohhh, we're about to have some fun."

"You're gonna have to kill me first," Clay said defiantly.

The man's smile grew wider as Clay's suggestion enticed him even more. He pressed his forearm up against Clay's neck, closing off his airway. "That's the way I like it," the man said, increasing the pressure applied to Clay's neck.

Clay's attempts to break free weakened with each passing second. The world was growing darker...

A blood-curdling scream from Megan pulled him back from the edge of oblivion. A switch had flipped, and, as if he had just been injected with the adrenaline of a gorilla, Clay's drowsy eyes sprung open as the muscles in his neck tightened, causing the man to lean harder.

The Screamer's smile only grew wider as Clay's resistance increased. He laughed as he seemed to relish every struggling movement his victim made. "Good," he said with a maniacal whisper, "I really hate it when people just give up without a fight. It makes things so much less...*satisfying* when I'm done..."

"Please don't," Clay pleaded with his attacker, making sure to keep the attention on his face.

"Yeah, that's it, sweetheart, keep begging..."

Being consumed with the feigned cries for help, the man hadn't noticed Clay's hand slowly reaching for his knife. Needing to complete the transaction in one swift motion, Clay unsnapped the sheath, pulled the knife out, and swung it upwards, driving the blade deep into the man's armpit.

Releasing his choke hold on Clay, the Screamer stumbled backwards, howling in agony. After refilling his lungs with air, Clay ran forward, lunging at the wounded man in front of him. As they hit the ground, Clay jammed the knife into the man's solar plexus, causing his body to go limp.

The man gasped in vain as Clay's unforgiving eyes watched him struggle to breath. Clay felt as if he was having an out-of-body experience; he was no longer calling the shots. He leaned in closer to the man's face, "Was it good for you, too?" he whispered in the dying man's ear as he pressed the blade even further into his gut.

The gurgling response from the Screamer's throat told Clay he was no longer a threat.

After a few very exhausted breaths, Clay stumbled back to his feet. He could still hear Megan pleading for the man to stop—it sounded like they were behind an eighteen-wheeler off in the ditch.

Quickly locating his Glock, Clay made his way around the semi and saw the man straddling his sister, groping and slapping her in the face. As far as the Screamer was concerned, she was *his* property now. Clay stomped up to the man and hooked his arm around his neck, dragging him off Megan and out into the middle of the road. The Screamer fought, but was no match for the almost-supernatural rage surging through Clay's body. When they reached the road, Clay threw the man to the ground; he landed on his back. Before he could recover from the fall, Clay had trained his Glock on his stomach.

He emptied the magazine.

The man was not dead, but his screams had morphed from terrorizing to suffering, and Clay wanted every last psychopath in the area to hear it. So, he let the man scream until there was no more air left in his lungs. It didn't take long.

Megan pulled herself together enough to come around the front of the truck. She saw Clay walking across the street toward a wounded man who attempted to flee by crawling like a lowly snake.

He walked up to the man as he swapped magazines. He pressed on the release, causing the slide to jerk forward as he towered over the Screamer on the ground. "Please," the man pleaded as he turned onto his back, "I-I-I'm sorry, just don't kill me."

It was the first time Clay had ever heard the slightest bit of remorse out of one of the sociopaths. It was strange—almost disturbing.

Nevertheless…

Three shots disrupted the now-silent night, causing Megan to flinch with each report.

With the threats finally neutralized, Clay walked back over to his sister. Her open coat exposed a ripped shirt, and her pants were still unbuttoned. Her face was bloodied and bruised and still displaying a look of fear.

"Are you okay?" Clay asked.

Megan, still in shock with what she had just witnessed, ignored his question and fired back one of her own. "What did you do?"

"Megan!" Clay shouted in frustration. "Are. You. Okay?"

Megan's glassy eyes reflected what was left of the fading day. "Uhm, yeah, I think so. You got there before he was able to..." Megan trailed off as her brain finally processed what nearly happened to her.

Clay nodded, not needing her to venture down that path any further. "Good," he said while dropping the magazine from his rifle and quickly replacing it with a fresh one.

Megan looked over at the grizzly scene in the middle of the road, a sight not too dissimilar from the ones that would have been left behind had the attackers been victorious. "Why?" she asked with a fear-stricken voice.

Clay took a brief glimpse at the body in the middle of the road before turning back to Megan. "I wanted to make sure that he *never* had a chance to hurt someone again," Clay responded.

"But Clay...you're—"

"Surviving!" he cut her off. "Listen, Megan, this is the world we live in now, and each year it gets a little worse. Trust me, I realize just how easy it is to forget how bad things are when you spend all your time in the comfortable confines of your home, but now you're seeing life the way it really is; in its raw and unfiltered state."

Megan reached her hand up and brought it across Clay's cheek. Ignoring the stinging sensation, she proceeded to stick her finger in Clay's face. "Don't you *dare* talk to me as if I am oblivious to the evil in this world, Clayton!" Megan roared, her anger temporarily holding the tears at bay. "I see it...I see it every *single* day, and some days I saw it in ways you could never imagine. So, don't you think for a minute that you're the only one who has it rough, because

I've got news for you, buddy boy, until you spend a day in my shoes, and have the nightmares I have, you are in no position to judge me."

Clay breathed heavily through his nose. "Let's go," he said with contempt as he turned away from his sister and continued down the road.

Chapter 32

The crackling ding of the elevator tone signaled their arrival, and then the doors parted.

"Welcome to my new home away from home," Clay said, the first words either of them had spoken since the heated exchange on the road. He stepped out of the elevator and turned down the hallway. "Here are a couple of bedrooms," Clay said as he walked past the first door. "There are plenty—" The sound of a metal door slamming shut disrupted Clay's comment. He turned around to a dim, empty hallway.

Clay deflated his lungs through a long, drawn out sigh as he leaned up against the cinderblock wall. The sobs and cries on the other side of the door quickly became unbearable, forcing Clay to move to the very end of the hallway, claiming the last room on the opposite side as his own.

He gently closed the door behind him, hoping the guilt would not follow him inside. He dropped his pack onto the rickety cot, the springs sounding as if they were going to snap under the sudden weight change. The pain in Clay's body seemed to grow exponentially as the adrenaline continued to diminish, making the simple task of removing his coat feel like he was bench pressing an elephant. If Megan weren't in the process of a nuclear, emotional meltdown, he would have already volunteered to test the potency of the pain pills in her pack.

A loud growl erupted from Clay's stomach, a reminder that his last bite to eat was nearly twenty-four hours ago. With growing concerns that their food wouldn't last the journey, Clay had opted out of his last few meals. He *had* planned on a hearty meal of freeze dried apple slices with some crumbled soy posing as sausage, but with the bout of nausea he currently battled, he immediately nixed that idea. He settled for a few sips of water instead.

He sat down on the side of the bed and dropped his face into his hands. A couple of slow, deep breaths persuaded his heart rate to return to a normal range. As he sat in silence, the fog in his head also began to lift.

Clay started to wonder if poor decision-making was what brought on such a tumultuous day of travel. After all, his track record of sound judgment these past few months were not exactly stellar. Was everything today his fault? The incident with the watch was unfortunate, but it was—for all intents and purposes—an act of God—something outside of Clay's control. *But still,* he thought, *maybe I could have done something different to avoid such a terrible day.* A day that nearly cost both his and Megan's life.

But the fact was, there wasn't much else he could have done. Clay constantly found himself thrown into a position where decisions need to be made with little to no information. And while some of those choices didn't pan out the way he had hoped, more often than not everything went off without a hitch. Still, it's easy to forget about the thousands of little victories while standing in the shadow of a massive failure.

Clay recalled one of his dad's favorite quotes from Eisenhower. *"In preparing for battle, I have always found that plans are useless, but planning is indispensable."* Perhaps some plans would never work out as expected, but just "winging it" was the kind of thing that would result in a great deal of trouble in the wild. The world, anymore, is out to kill; so, there was no need to give it an advantage by shooting yourself in the foot.

Foiled plans, however, were not always a bad thing. As Clay thought back to the fateful night of Liberty's attack—at the farm house where they found the kids—he remembered the first thing to go through his head after Geoff opened fire: *Why couldn't this have just gone as planned?* But as he sat in the dank room in the basement level of the FEMA camp, Clay realized that had Plan A worked out, he would have never gone inside the farm house, which meant he would have never found Madeline hiding in the closet. She would have been left alone with the remainder of the men waiting for a fate that made Clay cringe.

Everything happens for a reason, he heard Kelsey's voice in his head. It was a saying that, at times, appeared to be true. But the days of trusting that something good could come out of something so terrible were becoming few and far between.

But as the grim look on Madeline's face flashed to the front of Clay's mind, he was thankful that on *that* night, the adage had been true.

After failing to fall asleep for over an hour, Clay warily put his coat back on and left his room. He walked to the end of the hall, past the elevators, and climbed up the stairs. He avoided the elevator as to not disturb Megan, who seemed to have finally cried herself to sleep. Each step was accompanied by a terrible ache in his legs and shoulders—a painful reminder of the dreadful evening they had endured; one that would be sure to visit Clay in his sleep for many years to come.

The sound of a flapping tarp reached Clay's ears as he conquered the final stair and rounded the corner, revealing the observation deck. Snagged on a broken section of window frame, the tattered blue tarp—a FEMA logo still just barely visible—clung on as the intense wind shot through the tower. Suddenly, with a slight shift in the wind, the tarp slipped just enough for it to release its grasp on the window frame, causing it to fly across the room, smacking into a table where it made its way to the floor.

The wind whipped the snow and everything else light enough all across the room, making a complete mess of the observation deck. The whooshing sound of the wind racing through the second-floor windows was eerily reminiscent of the creepy forest from earlier in the evening. Clay wasn't sure if the chills that shot through his body were from the cold itself or the haunting orchestra playing out in front of him.

He remembered the relief he felt when he and Megan finally exited the wooden cemetery—it was indescribable. However, unbeknownst them, the real danger waited for them up ahead.

Feeling lightheaded and a little weak, Clay grabbed a nearby chair and sat down. He was out of the direct wind but close enough to still feel its effects. He stared almost lifelessly out the windows, watching as the snow and ice bounced off the jagged remnants of the glass panes.

What did I do, he echoed Megan's question. Clay had executed two men tonight. Two men who, at that moment in time, posed no threat to him or his sister. He had rationalized his first kill as a preventative measure, even though his vulgar comments about Megan was what made him the first target. And those he slayed after were cut and dried self-defense. But could he justify what he had done to the last two?

Probably not.

But as his mind flashed back to the sight of the man attempting to rape Megan on the side of an abandoned road. He didn't care if the steps he took were excessive or not. That man deserved nothing less than a bullet, and Clay's attempt to feel remorse for taking his life—or *any* of their lives for that matter—had turned up empty. That ship set sail the night he spent in the bathroom in the Screamer's lair.

What bothered him more than anything was the look on Megan's face after she witnessed the event. Those brown, judging eyes that pierced his soul. *She has no idea what it's like to be out here so much,* he thought to himself. Clay loved his sister dearly and he still respected her and everything she had been through, but that was her first run-in with the Screamers. *If she saw half the things I've seen them do, she'd understand...*

Ignoring the pain and fatigue hounding his body, Clay stood up from the chair and hobbled over to the windows. The cold air sliced through his coat like a katana blade crossing silk. Small pellets of ice stung at his face as he stepped up to the floor-to-ceiling window frame, gazing into the darkness where he had put Smith's body in the ground not even two months before. He couldn't see the grave, but he knew it was there. He thought of the joyful sorrow the Marine had borne before finally deciding that eating his own bullet was more desirable than taking another breath in this God-forsaken world.

The tears on Clay's face froze before they reached the bottom of his cheeks.

Bringing Smith that flash drive had been one of the single greatest honors, and most regrettable decisions, of Clay's entire life. Even now, as he stared out at his friend's frozen tomb, Clay found that there were no words to describe how he felt. He was more than willing to answer to the good Lord on judgment day for all the lives he had taken—even of those who departed tonight—but if Smith's blood was indeed on his hands, Clay could only beg for forgiveness.

His stomach writhed just thinking about it all. He knew coming back here would not be without its guilt, but the tremendous weight he felt, along with the violent encounter earlier, was becoming too much to bear. The temptation to follow in Smith's footsteps was gnawing at the back of his mind. As always, his vow to protect and provide for his wife and children was the only thing keeping that enemy from busting through the gates, but with each friend lost, each child-sized grave dug, the tides of that war turned just a little further.

****

Sleep never came.

However, Clay was afforded another opportunity to sleep by the raging snowstorm outside. It had only gained in strength overnight and still hammered them with snow. With visibility next to nothing and the temperatures by far the coldest of the season,

Clay and Megan decided to wait out the storm. Well, not so much Clay and Megan as it was Clay. Megan merely shrugged her shoulders and said, "Okay," before shutting the door.

Clay took the unexpected downtime to do a thorough search of the bunker, making sure he hadn't missed anything the last time he had stayed. Given the circumstances, it was understandable that he might not have been as thorough a scavenger as usual. And since there was nothing else to do and he didn't want to try to sleep again until later in the afternoon, he got to work.

The search paid off when he uncovered several goodies—among which were a few extra PMags, a small bottle of CLP, and a few hundred rounds of 9MM. Amazingly, the pistol cartridges were not only factory loads, but they were Federal HST's—a high quality defense round. Despite the good fortune, Clay was disappointed that he was unable to find more .300 blackout.

In addition to the mags and ammo, Clay found Smith's food pantry inside a couple of lockers next to the "dining room." After dragging Smith's body out for burial, he had avoided the dining room as if it had been radioactive and had missed the nutritional find. There were nearly twenty packs of saltine crackers, a half dozen MREs, and a handful of smaller, prepackaged snacks—mostly protein and oatmeal bars. He imagined everything would need to soak in water for a few moments before consuming to avoid chipping a tooth, but it was still food, slightly easing the heavy burden on his shoulders.

Because he and Megan had decided they would leave the bulk of the pilfered assets in the bunker to be retrieved on their return, Clay decided to lay them out in Smith's old room and prioritize what to pack.

Reducing the weight in their packs for the next leg of their journey provided more space for future finds and was the logical choice, but Clay still felt uncomfortable leaving such resources behind. The plan was to swing by a little town called Douglas Grove before looping back around and heading south on a different route. They would return to the FEMA camp to collect the things they left behind before heading out on the final leg back to Liberty.

After examining his pack, Clay could only justify two additional PMags for his bag, and left the rest on the bed next to the case and a half of 5.56 and the SKS he had left behind earlier. He filled his empty Glock magazines with the HSTs he had found, giving him two full-sized magazines of hollow points and three magazines of FMJs. He also had a just-in-case thirty-three-round magazine for the pistol. Before the collapse, the oversized magazine was considered more of a novelty than practical because the lower half stuck out a good ways from the bottom of the handle. If push came to shove, however, Clay would be happy to reach for the awkwardly long magazine.

With nothing else to do and boredom setting in, Clay did yet another pass around the basement and first floor, turning up nothing new. It wasn't even lunch yet and the time was crawling, so Clay found the deck of cards that he and Smith had played with the night they met and sat down to a grueling game of solitaire. Megan's door remained shut, and with the exception of the occasional card being flipped over, the day passed away in silence.

Chapter 33

The last day and a half had been among the worst—if not *the* worst—stretch of time Dusty had ever experienced. And the kicker was, she volunteered for the op. At first, Shelton had been reluctant to let her go, but he couldn't deny that she was the right person for the job. But, as she lay under a half-dead pine with snow piled on and around her, she started to wish he hadn't been so easily swayed.

Most of the snow sitting on top of her petite frame had dumped down over the past six hours. The storm had intensified around midnight, and only let up shortly before dawn, making for yet another long, sleepless night. Dusty was down to her last hand warmer—which was just enough to take the edge off hypothermia. The sleeping bag she was nestled in was rated for subzero temperatures, but it took less than an hour for Dusty to call that lie out.

Despite her best efforts, Dusty's body trembled aggressively. She had to find a way to control the shaking; the success of the mission was riding on her having the hands of an experienced surgeon. Her hope was that when "go-time" finally arrived, her adrenaline would start a neurological coup-de-tat and take control of her nervous system.

To combat sleep, Dusty mentally field stripped her Browning X-Bolt, cleaned it, and reassembled it again. Of course, in her head, she did it all in record timing, but the imagery helped keep her eyes open, even if her mind wasn't all there. She had been awake for nearly forty hours, save the few times she nodded off for less than fifteen minutes. As the sun came up, room for error would decrease; she had to stay alert. Dusty wanted a quick and successful mission as much as Kohler did, and she wasn't about to blow the opportunity by sawing logs. She knew what this victory would mean for everyone back inside Liberty.

She shifted her body around the sleeping bag in an effort to find a more comfortable position. No such luck. Each one of her ribs felt bruised from lying on her stomach for almost the entire time she had been out. Her misery concerned her—how agile would her body be when it was time to move—especially if she had to make a speedy escape? It wasn't as if muscle atrophy would have set in already, but her legs would be stiff after lack of significant motion in nearly two days. Needing to go from inactivity to an 800-meter dash in the blink of an eye would not likely be a smooth transition.

Finally finding the *least* uncomfortable position, Dusty's thoughts drifted to her parents. She had thought about them a lot since they came up in conversation a few nights ago. She couldn't help but wonder what they would think of who she had become. She wasn't worried that they would have disapproved—she already knew the answer to that and didn't care. But, if they were to come back from the dead and saw her now, would they still love her despite their disapproval? Or would they completely disown her altogether? It was a question that would forever be unanswered.

She expelled the emotional thoughts from her head as dawn approached. She needed to focus, which was no small feat as she continued to wrestle with the nauseating headache she had had all night. Dusty reached for the Savage Mark II next to her right leg and brought it up from the relative warmth of the sleeping bag. Repeating her routine from the previous morning, she triple-checked that the gun was ready to go. The small bolt action .22 long rifle was outfitted with an unused oil filter attached to the end of the threaded barrel. The functional, albeit makeshift, silencer, coupled with subsonic rounds would make her almost impossible to pinpoint after the shot.

The problem, however, was distance—the gun wouldn't have much. Between the weight of the bullet and the smaller than normal charge, it was a *big* question if the lightweight copper-jacketed bullet could get the job done if Dusty's aim was on the mark. However, using the .22 long rifle would likely afford her a slow and invisible retreat back to Liberty—back to safety. And that didn't just sound nice. It started to become necessary with the increased rigidity in her muscles.

After giving the oil filter a snug twist and making sure the sight picture on the scope was not obstructed with frost, Dusty carefully slid the rifle back into the sleeping bag before grabbing her Browning X-Bolt next to her left leg. She loved the Browning and had no reservations about using it for the mission. In fact, part of her hoped she needed to, because she felt more confident with her accuracy using the trusty .270. Much more so than she did with the .22 rifle she'd only first held less than forty-eight hours ago. But after dispatching the hefty soft point round, she might as well hold up a big red sign that says, *I'M THE SHOOTER!* Each rifle had a major con along with a series of pros, and Kohler trusted Dusty to pick the appropriate weapon when the time came.

With dawn officially in the record books, Dusty deployed the bipod on the X-Bolt and kept it just off to the side as she waited for the target to arrive. Because Morgan's vision was blurry, she was unable to give details on the location of the muzzle flash. She was able to give a narrow stretch of tree line where she was confident she'd seen the sharpshooter, and both Kohler and Dusty agreed that the location was in line with their theories.

No more than ten minutes after dawn, Dusty saw a shadowy figure moving through the woods, creeping slowly toward the edge of the forest. Moving like a sloth dipped in tar, Dusty reached forward and flipped up the scope covers and peeked through the lens. It took longer for the image to come into focus than it should have. *Stupid headache.*

The target was dressed in white camo snow gear complete with a solid white ski mask. Clutched tightly in his left hand was an old scoped rifle—a Karabiner 98—the standard service rifle for the German Wehrmacht in World War II. The mask made it difficult to tell, but based on the wrinkles around the man's eyes, Dusty guessed him to be in his 50's or 60's—an old-school shooter for sure. But old school did not equate to ineffective, as the sniper proved repeatedly since the opening remarks of the war.

Dusty watched as the man knelt behind a thicket of trees and shrubs. From Liberty's vantage, he was impossible to see. But with several large gaps between the twisted branches right in front of him, the sniper, at that range, had a wide view of the town. It was absolutely perfect—for *him.*

Dusty slowly lifted her head above the scope to try and gauge distance. He wasn't far, but he wasn't close, either. *Of course, the decision couldn't have been easy.*

She estimated between eighty and ninety yards. She had told herself that anything under fifty was obvious, and it was the same for anything over a hundred. But that nebulous fifty-yard range...that was where she kept going back and forth. So, naturally, when the moment of truth had arrived, the shooter would fall within that range. On the plus side, though, Dusty noticed her shivering had already stopped.

Looking through the scope again, Dusty watched as the man patiently set up for the morning. With several stripper clips neatly lined up on a nearby fallen tree, a set of binoculars hooked to a branch, and a canteen hanging around his neck, the man was ready for a busy morning.

With one knee on the ground and his right shoulder leaning against a tree, Dusty watched as he tightened his grip on the war relic, resting the muzzle on a branch just in front of him. He positioned his eye behind the scope and swiveled the rifle from left to right.

Dusty's eye remained glued to the convex piece of glass as she considered her options. She was in decent position, having a perfect profile of the man's head in her crosshairs—which would be crucial if she opted for the Mark II. However, her head was swimming, and if her fuzzy vision were any indication, she wouldn't exactly be on her "A game" this morning. She was no closer to making that decision than she had been when the man first arrived. Fortunately, however, the shooter wasn't going anywhere, at least for the moment. Nevertheless, time was not her ally, and she had to act fast.

She closed her eyes briefly and took in several deep breaths. *I know I can make this shot,* she thought to herself.

After a moment, her eyes sprang open. Her vision was clear, and, at least in the moment, the fog in her head had lifted. Casting all doubts aside, she reached down and grabbed the Mark II, psyching herself up to take the shot. She stuck her right index finger into her mouth and lightly bit down as she pulled her hand out of the bulky glove, immediately feeling the temperature change. She chambered the insignificant bullet, hoping that it would have a significant impact and positioned herself to fire. To help combat her unstable extremities, she rested her left elbow on the ground and tucked her right arm in as close to her body as she could. She looked through the scope: the target on the other side was crisp and clear. Her heart rate was borderline cataclysmic, so she began taking slow, controlled breaths. It was working.

Dusty continued with her rhythmic breathing as she flicked the safety off. The jittery crosshairs slowly came to a standstill, finally resting on the man's temple as he looked for a target of his own.

It was almost poetic.

Her finger rested on the polymer stock just above the trigger while she waited for the wind to die down. Knowing she would only have one chance, she waited patiently for the right moment. As quiet as the round was, there was no mistaking a hunk of lead whizzing by at 900 feet per second. If she failed to deliver a kill shot on the first trigger pull, the sniper would be gone before she could cycle the next round. It had to be perfect.

The wind weakened, but anything more than a gentle spring breeze would affect the slow moving 40-grain projectile. She had planned to wait just a little longer but the man's rifle suddenly stopped panning the horizon and jumped back to the left. He stayed put for several seconds, then pushed the rifle stock harder into his shoulder; his entire body tensed up.

The conditions were not ideal, but Dusty wasn't going to let him strike again. Calmly, she moved her finger to the trigger and took another deep breath. She exhaled slowly; halfway through, she stopped. Her pounding heart was all she felt—all she heard—when she squeezed the trigger.

Clack

The noise, along with the recoil from the Mark II was anticlimactic. Dusty never lost complete focus on the scope, but it took a moment to reacquire the target. He was still there and still holding his rifle.

"What?" she said in quiet disbelief as she moved her eyes off the scope to cycle the next round.

She thought for sure when she looked back through the scope the man would be gone, shouting to the others about the botched assassination attempt, but he was still lining up his shot. Miraculously, the man had not heard the miss. Dusty had no idea where her bullet had gone, and without a spotter she wasn't even going to venture a guess. Unwilling to throw away this gift of a second chance, Dusty placed the Mark II off to her side and reached for the X-Bolt. The comfortable familiarity of the rifle allowed her to quickly chamber a round, locate her target and press on the trigger, finding that nanometer gap that separated the man from this life and the next.

Ready to fire a follow up—and more devastating—shot, Dusty aimed at the shooter eighty or so yards out. With *that* rifle in her hands, however, the man might as well be sipping on a cup of coffee five feet away. She hesitated for a moment as her mind questioned her exit strategies, but she had already gone over her plan a thousand times; now was not the time for reevaluations.

"Lights out, dude," she mumbled as she prepared to fire, but suddenly, alarms inside her head sounded off, causing her to pause once more.

She eased her finger off the trigger ever so slightly as she noticed a small black dot appear on the side of the man's ski mask. Dusty reached up and twisted the zoom on her scope, maxing out the magnification which was not practical for the shot she planned to take, but enough to see the strange anomaly in more detail.

The black dot had a tinge of red to it, and it was slowly consuming the surrounding white wool.

Dusty fully released the trigger, but kept her eye on the scope. "No way," she mumbled under her breath. She watched in awe as the German rifle slowly broke out of the man's grip, smacking into a few branches before disappearing into the snow at his feet.

After another thirty seconds, the small dot had grown to the size of a silver dollar. The man hadn't so much as flinched since dropping the rifle, and the lack of vapor flying away from his mouth confirmed it.

Tango Down.

Though she was still in shock from the historic kill, there was no time to revel in her absurd accuracy. The sniper's presence meant an assault could begin at any moment, and she needed to be back inside the walls by that time.

She put the X-Bolt back on safe and then did the same with the Mark II. She then wriggled her way out of the sleeping bag and started her long, painful belly-crawl back to safety. Having spent nearly two straight days in the sleeping bag, never leaving once, she would *not* be taking it back with her. Being a patient sniper was not for the faint of heart.

Dusty was a few hundred yards from her exfiltration point when the assault began. She climbed to her feet—her legs even wobblier than she had anticipated—and started to run. Her mission was accomplished; the sniper was dead. At this point it didn't matter whether they saw her or not, all that mattered was getting to the other side of the fence before she caught a bullet.

The gunfight toward the front of the town had intensified, but as far as she could tell, no one had spotted her yet. "Kilroy!" Dusty yelled as she approached the fence. The code word was the signal to toss a rope over the fence, but panic hit hard when the rope didn't come. "KILLROY!" she shouted again, straining her vocal cords until they burned.

Nothing.

Convinced that nobody was around to hear her cries, she immediately started thinking of a backup plan. Then, like a nylon guardian angel, a rock climbing rope launched over the top of the fence, the knot on the end smacking down onto the other side with a thunk. *Thank God!*

Dusty could no longer feel her legs, and she wasn't totally convinced her brain was even the one giving the orders—it seemed adrenaline had once again taken over the operation entirely. But she was moving in the right direction, so she didn't care to question how.

When she got within a couple yards of the fence, Dusty lunged forward, expelling the last bit of strength her body had to offer. She smacked into the reinforced fence and grasped onto the rope as if the braided fibers were life itself.

Reaching the fence was the easy part. Scaling it, however, was too much to ask of her fatigued body to take on. But she didn't give up. Dusty screamed out in pain as she forced her muscles to work well beyond their limits. It felt like hours had passed by the time she managed to get halfway up the fence when suddenly...

PING

A bullet struck a lightweight I-beam just a few feet away. The deafening concussions from the impact further disoriented Dusty's already muddled head, causing her to lose her grip on the rope. The pain from the fall was intense, but as she stared up at the rope still bouncing off the side of the fence, she watched several bullets pound the fence right where she had dangled seconds earlier. She reminded herself that if she felt pain, she was still alive.

"Dusty!" A voice cried out from the other side of the fence. The ringing in her ears had waned enough to just barely make out Morgan's voice. "North border!"

Before she could get to her feet, the rope had slithered back over the top, hopefully making its way to the back of the property.

With the world spinning, Dusty stumbled forward, increasing her speed with each step. More shots peppered the fence, a melody of metal ricochets and small, wooden explosions gave Dusty the proper motivation to not let up.

Focused on keeping her balance, Dusty never gave her attackers a glance. Returning fire would not only be completely ineffective, but probably a fatal mistake. The only option was to run. *What's another five football fields,* she thought.

As if her mind had briefly stopped functioning but her body kept moving, Dusty couldn't remember how she got to the north-western corner of the property, but there she was, still alive, and nearly home free.

Another close call from enemy fire snapped her from her trance. As she reached the edge of the fence line, she slapped the corner post with her right arm, using it, and her momentum, to swing her around the back. She was now out of the sightlines of the shooters.

The rope was already waiting for her at the nearest point without razor wire, just another fifty feet to go. Forty. Thirty.

Dusty's legs finally gave out, causing her to smack into the snowy ground with a breathless thud. A loud, furious voice inside her head demanded she get up, but her muscles were no longer taking orders. *I was so close,* she thought, her spirits throwing in the towel along with her body.

She could hear shouting coming from the other side of the fence and scrambled movement between the slats, but none of it made any sense. It didn't matter. Arlo's men would round the fence corner at any moment. It was over.

"Ow!" a voice cried out from above.

Dusty mustered enough energy to look up as Morgan hiked her leg over the top of the fence trying to avoid the razor wire.

"No, don't come for me," Dusty said, her words barely loud enough for her to hear, let alone Morgan.

Morgan landed on the ground a few feet in front of Dusty, absorbing the impact about as perfectly as one could. Her hands bled and her coat and pants were sliced in several spots. "Get your ass up, Dusty! It's time to move!" she said as she grabbed Dusty's arm, pulling on her.

With Morgan's assistance, Dusty got to one knee, and then the other. Shortly after, she was on her feet again, hobbling forward. With one arm over Morgan's shoulder, the pair limped the rest of the way to the rope.

"Get ready, guys!" Morgan yelled as she leaned Dusty up against the fence next to the rope.

Dusty's world was getting darker.

"Stay with me, Dusty, you're almost there," Morgan said, trying to sound calm. "Hold your arms up," she said.

Dusty was unable to oblige.

Morgan fished the rope around Dusty's back, keeping it under her armpits. She pulled the rope to the front and tied a haphazard knot across her chest.

"Go! Go! Go!" Morgan shouted.

Dusty felt a sharp pain as her shoulders jolted upward, and the ground dropped from beneath her feet. The awful grind of the rope sliding across the top of the fence brought her back from the grips of unconsciousness just long enough to see Morgan standing below, wounded and unarmed, waiting for the same lifeline to be thrown back to her.

Chapter 34

"You ready to go?" Clay asked as he peeked his head inside Megan's room.

"Almost. Just need to get my socks and boots on," Megan replied casually as she pulled a sock over her foot. "By the way," she added, "I know you're pretty confident this place is secure and all, but I'm really not digging the idea to leave all of the pills here. If by chance someone *does* get in here, then we just handed over the high of a lifetime. And besides, it's not like they take up much space in my pack."

It was true, the place was not exactly Fort Knox, but besting the wall surrounding the bunker itself would be no easy feat without the key code. However, once inside the walls, it wouldn't take much effort to gain access to the bunker through the observation deck, just as Clay had done himself. But, at the same time, they were about to trek into uncharted territory, and Clay was not the "put all your eggs in one basket" kind of guy. "How about this," Clay said, "leave one of the bags here—we'll find a good place to hide it—and bring the other with us?"

Megan nodded. "That seems reasonable," she said as she fished one of the bags out of her pack.

Clay also didn't mind the idea of having some pain meds on hand while traveling, should a need arise. The weak, over-the-counter pills were only so effective back when they were fresh off the shelf, let alone seven or eight years past their prime.

Slapping her hands on her thighs, Megan stood up from the bed. She picked up her pack and the bag of pills and said, "All right, let's find a place to stash these so we can head out."

Clay was both surprised and relieved with Megan's abrupt shift in mood. He wanted to prod her over the complete about-face from yesterday, but thought better of it. The need to avoid distractions while traveling today overpowered his curiosity. *Sleeping dogs would just have to stay put.*

Clay pushed the call button on the elevator, and the doors immediately opened for them. They both walked inside and Clay pressed a button.

"Oooh! SB-Two?" Megan said with a mysterious tone in her voice. "Have you been down there before?"

"Unfortunately."

"Unfortunately?" Megan asked, but quickly understood what Clay meant as they were met by the god-awful stench of Sub-Basement Two.

"Oh, sweet mother, this is awful!" Megan said, breathing through her mouth.

Even Clay was taken aback by the appalling smell, and *he* had braced for it. The smell got worse as they walked down the hall, as did Megan's gagging. She tried to distract her brain by focusing on the echoes from her and Clay's boots. The mental trickery only lasted so long, and by the time they had reached the cell Clay had stayed in during his first night at Smith's, the pungent odor had overpowered Megan's stomach.

"I'm sorry, I can't—I mean, I-I think I'm gonna—" Megan turned and left the room in a hurry.

"Yeah, try sleeping in it," Clay said, certain she couldn't hear him over the sound of her dry heaving. Shortly after, the shrill squeak of the elevator doors splitting apart filled the concrete hallway before the elevator's grinding motor kicked on.

Eager to get out of the toxic air as soon as possible, Clay got to work. He moved the cot in the back corner of the room, uncovering a small vent near the bottom of the wall. He used his multi-tool to break loose the crusty screws from the wall before finishing the job by hand. He placed the bag of pills a foot or so back and then quickly replaced the vent cover. Confident nobody would discover the pills inside—after all, it's not as if the DEA would be raiding the place, checking every nook and cranny for narcotics—Clay turned around and urgently walked back down the hall. Thankfully, Megan had been kind enough to send the elevator back down.

When the doors opened at Basement One, Clay saw Megan sitting against the wall, pinching the bridge of her nose with her finger and thumb. Her eyes were closed and her face was green.

Clay laughed. "You okay?"

Megan replied with a nauseated groan before she slid her thumb and finger off her nose and rubbed at her eyes. "That was, without a doubt, the worst smell I've ever experienced," she said, gagging just from the thought of it. Her closed eyes began to water.

"Well, *I* put the pills in there, so *you* have to be the one to go get them when we get back," Clay joked.

Megan shook her head, "Uh uh, no way. You can leave the gate open and tape a detailed map to the pills on the front door. Let some junkie have them, cuz' I am *not* going back down there without a hazmat suit or something."

"If I recall correctly, when we were kids you once told me that you had an iron stomach," Clay jabbed.

Instead of taking the bait, Megan focused on not throwing up. It took several minutes before she was finally able to stand back up—the threat of horking up her breakfast finally subsiding.

"You good?"

"Yeah," Megan said, blinking her eyes rapidly. "I think."

Clay was antsy to get going. With a snow day yesterday, and the shorter days already putting them at a disadvantage, it was imperative Clay and Megan made up time over the next few days of traveling.

Megan opted for the stairs to avoid a relapse from the lingering smell in the elevator. Clay didn't put up a fight. The color in Megan's face returned more and more with each step away from the basement. And by the time they had reached the security checkpoint just inside the front door, she was back to normal.

Clay unlatched the deadbolt and pushed on the green, metal door.

It was stuck.

Repeated attempts to push the door open were all met with failure. "Guess we're climbing out the windows," Clay said as he walked back toward the stairwell. Megan lagged behind.

Just before they reached the observation deck, Clay stopped Megan. "Wait here."

He was serious about making smarter, more thorough choices moving forward. He would no longer allow time and convenience to dictate his actions; that kind of lazy behavior would stop immediately.

Stopping just short of the doorway, Clay flipped the ARAK off safe and pushed the rifle into his shoulder. He leaned out into the room and looked around, focusing his attention mostly out the windows. His chief concern was not of danger lurking around the corner, but a thief watching from afar, waiting to jump on an opportunity.

Though the sky was gray, it had stopped snowing hours ago, providing a clear, near-white canvas of terrain that would make movement of any kind easy to spot. Clay took his time scanning his surroundings, looking for anything out of place. Apart from the tattered remains of an American flag hanging near the front gate and a few feral dogs far off in the distance, the scene was perfectly still.

Clay turned back toward the hallway, "All right, you're good."

Clay stepped through the window onto the shaky metal catwalk just outside. It creaked and groaned as he leaned over the railing, looking for the best way down. He noticed several snow drifts climbing up the wall, one nearly reaching the bottom off the catwalk. He turned around and gave a quick nod to his sister.

"Just don't fall and break your neck," Megan added her two cents.

Climbing over the handrail, Clay slowly lowered himself down onto the tightly packed snow mound and eased his weight down while still grasping the railing of the catwalk. After nearly sinking a foot into the drift, Clay was able to regain his balance and trudge his way to the ground. Even on the ground, though, the snow was up to his knees. *So much for making up for lost time,"* he thought to himself.

Clay moved over to the gate as Megan climbed down, following the same path he had taken. Without a shovel, it took the better part of fifteen minutes to get the gate cleared enough to open, and even then, they had to side-step their way out. If another blizzard were to hit on their return trip, they might not be able to get back in. Clay shrugged that concern off. *Today has enough problems.*

Slogging through the snow was a grueling battle of strength and endurance. By the time they lost sight of the FEMA camp's boundaries, half the day had come and gone—a testament not only to their slowed pace but also to the massive size of the camp.

"So where are we headed?" Megan asked from a few yards behind, puffing for air between words.

Clay reached into his pocket to check the map. His stomach sank when all he came up with was lint. "That's just freakin' wonderful," Clay said with a sardonic laugh.

Finally catching up to him, Megan stopped next to her brother. "What's wrong?" she asked, Clay's anger vividly on display. "You don't have the map?"

Her question was answered by a furious sigh. "I opened it up last night to chart out our course for today..." Clay said in disbelief. "And, to top it all off, we're not even halfway to where I expected us to be by this point." Clay's shoulders slumped as he radiated frustration.

Megan remained silent for a few moments before finding the right words to say. "Hey, it's really just not a big deal, okay? We'll figure it out. It's not like you haven't done this before. I've seen the stuff you've brought home in the past—you've never needed a map to find the treasure," she said with a reassuring smile as she reached up and rested her hand on his shoulder.

To Clay's surprise, Megan's calming, sisterly words had disarmed him. It didn't change how pissed off he was that he, once again, made such a foolish mistake, but it did suppress his anger enough to see the forest through the trees, giving him a shot of optimism he so desperately needed. Clay was indeed no stranger to long expeditions without a map, and he was confident that they would find some fortune during the rest of the trip. But it would be a whole lot easier to plan with the map.

Clay forced a quick smile at his sister, which was all the thanks she needed. "All right," he said. "Let's keep moving. I know we keep heading west on this road for quite a while before it swings north. A few miles after that should be a small town. I had planned on us stopping there for a quick lunch and scavenge before continuing north, but I think it might just have to be our pit stop for the night."

Megan gestured ahead, "Lead the way, little brother."

****

With nearly an hour before sunset, the minute, rural town came into view. Thankfully, they managed to steer clear of unwanted travel companions, and as they got further from the campsite, the snow became easier to negotiate, increasing their speed.

As they walked into what Clay could only assume was downtown, he laughed as he looked around. "I've seen small towns before, but this one might take the cake."

Megan looked to the left: a mediocre strip mall, a gas station and strangely enough, some sort of war

355

memorial. To the right: a few older brick buildings of various retail shops—mostly antiques and other trinket stores with a Subway plopped right in the middle of them all. Beyond the small town, no matter which way they looked, were towering grain silos, several of which were crumpled or leaning over.

"Yeaaaaah, this is pretty small," Megan added.

"Pretty small..." Clay mocked. "I've seen intersections in Fort Worth bigger than this."

Megan chuckled.

Before getting started on their search, curiosity had gotten the best of Clay, and he walked toward the war memorial. Recognizing the jet as an F-4 Phantom and the helicopter as a UH-1 "Huey", Clay quickly pegged it as a Vietnam Memorial.

The flying war machines, which looked like toys from the road, appeared to be life-size as he and Megan got closer. Their father had served aboard the USS Harry S. Truman arming F-18s. Though he never got behind the throttle himself, the man loved avionics. Clay spent many nights helping his old man assemble scale models of various military jets, listening as he talked about what each one could do and how they were used in war. He even had a plastic A-10 Warthog hanging from his rearview mirror in his squad car. Bittersweet memories.

As Clay walked toward the Huey, he saw three metal statues of U.S. soldiers bravely charging into battle. With one hand pointing toward the road, and the other tightly gripping a 1911, a Lieutenant led the way as two men behind him followed, clutching to their M16s.

Whoever had sculpted the statues had managed to capture both valor and fear in the expression of all three men. Each one of their rust-stained faces seemed to tell a story of their own. It was beautiful.

A plaque in front of the soldiers read:

Success is not final; failure is not fatal: it is the
courage to continue that counts.
Winston Churchill

Beneath the quote it said:

In memory of Lt. Franklin Fontaine Jr. Husband.
Father. Son. Gave his life to save those in his charge.
February 1, 1968

It hardly seemed to matter now, but Clay whispered a thank you to the late Franklin Fontaine Jr. for his dedicated service to this country.

As Clay and Megan left the memorial, another plaque caught Clay's eye. It was a list of people, groups, and businesses that had contributed to the erection of the memorial. The only name on the first line was:

Mayor Franklin Fontaine Sr.

Clay also whispered a thanks to the Mayor for the sacrifice of giving up his son as he left the memorial to search the town.

With daylight running out, Clay and Megan covered as much ground as they could. Unfortunately, the entire strip mall had long been picked clean. However, as night arrived, Megan spotted an old fire station out the back door of a liquor store.

"What do you think?" Megan asked.

"Looks good to me."

Chapter 35

Clay's feet had already swung off the bed and his hand reached for his rifle before he had fully woken up. The shattering glass sounded as if it had come from downstairs. Without thinking, he swiftly walked across the bunkroom with his rifle at the ready. "Stay here and get your gun out," he said to Megan, keeping his eyes on the door he approached.

He walked out into hallway and squinted; the orange glow of the windows from the rising sun wreaked havoc on his tired eyes. A crisp, clear dawn was a sight to behold these days, but at that moment in time, Clay would have given anything for yet another drab, lifeless sunrise. He tried to blink away the blinding radiance, but to no avail. The best he could do was keep his vision low, and be ready to fire at the first set of feet he saw.

He heard footsteps echoing around the cavernous engine bay, but when he stepped off the stairs, it was empty. The sound came from the kitchen. An L-shaped hallway was all that separated Clay from the intruder. Quietly, he moved to the corner of the hallway and put his back up against the wall. He waited and listened as he continued to hear the footsteps. He felt a tinge of relief when he realized it was just one person.

One person could still do a whole lot of harm though, and the truth of the matter was he couldn't know for sure that there weren't more. He needed to be smart. He needed to get the drop on the burglar and assess the situation before they had a chance to react. Based on what he could hear, the individual was on the left side of the kitchen.

With his heart thumping and every muscle sufficiently constricted, Clay began the silent countdown to make his move. *Three...two...one.*

He pushed off with his right foot as he pivoted his body around the left. The spin transitioned seamlessly into a sprint as he made his way down the short, carpeted corridor. As he stormed into the kitchen, Clay planted his foot on the linoleum tile and twisted his body to the left.

"Don't move!" he shouted before he realized his socks had kept him moving long after he wanted to stop. The whole sequence had been a blur and before he realized what was happening, Clay had fallen to the ground, his back taking the brunt of the impact.

With a thousand thoughts going through his head, the only one he could hear was, *Is the intruder armed?* Then it was, *Are you really going to go out like this? Slipping on cheap kitchen flooring?* Before Clay could snap out of his daze, he heard snorting laughter come from the direction of the intruder.

Clay looked up and saw Megan covering her mouth with her hand, her eyes squinting as she snickered at the sight of her brother on the floor.

Next to her head was an open cabinet, and there was a pile of broken dishes at her feet.

Megan's attempts to corral her amusement were not going well. "That was very Schwarzenegger of you there, little brother," Megan said, fighting back more laughter as she stepped over the larger chunks of porcelain to help Clay up.

Clay winced as he took in a sharp breath. Finally finding his feet, he looked over at Megan and shook his head, "Do you want to get shot? Because this is the kind of thing that will get you shot."

Megan leaned back, as if Clay's breath was offensive, and gave him a snarky look. "You're one to talk, Rambo. If I had been who you thought I might be, *you* would be the one on the ground right now."

Clay rolled his eyes. "Seriously, Megan..."

Megan's laughter finally waned. Sincerity struck her voice. "Look, Clay, I know it's been a rough couple of days for you...I woke up early and you seemed to be sleeping pretty soundly, so I thought I would get a jump start on the day by looking around downstairs while you caught a few extra minutes of sleep." Her sincerity morphed back to comedy. "And all was well until I opened that cabinet and got blitzkrieged by some cheap china."

Even though he wasn't in a laughing mood, Megan's comment caused Clay to chuckle. He knew his sister meant well, even if her execution had been less than stellar. Of course, Megan was right, he had no room to comment on execution based on this morning's performance.

"Well, while I do appreciate the extra sleep, if it's all the same, let's just go ahead and stick together in the future, okay?"

"Fine by me." She noticed Clay still held onto his side. "Anything hurt? Besides your pride, of course?" she jabbed.

"I think something might've pulled when my legs decided to keep going after the rest of my body had stopped," he replied as he absentmindedly rubbed the side of his abdomen.

"You going to be able to move today?"

"Believe me, I've traveled with much worse." Clay looked over at Megan's backpack sitting on the counter next to the sink. "Find anything good?" he asked, nodding toward the open pack.

"A few things here and there. Found a few needles and a couple of bags of IV tubes in the bus out in the bay. I think the thing had been decommissioned or something beforehand."

"Why do you say that?"

"No gurney for one. Everything was gone, but it was still clean, which I find very unlikely if someone had torn it apart looking for drugs. I mean, even the defib was missing. I just happened to find the needles wedged between one of the seats and the wall, and the tubes were stashed in one of the drawers." Megan looked around the disheveled kitchen, "But, besides that, it's been slim pickin's. Oh! I *did* find a sample bottle of dish soap underneath the sink just before your epic fail," she added, grinning ear to ear.

Clay sighed. "I suppose you've already decided that I won't be living this down for a little while, huh?"

Megan bellowed a fake, sinister laugh as she walked over to her backpack. "You have no idea, little brother." She gave the zippers on her pack a quick tug and then slung the strap over her shoulder. "There's just another room or two I need to check out, so while I am doing that, why don't you go get packed up and meet me back down here in a few minutes?"

"All right, sounds good."

As Clay gathered up his things in the bunkroom, he suddenly found himself laughing over the events of the last few minutes. Pushing aside the thought that he could have accidentally shot Megan or that he could have been killed had Megan actually been an intruder, the whole thing was pretty comical. Even though a lot of things could have gone wrong, it ended with merely a bruised ego and a lot of laughter—the latter of the two was a welcomed change.

The final two rooms Megan searched yielded several useful items including a pair of utility scissors, a full box of antiseptic wipes, and various sized trauma pads. Already, the day was off to a much better start than the previous day.

The shops across the road were filled with mostly useless items. Megan found a half dozen travel-sized sewing kits and a vintage scarf. They both found coats that were in much better shape than the ones they wore, boosting their moral that much more.

While Megan continued to shop around the antique store, Clay ventured up the stairs into the apartment above. The home's décor was too similar not to have been the owner's place. Boxes of inventory overpowered the dining room, a gaudy chandelier suspended just above the small round table. The boxes spilled into the living room where a bright orange floral couch—a design that could have only been conceived in the 70's—sat up against one wall, a small tube TV entombed in oak sitting on the opposite wall. In front of the couch stood a single TV tray with an empty plate collecting dust on top.

It would take hours, if not a day or more, to thoroughly pick through everything in the cramped apartment, and since Clay was not expecting to find much, he focused his efforts to just a few areas.

When he walked into the bedroom, it was more of the same. A mess of boxes and random junk strewn about. The room was a wreck except for the beautiful dresser just beneath the only window. Besides accumulating dust over the years, the antique piece of furniture was immaculate. At the very center of the dresser was a flag box, picture frames flanking either side. On one side was a black and white photo of a good-looking man in an Army uniform, sergeant stripes sewn to his arm. The other photo was the same man, his arm locked around a beautiful woman wearing all white, their smiles as bright as the sun.

Investigating the dresser more, Clay found a shoebox in one of the bigger drawers. *Max's things* was scrawled across the top with a thick, black marker. Clay opened it up to see personal photos from Europe, letters exchanged between the man and his wife, newspaper articles, and multiple medals tucked away at the bottom.

In the next drawer, Clay found an old .25 caliber pistol and two boxes of ammo that looked older than him. The pistol was tiny, and felt terrible in Clay's hands, but he wasn't about to pass up a perfectly good gun and ammo—*someone* back in Liberty would feel slightly more at ease having the sidearm on their hip.

Clay set the pistol and ammo on top of the dresser and kept searching. Jackpot! A box of .45 ACP. Sadly, the accompanying pistol was nowhere to be found. But it was no matter, Clay was thrilled to have some additional cartridges for his newly reacquired M1911.

Megan joined Clay upstairs as he finished up his search. In addition to the gun and ammo, Clay found a bottle of Benadryl, Ibuprofen, and a box of bandages. Megan spotted an automatic blood pressure cuff buried beneath a pile of coupons. While they both agreed it was unlikely that the thing still worked, it was worth grabbing with the understanding that if they ran out of space, it would be among the first things to discard.

"Find anything else down there?" Clay asked.

"Yeah, actually. A couple of things. It's funny, I almost told you we shouldn't waste our time with this place, but it's not been half bad."

Clay shook his bag, the sound of the ammunition jiggling in their boxes caused Megan to tilt her head—it was a sound she was very familiar with. "Nice! What caliber?"

"Twenty-five and forty-five."

"We got anything with us that shoots it?"

"Just this," Clay said as he held up the gun, its size even humorous to Megan. "But I'm not complaining."

Megan made fists with her hands to get the blood circulating and restore feeling to her fingertips. "Not bad at all," she said, slapping Clay on the back. "So, are you about ready to hit the road?"

"Yeah, I think I'm set."

As they walked across the tiny apartment, Clay suddenly stopped, his gaze stuck on the window.

"What do you see?" Megan asked, a touch of panic in her voice.

Clay held his finger up to his mouth and signaled for Megan to stay put. He tiptoed toward the window and knelt behind it, ensuring he hadn't been seeing things.

He hadn't.

Leaning his .300 blackout up against the wall, Clay slowly unzipped his pack and retrieved the M6 Scout rifle. The oddly designed gun looked even stranger when folded up. Clay unfolded the rifle, leaving it slightly broken. He reached into his bag and retrieved both a .410 shell and a .22lr cartridge, holding them in his hand as he debated on which to use. The .410 would improve his chance of success at that distance, which was a serious concern for a gun Clay had never fired before. But, with only four shells from Kohler, and two in his random ammo bag he always kept with him, there wasn't much ammo to spare. Nevertheless, with his shot demanding perfection with the .22, Clay didn't want to risk exposing his and Megan's position *and* come up empty-handed. The small shotgun shell was the way to go.

Clay inserted the .410 shell into the barrel and quietly snapped the gun closed before leaning it up against the wall next to his ARAK-21. Opening the window was no easy task, especially quietly, but all he needed was a few inches.

He picked up the Scout rifle and rested the barrel on the rotted windowsill. He gently eased the hammer back as he took aim.

"Clay," Megan whispered, "what are you doing?"

Clay remained silent as his fingers wrapped around the strange trigger on the bottom of the gun.

The rifle bucked up from the windowsill as the .410's blast filled the room. It was louder than he had expected, but still pretty quiet.

"Clay!" Megan exclaimed, trying to keep her voice at a whisper. "What did you just shoot?"

He stared out the window for another moment before turning back to his sister, a smile on his face. "Our dinner for tonight."

Chapter 36

"I think she's waking up," a woman's voice said from the darkness.

"Good. Send someone to get Shelton. He wanted to be notified as soon as she was conscious," a man responded.

Silence.

Then pain.

Dusty's eyes opened to a blurry world filled with blobby people walking to and fro, paying her no attention as she labored to breathe. It wasn't that her lungs didn't work, but with each drawn breath came the sensation of an elephant tap dancing on her ribs.

After hearing the hushed murmurs of several different conversations around the room, there was no question where she was. How she got there, on the other hand, was a different story—one she wanted to know.

As her surroundings slowly came into focus, she made eye contact with Doctor Sowell. He spoke a few more words to a patient lying in one of the dozens of beds in the room before turning around to head her way.

"Good morning, Dusty," Doctor Sowell said, his deep, raspy voice surprisingly soothing to the teenaged girl. "You gave us all a bit of a scare there." He reached for her chart, giving it a quick once over before continuing. "But I think it's safe to say you're out of the woods now." His words were washed in relief.

"How did I," Dusty said, her voice cutting out several times. She cleared her throat, but it had no impact on her hoarse voice. "What happened?"

"Well, as for the details, I cannot say. But, from what I understand, you suffered from a nasty fall or two during the last attack. That, however, was the least of your problems when they brought you in two days ago. You were *quite* dehydrated." Doctor Sowell sat down on the edge of the bed and put his hand on top of hers, taking care not to disturb the IV taped to the top of her hand. "Even in the cold, you've still got to make sure you're taking in fluids, even if you don't feel thirsty."

Dusty's mouth twitched as the fragmented events from the other day started to piece back together. "I was out on a mission—outside the gates—and I guess I-I just forgot to drink."

Doctor Sowell nodded. "I understand. Chalk it up to experience. You were lucky this time, but I wouldn't test luck's patience in the future."

Dusty nodded before being surprised with a sneeze, causing her to cringe afterwards. Her tolerance for pain was higher than most adults, but as with everything, there was a limit to what she could handle. She began to whimper, barely able to hold off the tears. "Why the hell does my chest hurt so much?"

"It's likely that you cracked a few ribs during one of your falls, or at the very least, bruised them. Without an X-Ray, I can't be one hundred percent certain, but your lungs sound clear, so the only thing to do now is give it time and rest."

As the intense sensation in her chest diminished, an image of a dark bloodstain spreading across a white ski mask flashed across her mind. The vivid sight, after hearing just how dehydrated she had been, caused her to worry that her mind had played tricks on her. That not only had she not taken out the sniper, but that she had never even seen him in the first place. "Can I ask you something?" Dusty asked timidly, not sure she wanted to hear the answer.

"Of course," Doctor Sowell said.

"Can dehydration cause...hallucinations?"

Doctor Sowell slowly nodded his head. "Yes, they can, in severe cases."

"Was I severe?" she asked.

"Uhhh," Doctor Sowell contemplated. "I would say you were close, but not quite bad enough for *that.* However," he continued, dashing Dusty's brief hopes that she was in the clear. "When other factors are at play, such as hypothermia, mild starvation...*stress*...those things can exacerbate most ailments and cause a few of the symptoms by themselves." Doctor Sowell detected Dusty's angst. "Is everything okay, darling?" he asked, revealing a caring, fatherly side to him.

"Hope so," Dusty said before closing her eyes and pressing back into the pillow.

"Well, you let us know if you need anything, okay?" Sowell said, picking up on her hint to be left alone.

Dusty kept her eyes shut and gave a nod. As much as she hated to be down and out, fighting in this condition was not something she could do—not well, anyway.

Dusty's mind started to slip into that NetherRealm between oblivion and reality as she began to drift to sleep. When she heard Shelton and Kohler approaching, she thought about keeping her eyes shut—faking sleep—but knowing what happened over the last forty-eight hours was more important. And from the sounds of it, she would have plenty of time to sleep later.

"Dusty, it's good to see you. How are you feeling?" Shelton asked as he pulled a folding metal chair up to the bed and sat down.

"Like I was kicked by a mule," she said matter-of-factly.

Kohler, who remained standing, responded, "It could have been a helluva lot worse, kid. All things considered, I'd put a kick by a mule in the win column."

"So, what did the doctor say?" Shelton asked.

"He said I'm going to be fine. Just need a couple of days to rest."

"Good," Shelton replied. "Well, I imagine you are pretty tired, so we won't take up too much of your time, we just wanted to see how you were doing, and to congratulate you."

Dusty tilted her head. "On?"

"The sniper," Kohler spoke up. "Kid, I don't know how close you were to him, but you couldn't have placed that bullet any better."

Dusty's relief came out in the form of laughter, disregarding the ache in her ribs. She smiled as it sank in that she had not hallucinated after all. "How did you find out?" she asked.

"We sent a team out the night of the attack. It took a while, but they were able to retrieve the body *and* the rifle," Kohler said. "It was truly a one-in-a-million shot." A rare smile flashed across Kohler's face. "Well done, soldier," he added, giving a salute.

Dusty couldn't help but smile. She might have singlehandedly changed the course of this so-called war. "Thank you, sir," she replied, mustering up the most proper salute she was capable of.

The smiles faded and Shelton's face went grim. "Uhm, there is one other thing that I need to tell you."

Dusty's first thoughts were of Clay and Megan. *Did something happen to them?* They weren't expected back for another week at the minimum, so she quickly dismissed that idea. What else could it be except for...

No.

"Morgan Rowley was killed in action," Kohler stepped in, detecting Shelton's reluctance to utter the words.

The world went blurry again as Dusty's eyes filled with liquid sorrow. Her chin began to quiver as the guilt burrowed deep into her soul.

"As I understand it, you two had become pretty close, so I didn't want you to hear the news of her passing through the grapevine." Shelton took his glasses off and dabbed at the moisture in his own eyes. Every death weighed heavily on Shelton's heart, but Morgan's death was even harder because she was the youngest combatant—just a few months younger than Dusty—fighting for Liberty's existence.

"Uhm..." Dusty shook her head as if hoping she had misheard Kohler's words. "Are you sure?" she asked after realizing she hadn't. Her eyes filled with tears as Kohler informed her that her nightmares of Morgan's death were in fact memories.

Shelton's eyes closed as he lowered his head. "There will be a memorial service for her later today.

If you are up for it—and Doctor Sowell agrees—I think it would mean a lot if you were there."

Dusty's blank stare held firm as the tears started to stream down her face. She didn't say a word.

"I'm sorry," Shelton added as he slowly stood from the chair. "Get some sleep, Dusty. You've been through a lot."

Not as much as Morgan, she thought to herself.

Her wide eyes refused to blink as she struggled to cope with the news of Morgan's death. A death she, herself, was responsible for. The blame Dusty felt quickly became smothering, making the cracked ribs feel like a playful snuggle from a puppy.

The tears of sorrow were slowly replaced with rage. She wanted Arlo and every last one of his men to pay for Morgan's death with their lives, even if it meant Dusty would pay with her own.

The anger continued to build up as she blamed herself for not being stronger—for not doing things differently. If she had, then maybe Morgan would still be alive today, sitting by her bed while they chatted about the stupid things teenaged girls talked about—and loving every minute of it.

She recalled the long talks they had in the clock tower each night, not to mention the ridiculous all-nighter they pulled so that Dusty could teach her how to fieldstrip and clean her gun. Morgan was unwilling to call it a night until she could do the whole thing with a blindfold. She wanted Dusty to teach her everything she knew and vice versa.

Dusty appreciated Clay and Megan taking her in, and she looked at them as friends—*good* friends—but she felt a connection to Morgan that she had not experienced with anyone back at Northfield or anywhere else for that matter. Dusty felt like she had a sister—someone she could actually lower her guard for and be who she wished she could have been. The two of them had even decided that either Morgan would come live at Northfield after the war or Dusty would stay in Liberty. They talked about being "professional" scavengers, eventually opening their own little shop. They had big plans together.

Plans, now, that would never be.

Dusty took short, rapid breaths. Her grief and rage finally reached its crescendo. She let out a furious scream, startling the quiet morning inside the infirmary. The shriek caused a host of concerned faces to look her way, including Doctor Sowell. Suddenly, her bed was surrounded by a myriad of voices asking her questions, but they all melded together as one, incoherent babbling. Her throat scorched from the cathartic release, making the mere thought of talking painful.

"Dusty!" Doctor Sowell's voice broke through, echoing above the rest. "Are you okay? What happened?"

With at least a dozen worried eyes on her, Dusty finally spoke. "Can I get a glass of water?"

Chapter 37

"Are they gone?" Megan asked in a hushed voice, sitting on the hood of a Buick LeSabre.

Clay leaned up against the wall, peering out of the filthy garage door windows. A group of bandits had wandered by just moments earlier, forcing Clay and Megan to seek cover inside a nearby mechanic's shop. "Almost," Clay replied.

The four men and one woman paid little attention to the various shops, diners, and motels surrounding them as they strolled down the road. Their casual demeanor, along with the absence of useable goods inside the buildings Clay and Megan had already searched, pointed to a scary realization: they were in claimed territory.

While only two of them were carrying rifles, all five had a pistol on their side. With fatigue impacting his every movement, Clay was certain any gunfight to erupt between him and the group would be quite short and not in his favor. So, even though the group was little more than specks on the horizon now, Clay erred on the side of caution and gave them an extra few minutes to disappear. There was no need to rush out and get spotted just so they could get back out on the road. It was still early enough in the day that time was not a big concern.

Traveling along the road as much as they were was dangerous, but due to the nature of their mission, there wasn't much to be done about it. They weren't going to find guns, ammo, and medical supplies in the middle of a hay field. If they wanted a shot at finding meaningful supplies, they had to go where the people used to be. And wherever people were, roads were built. Clay still made it a priority to travel off the beaten path whenever possible, but in an area that rural folks considered rural, there just aren't many places to keep out of sight.

Clay walked over and sat down on a short stack of tires next to the LeSabre to finish out their wait. He pulled a pack of crackers out of his bag and took a few out, handing them to Megan.

"Thanks," Megan said as she took a small bite out of the stale, white square. "So, I've gotta say, if ten years ago someone told me I would be hiding from a group of bandits in a dingy old garage with my brother while we searched for supplies to help us win a war…"

Clay grunted out a laugh. "Yeah, you're not alone. I never thought things would have gotten this bad—even after the eruptions. I mean I remember watching all the reports on the news and I knew it was going to be bad, but I just kept believing that we'd find a way to bounce back. That somehow stuff would eventually go back to normal, Dad would fly home, and it'd be business as usual by the end of the month." Clay gestured around himself. "But here we are," he said through a sigh.

"Do you ever wonder if Dad is still out there somewhere? Still fighting to get home to us?" Megan asked.

"Wow," Clay said, a little caught off guard with the question. "I haven't really thought about that in a while. I used to think he was; I even thought about going back home after we moved into the tower to leave him a note." Clay paused to mull over his next response. "But…I think Dad died ten years ago; I don't think he ever made it out of California."

Megan stared down at the half-eaten cracker in her hand. "Yeah," she said with a sniffle, "me too."

"One thing's for certain, though; I know he fought like hell to try and get back to us."

Megan smiled at the thought.

"But," he added, a hint of optimism in his voice, "there's no way to know for sure. And if a couple of kids like us could survive all this time, it's not a stretch to think that someone with *his* training and experience could, too."

"Yeah," Megan's smile grew wider.

Clay hopped off the tires and walked back to the door to confirm the group was no longer in sight. He turned around and asked, "Do you want to look around here some? Or just move on?"

"There wasn't *anything* at the motel or the diner, so I'm thinking we'd probably just be wasting our time here."

Clay nodded. "All right, then, let's get going."

Back on the road, Clay and Megan continued to head north. And though they had not gone as far north as they had originally planned, they had both decided it would be their last day traveling that direction. They would find a place to stop for the night, and then they would head south in the morning, taking a slightly different route back to the FEMA camp. From there, they'd return to Liberty with as few stops as necessary.

Clay felt some relief knowing that, after tonight, they would stop moving further away from their friends and family back in Liberty, and would be coming "home" to return to the fight—if home was still there.

Clay and Megan walked up the road for several hours and didn't so much as see a farmhouse. It was getting to be about the time of day when Clay would start thinking about a place to camp for the night, which worried him. He stopped walking and did a quick survey of the area. The featureless road they were on vanished into the horizon. To his right were rolling fields—no sign of civilization. To his left were more fields with an expanse of trees off in the distance.

"What are you thinking?" Megan asked.

Clay was less than thrilled to share his plan with Megan, mostly because he knew exactly how she would react. "I think we need to head for the tree line over there."

Megan shot him a look. "Uh, yeah...that's not gonna happen."

"I'm serious, Megan."

"Clay, there is *no way* I am walking through another forest."

Clay was empathetic to his sister's fears— walking into another ocean of trees sounded about as desirable as drinking kerosene and pissing on a brushfire. But as he took another look around, the choice was obvious. "Listen, if there was a better option, *believe me*, we'd be doing that. But there is absolutely nothing around us. It's going to probably take the better part of an hour to reach those trees out there. And with a little luck, it's just a small patch and we'll find something better on the other side."

"And if we don't?" Megan asked, glaring him down.

"Then we're better off building a shelter in the woods than staying out in the open. The trees will help with the wind, and I can build a quick lean-to with some branches and one of the space blankets to shield us from the rest. We'll really have to burrow into our sleeping bags, but we'll survive," Clay said. *I hope,* he added to himself.

"And what about the ravenous mob of lunatics that seem to be attracted to creepy forests in the night?"

"We haven't heard them in at least three days—I don't think they are this far north. We still have to worry about bandits, obviously, but I'm not terribly concerned about that at night," Clay said, trying to sound confident in his plan. "It'll be okay, Megs. I promise."

Megan exuded apprehension, but she had trusted her brother thus far and he had kept his promise to keep her safe—for the most part—so she finally relented.

Clay trudged through the snowy field, angling his body toward the trees up ahead. With each step, he felt less confident in the decision. There was no telling what would be on the other side of those trees, *if* they could even reach the other side by nightfall. He considered climbing atop one of the hills off the right of the road to get a better view of the area, but they were nearly as far away, if not further, from the trees. And if he summited the hill only to see more fields on the other side, there would be little chance they could get back to the woods and set up any semblance of a shelter before visibility disappeared.

There was no easy call to make, so Clay took a gamble on the trees. Playing the odds had kept him alive this long...

Clay's confidence was deflated as they approached the trees and were unable to see through to the other side. Dusk was a little over an hour away, so Clay decided they would keep walking. If they didn't reach the other side in thirty to forty minutes, he would scramble to set up a crude shelter for the night. Fortunately, dead trees littered the forest and would provide an excellent foundation for his lean-to. The small axe Clay had hanging from his pack and a small spool of paracaord would take care of the rest.

As if Megan's prayers had been answered, there was not much wind to speak of. The trees were calm, and there was no terrorizing howl—it was actually quite tranquil. The serene view offered a rare sense of peace; unfortunately, they were both consumed with too much anxiety to appreciate it.

A half hour quickly passed and the light had started to diminish. There wasn't much sunlight to speak of that day and being among the trees stifled the sun further.

Forty minutes. It was time to stop, but Clay's gut told him to keep going. He hated trusting his gut. Not because it was usually wrong—on the contrary, it was often right—but rather the inexplicable instinct typically only came around when it was a life or death decision. And trusting your life on a hunch was never easy.

Just five more minutes, he told himself, noting a fallen tree that would make an excellent platform for his makeshift lean-to shelter. Megan, the trooper she was, kept pace and kept her concerns to herself. Even though the walk had been nothing short of a pleasant stroll compared to their journey several nights ago, the fact they hadn't found a place to sleep for the night pecked at her psyche.

"There!" Clay said excitedly, pointing to a clearing up ahead. "We're almost out."

At the prospect of escaping the woods before nightfall, relief washed over Megan. The clearing provided a sliver of hope that a more-comfortable night was possible.

Night had all but taken over the sky, giving off just a hint of light that barely illuminated the field just past the clearing. It was bright enough, however, for Clay to see a small cabin on the other side of the field. As they reached the clearing, Clay knelt down in the snow and reached for his binoculars. He observed the cabin for a few minutes, looking for any signs of activity. Whether or not someone lived there wouldn't change that they were going to walk up to that front porch, but it *would* change how they approached it.

All was quiet. "Doesn't look like anyone's been there in a while...like, a *really* long while," he said, noticing several cords of firewood stacked up along the side of the wooden structure. He spotted what looked like multiple ATVs sitting beneath worn out tarps. It almost looked as if this little oasis had not yet been discovered since the eruptions. With trees completely surrounding the clearing, the only way to see it from the outside was by sky—and it had been quite a while since Clay had seen a plane fly overhead. He looked over at Megan with a smile. "I think we've found home for the night."

Clay stood up and walked toward the field— Megan followed. As they tromped forward, Clay couldn't help but daydream about owning a cabin like this in the pre-eruption days. A quaint little cottage in the middle of the nowhere; no loud neighbors, no city pollution. Just him, his family, and a healthy dose of nature. Even now, he would love to stake his claim on the cabin, but a week and a half hike through hell hardly seemed worth it for a family vacation.

"I am really kicking myself for forgetting that stupid map. This is a find worth saving," Clay said, trying to recall details of their journey so he could locate this spot on the map when they got back to the FEMA camp.

"I never really liked the outdoorsy stuff when we were younger," Megan said. "I never told him, but I *loathed* the annual camping trips Dad took us on. But, I'll be honest, if we had had a place like this, I probably wouldn't have minded so much," Megan said, her mind in a different time. Clay loved those trips, but he was with his sister—a setup like this would have drastically improved matters.

Both lost in alternative histories, Clay and Megan marched forward, a little less than half a field separating them from sleep. It was the sudden cracking sound that snapped Clay out of his fantasy, bringing him back to reality. Megan had heard it too—more ominously, she felt it. They both froze in place, Clay slowly turned around.

Megan looked down, her panicked eyes slowly made their way to Clay's as a paralyzing fear sunk in. Her chin began to tremble as she took in a shaky breath. "Clay...I don't think this is a fie—"

"MEGAN!" Clay shouted just as the ice broke beneath her feet.

Chapter 38

"We *have* to figure out where their camp is," Kohler insisted, his patience well beyond thin.

Shelton leaned back in his dining room chair and stared across the table at his good friend Captain Kohler. The two had been at each other's throats for the past few days—though it had mostly been a one-way street. Shelton had been hesitant to relinquish too much authority to the Army veteran since the war started, a poor choice that was now starting to catch up. It wasn't that he thought Kohler was incompetent or unwilling to lead the town—quite the opposite, actually—which was why Shelton had been reluctant. He worried that Kohler would look at the situation the same way a General might: do whatever it takes to win. Though every individual under his command had volunteered to stay and fight, they were not soldiers—names and ranks that could be replaced with someone fresh out of boot camp. These were people—members of this community who were husbands, fathers, wives, and mothers. And some of them...some of them were just kids. Shelton was afraid Kohler wouldn't see them that way if he took over at the helm. But he knew the man better than to think so lowly of him, as he had personally witnessed multiple instances when Kohler successfully walked the tight rope between drill instructor and concerned friend. He never put someone in harm's way just to gain a slight advantage over the enemy. He was methodical, intentional, and planned tirelessly to avoid casualties. Shelton would have been right to grant such leadership more freedom early on, but he was a day late and a dollar short.

"I understand that, Captain, but we just don't have the manpower to spare," Shelton replied.

"This is something I brought up with you on day one..."

"Hindsight is twenty-twenty, Daniel. Don't you think if I had known then what I know now that I would have given the okay for such an operation?" Shelton responded, matching Kohler's frustration. "I know that Arlo is a cold, relentless SOB that goes to great lengths to get his way, but I truly thought after encountering some stiff resistance, he would realize that capturing this town wasn't worth the cost." A lengthy sigh escaped from Shelton's lips. "But, I was wrong. Arlo's not going to stop until he gets this town, and he doesn't care if it costs him ten or ten-thousand men to accomplish it."

Kohler seemed to give a look that said, "I tried to warn you."

"Look, I realize now that I should have stepped aside a long time ago and given you the reins. But I can't change the past."

"You can change the future," Kohler replied. "Give me three men—I already know who I want—and we'll get it done."

Shelton folded his arms as he wrestled over the decision. Once again, he was undermining Kohler's experience for his own, personal concerns. Either Kohler was not overly concerned with being down a few men for a couple of days or he felt the risks were far outweighed by the reward. Nevertheless, Shelton shook his head. "No, I'm sorry, but I think that would be a mistake. We can't afford to lose another man for a single day, let alone three."

Kohler responded by slamming his fist down on the dining room table. "We will *not* win this war by constantly trying to stop them from carrying the ball into the end zone. If we can't get on the offense—and soon—then we would have been better off handing Arlo the keys."

Shelton stared down at the walnut table like a troubled boy avoiding an angry father.

"Look, you were the one who asked me to find a way to get us off our heels. I can't do that unless we know what we're up against and how to hit them," Kohler said calmly, slowly wrangling his anger. "Right now, we're blind and we can't keep fighting like that."

The weary old man wanted to say yes, but he couldn't. Not at this point. Not with all the losses they had already suffered and the people laid up in bed from numerous injuries, several of whom would be unable to return to their posts. Clay and Megan's absence didn't help matters, either. Shelton had been wrong up to this point, and he was the first to admit it, but he felt confident in this decision.

"I will consider your request and get back to you first thing in the morning," Shelton said.

"I've heard that load of crap before," Kohler said as he kicked back from the dining room table and stood from his chair. He gave Shelton a disapproving glare for a moment before he turned around and left, slamming the front door for emphasis.

The man is making a terrible mistake, Kohler thought to himself, shaking his head in disbelief. It was clear that Shelton was doing what he thought was best, but his lack of combat leadership had a detrimental impact on this war. And Kohler had had enough.

Breaking rank was not a decision Kohler took lightly, even in the ad-hoc militia he was currently serving in. He understood the value of the chain of command, and that every link, no matter how high up they were, must respect the one above it. Kohler had fully embraced this mentality within a few hours of stepping off the bus at Fort Sill, which is why he had bitten his tongue for so long with Shelton. In their current hierarchy, it was not for Kohler to make those calls, but rather provide Shelton with pertinent information from a veteran's perspective. Beyond that, he would be stepping out of line. But the time for chain of command was over. If there was *any* chance of them winning this war, he had to stop asking for permission and just act. And just before sundown, the captain would give his first unsanctioned order.

As he reached for the door, a part of him wanted to just turn around and leave. Even under such dire circumstances, he hated the idea of going against a direct order, especially from a man he greatly respected. But Shelton had asked him to lead the town to victory, and that was what he would do.

He stepped inside and gently shut the door. It was getting late, so the only noise in the room was from Kohler's worn out combat boots lightly treading the wooden floor. He walked across the room and stopped next to her bed. He sat down in the chair Shelton had used that morning.

Lying in bed, Dusty stared into his bloodshot eyes. His grim expression had her both concerned and excited. "What is it?" she asked.

Kohler exhaled deeply through his nose. "Are you ready to take the fight to them?"

****

After a fierce battle that had lasted nearly ten minutes, Kelsey finally gave up. The stain on the quilt held its ground and the weary mother had no more fight left in her. Conceding defeat, she spread the large, white blanket across the living room floor to dry out in front of the fireplace.

When Kelsey got down on the floor to stretch out each corner of the blanket, she caught Madeline looking her way—that same, hopeless expression plastered on her face. Kelsey's heart ached for the girl. It was bad enough she had to experience firsthand just how dark a man's heart could be. But locking the pain away with no way to escape was only adding to her agony. Kelsey was intimately familiar with such despair; it was a miracle that she had been able to escape it. But Kelsey had had something that Madeline seemed to be missing, something she didn't even seem to want.

Hope.

Kelsey had tried to help ever since they got back to Northfield, and all she got in return was silence. It felt wrong to write the girl off, but Kelsey's own family needed her undivided attention. They were her priority.

"Chip, get off!" Kelsey said, shooing away the little dog that had assumed Kelsey had spread the nice, big blanket on the ground for his benefit. Chip let out an irritated growl that was about as threatening as a hamster. Kelsey shook her head, "Devil dog, indeed."

"Mom!" Dakota called from the top of the stairs. "He's sick again!"

Kelsey pushed off the living room floor and stumbled to her feet. Exhausted, she ran up the stairs, heading to the bedroom. Covered in vomit, Charles screamed helplessly in bed, the three-year-old unable to fully comprehend what was happening to him. In outer appearance only, Kelsey calmly got him out of his soiled pajamas and cleaned his face before picking him up.

The boy was burning up and there was nothing she could do about it. Charles wasn't the first to get hit with the virus terrorizing Northfield, and he probably wouldn't be the last. The good news was that it only seemed to last forty-eight hours. The bad news was every one of those hours was loaded with misery.

"It's okay, baby," Kelsey said as she tried to lull him back to sleep. "Shhhhh, you'll feel better soon. I promise."

Charles quickly calmed down from the soothing touch that only a mother had. He quietly laid his head on Kelsey's shoulder, only the occasional sniffle breaking the silence as he drifted back to sleep.

"Can you go find him something to wear, please?" Kelsey said to Dakota.

"Okay," she said as she turned to go rummage through the closet.

Kelsey glanced over at Bethany on a small cot. Amazingly, she was still sound asleep even after

Charles's screams. *That kid could sleep through a tornado,* Kelsey thought.

Even though she stared down both barrels of yet another long, sleepless night, Kelsey was just glad to have the day behind her. A few nights ago, the wind sent some debris crashing into Rudy's pen, breaking the wooden fence and allowing the cow to escape. This morning they found a pack of feral dogs feasting on her for breakfast. Even though the failed search and rescue mission turned into a successful emergency butchering, there was a legitimate concern that the dogs might have tainted the meat with a number of diseases. Therefore, it was unanimously decided that the meat would not be dispersed among the people until starvation was imminent. The meat was stored in a large freezer chest sitting outside the workshop, snow and ice packing every spare inch of space on the inside.

The news of Rudy's death—and her meat possibly being spoiled—devastated the community and stirred up angst among both residents and guests alike. Hunting and even scavenging teams had already been working overtime trying to replenish the dwindling food supply, but even a good-sized buck would only stretch so far with so many hungry mouths to feed. Though the hunters had some success, and with each kill came some respite, the reality of the situation was one step forward, three back.

Then, shortly after lunch, two boys from Liberty started roughhousing, and the younger of the two ended up smashing through Kelsey's living room window, slicing his arm wide open. The amount of blood looked like something out of a horror movie, and if it hadn't been for Lona's quick first-aid response, things could have turned out much worse for the poor boy. The blood-soaked hardwood floor would remain a permanent reminder of this dreadful day.

To top everything off, there was a kitchen fire in the main house. It wasn't anything too serious, and nobody was hurt, but Ruth did have to use some flour—a commodity they were nearly out of—to put it out. They tried to salvage as much as they could, but they easily lost two or three loaves of bread out of it, which was no small thing during such lean times.

So, to end the day with her baby boy spiking a fever and throwing up just seemed par for the course. Kelsey was not just deflated; she was utterly demoralized. Her thoughts of her husband had gone from a longing desire to feel his embrace to a hostile bitterness over his absence. She needed him at Northfield helping to take care of his own family, not risking his life to fight someone else's war. Deep down she knew she was being selfish, but she didn't care—especially not as she clung to her sick toddler.

Kelsey laid Charles down on the floor so she could change the bed sheets. It was the last clean pair she had, after that only the mattress pad would separate the mattress from devastation. With Charles tucked back into bed and Dakota reading by candlelight in the corner, Kelsey climbed into bed, getting her feet off the ground for the very first time all day.

Though her body wouldn't allow her to forget the day's labor, sleep would come fast. Just as her eyes closed, there was a knock at the door.

What now, Kelsey screamed inside her head. She considered ignoring the request, but then another light rap on the door made her get out of bed. "I don't have it in me tonight," she said under her breath as she made her way to the door. She thought about the scathing words she might deliver to the unfortunate soul on the other side who had disturbed what little precious sleep she might actually get.

Suddenly, as if the pain in her body had ceased to exist, as if every worry, concern, or frustration fled her mind, Kelsey stood in the doorway in shock.

"I know it's late, but I was wondering if you had a few minutes to talk?"

Kelsey's thunderstruck look shifted to a tired smile. And at that moment, a sense of peace blanketed her heart. "Of course, I do, Madeline."

It was a good day.

Chapter 39

The air was stolen from her lungs the instant her head fell beneath the surface. The shock of the sudden environment change gave her the sensation that she was both upside down while also lying flat on her back. Her arms and legs felt as if they were covered with millions of vicious stinging wasps depleting their venom. The excruciating pain would have triggered a bout of vomiting if her brain wasn't already overloaded processing everything else. After several agonizing seconds, the stinging trailed off, and the numbness swooped in, bringing a terrifying relief as her body started to shut down. Though all the thoughts in her head were little more than static, a moment of rational, coherent thinking could be heard over the white noise, demanding she kick her legs and swing her arms. She complied.

As Megan's head came out of the water, she gasped for air as if she was taking her first breath of life. She thrashed around the surface, desperately seeking refuge from the biting cold that grew more intense by the second, but her hands only found more broken ice.

She heard a voice screaming; it sounded like Dad, but she knew it couldn't have been him—he was already gone for the day. *Maybe he took the day off.*

Megan's body waved the white flag. The brief but vigorous battle had drained what little energy she had left to fight. As her lungs deflated, she began to sink back down to the abyss below, her body no longer fighting.

Clay spread himself out, distributing his weight across as much snowy ice as possible in hopes that he wouldn't also break through. As his sister began to slip below the surface of the water again, Clay grasped her wrist and stopped her descent. With no real leverage to utilize, he growled violently as he relied solely on his biceps to pull Megan up, barely getting her head above the water. She gasped again as the frigid air painfully refilled her lungs. Having thrown in the towel already, Megan's near-lifeless body was only kept afloat by Clay's fading strength.

"Megan!" Clay said with a throaty shout, trying to bring his sister out of the deadly trance she was stuck in. "You've got to help me, I can't...I don't have the strength."

She gave him a delirious smile. "Five more minutes..." she replied.

Lifting Megan's body from the icy waters might have been possible for Clay under different circumstances, but the added weight from her pack and rifle made the task just out of reach, even with the endless supply of adrenaline coursing through his veins.

Operating on instinct, Clay kicked the steel toes of his boots down into the snow, each kick driving a little deeper than the last. His arms didn't have the strength, but his legs would. Or, he hoped they would, anyway.

With the tips of his boots anchored deeply into the snow, Clay didn't bother testing to see if it would hold. It had to. Using both his legs and arms, he pulled Megan out of the icy waters of the lake—engaging in a grueling game of tug-of-war with the Grim Reaper himself. Inch by inch, Clay snatched his sister away from death's gripping claw. As he got her upper body out of the water, he moved his feet back and quickly hammered his toes into two new anchor points, allowing him to repeat the process. With the bulk of her weight out of the water, he was more easily able to pull her legs from the water and drag her away from the danger.

Even though Clay had successfully pulled Megan out of the water, the battle was far from over. He needed to get her out of the cold and next to a raging hot fire. Though it had felt like hours, Clay was sure it had only been a minute or two since the ice had broken. Nevertheless, every second was vital. Clay threw his pack off his shoulders and used the quick detach on his sling, sending his rifle down into the snow. He detached the LaRue from Megan's sling the same way, and then pulled out his Seal Pup knife. Handling the fixed blade was more challenging than it should have been as he realized there was no feeling in his fingers. But, after a few seconds, he cut both straps, freeing Megan from the backpack.

With Megan slipping in and out of consciousness, Clay grabbed her arms and pulled her up over his shoulders. With barely enough strength to stand, Clay trudged toward the cabin—toward the shore—praying that the ice would hold their combined weight.

Clay held his breath as he walked across the crackling ice as fast as he could; despite his effort, his speed didn't match the urgency of the situation called for. There was no way for him to know when he finally stepped off the lake and onto solid ground, but he breathed a sigh of relief once he nearly tripped over a tree stump firmly rooted in soil.

The stumble jarred Megan back to consciousness for a moment. "I thought you had to work today, Daddy," Megan said.

I have to get her warm, Clay thought to himself, his quads and calves on fire as he covered the last bit of ground to the porch.

"Hello! I need help out here!" Clay shouted as he took the first step up the porch in the off chance someone was inside. Nobody came to their aid or tried to kill them.

The rickety porch groaned and trembled as Clay carried Megan to the door. As expected, it was locked, but, with a sharp kick Clay broke the door in, utilizing the extra weight on his shoulders. Shards of the rotted doorframe peppered the floor as Clay stumbled inside.

Keeping his grip on Megan with one hand, Clay used the other to grab a flashlight from his jacket pocket to illuminate the room. *There it is,* he thought to himself, moving straight ahead to the back of the cabin. He quickly navigated around the perfectly preserved furniture and around a large dining room table to enter what looked like the cabin's living room. He knelt down and carefully placed Megan on the floor just in front of the stone façade.

Clay wasted precious seconds Megan didn't have deciding which was most important: getting a fire going or getting the wet clothes off. He saw a blanket draped over the back of the couch and made a decision. After grabbing his knife, Clay cut Megan's shirt off, careful that his trembling hands did not cut her. He quickly unlaced Megan's boots and pulled them, along with her sopping wet socks, off her feet. He unbuttoned her pants and yanked them off her legs.

Clay walked on his knees over to the couch and grabbed the blanket. He placed it over Megan's naked body, and tucked it under her back, making sure to keep her arms and legs out of the covers.

Fire.

Digging deep and finding an auxiliary source of energy to pull from, Clay jumped to his feet and ran out the door. Practically jumping off the porch, he ran around to the side of the cabin, grabbing a couple of logs from the pile. On his way back to the front, he spotted a charcoal grill sitting beneath a cover. He tore off the tattered tarp and spotted the big white bottle on the shelf just beneath. *Lighter fluid.*

"Yes!" he said as he shuffled the logs into his right hand and grabbed the bottle with his left—it was nearly full.

Clay darted back inside, this time clipping several pieces of furniture as he hurried to the fireplace. Wasting no time, he tossed the logs inside and began dousing them with the lighter fluid. He set the bottle off to the side and reached for a lighter in his pack.

My backpack!

"Ahhh!" Clay screamed in frustration as he hobbled back to his feet. He looked down at his sister as she lay unconscious on the floor. "Hang in there, Megs," he said as he made his way to the door.

Clay sprinted out of the cabin and back to the shoreline. It took a great deal of restraint not to attempt a world record at the hundred-meter dash, but if he were to fall into the water, then *both* of them were dead. Clay moved with urgency but took great care not to test the ice's patience.

Having finally found his pack, Clay also grabbed his ARAK-21 before making his way back to shore. Feeling a bit like groundhog's day, Clay once again juked around the furniture and back into the living room. Having already retrieved his lighter, Clay dropped the pack and crouched down in front of the fireplace. He flipped the top of the lighter and gave it a flick.

The fire roared to life as it consumed the flammable liquid Clay had squirted on just a few minutes earlier. The heat was remarkable, and as much as his body fought him on it, Clay stepped out of the way so that Megan could take the brunt of it.

Her face—her body—was ghostly. He saw her chest rise as she drew in a shallow breath, giving him hope. Though Megan had taught him a few things about cold-water rescue, at this point, he had done everything he knew how to do. She was out of the wet clothes and next to a scorching fire. A scorching fire that started to fade.

"Don't you do it," Clay said as he walked back to the fireplace, hearing the sizzle from the log. "No, no, no..."

It only took another minute for the fire to finish off what remained of the lighter fluid before snuffing itself out.

It's too wet, Clay thought. He could try pouring the rest of the fluid on the logs again, hoping that it would get hot enough to dry the log *and* keep the flame going, but he wasn't going to risk the rest of the precious fluid on such a long shot. Clay got to his feet and grabbed some newspapers, books, and a few cardboard boxes and stuffed them inside. He then dragged one of the chairs away from the large dining room table and threw it to the ground. He stomped on the leg, snapping it clean off. He repeated this process until the chair was in nearly a dozen pieces before he stuck it inside on top of the various papers. Using the lighter fluid, but not nearly as much as the first time, Clay got the fire restarted, the paper quickly igniting the rest of the kindling inside.

While that burned, Clay ran back to the table and demolished a second and third chair. He filled the fireplace as full as he felt comfortable, with several chunks of broken chair to spare. Confident the fire would keep burning, Clay ran back to the log pile outside, and felt around. Grabbing a few smaller logs from the middle of the stack, Clay hauled them inside and began stripping the bark off. By then, the fire quieted down, so he added the rest of the pieces of chair. As he removed the bark from each log, he placed it in front of the fire to dry it out.

Several distressing minutes passed as Clay waited for the fire to reach a good temperature. He didn't want to have to start the process all over again by throwing damp logs on a fire that was not ready to handle such fuel. When it was ready, he carefully positioned each log in the fireplace, as to not disturb the kindling that was already ignited. He winced as he felt his skin sizzle from the heat, but it barely fazed him. All he could focus on was warming up Megan.

Once again, stepping out of the way, Clay sat down on the floor, his body starting to feel the effects of everything the night had thrown at him. He stared blankly into the fireplace, becoming mesmerized by the dancing flame as he waited to see if the logs would ignite. It felt like an eternity, but the flame finally sunk its fangs into one of the logs. Then another. And before long, the fireplace was burning hot and steady.

Clay retrieved several more logs from outside and repeated the steps from before: strip the bark and dry by the fire.

Though he was reluctant to leave Megan's side, losing the LaRue and Megan's pack would be detrimental to the success of their mission—even their survival—so Clay went back out onto the lake to retrieve both. Once he returned to the cabin, he secured the damaged front door before making his way back to the living room.

Sitting on the edge of the hearth, Clay warmed himself with the radiant heat as he looked down at his sister, her skin still so pale, and prayed for a miracle. He had done everything within his power to save her—the rest was up to her.

Chapter 40

Clay monitored Megan's condition throughout the night while he continued to feed logs into the fireplace, hoping the fire gods would remain pleased with his offerings. Finally succumbing to his exhaustion, he passed out around 3:00AM.

Much to his displeasure, Clay woke at sunrise. He kept his eyes closed as he listened to the gentle pops of the dying fire a couple feet away. As a kid, he spent many a Christmas Eve out in the living room with his blanket and pillow, listening to the same soothing sounds as he waited for morning to arrive. The nostalgic memories of better days brought with it a much-needed intermission from the grueling weeks—especially the past twelve hours—that had been battering him.

Having fallen asleep while sitting on the hearth, Clay's body was stiff and riddled with muscle spasms. He made an effort to rub the pain out of his back—a throbbing reminder that the past twenty-four hours had not been kind to him. And even less so to Megan.

Megan!

With his brain still duking it out with the morning grog, Clay had not yet checked on his sister. The guilt that the thought had not crossed his mind sooner hit hard; she should have been his very first conscious thought. He looked down to see her lying on the floor, almost exactly as she was last night. The color had returned to her skin, and a long, drawn out breath confirmed that she had pulled through. Clay's head fell back against the fireplace as he thanked God for the fortunate turn of events. And for the first time since they had left Liberty—perhaps even since the first attack—Clay felt a true sense of peace fall upon him. He hadn't forgotten about the daunting return trip still ahead of them or the looming battles they'd face once they arrived, but Megan had survived something that she shouldn't have. And *that* was more than enough reason to find some peace with the day.

As Clay looked around, he mentally smacked himself for not venturing over to the Lay-Z-Boy across the room before drifting to sleep. After the kind of night he had had, his body could have used some time in the oversized "throne" to heal. That was a mistake Clay would not make again. He had already decided they would be staying in the cabin for at least another day or two; Megan would be in no condition to travel. The added stay was yet another delay in their journey, but they both could use a couple of days to rest before making the trek back. It wasn't a matter of luxury; it was a necessity.

Glancing over at the fireplace, Clay smiled as he cherished the life-saving heat flowing out. Even though there was no longer a flame to speak of, the room was still warm, maybe even uncomfortably so. Grabbing the poker, Clay stoked the logs a bit before tossing the last two inside. He would have to venture out into the cold soon to get a few more drying off. But, since the sun was up, he decided to have a quick look around the little cabin first.

Standing to his feet was a painful endeavor that yielded far more grunts and growls than it should have. It felt as if he had been swallowed in an avalanche halfway down Everest, his body managing to find every tree and boulder along the way. The blinding pain in his legs made each step wobbly and raw, and his shoulders felt as if he had a sack of bowling balls slung over each one. Clay started to wonder if the near constant flow of adrenaline his body had produced lately was as much to blame as the physical punishment he had taken. At that moment, however, it didn't matter. The pain was real, regardless of its origin.

The décor of the cabin was expected for a cottage out in middle of the woods in Texas: wood-paneling slapped up in every direction, an abundance of mounted fish and animal heads crammed into the living room, the biggest mounted directly onto the chimney. There was a long, hand-made dinner table sitting almost perfectly in the middle of the cabin, acting as a divider between the four living spaces in the giant open room. Above the table was a tacky deer antler chandelier. The cabin was the epitome of cliché, and if Clay owned the place, there wasn't a single thing he would have changed about it.

Sidestepping the dinner table, Clay headed straight for the kitchen nook. Whoever built the cabin spared no expense. With granite countertops and slate tile on the ground, this cabin, although decorated in a way most would describe as rustic, if not redneck, was nicer than a lot of homes. Clay laughed when he saw a cute little ceramic bear hanging on the side of one of the cabinets; the bear was holding a sign that said, *Please feed the bears.*

Next to the stove was a tall, oak pantry cabinet just begging to be opened. He wasn't planning on doing a thorough search of the cabin just yet, but his curiosity forced a peek inside.

Food!

The small pantry might as well have been a grocery store—there were dozens of cans, boxes and sealed packages neatly placed on three different shelves. Several sealed two-gallon buckets sat on the floor—the contents inside a total mystery—adding to Clay's curiosity. There was easily more than they could carry back with them, and that was just one small closet.

Clay could feel his smile reach his ears. He hadn't found a score like this since the first year—it was just unheard of these days. Fueled by such a success, he decided to take a quick, high-level look around the rest of the cabin before braving the blustery cold outside to prepare more firewood.

The food in the pantry confirmed Clay's suspicions that he and Megan were the first to visit the old cabin since the collapse. Whatever the former-occupants had left behind for the following season was still there. And as Clay explored the downstairs a little more, he discovered a glut of miscellaneous goods that he itched to take back home; he was not looking forward to deciding what was essential and what was indulgent.

As he looked around, his eyes caught several Ugly Stiks stacked neatly in the corner, just waiting to reel in a monster bass. He told himself that it wouldn't take up much space if he broke the rod in half and fastened it to his pack. *But how will that help Liberty,* he heard the voice of reason ask, reminding him of the real reason they were at that cabin in the first place. Clay's personal shopping list would have to wait until he, Geoff, and Dusty could return to the cabin in the spring.

A narrow staircase sat against the wall just in front of the door. The stairs led up to a loft-like area that covered nearly three-quarters of the cabin. Clay clenched his teeth and winced as he hiked his leg up on to the first step. The turtle-like speed Clay could climb the stairs allowed him to get a good look at the long stretch of family photos following the wall. The first picture was labeled *1988,* and had a man holding hands with a *very* pregnant woman, standing just in front of the same cabin Clay stood in. Each subsequent frame held the same couple, the number of children and fashion styles changing every few steps.

Clay's emotions pinballed as he saw the family's story unravel through annual snapshots of their life. By the time he reached the last photo, the year before the eruption, the young couple proudly sported a bit of gray in their hair and some wrinkles around their eyes. The children were mostly grown, with the youngest appearing to be in her late teens. A beautiful woman stood next to the oldest son, a child in her arms. They all looked at the camera with joyful expressions as they looked forward to another year together as a family.

Clay wanted to believe that this big, happy family managed to safely stay together after the collapse, but experience told him that was just a fairytale. Even if they had all stayed together, he had yet to meet a single person in the last five years who hadn't lost loved-ones since the ash smothered the earth...and his jaded sense of reality told him this family was no different, whether he wanted to accept it or not.

But he willingly chose to believe this family was the exception to the rule.

Clay was out of breath by the time he reached the top stair. He stepped into a small family room with a loveseat and a few beanbag chairs in front of a flat screen. Down a very small hall were three doors, each one opening to cramped bedrooms not much larger than the holding cells back at the FEMA camp. One room had a triple-stacked bunk bed along the wall and the other two had queen-sized accommodations. The third room—which was a little bigger than the others—was decorated with more photos documenting the happy family's history.

His eyes immediately landed on the rifle safe on the far side of the room. It wasn't anything heavy-duty—just a thin-gauged steel with a piano hinge—you could pick up at a department store for a hundred bucks. It was enough to keep inquisitive kids out of trouble or unmotivated thieves from a quick score, but it wasn't good for much else. Clay didn't liken himself to a thief, but he was motivated. And if he didn't find the key lying around the cabin somewhere, he already had in mind a few alternative methods to crack the door.

He gingerly made his way back downstairs, grabbed his coat, and headed outside. The picturesque setting was even more impressive in daylight; it was truly a haven in every sense of the word. He walked around back and spotted a small toolshed about thirty feet behind the cabin. Right next to it was a large propane tank. He rapped on the side, hearing a loud, metal echo. He had no idea how much was left inside, or whether the lines running to the house were still in working order, but the prospect of a hot meal tonight made him feel like a million bucks.

After stripping the bark off a half-dozen logs, Clay carried them inside and positioned each one in front of the red-hot remnants in the fireplace. After preparing another ten logs, he needed something a little less physically taxing to pass the morning, so he decided it was a good time to investigate the contents of that pantry a little closer.

Until he heard Megan stirring.

He turned around to see his sister lifting the blanket, looking down at her body.

"Uhm, Clay," she asked nonchalantly.

"Yes?"

"Why am I naked?"

Chapter 41

Megan stared blankly at the floor as Clay painfully recalled the events from the day before. At first, she thought he was joking—she didn't remember any of that happening. But the grim look on her brother's face assured her that this wasn't just some twisted prank. She struggled to retrieve memories from her head that would corroborate Clay's account, but she barely recalled walking into the woods with him. After that, it wasn't even a blur; it was a black hole.

She felt like she should cry over the near-death experience, but she couldn't. She should feel shaken, but she wasn't. It just didn't feel real to her, so why stress over it? Megan had enough things terrorizing her mind; she didn't need the added angst from what felt like fiction.

Clay insisted she take it easy throughout the day, letting her in on his plan to crash at the cabin an extra day or two. Megan, rarely giving herself a break, told Clay the best thing to aid in her recovery was to be active. With no way of verifying her statement, Clay relented, trusting that Megan would listen to her body, and rest when she had hit her limit.

So, the siblings began to search the house more thoroughly than Clay's initial walk-through. The squeal that came out of Megan's mouth when Clay showed her the pantry could have shattered crystal. Having lived off stale crackers and extra gamey rabbit meat over the past week, the variety the pantry offered was nothing short of incredible.

After sorting through the food, and discarding more than half that was inedible, they still had more than they could carry back with them. Megan rummaged through the bathroom while Clay poked around the main living space. His mind kept drifting to what might be waiting inside the safe upstairs, but he was not quite yet up to the physical challenge of breaking the thing open. He was hopeful that he might get lucky and find the key hidden amongst the clutter, saving him time and energy.

Clay was encouraged with the various, useful items he found while searching the first floor. He started with a cardboard box he had noticed sitting on top of a coffee table in the corner, *ORM-D* stamped across the side. Inside he found several boxes of shotgun shells, both twelve and twenty gauge, in a variety of loads. Next to the box was a Rambo-sized hunting knife that was on the edge of ridiculous. But the blade was as sharp as any of his own knives, so it was a viable contender for bag space. As he expanded his search, he found a wide array of items from matches and fishhooks to an ancient break-barrel twenty gauge.

Clay had placed a few of his findings on the dinner table when Megan came out of the bathroom smiling. "I take it you had some luck in there?" Clay asked.

"Yep," she replied as she dangled a plastic shopping bag between two fingers. She set the bag down on the table and opened it up, pulling items out one by one. "A premade first-aid kit, *several* boxes of bandages, tweezers, scissors, antiseptic, and..." Megan said, a huge grin on her face, "an unopened box of Celox!"

Clay looked at the box in her hand and tilted his head. "What is it?"

"Clots blood. *Fast.* Not a permanent fix, mind you, but it might stop someone from bleeding out before they can get to the infirmary." Both knew that that was a problem several people had faced since the war began.

"Sweet!" Clay said enthusiastically. It sounded like a vital product for a field medic to have on hand; he just hoped he never had to test its effectiveness. "Anything else?"

"Nothing pertaining to my expertise so much, but I did find this—thought it might be of some use," she said as she handed Clay a flare gun, still in the packaging.

"Nice!" Clay exclaimed. "Find any more flares?" he asked, looking down at the three that came with the gun.

Megan shook her head. "Sorry, that's it."

"Don't be," Clay said. "It's still a good find."

Megan looked down at the table of goodies Clay had found. "I see you've had a productive morning as well," she said, a genuine enthusiasm filled her voice. "What's all this about?" She motioned to the separated piles on the table.

"Everything on that half of the table is the 'must go' pile," Clay said, gesturing to his left. "Stuff on this side of the table," he looked to his right, "is TBD. We can cherry pick after we see how much space we have left in our bags."

Megan bit her lip as she nodded along. "Okay, that sounds good. Speaking of bags, where's mine?"

Clay tilted his head toward the front door. "I tossed it somewhere over by the door," he said as he contemplated moving a few items from the "maybe" pile to the "must go."

Megan walked over to the front door and quickly found her pack. She crouched down next to it and unzipped the main compartment.

"Shoot!" she said under her breath as she looked inside. "Everything is soaking wet, Clay."

Before Clay could respond with a sarcastic comment about the little-known fact that water is wet, he remembered some of the items in Megan's pack. "Are the pills...?"

Megan pulled out the baggie and held it up. The mixture of pressed capsules and gel caps made for a chunky, colorful paste.

"Crap!"

"I did manage to make use of the empty space in that prescription bottle you found in the desk," she said as she popped the lid off the orange, plastic container and looked inside, "Well, except for the top couple of pills, everything in here looks okay, but..." Megan gave off a remorseful sigh as she moved her eyes back to the ruined bag of pills, "that's a whole lot of pain people are going to have to feel now."

Clay scratched at his itchy scruff as he shook his head. "There's absolutely *nothing* you could have done, Megan. In fact, you were thinking ahead by filling up the prescription bottle. So, with that plus what we still have back at the bunker, we're still in a whole lot better shape than we were before we left."

Megan shrugged. "Yeah, I know. It just sucks—these pills could have made a big difference in somebody's life."

Megan's frustration only grew as she dug deeper into the bag, discovering that bandages and various other items were now ruined. By the end, she had a small pile of wet, useless junk next to her feet. With an irritated groan, Megan picked herself up off the floor and walked back over to Clay at the table, placing the remaining contents of her pack onto the table before continuing to search the rest of the cabin.

By the time lunch had rolled around, there was no space between the two piles on the dinner table—and that didn't include the food in the pantry or a thorough sweep upstairs. As Clay surveyed their findings, even with the two additional duffel bags they had brought, there was no way it was all going to fit. It was a good problem to have, but a problem nonetheless. Weight was just as much of a factor as size. Clay's backpack was already pushing forty pounds, not to mention his chest rig. He guessed the duffel bag would easily double his pack with all the things he wanted to bring—if he could even cram them all into the bag.

The realization that they would likely be taking back less than he initially thought irked him. But this wasn't a movie, and he wasn't some buffed out action hero. Both Clay and Megan were, medically speaking, malnourished. They were also exhausted, having managed to find a way to burn the candle at three ends. There was no way to know what was in store for them on their return trip, and strapping more than 150 pounds to his back was not realistic. It was time to whittle down the "must go" pile even further.

Underestimating the hypothermal thrashing she took the previous night, Megan's body grew tired much quicker than she expected. Clay suggested she go up to the loft and take a nap in the far bedroom— she put up very little fight.

As soon as the bedroom door shut, Clay began to comb over the areas Megan had already been through—just to be sure. He was pleased and disappointed with his efforts. Pleased that Megan had done such a thorough job, disappointed there was nothing new to find.

Evening came fast, catching Clay by surprise when he noticed the muted sky start to fade. A ferocious growl echoed in his stomach, a not-so-subtle reminder that he had skipped breakfast and lunch. *Again.* And with the overabundance of food at his disposal, there was no excuse to be doing that while they stayed at the cabin.

With Megan still conked out in the master suite, Clay decided it was time to see if the propane tank out back had any fuel left. He grabbed a couple of cans from the pantry and then a couple of smaller pots next to the sink. Giving the oven knob a sharp twist, the igniter clicked persistently, but the burner wouldn't light.

He turned the knob off, wondering if it was out of propane or if the line coming into the cabin had been damaged until the putrid smell hit his nose. The propane was flowing, the igniter, however, was not functioning. Clay fetched his lighter from his bag and waited a few minutes to let the excess propane dissipate. Cranking the knob once again, he opened his lighter and flicked the flint wheel.

Success!

Dumping each can of food into a separate pot and letting them come to a simmer over the stove top, Clay found himself bouncing up and down on his toes, eagerly waiting for them to reach the optimal temperature. Dinner's aroma slowly drifted around the cabin, eventually enticing Megan to get out of bed.

"I don't know what you're up to down there, Cheffy-Boy, but that smells amazing," she said as she walked down the stairs.

"Go have a seat in the living room, it'll be ready in a few minutes," Clay replied.

Megan slowly finished the descent before heading over to the living room. She pulled down the clothes she had hung to dry on a stretch of paracord and placed them on the couch before plopping down on the opposite side. "I don't think I've ever been to a bed and breakfast before."

"Well, more like a bed and dinner," Clay said as he grabbed a ladle from a ceramic pot next to the sink and portioned out their dinner.

"Well, whatever you want to call it, it's food and it's hot, so I'll take it."

Clay came out of the kitchen holding a plate in each hand. "I slaved over that stove for like, five whole minutes preparing this meal, so you *better* like it."

Megan chuckled from her excitement. She licked her lips as Clay passed her the plate. Her eyes grew as wide as her smile when she looked down at the plate. "Refried beans and corn!" she said with nostalgic joy. "You remembered my favorite!"

"Sorry, I didn't see any rice."

In their previous life, when being choosy over your food wasn't going to mean starvation, Megan had become a vegetarian. For years, the family had made it a Friday night tradition to have dinner at Chuy's. Megan had become so obsessed with the chicken fajitas that the servers stopped asking what she wanted to order. But, the Friday before her fifteenth birthday, she ordered a bowl of rice and corn with a side of refried beans, and never had a fajita again. So, when Clay opened the cabinet that morning, and saw those two cans sitting right in front of his face, he knew what he'd make for dinner.

Megan grabbed the fork out of Clay's hand and immediately dug in. A lengthy "Mmmm" immediately followed. "Oh, sweet mother, this is heavenly."

Clay walked over to the recliner and sat down before shoveling in more food than his mouth could fit. "So," he said, several kernels of corn spilling from his mouth, "what made you decide to stop eating meat."

Megan laughed through a chew. She shook her head with a smile before taking another bite. "Alex Charters," she said before taking a sip of water.

"I knew it was a guy!"

"Yep. Alex Charters. He was a grade ahead of me and I had the biggest crush on him."

"Why didn't you ever mentioned him to us?" Clay asked, continuing to throw dinner etiquette to the dogs as food shot out of his mouth with his question.

"Well, let's see, he was a vegan, and...yep, that alone would have bugged the daylights out of Dad."

Clay laughed. "Yeah, Dad was not exactly subtle when it came to his thoughts on men refusing to eat meat."

"Nope," Megan said with a full mouth. She gulped down her big bite before adding, "And what he would or wouldn't eat was just the beginning."

"Wait a second," Clay said, his eyes looking up toward the ceiling as he recalled a distant memory. "I can't believe I remember this, but is he the guy that kept posting all that political crap on your Facebook wall?"

Megan nodded. "Yeah, that was him."

Clay let out a deep laugh from his stomach. "Yeah, Dad would have had that dude hanging upside down from the big oak tree in our front yard if he ever came to take you out."

"And that's why I never brought him up," Megan said with a smile. "Actually, though, once I spent a little bit of time with him and stopped idolizing him from afar, he turned out to be a pretty big jerk. But by then, I had gotten used to eating rabbit food, so," she said as she took the last bite on her plate, "I just kept at it."

With their stomachs full and a roaring fire, the two reminisced for a while, mostly talking about the pre-eruption days. Clay couldn't remember the last time he felt so relaxed. After everything they had been through the past couple of months, it was nice to be able to sit down and just talk to his sister again—like he used to back in the tower.

As the conversations died down, Megan began to shift uncomfortably in her seat.

"You okay?"

"Yeah...no...sort of, I guess."

"Wow, that wasn't vague or anything. What's going on, Megs?"

Megan twirled her hair around her finger as she tried to convince herself that she didn't have the energy for the conversation about to happen. "I really don't know how to say this, so I'm just gonna say it."

Clay gave her a funny look. "Uh oh, should I be scared?" he joked.

"I'm worried about you."

"Worried?"

Megan took a deep breath as she tried to keep her composure. "Ever since Mom died, and you stepped up to the plate to fill Dad's role, I've always labeled you as my 'big little brother'. Yes, you are younger than me, but I still look up to you. I still remember just how impressed I was with how you handled every situation thrown our way. After Michelle died, I thought you were going to finally lose it. And then there was Charlie and then we had to pick up and leave the tower...I thought for sure that eventually it would all catch up to you, but it never did. Whenever you got knocked down, you stood right back up, standing taller than before, and carried on. And no matter what, you followed a moral compass even when nobody else bothered to. You did not allow yourself to become a product of your situation."

The tears in Megan's eyes quickly built up and started to fall down her face. She sniffled a few times before continuing. "But after watching you kill those men outside the camp...you're not the brother I looked up to..."

"Megan, those men—"

"I know," Megan interrupted, "I know what they would have done to us—what they would have done to *me*. I know that you did what you had to do to keep us alive. But those last two, Clayton...they didn't have a chance in hell before you sent them there," she said as she rubbed her bleary eyes. "And it's not even just that you killed them, but you...you didn't even seem bothered by it. It was just another day at the office for Clayton Whitaker."

Clay remained silent for a moment as Megan's searing words scorched his conscience. "You're right, I have changed, Megan, but as you've seen firsthand," Clay said, gesturing toward the door, "things aren't getting any prettier out there. In fact, it's the opposite of that. And if you had spent as much time out there

DARKER DAYS

as I have, you'd understand where I'm coming from,"
he said, resorting back to his argument on the road.

Megan nodded along. "I know. And I'm not going
to pretend like I know what all you've been through
over the years, Clay, but you of all people should
know that I've battled my fair share of demons, too,"
she reminded him again. "You're not the only one
suffering, the only one praying that God would just
rain down fire and brimstone and just end it all.

"I remember that story you told Charlie years
back," Megan said as she leaned toward Clay, causing
him to look up at her bloodshot eyes. "*Stop* feeding
that wolf, Clayton. Because if you don't, it *will*
consume you, and I'd sooner dive headfirst back into
that lake out there than watch my brother become
the very thing he's fought against his entire life."

Clay's tormented eyes looked deep into Megan's;
he remained silent.

"I understand the world has changed, Clay.
Taking a life to save one has become a terrible
standard, but I realize that it's a necessary one. The
instant you forget that they are still people, though,
you're going to find yourself on a dark path, and it's
not going to end well for you. *Or* your family."

Unable to speak, Clay reached out and grabbed
Megan's hand, squeezing it tight.

"Men who are unwilling to compromise their
values just to survive is the only chance this world
has to ever being restored. That man is still inside
there, little brother," Megan said, pointing to Clay's
chest, "but you need to stop believing that *that* man is
too weak."

Clay gave her hand another squeeze before
standing up. "I need to, uh, go get some ice from the
lake so we can have something to drink in the
morning." His hand slipped out of hers as he walked

toward the kitchen, grabbing his coat and a large pot off the counter. He stopped just short of the front door and turned around. "Megan, I..." his mind was filled with a million different things he wanted to say, but only one word came to his lips. "Thanks."

"I love you," Megan said with a tired smile, feeling like she had gotten her message through to him.

"I know ya do," he replied before grabbing his rifle and walking out into the moonless night.

He hadn't made it halfway to the lake before his emotions got the best of him. Clay had not been oblivious to his dark demeanor lately, but hearing how it affected Megan, and likely everybody close to him, had knocked the wind out of him. There was no doubt he had been headed down a bad path for quite some time, but the murky veil that had been smothering his conscience made him believe that he was still in control of himself; that he was only doing what was absolutely necessary, given the circumstances. But as images of that Screamer's terrorized face illuminated by the fierce muzzle flash of his Glock 17 assaulted his conscience, he realized that he was anything but in control.

The delayed guilt, compounded with interest, hit hard as the full weight of Clay's actions fell squarely onto his shoulders. The nausea he felt for cold-bloodedly taking that man's life was a welcoming sensation. He still didn't know whether he could justify the action itself or not, but his callous indifference over those kinds of choices had to stop. As twisted and ugly as the Screamers were, they're still people, and Clay had to remember that. Always. And though he had no intention of laying his arms down so long as the rule of law was not present, the state of his mind and heart when he pulled the trigger mattered.

At least, it did to him.

Chapter 42

One by one, Dusty tossed several twigs into the small fire she had made just a few feet away from her tent. Having a fire in the middle of the woods at night was downright stupid, but the alternative—freezing to death—didn't sound all that appealing, either.

She sat down on a rock, her rifle sitting across her lap, and looked down at the dancing flames. As she watched small embers pop out of the crackling fire and float high into the trees, Dusty racked her brain as to where Arlo and his men could be. She had already crossed off the list of suggestions Kohler had given her before she left, as well as a handful of other promising locations she stumbled upon during her travels. But there were no signs of them anywhere. The tracks went cold just a couple of miles away from Liberty, giving Dusty a general idea of their direction, but still an impossible amount of ground to cover in the time that she had.

Of the week's supply of food she had brought, there was only a day, maybe two left if she starved herself a bit. Rationally speaking, she should head back to Liberty at first light, but Dusty wasn't the rational type. The girl had spent nearly seven years of her childhood fending for herself, so she wasn't about to sweat a few extra days without a safety net.

As she nibbled on a few morsels of food, she thought about the remorse on Shelton's face when she lied to him, telling him that she couldn't fight anymore and wanted to go home. After Morgan's death, Dusty *did* want to throw in the towel and go back to Northfield. She even considered going back out on her own again—after all, she couldn't feel the pain of losing a friend if she didn't have any to begin with. However, her desire to settle the score was much greater than her wishes for solitude. And while she lay in bed, thinking of how she could accomplish that goal, Captain Kohler walked in with his proposal. Knowing that Shelton would never agree for her to take on such a dangerous, if not suicidal, mission, she lied.

Shelton didn't bat an eye with her false request and offered his heartfelt gratitude for all that she had done before apologizing for what she had lost. He made sure she was well equipped for her journey back to Northfield and even woke up early to see her off, giving her his very own pistol on her way out the gates. Shelton was by far the kindest, most genuine man she had ever met, and it was evident that *every* decision he made had the well-being of others right at the center.

Lying was a skill that Dusty had become quite proficient at over the years, and after a while she became completely desensitized to it. But as soon as she bluffed the old mayor, the look of grief on his face was seared into her memory as if she had stared into the pre-eruption sun. It felt like she had lied to her own grandfather. Feeling guilt for lying to someone was uncharted for her, and she used this unpleasant feeling as additional motivation to find Arlo. She didn't want to come back empty-handed, but *especially* not after deceiving Shelton.

With the fire burning and "dinner" consumed, Dusty was about ready to turn in for the night when she heard footsteps shuffling through the snow. She jumped up and aimed her rifle in the general direction of the sound. "Don't come any closer!" she commanded.

"Whoa! Easy there, girlie," a man appearing to be in his late twenties replied, a similar hunting rifle slung over his shoulder and a pistol holster hanging off his belt. He slowly raised his hands into the air and talked with a calm, gentle voice. "I didn't mean to startle you none, I was just headin' back home when I smelled your fire."

The man continued to close the gap between him and Dusty. She pressed her shaking gun—which was more for show than nerves—tighter into her shoulder. "I told you to stop," she barked, "unless you have some sort of lead fetish, I wouldn't take another step if I were you."

Dusty's threat did not fall on deafened ears and the stranger stopped walking. The small fire dimly illuminated his odd facial features, his pale white skin and his intensely bright blond hair. The man was in desperate need of a set of braces, twice, and his tattered coat barely made it down to his hips, yet seemed to swallow him. The man couldn't have weighed more than a buck forty with a full tank of gas.

With his hands still in the air, posing no immediate danger, he continued to talk. "It's awful dangerous for a sweet, young thing like you to be out here on your own—'specially this time of day," he said, looking up through the scraggly canopy above to the darkening sky.

"I've been on my own for many years, mister, this ain't my first campout under the stars and I'm sure it won't be my last."

"Well, it doesn't have to be that way, ya know," he responded with an earnest smile, attempting to mask the menacing one.

Dusty lowered her rifle slightly and raised her eyes above the scope. "What are you talking about?"

"Well, like I said, I was just heading back home when I smelled your fire. It's just a few miles from here, and we're always looking for new, friendly faces to join our community. And I gotta say, you've got the friendliest looking face I've seen in quite some time."

Dusty played along and forced a smile. "How many in your group?"

"Oh, we've got boats of people back home," he said enthusiastically. "All different ages, too. I know for a fact there's quite a few teenagers always gettin' themselves into trouble, ya know, just doin' what teenagers do." The man sounded sincere, but Dusty wasn't taking the bait. "Anyway, I think you'd like it there, I bet you'd fit in real good."

Her rifle came down even more as she feigned interest in the man's offer. "How long you guys been there?"

"Well that's the beauty of it, this place is nice and all, but we've got our eyes set on greener pastures. We're in the process of negotiating a deal with another group to let us live on their farm. A place where we can grow our own food, access to fresh water…a comfy, warm bed to sleep in," he said as his lustful eyes narrowed on Dusty's physique. "So, what do ya say? Why don't I help you pack up this here tent, and you can come back with me? Like I said, it's not much for now, but it beats sleeping out in the cold like this, waiting for those Berserkers to come walking by."

She had all but lowered the gun now, giving the man a false sense of hope, but he still respected her wishes to keep the distance. "Where is it?" she asked.

"Well," the man replied, dragging out the word. "I can't just go and tell you that…"

"But you're willing to up and take me there?"

"Well, while we do have an open-door policy for new folks such as yourself, we do have some…precautions that we like to take before letting newcomers inside. We've had a lot of people trying to attack us lately, to take what's rightfully ours, so we can get a tad antsy when a stranger just walks right up to our doorstep, ya know? It'd just be easier—and safer—if I was with you, just to make sure no one sees you as a threat or somethin' like that," he said, stammering over his words.

Dusty acted as if she was truly contemplating his proposition before declining. "Well, mister, I do appreciate the offer, but there are a few precautions of my own that I like to take, and it has kept me alive this long. As it turns out, following a stranger who just surprised me in the woods back to his place is *not* one of them."

The man gave a light-hearted chuckle. "Look, I totally understand. I'd probably say the same thing if I were in your shoes," he said as he shrugged off her rejection. "Well, it's not as if I can give you my phone number in case you change your mind, but if we ever cross paths again, consider the offer a standing one."

"Thank you," Dusty replied with a flirtatious smile.

"Well, stay safe, uh…"

"My name's Morgan."

"It's good to meet you, Morgan. I'm Rhett. Anyway, stay safe, maybe I'll see you again someday."

Without another word, the man turned around and left the same way he had come. Dusty thought about following him, but she would be one broken twig away from getting into a shootout with him, at which point she'd either lose the trail or lose her life. Neither outcome was acceptable, so she decided to practice patience instead and wait for another opportunity.

She didn't have to wait long.

Sometime in the middle of the night, Rhett crept back into Dusty's camp and silently approached the tent. He pressed his knife into the fabric just to the left of the zipper and began cutting. As he pulled the cut fabric away, he could just barely make out the sleeping bag. "Oh, little girl, you have no idea the kind of night I have in store for you," he panted quietly. As he leaned inside the tent, his stomach sank when he felt the barrel of a gun press firmly into his temple. Then came the unmistakable sound of a hammer being wrenched back.

"In case you are wondering, that is the business end_of a Browning Hi Power up against your skull. And I gotta warn you, this thing has a custom trigger job on it; a duck farting in Texarkana would set it off, so don't make any sudden moves."

"Morgan? It's me, uh, Rhett. I was actually coming here to warn you about a group of bandits I saw heading your way and uh—"

"So, tell me about this night in store for me?" Dusty interrupted as she flicked her flashlight on, revealing a look of terror on Rhett's face. "Drop the knife, and get over there, now," she ordered, pointing to the opposite side of the tent. "And God help you if I see your hand move anywhere near that holster.

Rhett swallowed hard as he walked on his knees to the other side of the tent. "Okay, okay. Take it easy, Morgan, there ain't no reason for that kind of talk. I ain't gonna try nothin' stupid. Like I said earlier, I like ya, and I think you'd fit in real good with our group. Even more so, now," he said followed by a nervous chuckle. "You've got a spunk about ya that I think everyone back home will appreciate."

"Well, it *does* sound like a nice place. Why don't you go ahead and tell me where it is, and I'll swing by and give it a look-see."

Rhett played every bit the part of a stupid redneck, but he had already figured out what was going on. Realizing that she wasn't buying his act, his demeanor shifted. "So, I'm guessing all the men back at your camp were all too gutless to come find us themselves, so they sent a little girl to do their dirty work."

"Hmmm," Dusty replied, "*or* they sent the right person for the job. After all, here I am with the very person who is going to tell me what I want to know."

"And what makes you think I'm going to do that?"

"Either ya do, or you experience firsthand what it's like to breathe out of your forehead."

"Oh, come on, Morgan," Rhett said with a smirk. "We both know you ain't got it in ya."

"Is that so? If you're so sure I'm not willing to pull this trigger, then tell me why you haven't reached for that CZ 75 in your holster there?" Rhett gave her a surprised look. "Yep, the little 'girlie' knows her guns. Actually, I find it a little ironic that

that's what you're carrying, seeing as it's the Czech knockoff to this American beauty here," Dusty said, giving her Hi Power a tilt. "Speaking of which, why don't you go ahead and use your left hand and take the gun out of the holster, *slowly*, and toss it out the tent."

While Rhett complied with the command, Dusty kept the Hi Power trained on his head, her finger ever so slightly squeezing the trigger.

After tossing the gun out of the tent, Dusty continued. "I *do* think you are scared of me, and if I am being honest, you really should be. So, why don't we just skip all this back and forth, and you just tell me what I want to know?"

Rhett looked Dusty in the eyes; he knew she wasn't bluffing. "All right, I'll make a deal with ya," the man said with a twisted grin on his face. "Lately, I ain't been too crazy about that Arlo guy—I don't think he's all there, if ya know what I mean. I've already been fixin' to leave his outfit for a few weeks anyhow, so why don't we turn this into a win-win for both of us.

"How is that?"

"How about you and I spend a couple of quality minutes over there in that nice, warm sleeping bag of yours, and then I'll tell you *everything* you want to know. After that, we go our separate ways."

Dusty had to swallow the bile that skulked up her throat. "You promise to tell me everything?" she said, stringing the man along.

"Scout's honor," he said as he held up his right hand, a look of hope flashed in his eyes.

"Well, I've got something of a counter offer for ya. You tell me where they are first," she said, a mocking smile on her face, "and I...won't...kill you. I realize it's not quite the deal you were hoping for, but I'm afraid it *is* the only one on the table."

The man's grin turned into an insolent sneer. "All right, all right, I know when I am beat. What you want to do is take that road just to the north of where we are now, then you can follow it all the way to hell."

Dusty's response came in the form of a 124-grain hollow point.

Rhett screamed out in pain as he clutched his shoulder with his left hand. "You crazy little bi—"

"Ah, ah, ah...I'd watch that tone there, mister. You're only on strike one; strike two is going to be a whole different ballgame," Dusty said as her slack wrist dropped the gun's barrel toward the man's groin.

Rhett breathed heavily through his nose as he shifted his clenched jaw side to side. "Fine," he grunted. "Fine! Screw it, they ain't worth dying for."

"That's a good boy," Dusty said as she set the flashlight on the ground and leaned back on the palm of her left hand, while the other rested the gun over her knee, still aimed toward Rhett. "Go on."

After some angry grumbles, Rhett started talking. "Head south from here, in about two or three miles you'll come out on a big field. On the other side of that field is a rural highway—can't remember the name but it's the first one you cross. Take the road east about another mile then you'll see a sign for Texas Premiere Cattle Auctions, take a right at the driveway and you'll find them inside," he said, his nostrils flaring as he growled through the pain.

"See, that wasn't too hard, now was it?"

"So, I kept up my end of the deal," Rhett said as he shifted his weight, trying to get to his feet.

"Whoa there, slugger, you aren't going anywhere just yet."

Rhett sat back down, his face red. "You said that you would let me go when I told you what you wanted to know."

"No," Dusty replied sarcastically, "I said that I wouldn't *kill* you. Do you really think I am dumb enough to just take you for your word? I'm going to make sure you *actually* held up your end of the bargain before I cut you loose. So, on that note," Dusty said as she pulled out a zip tie from her pocket and tossed it over to Rhett. "Never leave home without one. Now get to it."

Rhett started laughing. "Boy, you must think you're pretty tough there, don't ya?"

"Well, I'm not the one with a bullet hole in my arm, so..."

Rhett leaned back as he laughed loudly, but when his body came back forward he leapt toward Dusty, knocking the gun out of her hand. The two of them wrestled around the tent as each frantically searched for the pistol. Rhett managed to get on top of Dusty momentarily, but his slender frame did not give him much advantage over the girl. As he used his left hand to try and choke her, Dusty managed to land several blows to his injured shoulder.

While Rhett was dazed by the pain, Dusty knocked him off her and anxiously resumed her search for the gun. Her hand had found a handle—it wasn't the one she was looking for, but it would do. As Rhett stood to his feet, the Hi Power in his hand, Dusty's arm swung around and plunged his own knife deep into his stomach. The air rushed out of his lungs with a look of horrific surprise plastered across his face. He tried to bring the pistol up but Dusty batted his arm away. She drove the Tanto blade deeper into his abdomen as she twisted the handle—Rhett's blood poured out onto her arm, splattering all over the tent floor. He made another feeble attempt at shooting her, but Dusty once again defeated his efforts.

With another good push, Dusty shoved Rhett back, causing him to fall out of the tent. He made noises that no human being long for this world could make, and it was only a matter of time before the man would take his final breath.

With the knife still lodged in his gut, Dusty easily overpowered the dying man and regained control of her pistol. She stood up and towered over the gangly man as life drained from his body. She looked at his face, the subtle glow of the flashlight inside the tent revealing nothing more than a scared little boy as he saw death approaching. Unable to find his voice, he pleaded for help with his eyes.

She lifted her arm and leveled the Browning's sights on Rhett's head. Images of Morgan staring up at her flashed through Dusty's mind as she curled her finger around the trigger. Her breathing was irregular, her heart pounding rapidly. She closed her eyes and fired, ending Rhett's suffering.

The echo of the nine-millimeter seemed to go on for days as it made its way through the forest.

Dusty leaned against a nearby tree and slowly slid down to the ground, folding her arms across her bent knees. Her stone-like exterior had started crumbling the moment she learned of Morgan's death. And after her scuffle, it was merely a heap of ruins surrounding her. At that very moment, Dusty experienced a plethora of emotions: anger, fear, sorrow, satisfaction and accomplishment. It was like a tornado of emotions tearing through her mind and soul. She had no idea how to feel, but her body had its own response in mind. Confident that nobody was around to witness such vulnerability, Dusty buried her face into her crossed arms and sobbed.

Chapter 43

Sitting in the bed of an old pickup truck just a few hundred feet from the driveway, Dusty propped her elbows up on the truck box behind the cab, and observed the old livestock auction house through a pair of binoculars. The binoculars had been glued to her eyes for nearly a half hour before she saw any sign of activity—a man walking out from a side entrance of the large building. It was promising, but it was going to take more than one man smoking a cigarette to convince her that Rhett had told the truth. It could just as likely be a coincidence that someone else had taken up shelter there for the night. However, as the rising sun washed away the contrasting shadows, Dusty spotted an armed man walking the perimeter of the roof.

Guess he wasn't lying after all.

Dusty watched as the man by the side door took one last drag on his hand-rolled cigarette before flicking what little remained into the snow. He walked toward a rusted-out cattle trailer parked just beside one of the dozens of corrals on the property. She could see the man had shouted something as he approached the trailer, but there was no guessing what he had said. By the time he had reached the trailer, a man holding a scoped M76 was hopping down from the back.

The man from the trailer quickly dumped the Yugoslavian rifle off on the other man before he placed his hands on his sides and stretched out his back. They chatted for a few minutes, laughing and joking as they fired up more cigarettes. Passing the baton in the form of a slap on the shoulder, the man from the trailer walked back toward the building, thus completing the shift change. His replacement stepped up into the trailer and found as comfortable a position as he could on the rotting, wood floor, his hard-hitting rifle aimed straight down the driveway leading to the road.

As the morning passed, Dusty continued to spot more sentries patrolling the area. She also discovered two additional sniper nests, realizing that there were likely even more still hidden. As much as she hated these people, she couldn't help but be impressed by their current arrangement. With very little in the way of actual borders to protect their stronghold, their defensive strategy was quite remarkable. Although the location was far from ideal for a long-term place to call home, it did seem to be more than adequate to serve as a Forward Operating Base.

Dusty spent hours watching the property, scrutinizing every little detail so she could provide as much intel as possible to Captain Kohler when she returned. Though she was far from an experienced soldier like Kohler, she already knew this would not be an easy place to assault. With multiple snipers covering the area, and miles of open sightline in every direction, attacking this compound without incurring heavy casualties would be a logistical nightmare, probably an impossibility altogether. Liberty just didn't have the manpower to be able to absorb that kind of loss. Arlo had chosen an ideal location to station his men.

Swinging her binoculars to the back of the building, Dusty watched as one of the garage doors shot upward, revealing a large group of armed fighters standing just inside. The man at the front, holding an AR-15, briefly turned around and said a few fiery words to his troops before signaling for them to move out.

The group, consisting of at least fifty men and women, poured out of the garage door and funneled their way between two of the cattle pens. Dusty watched as they walked down the long driveway, heading toward the road—the road she sat on.

"Please turn right," she whispered to herself as Arlo's men approached the rural highway, knowing it was wishful thinking. Once she saw the point man turn left—coming right toward her—Dusty slithered her body down into the bed of the truck, making herself as small as possible between the wheel well and the cab on the driver's side. "This is bad," she whispered.

The sound of the marching soldiers produced a violent tremble throughout her body that made her queasy. Just one glance inside the bed and she was dead. She could be cradling a belt-fed M240b right now and *still* not make it out of that gunfight alive. Closing her eyes, all Dusty could do is wait, and hope that they wouldn't hear the thumping in her chest that eerily matched the marching feet headed her way. She took a deep breath in, and held it.

The chatter amongst the fighters was minimal, as many of them were still waking up, but Dusty heard one man say, "I'll tell you what, these guys put up a much bigger fight than I thought they would."

"No kidding," another man said. "Hopefully the Judge will give us some reinforcements for the final push..." The man's voice trailed off as he walked away.

The Judge, Dusty thought to herself, trying to recall why that name sounded so familiar.

Moments later, the last of the footsteps faded, bringing with it a very thankful exhale from Dusty's tired body. Arlo's plans for reinforcements were critical intel, perhaps even more crucial than finding the stronghold itself. She wasn't sure what Kohler would do to prepare for increased waves of attack— she wasn't sure if there was anything he *could* do— but she needed to relay that information to him as soon as possible.

Dusty fought the urge to leap out of the bed of the truck, dump her pack, and sprint all the way back to Liberty, warning them of the attackers that just passed by. However, the information she had collected over the past few hours was far too valuable to risk such a dangerous move. In this snow, and with no real cover to move between, those rooftop snipers would spot her like a hobo at a gala before she could make it to the other side of the road. She would have to wait until nightfall, which would give her plenty of time to dwell on the nauseating game changer she had just overheard.

Chapter 44

Clay growled through the pain as every muscle in his body constricted. His face turned red and a jolt of pain shot through his jaw as he clenched his teeth. Having expended all his energy for the moment, Clay's body relaxed as he gasped for air. Feeling lightheaded, he sat down on the edge of the bed and took several slow, deep breaths as he tried to flex the pain out of his fingers.

"Need me to loosen it up for ya?" Megan chuckled as she leaned against the doorframe.

"Be my guest." Clay held out the pry bar toward Megan. After several seconds of Megan ignoring his offer, Clay's arm got tired. "That's what I thought," he said as his hand, along with the pry bar, plopped down to the mattress.

He had made good headway on prying the safe door open, but either the door was getting tougher with each pull or he was quickly losing steam; it was probably a combination of both. Either way, he had already spent twice as much time on it than he had expected, but he wasn't about to walk away now.

Taking in another deep breath, Clay got off the bed and wedged the pry bar between the door and frame. He placed a shirt over the pry bar and then used a framing hammer from the shed in the back yard to wedge it further inside. The impact was loud, but the shirt dampened the high-pitched ting it would have made, reducing the chances that anyone who *might* be in the area would hear it.

Tossing the hammer onto the bed, Clay began to push then pull the bar again. His grunts evolved into a full-on scream as he felt the door starting to give. The gap between the door and frame was now large enough that Clay could peek inside, ensuring that he wasn't wasting any additional time or energy on a fruitless endeavor.

The safe wasn't going to be the treasure chest he had been hoping for, but he did see a rifle toward the back, as well as a few boxes of ammo on the top shelf. He also noticed a plastic bag on the floor, on the left side of the center divider; he was hopeful for some more ammunition. Motivated enough by the discovery, Clay kept prying, pulling, and hammering at the budget safe. Twenty minutes later, he bested the steel box.

The door swung open and Clay immediately went for the rifle. He pulled the bolt open, revealing a small, empty chamber.

"Sweet!" Megan said, "Good find?"

"Hmm, maybe not," Clay said as he read the etching on the barrel. He shined his light inside, and looked at the six boxes of Hornady on the shelf—all of which were 30-30 cartridges—before looking back at Megan. "This is a .204 Ruger. I know for certain we don't have any ammo for it back at Liberty. So, with the exception of the..." Clay trailed off as he counted the .204 cartridges on the rifle's stock sleeve, "*nine* rounds here, this rifle is as good as a club."

"You still gonna take it with us?"

Clay chewed on the pros and cons of her question. On one hand, anything that goes bang would be useful. On the other hand, the added weight to an already oversized load plus the *very* finite amount of ammo did not make it a likely contender for the trip back. "Nah, I don't think it's going to make the cut."

Tossing the gun onto the bed, Clay turned the flashlight back inside and grabbed the plastic shopping bag off the floor. At first, he was disappointed when he saw that there were no ammunition boxes inside. Once he actually processed what he was looking at, however, he thought he was dreaming.

"What is it?" Megan asked, intrigued with the enormous, if not mischievous, smirk on her brother's face.

With his eyes remaining glued to the bag, Clay laughed in disbelief. "I can't believe it."

"Okay, you're killing me, Smalls," Megan said, referencing one of their favorite childhood movies.

"It's Tannerite."

"Tannerite? What's that?"

"Remember when Uncle Ted had that old tree stump right in the middle of where he wanted his new carrot patch to go?" Clay asked. "So, he had Dad come over to help dig it up, but Dad had other plans..."

"Uhm, maybe," Megan said as her mind went back in time. "Wait, oh...OH! Yeah, I remember that now. Wait, *that* is the same stuff?" she asked, pointing to the bag.

"Yup," Clay said as he nodded, "the very same."

Clay's smile had become contagious, causing Megan to join in on the excitement. "Is it dangerous for us to be carrying around?"

"No, the way it's packaged, we're totally safe. Besides, it needs a good hit from a fast bullet to ignite it.

Megan wasn't too reassured with Clay's explanation on how the explosives were detonated, seeing as shootouts during the travels were not a terribly far-fetched reality for them. However, Clay's relaxed demeanor as he handled the bag put her mind at ease. A little. "So, what will you guys do with it?"

Clay shook his head. "No clue. I'm just going to hand it off to Captain Kohler when we get back, I'm sure he'll have a few ideas."

Reaching in and grabbing the ammo boxes—five full and one missing six cartridges—Clay dropped them onto the bed next to the Tannerite before he grabbed the varmint rifle and placed it behind the safe. Megan gave him a look that told him she wasn't convinced that was a great hiding spot.

"Hey, if we were the first people to stumble across this place in the last ten years, what are the odds that someone else will in the next couple of months? Besides, even if someone does find the place, I'm hoping they'll see that the door is destroyed, the safe is empty, and just turn around and walk back out."

Megan shrugged. It made little difference to her whether that gun was still behind the safe or not when Clay returned. In her mind, Northfield was equipped well enough to outfit a small army.

Picking up the Tannerite and ammo, Clay and Megan headed downstairs and grabbed their bags

437

sitting on the dining room table. The duffle bags could be carried by handles or slung over the shoulders like a backpack. With Clay's duffle weighing upwards of seventy pounds—with spare space saved for the items back at the FEMA camp— he opted to shoulder the weight and carry his backpack with his left hand while his right stayed on the handle of his ARAK-21 hanging from its sling.

Megan's packs were full, but considerably lighter. As they divvied up the goods, Clay intentionally gave her items which took up more in volume, but less in mass, such as their clothes, sleeping bags, foil packs of pink salmon, and so on. It was all still vital to bring with them, but would be less taxing on her much smaller frame.

After trying to wear the duffle bag like a backpack, Megan decided to carry it instead. The long, canvas bag felt awkward on her back, making her feel off balance, and slowing her movement. She, instead, opted to wear her backpack on her shoulders. However, since Clay had severed both shoulder straps after pulling Megan out of the lake, a very crude surgery involving his knife and a length of paracord was necessary. The end result was surprisingly strong.

Walking out the back door, they decided to follow—as best as they could tell—the path the former owners of the cabin would have driven in on—which headed away from the lake. With the snow on the ground, they only used the unnatural gaps in the trees to chart their course. After a twenty-five-minute hike, they came out to a road, and started heading south.

Clay was already feeling the rigorous effects of the added luggage strapped to his back. He felt as if he was inside his favorite RPG game and had just picked up one bottle cap too many. He moved like he was smothered in molasses walking through wet cement.

"Where's some power armor when you need it?" Clay mumbled.

"Huh?" Megan glanced back.

"Nothing," Clay replied with a nostalgic smile.

A mile down the road Clay had finally spotted a road marker. He wanted to collect as much geographical information as he could so he could accurately re-locate the cabin on the map when they got back to the FEMA camp.

"So, what's the plan?" Megan asked.

"We walk. Except for the occasional rest stop, we don't quit walking until we need to find a place to set up camp for the night," Clay said matter-of-factly. "Unless," he continued, "that is, we happen to see a hospital or gun store with a neon *OPEN* sign glowing in the window."

"So, we're done scavenging?"

"You got room in your bag over there?"

"Good point," she quickly conceded.

"Plus, we *should* just be a day or two out from Liberty, so, we're obviously running a bit behind schedule. We can poke around the places we stay for the night, but we're at a point where if we take something, we're probably going to have to leave something behind anyway."

With the game plan settled, the two trekked quietly down the road, focusing on their movements for nearly an hour before Megan broke the silence.

"Do you think it's worth it?"

"Is *what* worth it?" Clay replied.

"This," Megan said, gesturing to their present situation, "Liberty...this war."

"You tell me," Clay said before puffing for some air, "you're out here risking your life for the town."

"No. I'm here risking my life for the *people* in the town."

"Fair enough."

"I mean I get why Mayor Shelton made a stand," Megan continued, "and I even get digging in and trying to tough it out, but I mean...at some point you gotta throw in the towel. At the end of the day, it's just a *place*. You can always find somewhere else to live, but you can't bring back the dead."

Clay had pondered the very same questions in recent weeks. Although he had a bit more skin in the game than Megan—given his history with the little town—he, too, wondered why Shelton was going to go down with the ship while there were still life rafts hanging off the boat. The more Clay thought about it, however, he started to see, perhaps, what Shelton saw.

"Well, to be honest, if you had asked me that question the other night—before our talk—I probably would have had a much different answer," Clay said, trying to catch his breath as he walked. "But, to these people, it isn't just some place where they survive...it's not just a home, something they'd be willing to trade for a bigger and better model someday down the road. It isn't even just a community of friends and family that they've grown to love. I think it's bigger than all that. The town itself is a sign of hope. A hope that is starting to fade for a lot of people...present company included."

Megan's head hung low with the response.

"So," Clay continued, "here we are, walking side by side down a snowy road, God knows how far from the nearest person we know, all on the slim hopes that the supplies we've found over the past couple of weeks will somehow make a difference," Clay said before laughing ironically. "I mean you are *willingly* risking your life for a town you visit maybe a few times a year, because it, and the people, mean something to you, too. So, think about how much more it means to those who helped build a community, literally, from the ashes."

Megan's silence was louder than any words she could have spoken.

"So, to answer your question, I don't know if it's worth it," Clay said, his answer catching Megan by surprise. "But, so long as they stay and fight, I will, too."

Chapter 45

Dusty was filled with both pride and shame as she stood in front of Shelton and Kohler. The hurt in the old man's eyes when he realized she had deceived him was less than subtle, tugging at a string in her heart that rarely got plucked.

That hurt, however, quickly shifted to hope as Dusty uttered three powerful words: "I found them."

She went on in great detail, from every sniper perch she had uncovered to the path Arlo's men took on their way to Liberty. With her scratchy throat drying up from the hours-long debrief, she ended the discussion by relaying what the one man had said—about the rumors of Arlo receiving reinforcements from someone called the Judge. The name didn't sound familiar to either of them, which made it all the more perplexing to Dusty.

"Outstanding job, Dusty!" Kohler said with optimism filling his voice. He stood to his feet and gave a salute. "Go get some chow, and if they give you any grief about waking them up or the extra rations, you tell them to come see me."

Dusty returned the salute. "Yes, sir!" The teenaged girl spun around on the ball of her foot and walked out of the house.

Kohler immediately looked over at Shelton, who still sat on the couch. "Barry, I know what you're thinking: I was way out of line to send her out against your wishes, but—"

"Yes, you were out of line, Captain," Shelton interrupted, silencing the veteran. He slowly made his way to his feet and walked over to Kohler. "And you had every right to do so."

"I know but—" Kohler said before registering Shelton's words. After a brief pause, he continued, "Uhm, I beg your pardon?"

"Daniel...I have no right making these types of calls. I've never been to war; I never even served in the military. I don't belong in this kind of role, telling a man who knows far more than me how to do his job."

"Permission to speak freely, sir?" Kohler said.

Shelton sighed, frustrated that the man had still not learned that he didn't have to ask permission for that. "Go ahead."

"You have had some critical errors in your judgment since this war started," Kohler stated bluntly.

Shelton started to regret giving him permission.

"But, you have done an excellent job leading the men and women of this town for so many years. There's no doubt in my mind that this town wouldn't even be here to defend if it hadn't been for your superb leadership, hard work, and self-sacrifices."

Shelton felt a little better after hearing the second half of Kohler's statement. "Well, I do appreciate the kind words, Captain, but I am feeling like the furthest thing from a good leader right about now."

"A leader can't be expected to do it all. You've more than proved that you would never ask anyone in this town to do something you wouldn't do yourself, but that doesn't mean you *should* do it yourself. A good leader knows when to take charge and when to hand off the reins."

Shelton stood in silence as he reflected on the statement. "You're right, Captain," Shelton said, "which is why, effective immediately, you are in charge of this town."

"Whoa, whoa, whoa, what are you doing, Barry?"

"Being a good leader, knowing when to hand off the reins to a more capable individual."

Kohler shook his head, "That was *not* what I was getting at, sir. I was just saying that sometimes you've got to just trust other people to do their jobs, even if you aren't sold on the idea yourself."

"I understand, Captain, but I also realize that I am no longer the leader this town needs. You are."

Kohler was honored that Shelton thought so highly of him, but the unexpected turn of events didn't sit well with him. "Sir, I don't know if this is the best idea. To be honest, I think it will do more harm for morale than good."

"Then we don't tell anyone—at least not until after this war is behind us."

"Wait a second," Kohler said, analyzing Shelton's last statement, "'until after this war is behind us?'"

Shelton walked over to the kitchen and poured himself some water. He took several large gulps before wiping his mouth with the back of his hand. "Daniel, you have been by my side almost every step of the way since this town was founded. You've let me bounce ideas off you; you've provided me with invaluable counsel. I tasked you with important jobs because I knew they would always be done right..." Shelton finished off the water before wiping the glass down with a rag and replacing it in the cupboard. "You said if it weren't for me, this town wouldn't have made it. But, the truth of the matter is, if it hadn't been for you, I would not have been nearly as effective at my job as I was."

"Sir, I don't know..."

"You know how much this town and each and every person in it means to me," Shelton said.

"Without a doubt, sir."

"Then you understand that I would never make a decision that I didn't think was in the town's best interest."

"Yes, sir," Kohler agreed.

"Daniel, I did not come to this conclusion lightly. It's been one I have been considering even before this war even started. But, as I stand here right this moment, I don't believe I could make a better decision for the people of this town than to put them in such capable hands."

Kohler was speechless.

Shelton extended his hand. "Take good care of them, Captain."

Kohler reached out and firmly shook Shelton's hand. "Thank you, sir."

Noticing the fatigue in his eyes, Kohler said, "You look dog-tired, Barry. You should try and get some rest."

Shelton nodded. "Yeah, I think I'll do that," the old man said as he turned and headed for the stairs.

The single-digit air assailed Kohler's lungs as he stepped out onto the porch and headed to his own house. It was late—easily past midnight—but he had stopped looking at his watch weeks ago. Anymore, there were only two hours in a day: daylight and night.

The newly appointed mayor of Liberty swung by his house, picking up the last map in his possession, and then made a beeline to the mess hall. He received a wrathful glare from Estelle, who waited for Dusty to finish her meal so she could lock up for the night—again.

"Why don't you go home, Estelle, I'll see to it that everything is secure before I leave," Kohler said.

The old woman grumbled something under her breath before putting her coat on and walking out.

Kohler sat across the table from Dusty, who had plated as much food as she could get away with. Given everything the girl had been through over the past couple of weeks, he wasn't about to comment on her indulgence—*especially* after the success of her most recent mission.

"How ya feeling?"

"Better now," Dusty mumbled through a mouthful of instant potatoes.

"So, I meant to ask earlier, but...what's that about?" Kohler asked, gesturing to the blood-soaked sleeve.

Dusty looked at her arm. "Oh, that? Well, I guess I don't have to tell you that interrogation is a dirty business," she said, giving the captain a deceptive smile. After the good, long cry she had endured in the woods, she managed to rebuild the wall that had crumbled down. But as images of the fatal wound she delivered to Rhett came to the front of her mind, she suddenly lost her appetite. Putting her plastic spoon down, Dusty nodded toward the folded map in Kohler's hand. "What's that about?" she asked, relieved to change subjects.

Dusty moved her tray of food to the next table over as Kohler unfolded the map and placed it in front of them. He pointed out Liberty's location to Dusty and asked her to locate Arlo's camp.

"It's riiiiiight..." she said as her finger hovered around the map, "there!" She gave the map a definitive tap with her finger.

"You're sure?"

Dusty picked at some food stuck in her teeth with her tongue before answering, "Positive."

Kohler used a red Sharpie to circle the area. Using the scale provided on the map, he used his finger and thumb to guesstimate distance. "Looks like it's a shade over eight miles away—as the crow flies."

"Yep," Dusty said as she took a swig of water from her bottle, "that seems about right."

"All right, Dusty, I know it's late and you're tired, but I need you to tell me *everything* you remember about this place. Layout, approach, nearby cars...whatever you can recall."

With Morgan in her thoughts, Dusty gave Kohler a sincere smile, the first one since her friend's death. "I've got nothing else to do tonight," she said, vengeance on her mind.

Liberty had endured her share of beatings for long enough—it was now time to return the favor. Tenfold.

Chapter 46

Arlo tapped his foot as he waited for over an hour on a bench just outside the Judge's "chambers." He had detested the self-importance the man felt entitled to back when the two regularly met in the courtroom, but it had grown beyond absurdity since society collapsed. It wasn't that Arlo was exempt from a bit of narcissism himself, but from the moment the Judge recruited his first minion, a dirty corrections officer who had been in his back pocket for years, he was no longer just some high-ranking official in the judicial system; he was a god in his own eyes.

It didn't take long for the crooked cop to round up a sizeable gang of criminals to do the Judge's bidding. With a relationship built on smuggling contraband inside the prison, the drug dealers, murderers, and rapists had no problem teaming up with the well-known officer.

The judge was no more corrupt in the fallen society than he was when he sat on the bench; the only difference was that the rule of law—as far as the US Constitution saw it—no longer existed. The judge had *his* law—and to break it was to sign your own death warrant.

Arlo heard footsteps on the other side of the door just before it popped open. A short, Hispanic man stepped out. "He's ready for you," is all he said before turning around and walking back inside.

Arlo followed the man down a long, narrow hallway. As they walked, they passed numerous windows and doors, each one looking into a depressing, jail cell-sized office; they were all equipped with the exact same desk, chair, and pair of cream-colored filing cabinets.

As they reached the door at the end of the hallway, Arlo's eyes couldn't roll back far enough at the sight of the handmade plaque hanging on the wall.

Hon. Joseph Patrick

Arlo's escort knocked twice.

"Come in," a muffled voice called from the other side.

The man opened the door and walked inside, Arlo followed closely behind.

The room easily swallowed four of the smaller offices just down the hall, and with room to spare. The beautiful Mahogany desk and the hand-stitched, leather chair no doubt came with a heftier price tag than the Swedish-made counterparts the rest of the former employees were issued. Sitting in the corner at a forty-five-degree angle was a tall armoire that looked as if it had been cut from the same tree as the desk. The office screamed executive, but still wasn't quite as posh as the Texas-native judge would have decorated his own. However, it worked for the interim.

"Thank you, Lorenzo. We'll just be a moment," the stocky man with an unfortunate comb-over said from behind the desk, nodding toward the door.

"Yes, your honor." Lorenzo slipped out the door, quietly latching it behind him.

"Have a seat, Arlo," the judge said. It was not so much an invitation as it was an order.

Arlo sat down. "Thank you for seeing me today, *your honor*. I know that it's quite difficult to pencil people in on such short notice with such a hectic schedule," Arlo said, still irritated with his lengthy wait in the hallway.

"Boy, I sure hope you didn't come all this way just to show me how dry your wit is," he replied with his heavy, southern accent.

"Of course not, sir," Arlo quickly backpedaled, sensing the annoyance in his tone.

"Then, I do hope it's because we're all set to move in," he said as he rolled up the sleeves on his Brunello Cucinelli button down, a shirt that cost more than a week of take home for some of his clerks back in the day.

"Soon. Very soon," he said confidently.

"Oh, you're gonna have to do a whole lot better than 'soon', Arlo."

Arlo gave a nervous smile. Even though he found the man despicable, he still needed him. For now. "Unfortunately, your honor, the people in this town were a bit more resolute than I had initially expected."

"Mmmmhmmmm," the judge said, as he leaned back in his chair and rested his folded hands on his stomach. "So, we've established that your visit isn't just a social call, and you're not here with the keys to my new home..." he leaned forward, transferring his clasped hands from his stomach to the desk. "Then tell me, Arlo, what is it exactly that you want from me today?"

Getting straight to the point, which was how the judge liked it, Arlo said, "Well, sir, it would be quite advantageous to us—and our commission—if we could add to our numbers slightly."

"You want more men?" he said in disbelief.

"Yes. Our efforts have been quite effective thus far, but—"

"Not quite effective enough, it would seem," the agitated man barked back.

Arlo lost his cool. "Well, if you would just let me finish what I was saying, Joseph, I would—"

"Your honor!" he shouted, interrupting Arlo again.

Arlo suppressed his indignation with the outburst and calmly continued. "Please forgive me. As I was saying, *your honor*, my men have successfully worn down this town's defenses. Our recent aggressions have indicated to us that they are low on supplies and would not be able to sustain another large-scale attack."

The judge shook his head as Arlo's proposal sunk in. "Heavens to Betsy, son, I gave you two hundred men when you first came up with this foolproof plan of yours, then I sent another forty—including my best sharpshooter—after your old friend decided he wasn't gonna just turn tail and run. So, here we are now, weeks past due, and you want even *more*?" the man said, his cheeks reddened from his tirade. "I gotta tell ya, Arlo, you're making me ill as a hornet right now."

Arlo managed not to flinch as the man spat out yet another one his southern idioms—they were the lowest form of expression in Arlo's mind. "You have indeed been very generous with your men, your honor, but it is quite unrealistic for you to expect us to go to war without incurring casualties. I do understand that this investment has cost you a little more than we had initially discussed, but my losses have not been so modest either," Arlo said, seeing that the man's disposition softened. "We both have much to gain from this opportunity in front of us; walking away now would be imprudent."

As the judge leaned back in his chair to consider his options, Arlo sat in silence, knowing exactly how the man would answer. Joseph Patrick was anything but a patient man, but once he threw some chips of his own onto the table, his ego would prevent him from folding. The dwindling resources at the office complex he currently stayed in only furthered Arlo's confidence that he would get his way.

"And just how many more do you need?"

Arlo needed about fifty men. "One hundred."

The judge grunted out a laugh. "Try fifty."

"Seventy-five."

"*Or,*" he sat up in his chair, "how about fifty?" he reiterated.

"Fifty," Arlo acknowledged with a smile. "Thank you for your generosity, sir."

"Lorenzo!" the judge said loudly.

The door to the office opened and the man walked inside. "Yes, your honor?"

"Please tell Hatcher to round up fifty of his finest men—they are to head out with Mr. Paxton here in the morning."

"Yes sir," the man said before promptly turning around to leave.

"Thank you, your honor," Arlo said, feigning a smile.

The judge stood up from his chair, causing Arlo to follow suit. He limped his way around the desk and walked up to Arlo—his face just inches from his old colleague. "Let me make myself perfectly clear, Arlo. There are no more men after this. If you fail me one more time..."

Arlo braced himself for another one of his brilliant southern sayings.

"You just better hope that you die in battle, son, because if your death comes by my hand, it will neither be quick or painless," he said, his sincere eyes piercing into Arlo's soul. "Do you follow me?"

The man's pitiless track record let Arlo know that his words were not empty threats. "Of course, your honor. I promise to return with good news within the next two weeks."

"You better," he said, his eyes still locked to Arlo's, "now get out of my chambers before I decide to expedite that process."

Chapter 47

Kohler had been hunched over the table, staring down at the map for the last five days. Except for intermittent breaks for sleep and a brief skirmish with Arlo's men, he had been glued to the dining room chair as he attempted to come up with viable strike options—there weren't any. None that he liked, anyway.

At that point in time, the best option he could come up with was to attack the group as they cut through the woods, but he was not thrilled with that idea for several reasons, the biggest concern being that there was no way to guarantee *where* they would enter the woods. If he were leading a group that size to an attack, Kohler would make sure they never used the same path twice.

Ambushing them from the side of the road wasn't even on the table. Based on Dusty's description, the road was long and empty. The biggest blockade she saw was an overturned semi, and many of the panels on the trailer were missing or rusted through, making it virtually ineffective as cover.

Both options came with minimal pros while sporting overwhelming cons. If he sent a large group of fighters out into the woods, there was a good chance the attackers would take a different path, missing the ambush altogether, which would leave Liberty without dozens of defenders. He could send just a few fighters out, picking the best spot along the road to wait until the enemy marched by, but Kohler knew there would be no homecoming for those men. He couldn't reconcile sending three or four men to their deaths just to take out some of Arlo's. War, in many ways, *was* like playing a game of chess, but Kohler was never willing to sacrifice a pawn to capture another pawn.

Peeling himself away from the table, Kohler walked into the kitchen and got himself some food and water. Just as he returned to the dining room, he heard a knock on the door. He set his food and drink down on the table and went to open it.

He immediately wondered if he had drifted to sleep at the table and was now dreaming. Or maybe the lack of sleep he had had over the past week had finally bested him. But when he shook hands with the visitor at the door, he knew it wasn't a delusion.

"Clay! It's mighty good to see you again," Kohler said, stepping out of the doorway to make room for Clay.

"You too, Captain," he said as he stepped out of the brisk, morning air.

"How are you? How is Megan?" Kohler asked as he closed the door.

"We survived," Clay said wearily. "We had more than a few close calls, but we're back now, so that's all that matters."

"Well, come in, have a seat," Kohler gestured to the living room. "I wish there was more time for us to chew the fat before getting down to business, but due to some recent developments, we are *really* up against the clock here," he said as he leaned on the arm of a recliner before Clay sat down on the couch.

Clay read between the lines and wasted no time getting into the meat and potatoes of his visit. He went on to tell Kohler about the food and medical supplies they had brought back, particularly the painkillers they had scored at the law office. Kohler was excited with their success, and was particularly thrilled to know that the wounded currently laid up in the infirmary would have some effective pain management, even if for just a little while. But he was, at the moment, more concerned with how the lives of his men on the battlefield could improve.

"Did you have any luck with things of a more tactical nature?" he asked.

Clay flashed a grin before plopping his backpack down with a heavy thud on the coffee table in front of him. He tore into the pack, starting with the loose boxes of ammo he had found sporadically during the trip. Kohler nodded with a smile as Clay pulled the last of them from the bag. Then, he pulled out the three .30 caliber ammo cans, each filled with 420 rounds of 5.56MM on stripper clips.

"Outstanding!" Kohler shouted with excitement in his eye. "That's the kind of find we needed, Clay. Excellent job!"

Clay's sly smile told Kohler there was something else left—something big. Reaching inside the bag, Clay said, "So, I found this in a cabin in the woods and thought 'eh, maybe Captain Kohler can find *some* way to put it to use,'" he said as he pulled the Tannerite out.

Kohler had the same expression on his face as Clay when he first discovered the explosives back at the cabin. He took the bag out of Clay's hand and inspected it closely, quickly recognizing that it had not been exposed to the harsh elements all these years.

"How much is here?" Kohler asked.

"Five pounds."

The wheels in Kohler's brain spun as a workable plan started to formulate. He walked back over to the table and looked at the notes on the map again. "How much time do you need before you're ready to go back out?" Kohler asked.

Clay was exhausted, and could easily sleep for a week if not disturbed, but he knew Kohler had something big brewing in his mind, and Clay wanted to do whatever he could to help. "I can be good to go after a few hours of shut eye," Clay said.

"Okay. Meet me back here at sixteen hundred. Dress warm and pack light."

****

With his suppressed .300 blackout pushed squarely into his shoulder, Clay crouched down in the back of the pickup truck, keeping guard as Kohler mixed the Tannerite. Having served multiple tours in both Iraq and Syria, there was no more qualified person in Liberty to setup an IED than Daniel Kohler, which was the only reason why the leader of their improvised military was currently behind enemy lines with just one person watching his six.

Working under the cover of a vinyl rain poncho, Kohler held a penlight between his teeth while he prepared the device. In his experience, the most devastating blasts often came from the most simplistic of designs, and this would be no different—or so he hoped.

With the Tannerite mixed, Kohler inspected the two Mason jars he had brought along. Each one was tightly packed with ball bearings, screws, nails, and other small, destructive metal pieces that would only add to the carnage. The very thought of using a device that had been responsible for the deaths and maiming of so many of his brothers in arms over the years made him nauseous, but he had exhausted all other options. Twice.

With everything ready, Kohler clicked the light off before removing the poncho. He picked up the large container of the explosive mixture and carefully placed it on the center of the truck box. He turned around and looked at Clay. "Hand me those, will ya?" he whispered.

Clay handed him a two-gallon plastic can of gas, and then another one filled with kerosene. Kohler placed both of them just to the left of the Tannerite, facing the road. He then put one of the Mason jars to the left of the gas cans, and the other one just behind the gas can, trying to maximize his area of effect. Kohler then crammed a few one-pound propane tanks anywhere he could fit them—only one of which was completely full. He didn't expect them to have much oomph by themselves, but coupled with the rest of the bomb, he hoped it would help.

"Think this will work?" Clay asked.

"It should," Kohler responded as he tweaked the position of one of the Mason jars. "I mean it's gonna go bang, so the real question is, how *well* will it work. And that, I do not know," he said as he slowly moved his hand away from the jar. "Hopefully...really well."

Kohler grabbed the poncho next to his feet and carefully laid it over the IED. He took several minutes neatly positioning it so that it covered as much of the bomb as possible while keeping the Tannerite itself in view. Kohler hoped that the soldiers had walked by this truck so many times already that they wouldn't waste the energy to turn their heads. But, if they did, at least they wouldn't see red gas cans and glass jars sitting out in the open.

With daylight fast approaching, Clay and Kohler hightailed it back to their shooting position—a rusted out hatchback around two hundred yards up the road. Leaning up against the trunk of the car was Dusty's X-Bolt and Kohler's M1A. Either rifle was more than capable of setting off the IED, but it was Clay that would take the shot with the .270 while Kohler acted as his spotter.

Prepared to dig in for the long haul, Clay and Kohler were both caught off guard when they saw a large group walking their way just after dawn. The mission was off to a good start.

"Get yourself in position," Kohler told Clay.

Resting his elbow on the trunk of the car, Clay propped the X-Bolt up and aimed through the back window and out the windshield, finding a clear line of sight between the headrests. All the windows, including the windshield, were absent, giving Clay an unimpeded shot at the Tannerite. He chambered the round and looked through the scope, finding Kohler's improvised explosive device behind his crosshairs.

Lying prone on the ground, Kohler slithered his way out from behind the car, only exposing himself as much as necessary to get an angle on the incoming troops. "All right, they'll be reaching the truck in less than thirty seconds, he whispered. "Standby."

"Roger that," Clay acknowledged.

As the group approached the truck, Kohler kept his finger near the trigger so he could attempt a quick follow up shot in case Clay was off target. "They're at the truck...on my mark."

Clay held his crosshairs on the bomb, trying to ignore the marching heads bobbing in and out of the bottom of his sight picture as the group walked past the truck.

Kohler wanted to let as many people pass as he could before giving the signal. Worried that the cab of the truck would deflect the explosion, he hoped to have the bulk of the group past the cab before detonating. "Standby..." he said again. Just then, he saw one of them glance over at the truck—the man quickly doing a double take. He stopped walking and stared at it for a moment, causing the others around him to take notice. It was as if he knew something was different, but didn't know what. Then he pointed to the poncho.

"Now, now, now, now," Kohler ordered.

Clay squeezed the trigger.

Just as he was recovering from the concussions of his shot, Clay was thumped in the chest from the shockwave of the fiery explosion two hundred yards ahead. Bits of debris and wreckage were already raining down around Clay and Kohler, with a few larger chunks narrowly missing them.

Shaking the cobwebs loose, Clay looked through his scope again to examine the destruction. The first thing he noticed was the flaming, twisted wreckage of the truck. The front door and hood were relatively untouched, but the back half was devastated. Swinging his scope to the left, he watched as a small group of men retreated to the auction house driveway, tripping and stumbling over their own feet as they scrambled to safety. With the disoriented group lacking any real threat status, Clay shifted his scope down lower and spotted numerous bodies littering the road; only a few even attempting to get up. After counting ten, lifeless corpses, which only accounted for a portion of the lives claimed in the blast, Clay pulled his eye off the scope—he had no desire to ever find out just how many people he had killed with the single pull of the trigger.

Meanwhile, Kohler shifted his attention to the auction house. As expected, there was a burst of activity on the premises, which meant that he and Clay needed to leave about five seconds ago. He saw someone run up to the edge of the rooftop and look out toward the smoking truck.

"Captain, I think we need to go," Clay said as he, too, noticed the soldiers gathering up outside the building.

Kohler heard Clay, but was distracted by the man on the other end of his scope. Estimating the rooftop to be around six hundred yards, Kohler found the appropriate hashmark on his reticle and placed it on his target, who, eerily, seemed to be staring right back at him. As his finger reached the trigger, he started second guessing the decision. It was never in Kohler's plan to start taking shots at people, they were to set off the Tannerite, and then escape amidst the chaos. But he hadn't expected this opportunity to present itself.

Wading through a slew of questions in his head, both moral and tactical alike, Kohler had only seconds to decide. *It's worth it*, he thought to himself, sealing the man's fate. He took in a deep breath before easing the air out through his mouth, and then squeezed the trigger.

The .308 kicked back as it spit out the smoking shell case before chambering the next. The picture in his scope came back into focus just as the bullet struck the man in the chest. Even from six hundred yards, Kohler could see the shock on his face when he looked down at his mortal wound for a fleeting moment before stumbling away from the edge. One of the nearby snipers ran to his aid, but by then the man had already collapsed. Kohler questioned whether it had been the right decision or not, but there were no take backs now. The deed was done.

Rolling over behind the car and getting to one knee, Kohler looked up at Clay, "Okay, *now* it's time to go," he said as he jumped to his feet.

As soon as Clay and Kohler were on the move, sniper fire rang out from the rooftop. There was nothing they could do except run. Spinning around and firing while jogging backwards or blindly shooting over the shoulder was the type of stuff that worked in movies, but in real life those kinds of action hero stunts would just slow them down and get them killed.

Snow and asphalt kicked up around them as they moved in a zig-zag pattern, making themselves nearly impossible to hit with a bolt gun from that range. After a few minutes, the gunfire slowed, eventually coming to a halt. They both managed to get out of the sniper's range with no new holes in their bodies. However, uncertain whether they were actively being pursued or not, neither man slowed his pace until after they were deep into the woods.

Feeling comfortable that they weren't being followed, they each found a tree to lean on while they gasped like fish out of water. "Glad I took your advice on the whole packing light thing," Clay said, deep breaths disrupting his remark.

"Yeah, I kind of thought something like that might happen," Kohler responded before coughing through the ache in his lungs.

"Did you think the explosion was going to be *that* big?" Clay asked.

Not wanting to waste precious oxygen on the response, Kohler just shook his head.

With their O2 and adrenaline leveling off, Kohler was anxious to get moving again. "Come on, we need to double-time it back home and get ready for their counterattack. Arlo is going to be furious."

"Well, I imagine so, seeing as we just took out a good chunk of his men with one shot," Clay said, quickly pushing the images of the gory road out of his mind before he threw up. After clearing his throat, he continued, "But don't you think he'll take a little bit of time to lick his wounds and come up with a solid response? I mean I don't know the guy all that well, but from the sounds of it, everything he does is pretty methodical and well-planned. After such a big blow, don't you think he's going to take a little time to recover?"

"Rational thinking goes out the window when you find out your son is dead—trust me on that one," Kohler said with a grief-stricken look in his eyes. He began walking and Clay quickly fell inline. "I assure you, Clay, Arlo is coming, he's coming soon, and he is going to bring everything he's got."

Was Brendan next to the truck, Clay asked himself. That was when he remembered Kohler's only shot of the morning. The feeling sent a chill down his spine.

Yes...Arlo would be coming very soon.

Chapter 48

Surrounded by four of his best men, Arlo braved the deadly evening temperatures as he led his new recruits to the auction house. Ordinarily, a journey like this would be spaced over the course of two days, but Arlo's fervor to stake his flag inside the walls of Liberty overpowered his own physical limitations. He wanted his newly acquired fighters to be well rested, fed, and properly motivated to storm Shelton's gates the day after next. So, as they passed their usual pit stop for the night, Arlo pressed on.

Arlo's enthusiasm, however, waned once the smell of burned rubber and plastic drifted into his nose. With each step, it grew stronger, as did Arlo's anger. Somehow, he knew what had happened. And there was going to be hell to pay.

"Jenkins, give me some light," one of Arlo's bodyguards said as they approached the pickup truck.

A few of the men flicked on their flashlights, revealing the disturbing aftermath the IED had left behind. Smoke continued to pour out of the shattered windows as the seats inside smoldered. The melted snow around the truck gave way to cracked asphalt covered with corpses, detached limbs, and pools of blood that had started to crystalize from the below-freezing temperatures. It was a massacre.

"What the...?" one of the men said, verbalizing what everyone else thought.

"Nobody move or you're all dead!" a voice in front of them cried out from the darkness, sounding more afraid than threatening.

Recognizing the voice, a man standing next to Arlo replied, "Hey Morris, when you're all done pissin' your pants, why don't you come over here and talk to us."

"Is that you, Elliot?" the man replied, his voice slightly bolder.

"Just get over here!"

Morris jogged over and was greeted with a furious look from his boss.

"Care to tell us what happened here?" Arlo asked.

"Uhm, well, sir, s-s-someone hit us," Morris nervously replied.

"Oh, someone hit us..." Arlo scoffed before bringing a closed fist across Morris's jaw. "Do you think that I am blind, son? Can I not see plainly that 'someone hit us?' How about you enlighten us and elaborate a little further."

Morris still held his jaw, using every ounce of strength to suppress his whimpers—he was just barely seventeen. "My apologies, sir. I did not personally see what happened. All I know is that someone had planted some sort of bomb on the truck, and it detonated as our troops were passing by." Fearing a reprisal from a lack of information, Morris's body tensed up. But he only heard an infuriated sigh flee from Arlo's nose. "I b-b-believe Simms was on the roof when the attack occurred."

Arlo nodded. "Thank you, Mr. Morris. I presume my son is inside?" he asked.

Morris feared for his life. "Yes, sir, I believe he is."

Without saying a word, Arlo continued walking toward the driveway up ahead. Elliot looked over at Morris with contempt. "Clean this mess up, boy," he said, pointing to the bodies around.

"Y-y-yes sir."

"Let's go!" Elliot said as he and the rest of the men followed Arlo down the road.

Morris busied himself with a corpse until the group faded into darkness. More willing to face the Screamers than Arlo's wrath for lying about his son, he turned and ran in the opposite direction, never looking back.

****

Barging inside the room with Simms and Elliot in tow, Arlo walked up to the old, metal desk on the back wall. "How did this happen?" he asked as he looked at his son's cold, lifeless body lying on top of the desk.

"After the explosion, Brendan came up to the roof. He couldn't have been over at the edge for more than a few seconds before he was hit by sniper fire," Simms said somberly.

Arlo winced as Simms's words came to life in his mind, making him wrought with grief.

"I tried to save him, sir, but he was already gone by the time I reached him."

Feeling lightheaded, Arlo caught himself on the edge of the desk before falling to the ground. Elliot rushed a chair over and eased him into the seat before giving the man space.

Grasping his son's hand, and putting his head on the desk, Arlo mourned silently over the death of his only son. "And...this sniper...did he shoot at you, as well?" he asked, his head still on the desk.

Simms thought about it for a moment. "No, sir. Come to think of it, I'm not sure they shot at anyone else after the explosion."

"*They*?" he asked, slowly standing from the chair, his back still turned to them.

"Yes, sir," Simms replied. "I engaged two targets that fled the scene immediately after Brendan was," he paused for a moment, realizing who he was talking to, "after your son was shot."

Arlo's knuckles throbbed from his clenched fists. "You shot at them?"

"Yes, sir, I did."

Arlo's seething eyes narrowed on Simms. "Then why aren't their bodies right here next to my son's?"

Simms swallowed nervously. "I'm sorry, sir, but they were quite far away and—"

"And yet, they were able to kill *my son* from the same distance?!" he screamed, kicking the back of the desk and leaving a furious dent behind. "Well, imagine that!"

Simms knew he would be wasting his breath to try and explain to the dejected man about the higher degree of difficulty when shooting at a moving, evasive target, as opposed to a stationary one. "I'm sorry, sir. There's no excuse for my poor performance."

Arlo shrugged off the man's apology and refocused his attention on the ghost-white face of his departed son. He had known the risks in having Brendan be part of this undertaking. With his involvement of the initial strike, as well as taking part in several other attacks since, Arlo was not blind to the reality that his son could very well die in this war, yet he was woefully unprepared for it.

As the lamenting father observed the traumatic injuries to his son's chest and Simms's words echoed through his head, Arlo realized that Brendan had not just been another casualty in this war—someone in the wrong battle at the wrong time. The twenty-seven dead and fourteen wounded from the explosion had just been the cherry on top of the real objective—the assassination of his son.

Shelton, no doubt, would be expecting a fierce retaliation from Arlo, and he had no plans to disappoint. Despite the bad blood between the two, up until now, Arlo had viewed this war politically rather than something personal. It was about satisfying his group's needs more than it was about revenge for his banishment. But when Shelton ordered the death of his son, he made it personal. And now, Arlo was going to see to it that the mayor of Liberty suffered a most excruciating demise, witnessed by every last one of the survivors from his beloved town.

"Go tell the others to get ready, we move out in one hour," Arlo said to Simms.

"Sir, if I may," Simms bravely spoke up—something he wouldn't have dreamed of doing if it hadn't been important. "I understand that you're upset, but our guys need to rest. It's already past midnight and with everything that happened this morning, and the new troops fresh off a fifteen-mile hike, I really think it would be best if we at least waited until dawn."

Arlo's shoulders dropped. He placed his hand on Brendan's face and lovingly stroked his cheek with his thumb. "I love you, son," he whispered before kissing him on the forehead. Arlo turned around and calmly walked across the room, heading for the door. As he passed Simms, he pulled his H&K VP9 from his holster and snapped it up to Simms's head. "If you make me repeat myself, I will have Elliot dig your grave right next to my son's." Arlo lowered the gun as he took a step closer to Simms. With eyes depraved of all mercy, he got within an inch of the jittery man's face and hissed, "So do you need me to go ahead and repeat myself?"

Simms forced himself to keep eye contact with Arlo as to avoid setting the man off further. "No sir, that won't be necessary," he said, his words unsteady.

Arlo took a step back and gestured toward the door.

"I'm very sorry for your loss, sir," Simms said as he walked out of the room.

"What would you like me to do, sir?" Elliot asked.

"I want you to make it very clear to the people downstairs that I am removing *all* restrictions on weapon usage. Minimizing destruction to the town itself is no longer of concern. We will storm that gate, and get inside those walls—even if it means burning the whole damn place down."

"Yes, sir," Elliot replied sharply before leaving the room.

Taking possession of Liberty was no longer a priority for Arlo. Claiming the town in the name of the "honorable" Joseph Patrick would merely be the cherry on top of *his* primary objective. The judge's threats over failure no longer concerned him, because after tomorrow, either they would both have gotten what they wanted or he would be dead. There was no middle ground, therefore no need to fear reprisal from his former colleague.

Walking to his quarters, Arlo picked up a Galil leaning against the wall next to his bed. Once practically an extension to his arm, the rifle now felt foreign in his hand. With so many people around willing to take a bullet for him, it had been a long time since the former district attorney had found a reason to pick up the old Israeli rifle.

But tonight, the reason had found him.

Chapter 49

The night was disturbingly still and impossibly dark. It was unnerving enough on its own, but throw in the fact that at any moment a throng of pissed off marauders could besiege the town with a ferocity not yet seen in the war only added to the contagious anxiety.

With his senses firing on all cylinders, Clay lay silently in the clock tower, his eye peering through the holographic sight on his AR-15. He scanned the abyss in front of him from south to east while Dusty, just a few feet away, covered south to west. The effort almost seemed worthless, as Clay wasn't even able to make out the front gate through the dense blackness, much less people walking through the field across the street. However, if just one of Arlo's men made a mistake, accidentally bumping a flashlight switch or lighting up a cigarette, Clay was certain they would spot it.

The entire town was under strict noise discipline. So long as the sun was down, no one was to speak unless *absolutely* necessary. With visibility practically zero, they would have to rely on sound instead of sight. Foreseeing this scenario, Kohler had ordered the placement of several noise traps outside the walls, including one particularly crucial trap halfway down the Deadly Eighth.

In addition to the noise discipline, light discipline was also in effect. Lights and flame of any sort were not allowed. The only exemption was the infirmary, which had blacked out its windows with canvas tarps, boards, and anything else that prevented light from escaping the inside. Kohler wanted to make any night assault as difficult on the enemy as it would be on them.

As the soundless night drew on, the waiting game began to have its way with Clay's psyche. Despite trying to stay alert, his mind drifted over the if's, when's, and how bad's of the imminent attack. And even though history told him that the bark was often worse than the bite, Clay was not optimistic that that would be the case this time around. When Kohler acted on the opportunity Brendan had presented, the Army veteran knew exactly how Arlo was going to respond—in fact, he counted on it.

"There's no greater enemy to a strategist, than emotion," Kohler had said to Shelton during their mission debrief after getting back to town. It was the sole reason why Kohler had decided to pull that trigger; why he dared to inflict a pain upon Arlo that he had never wished on his worst enemy. Kohler had bet the farm—literally—that killing Brendan would all but obliterate Arlo's judgment, making his attack strategy one-dimensional. A passionate, but shortsighted assault was the very thing that could finally give Liberty the edge it needed to end this war. "The flame that burns twice as bright burns half as long," Kohler said, quoting Lao Tzu.

Clay convinced himself that it was unlikely that just one final battle stood between him and returning home to his family, but it didn't stop him from daydreaming about waking up in his own bed on Christmas morning, his wife tightly wrapped in his arms as the kids played downstairs. *What a gift that would be.* But, with Kohler's words about emotions and war fresh on his mind, Clay quickly snuffed those happy thoughts out. He needed to keep his mind razor sharp, which was already a challenge with the crushing fatigue.

The closer it got to sunrise, the darker his surroundings seemed to be. With no way to check the time, Clay hoped that that hazy orb in space would soon make its appearance for the day.

Having not moved in several hours, Clay's idle state started to catch up with him. His eyelids became heavy as he used the stock of his LaRue to prevent his head from plummeting to the floor. Ordinarily, he would have already requested relief from someone else, but every capable fighter in town was already awake and each with their own assignment.

Reprimanding his brain for craving sleep, Clay pinched his forearm to the point of pain. The discomfort jolted his mind awake, but the desired effect was minimal and short-lived. He rubbed at his eyes, but stopped when he heard a faint noise in the distance.

THWACK

"Did you hear that?" Clay whispered softly.

"Yes," a barely audible reply came from next to him.

Seemingly impossible, the silence around them got even quieter as the soldiers of Liberty held their collective breath, waiting for a confirmation on the sound.

Then Clay saw a soft, green glow about halfway down the driveway. Having rigged a mousetrap and chemlight to a trip line, Captain Kohler had created not only an audible alarm, but a visual one as well. But the chemlight was more than just an alarm; it acted as a marker.

"Dusty, do you see it?" Clay whispered.

"Yep, I'm on it."

Dusty swung her rifle to the left and found the only source of light around. Having simulated this moment hundreds of times before sunset, she operated purely on muscle memory as she centered her crosshairs on the chemlight before dipping it down one hashmark. She couldn't see the Tannerite, but she knew it was there.

The call was Clay's to make. Though it was unlikely a wild animal would have wandered down the long driveway, tripping the trap, it wasn't impossible, either. And with the last pound of Tannerite—the final ace up their sleeve—at stake, Clay found the decision more difficult to make than he had expected.

With a deep breath, "You're green," left Clay's mouth; there was no point in whispering now.

When Dusty fired the rifle, every eye looking in that direction became blinded by the fireball billowing through the darkness. Having used just a quarter of the amount of Tannerite as they did in their ambush at the auction house, the blast was far less impressive. However, Kohler had made up for that by packing as many flammable materials around the explosive, creating a fiery wall across the Deadly Eighth.

Clay noticed a few bodies illuminated from the burning light, but there was no way to know just how many were taken out from the blast.

"Contact!" Clay heard Kohler shout from near the gate. This word was relayed around the whole town, alerting the troops that the enemy had arrived—as if there was any doubt after the explosion.

An eerie silence fell on the town once again, stirring up a flurry of emotions for everyone inside. Looking through his EoTech, Clay swung his rifle left and right, searching for a target. His stomach sank when he finally found one.

"Molotov!" Clay shouted as he saw the makeshift wick on the petrol bomb ignite. Clay placed his illuminated reticle on the only thing he could see, and fired several rounds, deafening him and Dusty inside the small, concrete room.

Suddenly, the flames spread, quickly engulfing the man who had held the homemade incendiary device. The burning man screamed in agony as he dropped to the ground in an attempt to put out the flame.

By the time Clay looked away from the man, he saw several other flaming bottles flying through the air, including one coming right at them. "Watch out!" he said as he shielded his face with his arm.

The glass bottle hit high, striking just inches above the window they were looking through. Though the bulk of the fuel was deflected, residual splashes had made it inside the window, burning both Clay and Dusty and igniting a blanket Dusty had been using.

After a furious growl, Clay looked up, through the dripping fire from above, and saw another bottle lighting up. He got to his knee and attempted to take a shot, but was forced back into cover from the hail of bullets screeching his way. He and Dusty grimaced as the bullets smashed into the wall, peppering them with small chunks of concrete shrapnel.

Dusty's efforts to put out the flame on the blanket were in vain, and the room started to fill up with smoke. Staying low, Clay and Dusty made their way to the trap door. "Go!" Clay shouted as he lifted the hatch. Dusty wasted no time getting to the ladder and made a quick descent. Clay dropped his legs through the hole in the floor, finding the ladder rungs with his feet. After climbing down a few feet, he reached up and grabbed the handle of the trap door. As he started to close it, he saw another Molotov cocktail flying in, this time the pitch had been in the strike zone. Clay slammed the door shut just as the bottle hit, but he had lost his footing on the ladder while doing so. The flimsy cabinet-style handle on the door was not strong enough to withstand Clay's weight and quickly separated from the door, sending Clay to the ground below. The drop was only eight or nine feet, but it took him several seconds to find his breath, and there just wasn't time to waste on such trivial things as breathing.

"Holy crap! Are you okay?" Dusty asked.

"I'm fine," Clay managed to eke out before rolling over and, with Dusty's assistance, getting to his feet.

As he and Dusty made their way to the first floor of the tower, the echoes of war from outside let Clay know that Kohler had been right—Arlo had brought the fury of Hell with him.

The first thing Clay and Dusty saw as they emerged from the clock tower was several structures on fire, including the one they had just vacated. Like looking at a train wreck in the making, Clay watched in horror as the buildings, already riddled with dozens if not hundreds of bullet holes, were gradually consumed with fire. The sensation of his stomach being torn out of his body made him want to double over in pain. There would be no efforts made to douse the flames—to save these buildings that were part of what Clay considered his second home. They would continue to burn until they were reduced to nothing more than a pile of ashes—almost symbolic.

A barrage of incoming gunfire snapped Clay out of his daze, bringing him back to the gritty reality of his present situation. With chaos in every direction, Dusty looked around, trying to figure out where she could be most useful.

"What do we do?" she asked. Having planned on being in the clock tower far longer, the teenaged soldier was unsure of her next move.

"Kohler's going to be somewhere near the pool house, go see where he wants you," Clay said. "I'm going to make sure the rear perimeter is secure, then I'll swing back around and meet up with you guys."

"Okay," Dusty said, a tinge of fear in her voice.

"Hey!" Clay said, grabbing Dusty's attention. "It's gonna be okay. Just be smart," Clay said, giving her a reassuring slap on the shoulder before turning around and jogging toward the northern border.

As Clay got further away from the front, each of the individual shots started to meld together, transforming into a constant, thunderous rumble. As was the case with the previous attacks, Arlo concentrated his efforts on the front gate. However, the lingering embers and melted snow from several unsuccessful Molotov throws around the foxholes suggested they were attacking on all fronts.

"DeMarcus, give me an update!" Clay shouted as he jumped down into leftfield's foxhole.

"Can't see nothin', brother, but as far as I know, ain't nobody dead back here," he replied, "but that goes the same for them guys outside the wall, too."

"So, no breaches?"

"Far as I can tell, no. But, like I said, we can't see nothin', so one of those fools could have tip-toed his way past us, and already be on his way into town."

Just then, another fiery bottle tumbled over the fence. The aim was long, and it landed about fifteen feet behind them, but as they all prepared for the impact, a rifle barrel squeezed between a gap in the fence and opened fire.

"Tag that SOB!" DeMarcus yelled as he raised his shotgun, squeezing off several shots along with a half-dozen other men. By the time Clay had raised his AR-15, the muzzle flashes from the fence had stopped.

"Cease fire!" DeMarcus shouted. "You all heard the Captain before, make 'em count."

Clay turned around to see the crackling fire behind them started to burn out. "You got your flare?" Clay asked, redirecting his attention to DeMarcus.

DeMarcus felt around his vest to make sure. "Good to go."

"Remember, if they get through, you paint the sky," Clay said.

With only two flare guns to share and three flares in total, it was decided that the two most vulnerable positions in town—the front gate and the northwestern corner—would be equipped with them. In the event the perimeter became compromised, a flare was to be deployed, and depending on who sent the signal up, a nearby post would act as a QRF (quick reaction force) to close off the breach.

"All right, keep your heads down, fellas," Clay said before heading out to the next group.

As Clay moved to the next defensive position, he looked to the horizon for some good news, but, once again, came up disappointed. It seemed that the longest night of his life would carry on just a bit longer.

His stops at the other two posts were very brief. Thanks to the steep drop off into the creek on the northeastern border, Levi had reported they had only experienced minimal contact in centerfield, while right field had not seen *any* attempts to break through.

Clay had started heading back to town to rendezvous with Kohler and Dusty when the sky lit up to his right. Whipping his head over, Clay watched as leftfield brilliantly lit up under the red-hot flare that drifted back down to earth. He realigned his body toward the distress signal and ran.

His aching lungs wheezed in agony as his overworked body crossed the several acres of snow that separated him from DeMarcus's group.

The QRF was already there and engaging the enemy by the time Clay arrived. The battle was intense, but pretty one sided at that point. Clay could make out several bodies scattered around a sizeable hole in the fence just before the flare overhead fizzled out.

"Need some light!" DeMarcus shouted.

Makeshift floodlights on either side of the foxhole, each one consisting of four separate Maglite flashlights, quickly zeroed in on the damaged section of fence, allowing DeMarcus's team to efficiently receive additional intruders with sixty-two grains of love. Clay noticed a man peeking around the corner, contemplating his strategy, but three dangerously close shots from Clay's AR-15 gave the man more to consider, and he quickly retreated.

"Contain! Contain! Contain!" DeMarcus screamed. Two men hopped out of the foxhole while several from the QRF broke away and ran outside the lit areas. Moments later, they returned, each one grunting as they pushed a Ford Explorer toward the hole in the fence. Clay ran over and assisted their efforts.

With a man inside persuading the front wheels to turn ever so slightly, the side of the SUV began to scrape along the fence as they approached the gap. Just as they reached the opening, the SUV wrenched to a halt.

"What happened?" someone yelled from the back of the SUV.

"You're stuck on a body!" DeMarcus shouted from the foxhole.

Clay ran around to the front, keeping as much of the mobile cover in front of him as he could, and grabbed the corpse's arms. He tugged, but the weight was too much for Clay's weary body to muscle. Amidst the gunfire, Clay heard heavy footsteps tromping through the snow from behind—it was DeMarcus.

He all but shoved Clay to the side as he crouched his gigantic frame down next to the body and pulled it out of the way. A furious growl erupted from DeMarcus as a bullet tore through the side of his stomach, causing him to release his grip on the body and fall backwards. Digging deep, Clay found the energy to finish the job, allowing the SUV to lurch forward again, finally sealing the hole.

The man steering the two-ton blockade scrambled out of his seat and over the center console to open the passenger door. As the door opened, the man fell to the ground with a thud, no attempt to brace his fall. Bullets continued to drill through the driver's door and over the heads of those in the foxhole.

After helping DeMarcus back to the foxhole, Clay took the opportunity to trade out his half-full magazine for a fresh one. "You all right, DeMarcus?" he asked as one of the other men dressed DeMarcus's wound.

He grimaced as he nodded. "I've taken harder hits with shoulder pads on," he said.

Clay laughed at the man's casual comment about his gunshot wound.

With the breach properly contained, Clay hopped out of the foxhole and headed south. Seeing the dozens of rooftops toward the center of town ominously silhouetted against the growing fires near the front gate gave him chills. Even when he closed his eyes, he could still see it—the devastation was indescribable.

As Clay's legs clumsily carried him toward the destruction up ahead, he heard a terrified scream for help.

Megan.

No longer bogged down by the effects of the physical beating he had taken over the past few weeks, Clay moved faster than he ever thought he was capable of. Megan frantically looked around for help as she stood just outside the infirmary door. She was covered in blood, and her expression was wrapped in fear. "I need some help here! Anyone, please!" she yelled.

"I'm here, Megan!" Clay announced as he approached the sound of her voice.

"Clay!? Thank God!" she said, the panic in her voice slightly diminished. "I was helping him back to the infirmary when he just collapsed, and I can't move him by myself," she said through rapid breaths, pointing to the dying man on the ground. It was Hicks, and he had taken a cannon of some sort to his gut. "I hit the wound with some Celox, but it's still bleeding. The wound is just too...I mean it's so massive! We need to hurry; he's lost a lot of blood."

A nearby fire provided just enough light for Clay to observe the damage on the man's abdomen. The only possible culprit for a hole that size was a twelve-gauge slug.

"On three," Megan said, grabbing Hicks's arm just beneath the armpit; Clay mirrored the position. "One...two...three!"

Hoisting the man's body up off the ground, Clay and Megan ineptly dragged him to the infirmary the last seventy-five yards down the road.

"Doctor Sowell!" Megan yelled as soon as they were close enough that she was confident the old doctor would hear.

The door to the infirmary swung open and Doctor Sowell took over for a struggling Megan, helping Clay bring Hicks inside. "Over there," Doctor Sowell said, nodding toward a vacant bed, its sheets having not yet been changed since it's last patient.

Both men grunted as they laid Hicks down, and Doctor Sowell immediately got to work. The look of exhaustion on Megan's face adequately described Clay's current state, but rest would not be found.

"*Stay* in here," Clay said to Megan.

"No way, there are others out there, Clay. We have to get them help!"

Before Clay could argue, a barrage of bullets pounded into the side of the building, two of which made it through, burrowing into the wall on the opposite side of the room.

Startled patients around the room screamed out in a mixture of surprise, fear, and anger. Clay looked at Megan, then down at her holstered sidearm. "If you're going back out there, that gun had better be in your hand!"

Megan's fingers wrapped around the handle of her pistol and pulled it out. "Okay, let's go."

As they walked back outside, Clay hesitated for a moment with the sight in front of him. Much like the first breaths after an asthmatic taking an inhaler, Clay finally felt some relief after seeing the vibrant purple, orange and blue start to fill the sky. "Dawn," he said wearily. Then the sky turned red. "Oh, no..." Clay said, his newfound hope quickly dashing.

"What does that mean?" Megan asked.

"They're inside."

Chapter 50

The entrance to town teemed with Liberty's armed fighters attempting to prevent the invaders from crossing a threshold that was once protected by a reinforced wrought iron gate—a gate that was now lying on the ground. The sounds of shouting and screaming as people tried to communicate were snuffed out from relentless gunfire, only adding to the total chaos of the scene.

As Megan broke away to help a wounded man who had managed to crawl out of the line of fire, Clay ran toward the screams and incoming bullets—toward the end of this war.

Slowly and carefully, Clay made his way up to the front entrance where a mountain of dead bodies had started to accumulate—he hoped it was Arlo's mountain. As he got closer, Clay could hear Kohler giving orders in between shots, doing his best to accomplish a goal that would have been a tall order for an entire special ops team. Standing right by his side was Shelton, smoke pouring out of his Mini-14's muzzle.

"Do not let them through!" Kohler shouted before blasting his M1A in the direction of a man gutsy enough to cross that line. "This is where we make our stand!"

With a short-lived lull in bullets being exchanged, Clay found cover behind a car that was positioned directly behind the gate. Two of Liberty's fighters took turns popping up like armed prairie dogs, getting off as many shots as they could before ducking back down behind the car. With his back to the front wheel, Clay spun around and up, dropping his elbow on the hood of the car to steady his shots. Five shots and two tangos down—not a bad ratio. Unfortunately, those shots proved to be dumb luck, as making his bullets find their targets became more of a challenge with each pull of the trigger.

Dropping down to his knee for a reload, Clay heard the brutal sound of a bullet careening through a human skull. The man next to him went rigid for a brief moment before falling straight back, smacking to the ground with a lifeless thud.

"No...no...Wesley!" The other man screamed, grief and hatred dancing throughout his words. "I'm going to kill you all!" he said as he stood up, carelessly firing his rifle as fast as his finger would allow. "I'll see you in Hell!" he shouted until his gun ran dry, an opportunity the enemy did not waste.

As the other man's body crumpled to the ground, hopelessness began to parade through Clay's spirit. This was, in fact, going to be the last battle, but the outcome would be much different than what Clay had envisioned.

With Liberty's defenses continuing to falter, Arlo's forces started stacking up in the Deadly Eighth.

Surrendering pawn after pawn to gain a little ground, each duo of men ran through the gate and inflicted as much carnage as they could before being taken out, getting in a little further each time. This method had been far less effective while the gate was still standing, but now it was like watching a lumberjack swinging his heavy axe at a trunk, swing by swing chipping away at the timber until one last blow finally brought the tree down.

Clay jumped up from his cover and fired multiple shots at an incoming attack, sending both men into a scramble for cover. Dropping back down, he suddenly felt a stinging sensation in his neck as the car shuddered from the return fire. "Son of a—" Clay said through clenched teeth as he felt the blood start to slide down his shoulder. Reaching up with his hand, his fingers found a flapping fold of skin just above his shoulder. He wasn't sure if it was a graze or shrapnel, but either way he counted his blessings it hadn't been an inch to his left.

Regrouping himself, Clay slid along the length of the car, stepping over the middle man's legs and stopping just short of the back wheel. With a few deep breaths, he jumped back up and fired his AR-15 over the roof of the car. With daylight in full effect, there was no more wondering where his targets were, but this tactical advantage was a two-way road.

To keep the enemy guessing, Clay changed his location on the car between each volley of shots. It was working.

While reloading his second to last magazine, Clay heard Kohler and several others all shout at the same time. Suddenly, it sounded as if someone mashed down the trigger on a minigun as five different men opened fire on the same target.

Clay saw movement out of the corner of his eye, causing him to turn his head just as the attacker's body started to fall to the ground just past the car, his legs still trying to walk. After smacking into the ground, Clay saw the flames spit up before he heard the bottle break—a bottle that had Clay's name written on it.

Dripping with blood, sweat, and rage, Clay stood to his feet and opened fire on the attackers advancing up the Deadly Eighth. Empty shells furiously kicked out of his rifle as he engaged a seemingly endless barrage of targets. He took out two more guns before his own rifle was silenced from a bullet punching through his left shoulder. The impact caused Clay to stumble back, tripping over a body.

As he lay bleeding in the snow, Clay gazed up into the near-perfect blue sky as he listened to the hypnotic sounds of copper-jacketed lead screeching overhead. What little energy remaining in his body absconded with the rifle bullet that tore through his shoulder. Winded, and feeling faint, he didn't try to get back up. He had nothing more to give for this cause.

His eyes welled up as the constant nightmares that he would never see his wife or children again became cemented in reality. After ten long years of surviving some of the most brutal situations a man could face, the end had finally come.

"Hold the line!" he could hear Kohler yell over and over. "We're still in this fight!"

Clay willed his body to move, but it refused to cooperate. Then his view of the clear, blue sky above was obstructed by a snarky sixteen-year-old.

"Get your ass up, Clay, it's time to move!" she echoed Morgan's final words to her. "You're coming back with us, I'm not going to babysit Geoff all by myself."

One by one, power seemed to restore to his muscles, allowing him to get to his knees. "Hey!" Dusty said, getting Clay's attention. The girl gave a sincere smile. "It's gonna be okay. Just be smart."

"Stand tall!" Kohler said. "Hold the line!"

Clay nodded at Dusty and made his way back over to the car. Propping the rifle on the hood, Clay clumsily aimed with just his right hand and engaged every charging body.

Dusty was down to her sidearm, but she was having success with it.

"Changing mags," Clay said as he knelt behind the car. After releasing the empty magazine from his LaRue, Clay dropped the muzzle of the rifle into the snow—the burning-hot barrel sizzled after being smothered with the frozen powder. Grabbing the final magazine in his chest pouch, Clay quickly inserted it into the magazine well, and tapped the bolt release with his knee. The snow that stuck to his flash suppressor melted away by the time he popped back over the car. Down to his final thirty rounds, Clay was more intentional with his shots.

As the herd up ahead started thinning, optimism began to flood his mind. They might just be able to win this, yet.

Still in the fight.

Feeling the bolt lock back, Clay verified he had run dry on 5.56. Wasting no time, his transition to the Glock 17 was seamless, and he immediately put the pistol to work. Seventeen rounds went fast. Reloading the pistol wasn't going to be as easy to do as it was with his rifle. Dropping the empty magazine, Clay looked over at Dusty, "Dust, need help," he said as he tossed her the Glock. Fishing a magazine off his belt, he tossed the magazine to Dusty, who promptly inserted it into the handle before giving a tug on the slide. She quickly handed it back to Clay.

Before he could stand back up, Clay heard something he hadn't heard in what felt like hours.

Nothing.

The gunfire had stopped; the screams and yells had ceased. Silence had taken over the town once again—beautiful, precious silence. An enemy terrorizing their spirits before, the sound of nothing was now warmly welcomed by those who were still breathing.

Slowly getting to his feet, Clay winced as he absent-mindedly tried to push off the ground with his left arm. Helping him to his feet, Dusty stood next to her good friend as Captain Kohler cautiously declared victory.

As the soldiers clapped, whistled and raised their rifles high up into the air, an overwhelming sense of peace fell upon the weary town. Against all odds, they had done it; Liberty had survived.

The celebrations were promptly cut short when Arlo himself walked through the gate, his empty Galil strapped to his back as he held his hands above his head and waved a white handkerchief back and forth. "Soldiers of Liberty, don't shoot; I formally surrender," he said through delirious laughter.

As he came to a stop just past the gate, every pistol, rifle, and shotgun in the area had given the man its undivided attention. His unhinged smile as he looked at his surroundings gave Clay chills. Knowing this was not going to end well, Clay stroked the trigger with his finger.

Arlo's eyes flashed with antipathy as they landed upon Shelton's face. After which, he feigned a smile. "Bravo, Mayor Shelton!" he said, lowering his hands to give an insincere applause, causing a lot of edgy soldiers to tense. "I'll be honest," he said, stuffing the handkerchief into a breast pocket on his coat. "I sorely underestimated what this little town was capable of. Quite frankly, I thought for sure you would have given up long before December, but you turned out to be quite the tenacious bunch, didn't you?"

"Damn straight!" one of the soldiers yelled.

"And Brendan!" Arlo continued, striking a nerve with Shelton, despite his lack of involvement in the decision. "Well, it takes a *lot* of cajones to order the assassination of a man's son—I didn't know you had it in ya," he said, followed by more deranged laughter.

Kohler took a breath in to speak, to make it clear that Shelton had not ordered the hit on his son, but Shelton, knowing what Kohler was about to say, held his hand up to him, shaking his head.

Lowering his Mini-14, Shelton replied, "Arlo, you've known me longer than any other soul here, so you *know* that I take no delight in killing another man, especially the son of a man I once called a friend..." The weeks of pent up frustration and anger finally started to come out, "But you, *once again*, gave me no choice in the matter!" he shouted. "Brendan's blood is just as much on your hands as it is mine."

"You would be wise to watch your tongue, *friend*," Arlo shot back, as if he had any edge in this fight.

"You see these people here?" Shelton continued, motioning to those standing around him. "I made a promise to them...to their wives...husbands...children...that I would do everything in my power to keep them safe—to keep this town safe. Sometimes, those decisions are black and white," he said, handing his rifle to Kohler before walking up to Arlo, "and other times they are cloaked in gray. But my pledge to the people of this town was never contingent on making easy choices. And someday, I will readily stand before my Maker to answer for those choices, so that these people won't have to."

Arlo had run out of moves the instant he stepped through the gate, but he wasn't about to leave without speaking his piece—without accomplishing his objective. Arlo looked at Shelton right in the eyes, giving a derisive smile. "Why wait for 'someday?'"

Arlo swiftly reached for his VP9 while Shelton scrambled for his Hi Power.

The crack of the pistol's shot tore through the silence of the morning, causing the spectators to jump. For the past six weeks, the men and women of Liberty—and her allies—fought valiantly against a merciless aggressor who wanted to take that which the citizens had worked so hard to build—to reap that which others had sown. The resistance had come with a heavy price tag, and for many, the ultimate cost, but it had been worth fighting for—worth dying for.

And with one final gunshot, Barry Shelton ended the war.

Chapter 51

As Clay walked through town, his arm in a sling and a slight limp, he witnessed the trail of destruction left behind from the war. The ruined buildings, destroyed lives, and horrific images would take up permanent residence in his soul.

"How's the arm?" Shelton asked as he walked up behind Clay.

Clay glanced down at the sling. "All things considered, not too bad. Doctor Sowell said it's going to be stiff for a good while, but he isn't expecting any loss of motion—long term at least."

"I am glad to hear it," Shelton said. After a moment of silence passed, he added, "Listen, Clay, there are truly no words to express just how indebted we are to you, Megan, Dusty, and Levi."

Clay looked up at the burned-out clock tower. "It was no problem," he said, knowing that Shelton wouldn't buy it for an instant.

Shelton laughed. "Yeah, and if I acted like I believed that, I'm sure you'd be trying to sell me a timeshare on South Padre Island—I hear it's nice this time of year."

Clay chuckled, experiencing true relief for the first time in what felt like years. "Well, I guess there were some *slight* inconveniences, but..." he said, turning to look at Shelton, "it was worth it."

The old man choked up. "Honestly, Clay, I don't know what I've done in this life to deserve such loyal friends, but there's not a minute that goes by that I don't thank God for them." He stuck his hand out to shake Clay's. "Thank you...from the bottom of my heart."

"Like I said," Clay said as he firmly grasped Shelton's hand, "it was worth it."

Wasting no time, the town buzzed with activity as it prepared to endure the rest of winter. Kohler, along with a few others, had already left for the auction house to ensure that no additional attacks would be coming. Though they would remain extra vigilant on security in the months ahead, with Arlo's body among the stack being prepared for burial, they were not anticipating further conflict.

"It's going to take a while to pick up the pieces," Clay commented.

"But at least we're alive to pick them up."

Truer words had never been spoken.

They walked into town, veering toward Vlad's house.

"I know it hardly seems like much after all you guys have done for us, but I want you to know that you, along with everyone back home, will *always* have a place here. If you were ever so inclined, that is," Shelton said.

"Thank you, Barry. That means a lot..." Clay said as they passed by a dozen bodies lined up on the ground, "especially in these darker days we live in."

"I pray those days become few and far between."

"Me, too," Clay replied, but his words lacked the same confidence Shelton's had.

"So, will you guys be heading out tomorrow?" Shelton asked.

"Today, actually."

Shelton was surprised with the response. After everything they had been through, he had expected them to take another day or two to recover. "I wish I had some horses to offer..."

"I think we'll manage," Clay said lightheartedly. The journey ahead would be a cake walk for the now-seasoned veterans.

"Well, if you change your mind, you guys feel free to take as much time as you need."

"Thanks, but I think we're all eager to get back home. Plus, I'm sure there are plenty of folks here equally as eager to have their family come back to them," Clay said, reminding Shelton that they would be the ones to tell the others staying at Northfield that it was now safe to return to Liberty.

"I understand that," Shelton said, longing for the day that he could see his own family again—a day that would never come.

When they arrived at Vlad's house, Shelton decided to forego another handshake, and gave Clay a hug. "Safe travels, Clay."

Clay gave Shelton a nod before running up the porch stairs. As he grabbed the handle to the door, he turned around. "I better get an invite to the anniversary celebrations next year," Clay said jokingly.

"You'll be the guest of honor."

Clay waved off Shelton's words and walked inside, nearly bumping into Dusty who was on her way out.

"Mr. Shelton," she called out, causing him to turn around.

"Dusty, my dear," Shelton said with a genuine smile. "I just want to say again—"

"I'm sorry," Dusty interrupted him; the guilt had been pestering her.

"Sorry? What on earth could you possibly be sorry for?"

"I lied to you."

Shelton walked over and put his hand on her shoulder. "You did what was necessary to help end this war, which means you did what was necessary to save lives. And you never need to be sorry for that, even if it means lying to an old man," he said.

"It just felt wrong—still does. But, I didn't want to leave without telling you that."

Shelton rightfully assumed any efforts to minimize her guilt would be met with staunch resistance, so he graciously accepted her apology.

With the burden off her shoulders, Dusty gave Shelton a salute.

Shelton returned the salute before carefully taking his Browning Hi Power out of his holster. "When I thought you were heading home before, I gave you this to help keep you safe. So," he said, holding the gun by the slide, the handle toward Dusty, "I aim to keep that promise."

Dusty looked adoringly at the pistol. "She's a gorgeous gun, and I do appreciate the offer, but I'll be okay. I have my entourage with me to help keep me safe," she replied with a chuckle.

Shelton's arm remained unmoved.

With minimal arm twisting, Dusty reached out and took the pistol from Shelton. "Thank you, sir," she said, stuffing the gun into her waistband.

Realizing he no longer had a use for it, Shelton took the holster off and handed it to Dusty as well. "I want you to know," he added, "if you ever need *anything*, we'll be here for you."

Dusty, caught up in the rare moment of friendly emotions, grabbed on to Shelton, giving him a hug and a kiss on the cheek. "I'll see you in a couple of months, Mr. Shelton."

Dusty walked back inside and Shelton headed home. As he observed the devastation the town had endured over the past two months, particularly yesterday, he knew there was a lot of work ahead of them. But more than ever, Shelton knew that Kohler and the rest of this town were fighters. There was no challenge too mighty for them to take on.

As he walked through the front door of his own home for the first time in many weeks, Shelton headed straight up the stairs to lie in his own bed. With tired eyes, he looked over at a picture of his wife that sat on the bedside table.

Sarah, his beautiful bride, was the last thing he saw before he closed his eyes and truly rested for the first time since the ballgame.

Chapter 52

Kelsey stared out the bedroom window watching the snow fall carelessly from the sky. Despite the circumstances, the picturesque scene never got old for her. There was just something so pure about the imagery that she loved—even if she was alone in that thought.

The serene moment was interrupted as the door flew open, with a rambunctious Dakota zooming in. "You never saw me!" she said as she darted for the closet, burrowing her way under a pile of clothes.

Moments later, Madeline walked in. "I know you're in here, Koty..." Dakota's muffled giggles had quickly given up her location, but Madeline played dumb. "I swear I saw you run in here," she said as she walked around the room "searching" for Dakota.

Temporarily suspending her search as she walked up next to Kelsey, she looked out the window. "It's beautiful, isn't it?" she said to Kelsey.

AJ POWERS

Kelsey put her arm around Madeline and gave her a hug. "It is…"

Madeline gave her a quick squeeze. "Okay, if I don't find her soon, she's going to suffocate under there."

Kelsey laughed—it was nice to do that again.

After discovering Dakota's hiding spot, Dakota chased Madeline out of the room, their shrieks and giggles muffled as they ran downstairs.

Returning her focus to the scene outside, her eyes began to tear up as she saw a small group walking through the gate to the farm. Whether her tears were of joy or sorrow could not be determined until she could see who was walking onto the property.

Storming down the stairs, Kelsey didn't bother to grab her coat as she reached for the door. With her mind focused solely on the figures up ahead, she barely noticed the twenty-degree temperature. Practically jumping off the porch, she ran toward the group.

They were tears of joy.

Kelsey ran full-speed into Clay's chest, all but tackling him as they fell into the fresh powder on the ground. So overwhelmed with the embrace of his wife, Clay didn't even flinch from the pain in his shoulder. After a lengthy squeeze, Kelsey kissed him over and over. Having no control over her emotions, her tears flowed heavily as she laughed with joy.

"Get a room," an unsolicited comment came from Dusty as the other three walked by.

"I missed you too, Dusty," Kelsey giggled, without breaking eye contact with her husband. She brushed the hair out of her face before bombarding him with more kisses.

Clay tightly wrapped his good arm around her as the snow gently fell on them. He had been dreaming of this moment since the convoy to Northfield blended into the horizon, and it had been far greater than he imagined. Her beautiful, smiling face renewed his spirits as if she was his source of life.

After a long, passionate kiss, Kelsey stared deeply into his blue eyes and said, "Welcome home, my love."

ABOUT THE AUTHOR

AJ Powers is an artist in the video game industry, working on some of the biggest franchises in the world.

He currently resides in Ohio with his wife Talia and their three children.

If you enjoyed this book, please consider leaving a review.

For more information on AJ, please visit
www.ajpowers.com

You may also join AJ's mailing list to keep up to date with the latest info on his books, free content and win prizes!
www.ajpowers.com/newsletter

You can also follow him on Facebook:
www.facebook.com/AuthorAJPowers/

Printed in Poland
by Amazon Fulfillment
Poland Sp. z o.o., Wrocław